Anne ... ...ained as l
Hospital, but after her ma... ... ...d
then in Nigeria. She e... ... ...
Birkenhead where she wor... ... ...ior over ten
years before taking up w...ng. She now lives with her
husband in Merseyside. Anne Baker's other Merseyside sagas
are all available from Headline and have been highly praised:

Praise for THE BEST OF FATHERS, Anne Baker's most
recent novel:

'A fast-moving and entertaining novel, with a fascinating
location and warm, friendly characters' *Bradford Telegraph and
Argus*

'[A]n immensely enjoyable read' *Coventry Telegraph*

Praise for Anne Baker's other novels:

'A wartime Merseyside saga so full of Scouse wit and warmth
that it is bound to melt the hardest heart' *Northern Echo*

'Baker's understanding and compassion for very human
dilemmas makes her one of romantic fiction's most popular
authors' *Lancashire Evening Post*

'A gentle tale with all the right ingredients for a heartwarming
novel' *Huddersfield Daily Examiner*

'A well-written enjoyable book that legions of saga fans will
love' *Historical Novels Review*

By Anne Baker and available from Headline

Like Father, Like Daughter
Paradise Parade
Legacy of Sins
Nobody's Child
Merseyside Girls
Moonlight on the Mersey
A Mersey Duet
Mersey Maids
A Liverpool Lullaby
With a Little Luck
The Price of Love
Liverpool Lies
Echoes Across the Mersey
A Glimpse of the Mersey
Goodbye Liverpool
So Many Children
A Mansion by the Mersey
A Pocketful of Silver
Keep The Home Fires Burning
Let The Bells Ring
Carousel of Secrets
The Wild Child
A Labour of Love
The Best of Fathers
All That Glistens

ALL
THAT GLISTENS

Anne Baker

headline

The right of Anne Baker to be identified as the Author
of the Work has been asserted by her in accordance with the
Copyright, Designs and Patents Act 1988.

First published in 2009
by HEADLINE PUBLISHING GROUP

First published in paperback in 2009
by HEADLINE PUBLISHING GROUP

6

Cataloguing in Publication Data is available from the British Library

ISBN 978 0 7553 4079 8

Typeset in Baskerville by Avon DataSet Ltd,
Bidford on Avon, Warwickshire

Printed in the UK by CPI Mackays, Chatham, ME5 8TD

Headline's policy is to use papers that are natural, renewable and
recyclable products and made from wood grown in sustainable forests.
The logging and manufacturing processes are expected to conform
to the environmental regulations of the country of origin.

HEADLINE PUBLISHING GROUP
An Hachette UK Company
338 Euston Road
London NW1 3BH

www.headline.co.uk
www.hachette.co.uk

ALL
THAT GLISTENS

CHAPTER ONE

Christmas Eve 1971

I T WAS ALREADY getting dark, though in truth this grey day of freezing fog had never reached full daylight. At half past four in the afternoon, sixteen-year-old Jane Jardine could wait no longer. Full of bounce and enthusiasm, she went to her father's office where she found his portly figure almost horizontal in his swivel chair. He was chatting to Sam Collins, who had been in charge of his watch and jewellery repair department for almost thirty years.

'Dad,' Jane said, her hazel eyes shining. 'Can we start?'

'If you're ready.' A smile lit up his plain heavy face. 'You can let the girls know it's time to come up to the rest room for the celebrations.' Edwin Jardine called the women on his staff 'his girls', though they were mostly well beyond girlhood.

Sam Collins got to his feet slowly. He was long past retirement age, gaunt and bent. 'I'll go down and help hold the fort,' he said.

Excitement was crackling through Jane as she sped down the stairs of the flagship store of E. H. Jardine & Son, Purveyors of High Class Jewellery. It was an elegant shop spread over three floors in the centre of Liverpool's shopping district, an Aladdin's cave of sparkling silver, expensive watches and glittering jewellery. Outside, she could hear a brass band playing 'Good King Wenceslas'. Church Street was lit up with coloured lights but it couldn't compete with the brilliance inside the shop. There were few customers at this late hour.

Earlier in the day, she and Pamela Kenny, the youngest assistant, had gone to Marks & Spencer to buy two dozen mince pies, a big iced Christmas cake, a chocolate yule log and a couple of bottles of sweet sherry. They'd set these out with glasses and paper napkins on the rest room table. Today, they would celebrate the start of the festive season before going home.

The girls were going up in twos and threes, chattering and beaming smiles at each other. Jane bounded up behind them. The staff rest room was decorated with paper streamers and Jane sighed with pleasure to see her father already there slicing up the cakes.

'Come and help yourselves now,' he said, pressing a plate on each member of staff. Jane handed round brimming glasses and Pamela poured boiling water into the big brown teapot for those who wanted their usual cuppa as well.

The elderly ladies were protective towards Jane. Miss Pinfold poured her half a glass of sherry, feeling that that was enough for someone of her tender years. It tingled on Jane's tongue and blended so well with sweet rich fruit cake that when Pam Kenny brought the bottle round again she didn't refuse.

All the girls gave of their best to the business. Edwin Jardine was popular with his staff. They found him a kind and sensitive man who treated them like an extended family. If they asked for help, he gave it. If he saw a need, he volunteered to fill it.

Of all the girls, Pam Kenny was Jane's particular friend. Small and birdlike, she'd come to work here when she'd left school at fifteen, and, though nineteen now, she still made the tea and ran errands as well as serving in the shop. Jane's gift to her was two pairs of tights.

The women began opening their bags and bringing out gifts for each other. Miss Hadley, plump, jolly and in her forties, was Edwin's senior assistant. 'I've made you and Jane a Christmas cake,' she said, presenting it to her boss.

'Thank you. My goodness, it looks too beautiful to eat!' Miss Hadley made them one every year and iced it herself to a professional standard. She taught cake decorating at night school.

'Thank you, Miss Jessop.' Jane accepted an impressive bundle wrapped in translucent blue cellophane and tied with trailing ribbons. Inside she could see many smaller packages. 'I know we'll both enjoy these.'

Miss Jessop always made them sweets like coconut ice and chocolate truffles. She was a large-boned woman in her mid-fifties and the only one to have a steady gentleman friend. They had been walking out for thirteen years and engaged for ten. From time to time, Jane had heard the girls urge Miss Jessop to push her fiancé for a wedding date, but it seemed she was too shy, and her fiancé Humphrey Biggs, a legal clerk, could not bring himself to commit to marriage.

In the early years, Miss Jessop had collected for her bottom drawer, but now Humphrey had become a bit of a disappointment. Still, they all remained somewhat envious that she had a man to take her out to the pictures in the winter and for trips in the summer.

Miss Povey was of retirement age and had made the Jardines a Christmas pudding large enough to satisfy ten people. Miss Bundy had made them a pork and ham pie to her special recipe.

'Thank you, thank you,' Edwin said. 'You're all very kind.'

Miss Lewis produced a large bunch of chrysanthemums from under the table, 'to decorate your home over Christmas', she said. Jane had known they were waiting there. The whole room had been permeated with their sharp fresh scent since morning.

Miss Pinfold had been Edwin's secretary for twenty-eight years, and helped him with the accounts as well.

ALL THAT GLISTENS

She was grey-haired and gaunt and always wore a grey suit with a long baggy skirt to work. She had the most reason to show her gratitude. Her mother was now in her nineties and very frail. Jane knew her dad allowed Miss Pinfold an extra half-hour at lunch time every day so she could go home to see to her mother's meal.

She was a quiet person. Taking two parcels from the Rexine shopping bag she brought to work every day, she said shyly, 'I've made little presents for you and Jane. I've knitted you a pair of socks, Mr Jardine.' Her cheeks were glowing with Christmas joy as he unwrapped them.

'Most kind, Miss Pinfold. They're lovely socks.' He held them up for all to admire, black and plain, not unlike those he wore every day. 'Beautifully knitted. They'll be a delight to wear.'

'And a cardigan for you, Jane.'

Jane's spirits bounded with pleasure at the thought of something new to wear. She had very little apart from her school uniform. She eagerly accepted the soft bulky parcel handed to her. 'I'd say a cardigan was a big present, not a little one,' she told Miss Pinfold. 'Thank you.'

It was neatly wrapped in pink paper and tied with scarlet ribbon. Full of anticipation, Jane tore it open. The cardigan was made of mud-coloured wool speckled with yellow and her heart sank when she saw it. She didn't like it. When she ran her fingers over it, it felt scratchy.

'It'll keep you warm, Jane,' Dad said with too much enthusiasm.

'Thank you, Miss Pinfold,' Jane said. 'You've put in such a lot of work for me.'

'Try it on, dear. I'd like to see if I've got the size right.'

Jane undid the buttons and pulled it on. The sleeves reached to her knuckles, and the body hung loose and empty round her slim frame.

'Just right,' Dad said jovially. 'Generously sized, so you can grow into it.'

Jane hoped she'd finished growing. She towered over Pam Kenny and was almost as tall as her father, but then he was only of moderate height. In fact the cardigan would be a better fit on him, because he was becoming quite rounded. The girls described him as dapper. In the shop he always wore a formal black suit with a stripe, complete with waistcoat, which he had pressed every week.

'It looks very nice, Jane,' he went on. 'It suits you.'

'D'you like it, lovey?'

'Very much, Miss Pinfold,' Jane choked. Dad had impressed on her that she must always be polite and grateful for what his girls did for her. She hugged the cardigan and searched desperately for something nice to say about it. 'There's something you can praise about everything,' Dad had told her, but sometimes Jane wasn't sure he was right.

'I want to see how I look in it,' she said. There was

a large mirror at the other end of the room, and she went over to it. Miss Pinfold crowded behind her.

Jane's anxious hazel eyes stared back at her from the glass. Dad said she had a pretty face and was like her mother, but she was afraid he was just being kind. She wanted a perm to improve her straight dark hair, but Dad said she was too young for that, and he'd prefer her to keep it long and tied back in its rather severe ponytail. Jane hunched her shoulders inside the cardigan; the colour made her skin look sallow. It was a hideous garment.

'Yes.' She tried to smile. 'It's very comfortable to wear and lovely and cosy. A good winter warmer. Thank you very much, Miss Pinfold.'

She'd wear it when she came home from school. She and Dad lived in the flat above the shop and she usually did her homework here in this room on the floor below, where the girls came and went and tea could be readily made. Her father's office was just across the landing. It would please Miss Pinfold to see her wearing it and it would please Dad too. While the shop was elegantly fitted out with thick carpet, the areas used by family and staff were utilitarian, tiled and draughty. She'd keep the cardigan on now.

Dad finished his slice of cake and said in his soft voice, 'I'd like to take this opportunity to thank you one and all for the help you've given me. It's been a difficult year, but you've all coped magnificently with the change to decimal currency, and I'm delighted to say we've had a profitable run up to Christmas.' The polished dome of his bald head rose from a narrow band of dark hair sprinkled with grey. A gentle man in his early fifties, he was nevertheless fiercely ambitious for his business. 'We couldn't achieve what we have without your enthusiasm and support, so there's a Christmas bonus for each of you added to your wages.'

He beamed round at them all as he handed the box of envelopes to Miss Pinfold to take round. 'And an extra day's holiday so you can all enjoy a well-deserved rest before we reopen on December the twenty-eighth.'

'Thank you, Mr Jardine,' Miss Hadley said. 'We are all very grateful for what you do for us.'

Jane had been sent out to buy small gifts of fancy soap for each of the girls, which she'd wrapped in fancy paper and done up with ribbon. Edwin nodded to her now, which meant it was time for her to hand them out.

'Now we'll close the shop so you can go home and enjoy Christmas. Jane, get Sam and Nick to come up and have some refreshment.'

Jane rushed downstairs, eager to find Nick. She met Sam coming up. 'I hope you ladies have left me some cake,' he said. 'Nick's still serving on the ground floor.'

When she reached him, he was just giving a customer his change and wishing him a happy Christmas.

Nick Collins was Sam's twenty-two-year-old

grandson, who was training to manage one of their branches. Tall and very slim, he wore the formal suit Jardine's required of male employees and always looked very smart.

A smile lit up his face when he saw her. He was a good-looking young man with brown eyes and a lot of unruly brown hair, which he'd told Jane was hard to keep under control in the shop.

'Make the most of it, lad,' his grandfather had told him, overhearing. 'You could end up like me, with thin wispy hair on your head but lots of curly grey whiskers on your face.'

Nick's parents were divorced; he'd been brought up by his mother who lived in Chester and was going to spend Christmas with her. He signalled Jane to come behind the counter and took a gift-wrapped parcel from a shelf below.

'I didn't want to give this to you in front of everybody else. You know what the girls are like.'

Her heart lurched. Anything from Nick would be lovely. She unwrapped a bottle of Coty L'Aimant toilet water.

'Oh, Nick, it's my favourite! I love this. Thank you very much.'

'Think of me,' he said seriously, 'every time you spray it on.'

Jane could feel herself blushing. 'I have something for you, too.' She'd put it in her pocket, ready for this moment. She'd bought him a ballpoint pen, though not one from their stock: her pocket money wouldn't run to that.

He smiled. 'I need a decent pen. Thank you.'

'It isn't all that good, I'm afraid.'

'It is, and it'll do me very well. By the way, I asked your father if I could take you to see the play of Dickens's *Christmas Carol* at the Empire. I told him I had tickets for the twenty-seventh.'

'What did he say?' Jane was eager.

'Well, he looked a bit doubtful but he said yes. I thought for a moment he was going to suggest coming along too.'

Jane laughed. 'It's usually Dad who takes me to places like that.'

'I know.'

'He'll be left on his own, though.'

'No he won't. He's invited Grandpa and me round for an early supper that night, so they can keep each other company while we go out.'

Sam had always lived in a flat over their Crosby branch, and since Nick had come to work for them he'd moved in with him.

The last job of the working day was to take apart the displays in the windows and interior showcases and store the valuables in the safes, one on the ground floor and one upstairs in her father's office. The girls were streaming round them, laughing and chattering merrily as a result of the sherry, as they set to with a will to get the stock locked securely away.

*

Mrs Hilda Sarah Thorpe felt lower than she ever had before in her twenty-nine years. She really couldn't be bothered with all this fuss about tinsel and turkey, she had too many other things on her mind. If it wasn't for Kitty, she'd have been happy to let Christmas pass unnoticed this year.

Her fourteen-year-old daughter had wanted to come up Church Street, in the centre of Liverpool's shopping district, to choose a present for herself, and she'd agreed.

'But you know I can't afford anything expensive,' she'd told her. The stone-faced buildings rose five and six storeys high and housed smart shops and department stores. Their huge plate-glass windows sparkled with lights and the desirable goods they offered for sale. It was a wide road busy with traffic; the pavements were wide too to accommodate bustling crowds of shoppers.

They were passing Jardine's jewellery shop when Kitty pulled her to a stop. 'Ma, just look at those necklaces. Aren't they drop dead gorgeous?'

In happier times, Hilda had sometimes paused to feast her eyes on the jewellery displayed in the three big windows of this shop. She admired expensive gems; she let her gaze linger enviously over the precious stones all flashing fire. All were set in gold and platinum and fashioned into the sort of jewellery women like her could only dream about.

11

Kitty was petulant. 'If I wished really hard, d'you think Father Christmas would bring me a necklace? I'd love that one, with the diamonds and those green stones, what d'you call them?'

'Emeralds. Sorry, love, but if you wish till you're blue in the face it won't help.'

'No necklace then?'

'Not like that one,' Hilda said. 'I bet it costs a fortune.'

It might be Christmas, but they'd be lucky to get a decent dinner. Things had never been easy for Hilda, though she admitted she'd had good times as well as bad. Right now they were very bad. She'd not been sorry when her partner Gary Bolton had recently been sent to prison for five years. He'd been arrested with several others while attempting a large-scale cigarette robbery. He'd also been charged with stealing a van, trying to evade arrest, damaging a police vehicle and assaulting a police officer.

Hilda had spent the best part of four years living with Gary and the last one had been pure hell, her nerves were still raw. It was a relief to know he was safely behind bars, but the thought of his release had been giving her cold shivers almost from the moment he'd gone down. She'd moved house to get away from him and his son, so neither of them would be able to find her and Kitty.

She now urgently needed to abandon the pretence of being Gary's wife and the name Gemma Bolton. On her birth certificate she was Hilda Sarah Frost. She'd been given the names of both her grandmothers and had always hated being called Hilda. As soon as she could, she'd called herself Sally Frost, but that name appeared on certain police records and she daren't use it without risking arrest.

She desperately needed to find work now, and to do that she'd have liked to ditch her real name of Hilda Sarah Thorpe, but the fact that Kitty shared the name Thorpe made it impossible.

They were both watching a plump woman lift the tray of necklaces out of the window. She looked up at them and half smiled as she reached for another.

Kitty sighed. 'Looks like somebody might get that necklace. Lucky beggar.'

The shop door opened, releasing a puff of warm scented air. A well-built man wearing a formal black suit and waistcoat looked out. 'It's getting dark early tonight,' he said to someone behind him. 'Have a good Christmas.'

Hilda took her daughter's arm. 'Come on. It's too cold to stand about, and we've got to get to the market before it closes.'

The market butchers were reputed to reduce the price of their birds in the last hour of pre-Christmas trading. She'd thought it was worth a try.

'I want turkey.'

'If they've got one cheap enough.'

'Ah, go on, Ma. It's Christmas and we haven't got anything, no decorations, no prezzies and no tree. Gosh, just look at that one.'

Her mother turned to admire the lavishly decorated twelve-foot-high Norway spruce at the top of the street. People loaded down with packages were swirling round them. Everybody seemed to have an air of jollity and anticipation as they headed home.

St John's Market was bright with lights and decorations and was warm inside. There were still fresh birds hanging up. She could have bought an enormous turkey at a bargain rate, but her oven was tiny and she had neither a pan nor a plate large enough to cope with a twenty-six-pound bird. Anyway, what was she thinking about? She should have gone to Tesco and bought a small frozen one. Instead, she bought a fresh chicken that had been reduced in price.

'We have chicken all the time,' Kitty complained.

'Only chicken pieces.' Hilda had learned only too well that teenagers could be difficult. 'I'll be able to roast this and do roast potatoes with it.'

'What about some of those sausages for supper tonight?' Kitty asked.

At a greengrocer's stall they discovered that the sprouts had all been sold. 'Good,' Kitty retorted. 'I can't stand them. I certainly don't want them for my Christmas dinner. Let's buy a bag of frozen peas. And a yule log, Ma, and there's those chocolate biscuits you like. We've got to have something for tomorrow.'

With her shopping complete, Hilda said, 'Let's go home.'

'Not yet,' Kitty protested. 'I only came with you so you could buy me a present. You said you would.'

'I'd love to get you something really nice,' her mother tried to explain, 'but the money's running out.' The trouble was, Kitty hankered for the most expensive things.

As they were passing the window of a small boutique, Kitty grabbed her arm. 'I'd love that coat,' she breathed. 'The white fur one. It's gorgeous.'

'Faux fur,' her mother corrected her. 'Nobody wears real fur any more – it's not popular these days.'

'Faux fur, whatever.' Kitty shivered. 'I need a warm coat.'

'It's not practical. You couldn't wear that to school.'

'I could. Nobody bothers much with uniform any more. Ma, I've got to try it on.'

'I haven't enough money left,' Hilda protested, but her daughter was already inside the shop, and she had to follow. She was in time to see the coat being brought out of the window. She hoped it was the wrong size and wouldn't come up to Kitty's expectations.

The coat couldn't have fitted better if it had been made to measure. Kitty turned round from the mirror beaming at her. 'Oh, it's lovely, Ma, isn't it?'

She was a good-looking girl who was doing her best to look grown up. Hilda couldn't keep her cosmetics and the stuff she used to lighten her hair away from her daughter, who was turning herself into an attractive blonde.

Hilda could see herself reflected in the background, looking a miserable spoilsport. She hadn't bothered to put make-up on and her hair was in need of a wash and a trim. She always used to take trouble with her clothes and had prided herself on being smart; today she looked a mess.

'Please, Mummy,' Kitty implored. 'Please get it for me for Christmas. I'll love it for ever.' She studied the price ticket.

Her mother shivered. She was cold and her spirits were sinking. Kitty only called her 'Mummy' when she wanted something. 'How much is it?'

'Forty pounds.'

'Oh, for heaven's sake.' She was impatient. 'You know I haven't got that sort of money.'

The shop owner said, 'I can let you have it for thirty-five.'

'Come on, Kitty. I can't afford it.'

'Thirty pounds.'

'No.' Mrs Thorpe had thirteen pounds left in her purse. It never would be possible.

'Sorry to have troubled you. It can't be done.' She picked up her shopping and headed for the door. On the step she waited, but Kitty was hanging back, still wearing the coat.

'I'll go without you,' Hilda threatened. 'I hope you've got your bus fare home.'

'No.' Kitty followed reluctantly, dragging her feet, at a distance. She was hostile. 'Ma, it's not fair,' she called. 'You promised to buy me a present.'

Hilda put her bags of shopping down on the pavement to rest while she waited for her daughter. Kitty was making a show of herself and embarrassing her. Only now did she realise she was outside Jardine's shop again. A woman was stripping out the few trays of jewellery that remained in the window. Only the Christmas baubles and tinsel remained. The shop was about to close for Christmas.

A prosperous-looking couple came out, middle-aged to elderly. The woman took the man's arm and smiled up at him. 'Absolute heaven to be able to choose my own present. I've never seen such beautiful earrings.'

'You can't wear them until tomorrow,' he teased, and the woman's laugh drifted back on the freezing air.

'Everybody's entitled to one present, aren't they?' Kitty whined. 'I'd love that white coat.'

'You know I'd buy it for you if I could.'

Kitty said in disdainful tones, 'You can't afford anything I want.'

'I'm sorry, love, I can't afford anything I want either,' she retorted crossly.

The shop door opened again and another customer was shown out.

'Compliments of the season to you, Mr Jardine,' he said.

'And to you, Mr Hamilton.'

Women with flushed cheeks came streaming out in a long line, all with broad smiles. 'Happy Christmas,' they were calling to each other.

'Looks as though they've been having a staff party.' Hilda drew her daughter further away from the door.

After the women came two men. The older one, who was stiff and grizzled, said, 'Run along now, Nick, you don't want to miss your train. Have a good Christmas.' Then he paused on the step and turned back to say to the man behind him, 'Don't forget to lock the Sun Diamonds away, Edwin, or you might not have an enjoyable holiday.'

'I won't, Sam. See you tomorrow at the Adelphi. About half twelve.'

For a moment, Hilda had a good view into the shop. Then the man in the striped suit closed the door and she heard the bolts being shot home.

'I bet he's the owner,' she said.

'There was a girl with him.'

'She could be his daughter.'

'Then she's lucky having a dad who owns all that,' Kitty said. 'And she must know all those people. That younger man who came rushing past us – wow, wasn't he something?'

That was enough to scare her mother. Kitty was growing up too fast. 'You're too young to be thinking about boys,' she said sharply.

'You weren't, Ma, at my age.'

Hilda Thorpe couldn't stop her sharp intake of

breath. Kitty had worked out from their ages that she must have given birth to her when she was fifteen.

'I was too young. It did us no good, and we're hard up now because of it. Better if you leave lads and all that alone until you're older.'

She meant sex, but she hadn't the energy to broach the subject again right now. It was good advice, but Kitty rarely listened to what she had to say.

'Come on, let's go for the bus.' Hilda pushed a bag of shopping at her daughter, and set off again. 'Help me carry some of this, please.'

Her mind was made up in that instant. She'd pull herself together and get the big changes that were needed under way, otherwise she'd find herself an ancient hag surviving on her old age pension. She had to learn to use her head and not her heart where men were concerned.

She'd do it; she'd had enough of envying what others had. She was going to make an all-out effort to claw her way out of poverty. She wanted to be able to buy Kitty a white fur coat and she'd like diamonds for herself. She was determined that, one way or another, they were going to have a better life from now on.

CHAPTER TWO

ON THE WAY home, Hilda Thorpe stared out of the bus window and mused that she'd had a bad start in life. She didn't know how old her mother had been when she'd given birth to her, but young, probably very young. Her name had been Rose and she'd looked after her baby to start with, but then, when Hilda was eighteen months old, things must have gone wrong for her because Hilda had been taken into care.

Throughout her childhood, Hilda had been in and out of foster homes, and though they'd tried to find adoptive parents for her none had wanted to keep her. She'd asked many times what had happened to her mother, and why she hadn't kept her, but had never received a straight answer.

What Hilda yearned for above everything else was someone to love her and look after her; someone who'd stand by her come what may. To begin with, she'd seen that person as a mother, but by the age of fourteen she'd wanted it to be a man and she'd been searching for him ever since.

ALL THAT GLISTENS

Hilda Thorpe knew exactly where she'd gone wrong. Time and time again, she'd fallen in love with the wrong sort of man. None of them had been in a position to buy her diamonds but that hadn't seemed to matter. Not when what she sought was love.

The first, Jack Tomlin, had got her pregnant at fifteen and abandoned her as soon as she'd told him Kitty was on the way. She'd been one month off her sixteenth birthday when she'd given birth.

She'd loved Kitty fiercely from the moment she saw her and was determined never to part with her. She was going to bring up her daughter herself; Kitty was going to have a better life than she'd had. She was a pretty baby and Hilda had given her the pretty name of Katrina. But choosing the right name wasn't easy; somehow she'd become Kat and that had metamorphosed into Kitty. There it had stuck.

By the time she'd met Paul Thorpe, she'd been looking for someone serious who would stay with her. He'd married her and adopted Kitty, who'd been three years old by then. He'd lasted longer than the others, but they'd lived mostly on social security which he'd managed to augment with a bit of shoplifting, pocket-picking and betting at the races. All the same, they'd never had enough money to get a decent house or do anything they wanted. She'd left him when she found he was carrying on with the red-haired barmaid at the Black Bull.

After that she'd got a job to support herself and

Kitty. For years she'd worked for a catering firm for low wages. On the whole, she'd quite enjoyed it and learned a lot. She'd been sent in a team into other people's houses to cook and serve food for dinner parties. Sometimes they'd gone into public buildings to set up for wedding receptions and birthday bashes, but she'd preferred the work in private houses. She'd enjoyed seeing how the well-heeled lived; what their houses were like and what they ate.

Mostly that had meant supporting her current boyfriend too, since they'd all been shy about getting proper jobs. There had been Brian, Graham and another Jack.

Gary Bolton was the brother of one of the women she'd worked with. His wife had gone off to live with a car salesman leaving him with a son to bring up. When Hilda moved in with him, Kitty was eleven and Jason fifteen, and together they seemed to make a real family.

To start with she'd found Gary very different and good fun. 'I'm an entrepreneur,' he'd told her. 'I work for myself.'

She'd guessed right away that his work wasn't entirely legal.

'I'm not a thief,' he'd said when she asked, but she found he was making big money as a fence: selling on property that had been stolen. The first summer they'd spent together Gary had earned what seemed a fortune and he began dreaming of moving a long way away where nobody would know him and he could enjoy his earnings in peace. Then two of the thieves he'd helped dispose of their ill-gotten gains were caught. Gary knew they would be subjected to close questioning by the police. He was afraid they would come looking for him. The tension was making his nerves raw, and his temper, always unreliable, flare up into ungovernable rage. When he'd suggested they escape to Spain with the kids and start living the good life, it had seemed an excellent idea.

Knowing that Gary was setting up the move to Marbella and expecting it to be permanent, Hilda gave in her notice. She'd worked for the catering firm for over four years and though she'd helped herself to some of their equipment and food from time to time, she'd still had a clean record.

She'd done a silly thing then; thinking she'd get safely out of the country, she'd helped herself to company money. She'd managed to hang on to it, but the police had moved more quickly than she'd expected and she'd been charged with theft. Fortunately, their move to Spain was all booked and she and Gary had skipped off before her case came up in court, but her name was still on the files.

They'd had two marvellous years in Spain, the best in her life. The kids had gone to the local school and had learned to chatter away in Spanish to the other children. Their troubles had only started when their money began to run out.

Hilda managed to get a job in a bar catering for English tourists but they'd lived at luxury level over the last two years and found it hard to cut back. They began thinking they'd have to return to Liverpool.

She knew Gary had a ferocious temper that could flare up from nothing. He'd turned on the kids from time to time when they got on his nerves. But during a night out together, eating and drinking in several local bars, he'd turned on a barman who he thought was charging him too much. It had been a very public quarrel and Gary had beaten the man to a pulp.

Somebody called the Spanish police and they arrived before she could get Gary out. They took him away and locked him in a cell for the night to sober up and the next morning quizzed him for hours. It was well on in the afternoon when he came home, very much in need of a shower and some clean clothes.

That had decided him. They started packing right away, and two days later set off to drive back to England.

Neither Hilda nor Kitty was in a good mood after their shopping trip. When the bus pulled in at their stop, Hilda heaved her bags off. Kitty was still dragging her feet a few yards behind. It was dark now and colder than ever; gaunt high buildings loomed over them.

Their new home was a flatlet in a barn of a house built in the last century. One of the massive gate-posts had the name Churton House carved into it.

For once, the front door was shut, but it was almost as cold inside as out. It felt dank and smelled of damp. They climbed the stairs to the second floor. The best that could be said of it was that the other occupants, mostly students, had gone home for the holiday and so it was quiet.

They had two large rooms with high ceilings and draughty windows that rattled in the gentlest of breezes. Hilda unlocked the door to their living room; each room had a Yale lock and they had to cross the landing to go from one to the other. They shared a bathroom on the other side of the house with the tenants of three other flatlets.

Kitty scuttled for the box of matches to light their one gas fire and sat on a stool in front of it with her coat on. In this weather, it was almost impossible to warm the place up. Hilda began unpacking her shopping on the scratched table.

'What are these?' She held up a net of mixed nuts and a chocolate Father Christmas. 'You didn't buy them, did you?'

'No, I nicked them. We have to have something.'

'Kitty! Don't you understand that's shoplifting? You could get a criminal record for that, if you're caught.'

'Well I wasn't.'

'It won't do you much good. We haven't any nutcrackers.'

Kitty slashed into the net and dropped a couple of

walnuts on the floor and then stamped on them. 'Shall I crack one for you, Ma?' Her tone was cheeky.

Their living room had a sink, a few cupboards and an ancient Baby Belling stove along one wall. There were three upright chairs and a settee with broken springs, lino on the floor and a threadbare rug.

They had to share the bedroom and the double bed, which had a mattress that sagged in the middle and made them roll together. There was frost on the inside of their window when they woke up in the mornings. The whole place looked dire.

'I'm hungry,' Kitty said. 'Let's start cooking.' She switched on the hot plate and clattered the ancient frying pan on top to warm up. 'Where are those sausages?'

Hilda cleared the shopping from the table and set out knives and forks. Kitty brought the yule log back from the cupboard.

'Christmas starts here, Ma. We've got to have something special. We can save half till tomorrow.'

'Right.' Hilda brought out a bottle of wine, a legacy from Spain where she'd learned to enjoy it. She'd brought two or three bottles with them from Gary's house together with the television set. Kitty switched it on.

Hilda poured herself a glass of wine and let the jollity of the show, which was making Kitty giggle, wash over her. They couldn't stay here. It was awful, and a dreadful comedown from their villa in Marbella and the pleasant house Gary had rented for them.

'I hate this place,' Kitty said. 'It's horrible. It's doing my head in. Why can't we go back and live with Jason? It wasn't fair to leave him on his own.'

'I had to do this. I had no choice.'

'You did. We didn't have to move. That was a much better place.'

Hilda was aware that she'd left Gary's house and then sat back as though she'd achieved her goal. She must carry on, move things along.

She refilled her glass and brooded some more, trying to think of practical ways and means. She was going to get them a better life, and she didn't care what she had to do to make it happen. For starters, she wanted a decent place to live with a bedroom to herself.

She'd need to smarten herself up if she was going to find herself a prosperous partner. Get her hair cut properly and some nice clothes. She'd start by looking through what she had and throw out the rubbish. She had plenty of smart summer clothes, though perhaps too many designed to be worn on the beach rather than for work. She'd need to go upmarket in order to attract a man with money.

It was half an hour off midnight when they went to bed and church bells were ringing out across Liverpool.

'Sounds lovely,' Kitty said dreamily, but Hilda couldn't get to sleep. She lay listening to the sound of the bells . . .

*

Jane shivered and pulled her scarf tighter as she stepped out into the night.

'It's freezing hard,' her father said as he locked the door behind him and pulled on his gloves. They walked briskly to his lock-up garage some streets away to collect the Rover. It would have been no further to walk all the way to church, except that they needed to pick up Miss Hadley from her home.

Edwin Jardine had been the senior organist at St Cuthbert's for many years, so regular churchgoing was obligatory. When Jane was very young, Colette, her nanny, had sat with her in church, but when she started school and was considered old enough to manage without a nanny Miss Hadley had volunteered to take charge of her during the service so her father could feel free to play the organ. It was now a long-established routine for Miss Hadley to accompany them to church, although for years Jane had felt perfectly capable of sitting through the service on her own.

Jane knew her father thought it unsafe for respectable ladies like Miss Hadley to walk the streets of Liverpool after dark, so for the Christmas Eve midnight service he always fetched her and took her back. The car still felt cold when it pulled up outside the Victorian red brick terraced house in which Miss Hadley lived with her sister Emily. Jane shot out to rattle the knocker but Dorothy Hadley appeared at the door almost immediately; she'd been watching for them and was ready with her hat and coat on.

It was her Sunday best – a heavy green tweed coat and green felt hat. Under it, her dark hair was arranged in its usual severe topknot. Tonight, as protection from the midnight chill, she was muffled in a green wool scarf as well. She wore large round spectacles with dark frames and her lips usually turned up at the corners, giving her the look of a good-natured owl.

Jane swung open the front door of the car, and while she held it for Miss Hadley to get in she glanced back at the house. Miss Hadley's sister Emily was not such a keen churchgoer as Dorothy but she sometimes came with them to the midnight service. Not tonight, though, and Jane was glad. She felt very much at ease with Dorothy; between them silences were companionable and she didn't need to make polite conversation.

The daytime fog had cleared; it was freezing hard now, but there were still lots of people out and the city was full of light. Dad parked the car, and when she got out Jane could hear the bells of several churches, some near and some far, ringing out over the city. The joyful sound seemed the very essence of Christmas.

It felt warmer inside, but the old-fashioned heaters gave off a whiff of paraffin that mingled with the smell of age and damp. The church's centenary would be coming up in the next year or two, and much thought was already being put into how they should celebrate that and raise some cash for the repair fund at the same time.

When the congregation rose to sing its first carol, Jane heard Miss Hadley's voice soar, strong, sweet and clear. Years ago, she'd asked her why she didn't sing in the church choir.

'That would mean I couldn't sit here with you.'

'But wouldn't you prefer to be in the choir?'

Miss Hadley had smiled at her. 'When I was young I joined every choir I could. I dreamed of earning my living as a singer. Going on the stage.'

'Then why didn't you? It sounds more interesting than working in our shop.'

'It isn't that easy, Jane. Half the girls in England want to be singers.'

'If you really wanted, you could do it now.'

Miss Hadley had smiled again. 'Only the young think all things are possible.'

Before the midnight service ended Jane began to feel sleepy. Miss Hadley opened a paper bag and offered her a caramel, in the fond belief that chewing sweets would prevent her charge from nodding off. It did, but barely, and it was the jubilant crashing chords of the organ heralding Christmas Day at the end of the service that really woke Jane up.

They dallied in the aisles on the way out exchanging Christmas wishes, because it took Dad a while to take his leave. Once in the car, Jane had a floaty feeling and knew she was drifting off, but when it stopped outside Miss Hadley's house she knew she had one last duty to fulfil.

ALL THAT GLISTENS

Because Dorothy Hadley provided services over and beyond those she was employed to perform, her father felt she must be presented with an extra gift. He usually chose something from the stock in his shop, and Jane gift-wrapped it and wrote out the tag. *With many thanks and good wishes from Jane and Edwin.*

The lapel of Miss Hadley's coat sported the opal brooch Dad had chosen for her last year, and Jane knew she'd have on her wrist the Longines watch he'd given her ten years or so ago. It was gold, very plain, and large enough for her to tell the time easily even with her bad eyesight. She wore it every day and was proud of it. None of the other assistants owned a Longines.

This Christmas, Jane had asked her what she would like to have. It seemed only sensible, because she'd already received a variety of brooches, a dressing-table set of brush, comb and mirror, a cut-glass powder bowl and a silver photograph frame.

'Have a look through the new stock, and see if there's anything you'd like,' she'd said. Miss Hadley had been a little embarrassed at the suggestion.

'Just whisper to me,' Jane had urged, and a day or two later Miss Hadley had taken her aside to point out a leather handbag. Now it was gift-wrapped on the back seat beside her. When the car stopped she got out after Miss Hadley, and leaned back in to collect the parcel. Dad got out too. Christmas wishes murmured across the gear lever was not his style.

'A little present to thank you,' Jane announced, as Dad had told her she should. 'You do so much for us and we're very grateful.' Miss Hadley was always kind and had been a comforting presence for as long as Jane could remember. She kissed her cheek. She truly was grateful.

Dad shook Miss Hadley's hand and pecked at her cheek too. Together they escorted her to her front door. He took the key from her hand and unlocked it for her, and with a final good night, and a flurry of Christmas wishes, she was gone.

On the five-minute drive back to the garage Jane fell asleep. However, the brisk walk home in the frosty air woke her up thoroughly, and when she finally got into bed, her feet were cold and sleep was miles away.

Christmas Day was exciting. As always, Dad was determined to make the most of the holiday, and at breakfast Jane found a gift-wrapped packet beside her plate. She knew what was in it before she opened it: the shape told her it contained LPs. Dad had not given up trying to reform her taste in music; he enjoyed highbrow stuff, requiems and dirges like that, and couldn't understand why she preferred something with a bit of beat to it. She enjoyed the popular songs of the day, rock and roll and jazz, and played them on the record player in her bedroom that he'd given her for her birthday. Dad was watching her so she started to unwrap them.

'From Father Christmas,' he said. 'He thought you might like the Beethoven symphony.'

The other was Pink Floyd. She agreed with the girls at school that they were the greatest band.

'Thank you, Dad. My favourites.'

Then he fastened a beautiful embossed gold bracelet on her wrist. 'This is from me,' he said, kissing her forehead.

Jane was thrilled. 'I loved this when I first saw it in the shop. Thank you, Dad.' He seemed pleased with the tin of tea she gave him. It was the sort with bergamot in it, which he particularly liked.

After breakfast she played the Beethoven and left her bedroom door open so Dad could hear it too. She felt she had to try to like it and in fact it wasn't bad. It had plenty of tune to it, but Pink Floyd was more to her taste.

'You'll enjoy it more when you're grown up,' he told her, but he had a twinkle in his eye.

At lunch time they walked up to the Adelphi Hotel. Dad popped into the bar to collect Sam Collins who was waiting for them there. He'd started working for Jardine's when her father was a boy, and had taught him a great deal about the business. Since his wife had died some years ago, Dad had invited him to have his Christmas lunch with them. Sam was a jolly sort of person, and his company made it more fun for them too.

They went straight to the dining room for a traditional Christmas dinner. With the decorations, the music and their fellow diners all bent on enjoying themselves, there was a lovely festive atmosphere. Jane really enjoyed it. The afternoon was drawing in by the time they returned to the flat over the shop.

'We should have put up a few decorations to make it more Christmasy,' Jane said, looking round. Their living room seemed bleak and comfortless despite the large vaseful of chrysanthemums Miss Lewis had given them. 'That big tree and all that holly and glitter at the Adelphi was lovely, wasn't it?'

Her father sighed. 'We were too busy to think of it until now, but if you want a tree, why don't you bring up one from downstairs? There's a nice one on the ground floor.' It was part of the shop decorations. 'We could have it here until we reopen. Would that cheer the place up?'

'Oh, yes!' It had lots of silver foliage and pretty colourful parcels with nothing inside. Jane raced down to get it.

In this five-storey building their flat was on the top. The floor beneath provided storerooms and two offices, one for Dad and one for Miss Pinfold, as well as the staff rest room.

Sam Collins ran a small repairs department on the second floor, though less work of this sort was done on the premises nowadays. Watches were usually sent back to their manufacturer except for replacement of straps, but Sam still repaired some jewellery, enlarged rings and polished up gemstones.

Also on this floor was an array of clocks and watches

and of domestic silverware: tea and coffee sets, cutlery, candlesticks, trays, cruets and photo frames. From here down, the staircase was carpeted and had mahogany rails.

The first floor displayed mainly gifts: expensive pens, cigarette cases and lighters, and ornate hip flasks, as well as signet rings, tie pins, chains and other gold jewellery.

Their main showcases were on the ground floor. When the shop was open there were scintillating displays of bracelets, necklaces, brooches and rings of every type imaginable. There was jewellery of gold, silver and platinum, set with precious sapphires, emeralds, rubies and diamonds. Equally lovely were the pearls, the opals, the jade and the coral.

The atmosphere of the whole shop was one of luxury, but today, with most of the stock locked away and the shutters on the shop windows, it was dark enough for Jane to switch on the lights. The place looked empty and the decorations of tinsel and holly drooped forlornly.

It seemed colder too, without the fiery glow of the Sun Diamonds. They were always locked alone in a glass cabinet occupying the most prominent position, and Dad allowed nobody to touch them but himself. They were rare yellow diamonds and the most valuable pieces in the shop.

Like most of their customers Jane often paused to admire them. Sometimes the stones looked yellow, but at others, depending on the light, they could be a deep orange; sparks flashed and burned in their depths with the warmth of the sun itself. Last night, she'd watched her father put on a pair of gloves and lift the pendant by its gold chain and lay it carefully with the ring and the earrings in their elegant shagreen case. He'd carried it straight up to his office and locked it in the safe.

Back in the living room upstairs, her father had lit the gas fire and sunk on to his favourite armchair. Jane arranged the tree in the darkest corner of the room and picked up the silver fragments it had shed.

'That's better, isn't it? More like Christmas?'

'Much more.'

The shop had a Christmas tree on each floor, and Jane brought them all up; one she put in their kitchen cum dining room and one she used to decorate the landing. 'That really livens the place up. It looks really festive.'

Dad's tone was guarded. 'Yes, but I'm glad it's only for a day or two. I have to turn sideways to get round that tree on the landing.'

She laughed. 'It isn't that bad.'

He sat down at his piano and started to play one of his tinkling Chopin favourites. 'Dad,' she said, 'do you really want to play your highbrow pieces now?'

He stopped. 'Do you want to watch television or is there something else you'd like to do?' he asked, his eyes twinkling.

'You know what I'll choose.' She knew what would engross them both. 'Let's go to your office. I want you to tell me all about the different pieces in Mother's jewel box.'

'Again?'

'Yes please, again.'

CHAPTER THREE

'YOU DON'T want a rest first, Dad?' Jane asked as she bounded downstairs to his office.

'No, love,' he yawned, following more sedately. She watched as he unlocked his safe.

After Elena's death, looking through her jewellery had provided both Jane and her father with a sort of comfort. It was what she always wanted to do on birthdays and anniversaries and sometimes on wet Sunday afternoons. She loved gemstones and jewellery and having Dad's full and enthusiastic attention, as he taught her what he knew.

Her mother had died twelve years ago when she'd been four. After the funeral, Jane had cried, 'I want Mummy.'

Her father had hugged her. 'I do too, little one,' he'd said, 'but Mummy was poorly, remember, and couldn't get out of bed. In a way, she's better off in heaven, though I think she'd rather be here with us if she could. We'll both miss her very much, so we must comfort each other,' and since then they had.

Jane had been only two when her mother first began to feel ill, and Dad had hired a nanny for her. She'd been very fond of Colette, who'd lived with them until she was nearly eight.

'I thought about boarding school for you,' Dad had told her. 'Everybody said it would be sensible, but I couldn't bear to be parted from you.'

So since then she'd done her school homework in the rest room where the 'girls' could keep an eye on her, and in the holidays Dad took her round his other shops when he visited them and put her into holiday clubs.

Jane felt very close to her father. Since she'd been a small child she'd seen herself as 'Daddy's girl' and tried to do what he wanted. She felt she belonged to him body and soul, but she'd been everything to Dad too. He'd always been pleased to receive her drawings and look at the work she did in school when she came home full of tales about what had filled her day. Every six months or so he would take her to the Birmingham Jewellery Quarter to choose more stock, and she'd sit quietly listening to the discussions between buyer and seller.

'When I'm grown up,' she would tell him, 'I want to work in your shops.'

'You don't have to make up your mind yet.'

'But I already have.'

'Your mother went to college to learn about art and design. Wouldn't you like to do the same?'

'No, Dad.' She attended a day school where

importance was put on high academic achievement. She could keep up with the rest of her form but she didn't want to train for one of the professions. 'No, I want to work in your shop.' She knew that hearing her say so pleased him very much, and that it was really what he wanted too.

Jane thought her father knew everything there was to know about jewellery, but he didn't love it in the way so many others did. He had very down-to-earth views about gemstones.

'Just rocks,' he'd say disparagingly. 'And very expensive. Pretty baubles that have no practical use at all.'

Now he had to move the shagreen case containing the Sun Diamonds before he could reach the much larger wooden box behind. Jane spread the piece of black velvet he kept handy over his desk and they sat down side by side. He handed her the key to unlock the box. It was strongly constructed and had her mother's name engraved on top, Elena van Straaten. Inside was a collection of small boxes and cases, each containing a piece of jewellery, most of it inherited from relatives.

Her mother had come from a large Huguenot family in Amsterdam who had earned their living in the jewellery trade for generations. Jane's grandfather had been a diamond cutter of some note, and Elena herself had designed jewellery. Many family members had been killed or starved to death during the Second

World War, but fortunately the trade had taken some of them to other parts of the world. Elena had been born in India, though she was mainly brought up in Amsterdam. To Jane, who knew only Liverpool, it all sounded very exotic.

She opened a leather case and took out a glittering brooch of platinum set with diamonds. Dad pushed his magnifying glass, which he had told her was called a loupe, towards her. 'Tell me what you see,' he said.

He'd trained her to think like a jeweller, to see the good points of gemstones and also their defects. She was now able to assess them for cut, colour, weight, age and value.

'This is a Victorian brooch from about 1880.'

'How d'you know that?'

'Platinum wasn't used in jewellery until about 1870. They didn't have machines to fashion it into delicate shapes. This brooch is like a bow of ribbon, with three baguette-cut diamonds on the knot in the middle, and two more of the same cut on the trailing ends.'

'Describe the diamonds.'

'They're not of the first water; they're very light in colour and there are slight inclusions.'

'What about this?' He laid a diamond and sapphire bracelet before her.

'I like this.'

'Most ladies would,' he said dryly. 'What can you tell me about it?'

'It's hallmarked London, let me see . . .'

41

'Look up the date mark.' He pushed his list of hallmarks in front of her.

'Yes, 1958. I think you gave this to Mum.'

'Yes, I did.'

'For Christmas?'

'It was a birthday present. In fact, I gave her that on her last birthday.' She saw him shudder. 'She hardly wore it. Describe it for me.'

'Six cushion-cut sapphires. Pale blue and of Sri Lankan origin, I think?'

'Yes. What would they weigh?' It was impossible to weigh them now because they were set into the bracelet, but dealers needed to assess their weight to have an idea of their worth.

'About one carat each?'

'Good.'

'Do you want me to count all these small diamonds?' She could see Dad was checking the certificate that had come with the bracelet to provide authenticity.

'There are twenty-six. Tell me about them.'

'Round and brilliant-cut. Some are quarter-carat and some half, all set in white gold.'

'You're remembering what I told you last time.'

'Yes.' Jane never tired of looking at Elena's jewels. Dad had told her that one day, when she was grown up, they would all belong to her.

He smiled. 'This is too easy for you now. You've done it too often. Let's try you on something from the general stock.' He was putting Elena's jewels away.

'Can we do the Sun Diamonds?'

'Well . . .'

'You've never talked me through those.'

'No . . .'

Dad encouraged her to learn all she could about jewellery and even to try pieces on, but he wouldn't let her handle the Sun Diamonds.

'You've never told me why I mustn't touch them. Why you won't let anyone touch them, come to that.'

'It's a long story.' But he was taking the shagreen case from the big safe. He opened it and she leaned forward to take in the sparkling glitter.

'Sit on your hands,' he said. 'You must promise not to touch.'

'I promise. But why?'

He smiled. 'I'm about to tell you. These stones were cut from a much bigger one that was mined in southern India in about 1780.'

'How big?'

'It was said to weigh eighty-one carats.' That made Jane whistle through her teeth. She'd seen a lot of diamonds but never one that big.

'Originally, it was thought to be a brown diamond and it was not a well-balanced shape, being more rounded on one side than the other. Its first owner was a maharaja, and he had it cut and polished into one large gem. It was worn by one of his elephants on ceremonial occasions.'

That made Jane laugh. 'Worn by an elephant?'

'But the owner was at war with the maharaja of a neighbouring state. They fought a ferocious battle which he lost, and afterwards he died of his wounds. The victor took over some of his land and added the Sun Diamond and some of his other jewels to his own collection.

'Within a year, his eldest son, who was ten years old, was mauled by a lion. Shortly after that his wife died in childbirth, leaving him with three daughters. He blamed the Sun Diamond, believing it to be cursed. He gave it to the wife of another maharaja who he thought was plotting against him, and was pleased when a few months later both of them died of some terrible fever. Their heirs feared the Sun Diamond and decided to sell it as soon as they could.

'Nothing was heard of it for generations, until at the beginning of the twentieth century an American millionaire bought it. He suffered a stroke that incapacitated him so he could no longer work. His wife sold it at a bargain price to another rich man to get rid of it.'

'It was cursed, then?'

'Many were afraid it was. Well, the new owner was young and prepared to take a chance; in an effort to beat the curse, he had the stone re-cut using modern techniques. It was now seen to be a yellow diamond, with streaks of intense orange in it and very rare, which meant it was even more valuable than had previously been thought. The owner was delighted, and believed that re-cutting would turn it into a good luck charm. He had four smaller perfect gems cut from the original stone and made up into jewellery as a gift to his bride.'

'And here they are,' Jane said, putting out her hand towards the case.

'No, you promised. Don't touch.'

'The necklace is absolutely gorgeous.'

'It's very ornate.'

'How big is that stone now?'

'Fifteen carats.'

'Wow, with a matching ring and a pair of drop earrings as well.' The Sun Diamonds were all set in white gold and embellished with smaller white diamonds and pearls. 'They're so beautiful. If they bring good luck now, why must we not touch them?'

Edwin sighed heavily. 'I haven't finished yet. In 1929 this owner lost much of his business and a good deal of money in the stock market crash; and the following year, his wife ran off with another man taking her jewels with her. Eventually, she sold them into the trade to have money to live on.'

'It sounds as though they're still cursed.'

'After the last war, there were a lot of stories in newspapers and magazines about precious stones that carried curses. Jewels that were said to bring their owners bad luck, most often disaster and death.

'The Maharaja of Baroda owned two pieces like that. There was a pearl necklace known as the Baroda pearls, and another called the pearl carpet that consisted of diamonds, rubies and emeralds as well as pearls.'

Jane smiled. 'With two he could have come to a very sticky end.'

'Well, I don't know . . . He died without children and his brothers fought long and hard over dividing up his jewels and the rest of his very valuable estate.'

'So how did you come by them?'

'They were bought by Elena's grandfather as a gift for your grandmother.'

'Oh, no! Did she come to any harm? And what about him?'

'He was killed fighting for his country during the First World War. Your grandmother was scared of the curse and it was said she never wore the diamonds after that. She lived on into old age.'

'So Granny wasn't harmed by the curse, and lots of soldiers were killed in the war so probably Grandpa wasn't either.'

Tales about jewels had been Jane's bedtime stories in childhood. But the fact that her mother had died as she had meant that Jane couldn't dismiss the story of the curse entirely.

'Just a myth, of course,' Dad said.

'You don't believe it?'

'Certainly your mother didn't. The Sun Diamonds were her favourite pieces.'

'I didn't realise they'd been hers.'

'Yes, she inherited them from her family. They'll be yours when you come of age.'

'Mine?' They were fabulous and worth a fortune, but . . . 'Yuk, I think I'd be scared to wear them after what you've just told me.'

'Just myths, Jane.' His dark eyes smiled into hers.

She said, 'But Mother wore them. D'you know, after all these years, I don't really remember her.'

'I know. I remember you being upset once when you were little because you couldn't picture her face. Do you remember that?'

'Yes. You brought out those photographs of her, and let me keep one on my dressing table so I'd never forget her face again.'

'Yes, the one where she has you sitting beside her. Those are in the ones I've put out in the sitting room; have you ever noticed?' He was pointing to the Sun Diamonds.

Dad had put pictures of her mother all round their flat then, and at the time it had seemed to bring her closer, but now Jane hardly noticed them. 'She was wearing the Sun Diamonds on her wedding day?'

'Yes. In the close-up of Elena taken in her wedding finery you can see the necklace and the earrings. She was wearing the ring, too, on her right hand. She wore them a lot. She was fond of them.'

Jane remembered painfully her mother suffering from breast cancer, and how after a long illness she'd died at the age of thirty-three.

47

'So now you know why I don't let you handle them.'

'Or anybody else in the shop.' He was even squeamish about touching them himself. He wore gloves whenever he went near them – just in case.

'So you do believe those myths?'

'Let's say I'm afraid there might be some truth in them, though logic tells me it's impossible. That's why I decided the best thing to do was to sell them on your behalf. You can use the money to buy something else.'

'But they've been on display in the shop for nearly a year,' she said.

'Yes, and though many customers stop to admire them, as yet they haven't attracted a buyer. Of course, they are expensive,' Dad told her. 'I should consider reducing the price, but I'm afraid it could be that the story of their curse is too well known.'

'But the next owner might . . .'

'It's just a story, Jane. All the world loves a story, and in the olden days people believed things like that. But in the modern world, we can't blame these stones for what happened to your mother.'

'But why mustn't I touch them, then? Why sell them?'

Edwin Jardine sighed heavily. 'Put it down to illogical fear. Aren't we all scared of what we don't understand? Scared of what might happen? With or without jewels, men go to war and get killed, others fall ill. Many more people lost fortunes in the 1929 stock market crash. And as for selling them, well, they're worth a good deal. If we could sell them, they'd give you a secure future.'

'Dad, I'll have that anyway. I'm going to work in your shop, earn my living.'

He paused. 'Do you want to keep them?'

Jane thought about it. 'No. Like you, I'm scared of what might be.'

Several hours later, up in their sitting room, Edwin Jardine found the canned jollity of Christmas night television wasn't holding his interest, though Jane was laughing at it. He opened the novel Sam had given him, which he'd thought to be to his taste, but found he couldn't get into it, not tonight. Christmas night was a night for ghosts.

He was remembering the Christmases gone he'd shared with Elena. Looking through her jewel case this afternoon had sharpened his memories of her. He'd been very happy in those days and had missed her terribly when she died. He told himself he no longer grieved for her, not after twelve years, but on nights like this he wasn't sure it was true. He knew his life and Jane's would be very different now if she'd lived.

Yes, he'd been lonely. He'd have welcomed a new love in his life who could be a mother to Jane, but he'd never met another woman who aroused feelings of passion in him. He should have made more effort. He'd liked the look of Mrs Biddolph, a war widow of his own age and a fellow organist at St Cuthbert's. Rowena

Biddolph played regularly at evensong and was a good-looking woman. They'd felt an instant rapport when they met, and even now were friendly, but he'd hung back for too long. He'd wasted the opportunity he might have had there.

He'd thought about marrying for companionship, and with that in mind had toyed with the idea of proposing to Dorothy Hadley. He had more in common with her than anyone else.

She was always cheerful. He liked to hear her laugh echo up the stairs and know she was down there looking after his shop. She was not handsome and had grown plumper with the passing years, but she could jolly any of them out of the doldrums, even him.

These days, women had come into their own, and at forty-seven Miss Hadley might feel happy and not want to change her life. On the other hand, she might feel she was not too old to find a man who could love her as a husband should. That had made him hesitate to offer marriage on a companionship basis. He found big decisions like that hard to make. Perhaps the ghost of Elena had stayed with him too long. Now it was probably too late.

He'd always tried to do his best for Jane but it worried him that he wasn't doing enough. Miss Hadley tried to help, as did the other women, but what did they know about young girls? She needed a proper mother.

He'd been taken aback when young Nick Collins had asked if he could take her to the theatre, although he should not have been, since he'd seen them chatting together in the shop and had known they were friendly. But she was only sixteen. Wasn't that very young to have a boyfriend?

He'd asked her if she wanted to go to the theatre with Nick and her eagerness had been disconcerting, almost hurtful. He'd made her his constant companion for years and now it seemed she wanted Nick Collins to take his place.

He sighed. He knew he mustn't discourage her friendships; she had to make friends of her own age if she was to be happy. It was he who must look elsewhere for someone to take her place. One day she'd want to leave him to marry and have children, and he must never stand in the way of her doing that.

He should count himself lucky that he knew Nick. He knew his background and that he came from a respectable family. He'd had him to his office for an hour or so on days when they weren't busy, knowing Nick had a lot to learn about the trade before he could be a competent manager. He'd found him eager to learn and quick to pick up what he was told. Miss Pinfold was showing him how she kept the daily accounts and she said the same. 'A bright lad.'

Miss Hadley, too, had nothing but praise for him. 'A good worker. Nothing's too much trouble for him. He's always polite to the customers – to everybody. He's popular with the girls.'

'With Jane too, it seems,' he'd said.

'She'll be safe enough with Nick.'

He let his eyes go round their sitting room. Jane was right, their home was bare. It looked shabby and lacked comfort. He had his piano, of course, he enjoyed that, but the furniture had been here in his parents' time: the sofa was nineteenth century, without springs and stuffed with horsehair; the carpets and curtains were faded and worn.

The next room was their kitchen. It was spacious but what appliances they had would have been quite at home in a museum. It was also their dining room and it housed a refectory table that would seat six in comfort and eight at a pinch. Against the wall behind it was a wooden bench with a high back and arm rests, and there were four Windsor wheelback armchairs to pull up to it. Old and of solid oak, it was the only furniture he had that he really liked, but it had all grown shabby. He'd been too preoccupied looking after Jane and running his business to notice, and now he was too set in his ways.

It was impossible in this day and age to get a proper housekeeper. He was lucky to have Mrs McGrath to do as much as she did for them. They ate a cold supper. It was the remains of the duck she'd cooked for their dinner on Christmas Eve, followed by a trifle she'd made and a slice of Miss Hadley's Christmas cake.

'I wish I had room for a slice of Miss Bundy's pie,' he said.

Jane smiled. 'That's for lunch tomorrow.'

CHAPTER FOUR

HILDA THORPE lay listening to the sound of the church bells. She couldn't sleep; she had too much on her mind. She knew she'd had very good reasons to get away from the Bolton family. They'd returned to Liverpool on a grey wet day, with very little cash. She couldn't imagine why she'd fallen in love with Gary Bolton – she must have been blind to let him attach himself to her. Their liaison had faltered as soon as money became short and the terrible rows had started well before they'd left Spain. She and the children were miserable.

'We'll be all right once we get settled,' Gary had assured them. 'We'll soon be back in the money.'

He was positive he'd be able to make a good living from fencing again and chose to rent, as a suitable base to carry on his calling, a large and comfortable house in Menlove Avenue. It was not overlooked and stood some distance from its neighbours, where he hoped any unusual activities would go unnoticed.

He refused to claim Social Security, because he

didn't want Social Services to know anything about him and his family, and it would have meant giving his address. He thought it wiser not to involve any of the authorities. To meet their living expenses, he sold his two-year-old Mercedes Benz saloon – part of his previous lavish life style – and bought instead a battered twelve-year-old Ford in order to get about.

Before he left for Spain, Gary's name had been known in the right circles to get fencing jobs. His reputation had been spread by word of mouth, but now his relationships with the people who needed his skills and with those to whom he'd sold had lapsed. Much had changed in the years he'd been away.

Money was so short that Jason found a job as a van driver at a dry-cleaning depot. He collected garments from agents all over the city and returned them when they'd been cleaned. But he let his family know he regarded it as a stopgap and he was eager to join his father in a following that would earn more money.

They found a school for Kitty and Hilda started applying for jobs for herself. She was prepared to take almost anything, but though she was interviewed twice no post was offered to her. She was unable to provide a reference from a previous employer, though she reckoned she'd been rated highly by the catering firm before she'd been caught stealing.

Gary did his best to help by writing a glowing character reference for her under a friend's name and address. He persuaded him to sign it and keep it ready should an employer write and ask for it. But they were afraid that big employers, councils and quasi-government bodies would check whether an applicant had a police record before taking them on.

Hilda achieved a third interview for a catering job at a small family-run hotel. When she was taken to see the kitchens and dining room, she met Don Freeman, a man she'd worked with many years before and with whom she'd got on well. He said he was due off shift and when he suggested they have a drink in a pub round the corner, she jumped at the chance. The wine loosened her tongue and she found herself pouring out her money troubles to him. His life had hit a bad patch too, and in return she learned that his wife had recently left him. They went for a meal and after that she went home with him and spent the night there.

It was, Hilda thought, more a matter of comforting each other than anything else. And why not? Gary no longer told her he loved her and he was showing little interest in her these days. She didn't get home until the afternoon of the following day and it was several hours after that when Gary came home.

'Where did you get to last night?' he demanded angrily.

She told him.

'You spent the night with a man?' He was outraged.

'He was just a friend . . . He gave me some money . . .'

'What? You bitch! That's prostitution!'

'No, it wasn't like that. He said I could pay him back when I was in funds.'

Gary put his face, working with fury, close to hers. 'Don't tell me you didn't have sex?'

Actually, they had. Hilda cowered away from him. It scared her to see him like this.

'You're going to tell me you enjoyed it now?'

'What if I did? You're too stressed out to be any good.'

The palm of his hand swiped across her cheek, and she was barely over the shock of that when he punched her chin, knocking her head back.

'Stay away from other men,' he blazed. 'Don't accept money from them.'

She had bitten her tongue; she could taste blood. 'Gary, it was a loan. We've hardly had anything to eat the last few days.'

'Where is it? Where is this money? I'll burn it.'

'Don't be such a fool. We were desperate for cash. I've paid a month's rent on this house, bought some coal and stocked up the fridge and the larder. The kids are eating the first decent meal they've had in a week. You should be grateful there's a meal here for you.'

He was almost incoherent with temper. 'I'm not having my bint going with other fellows. Cuckolding me.'

'Cuckolding is it now? You told me to get out last week and I wish I had. I should have done once I got hold of this money. You don't own me.'

'I'll knock your bloody teeth out.'

He came at her again with his fists. She'd seen him attack other people like this, but it was the first time he'd turned on her. To feel his fist crash into her face was a real shock. She screamed. He meant to give her a good beating and she really did fear for her teeth.

Kitty was eating in the kitchen and came rushing in, her mouth full of chocolate biscuit.

'Leave her alone,' she yelled and tried to pull him off, but she got a bloody nose for her efforts. It was only when Jason came rushing downstairs to join in the fray that Gary was overcome and forced to stop.

Hilda burst into tears and collapsed in an armchair in front of the fire she'd just lit. Kitty threw her arms round her and wept too. 'He's an animal,' she screamed. They were both covered with blood.

Hilda felt sick, her nose hurt and her cheekbone felt as though it was broken. He'd punched her in the stomach and she'd twisted her shoulder. She was scared to look in a mirror to see what damage he'd done.

If that wasn't bad enough, he'd been too cocky by far about his ability to earn another fortune. He'd gone on to ruin everything. Yes, Gary was to blame for the terrible mess they were in now. She should have pushed off and taken Kitty with her while she had some money, but with an empty purse that had been impossible. She'd eventually got over it and so had Gary. They'd had to, just as they'd got over the rows they'd had before.

She knew Gary had been doing his best to revive his old contacts. He'd taken Jason on a trip to Birmingham to visit a man who in the past had taken stolen jewellery from him, breaking it down and using the gems and precious metals in redesigned pieces. He'd fenced a lot of expensive women's wear in the past. They'd visited a large retail outlet for expensive ladies' wear in Liverpool to let the owner know he was proposing to go back into that business.

Not all the customers who had used his services in the past were still to be found in their old haunts, however. Some he heard were behind bars, while others had found new ways of realising some value from what they stole. He was told of a new fence on the scene who ran a team stealing to order, and was therefore very successful. Gary's confidence took a dip.

Cigarettes remained a very popular commodity. They were of high net value, light to lift and move about, and as they were sold in every pub, newsagent and corner shop they were easy to sell on.

Gary met an old friend who introduced him to a gang who were proposing to intercept a heavy goods vehicle fully loaded with cigarettes between the factory where they'd been made and the warehouse where they would be put in bond. The HGV would then be driven to a disused dock where its cargo could be unloaded away from prying eyes. There were many such docks along the banks of the Mersey these days because goods to be shipped by sea were now being containerised and shipped through a new container terminal,

The gang had a buyer lined up in Holland for the articulated vehicle itself and were anxious to get it away before the alarm was raised. Two Dutchmen were going to take it across the Channel; they had Dutch papers for it and Dutch number plates to put on it, and they intended to give the paintwork a quick respray to disguise it. Then it would be driven down to Dover under cover of darkness.

The plan was for one team to work on the truck while another transferred the haul of cigarettes to the vans that would disperse them to various British cities. Gary had told them he had a suitable van for this task when he had not. He had in mind stealing one earlier in the day and leaving it parked nearby. Jason was keen to get in on the act and already had a van provided by his employers, so Gary mentioned his name and got him on the job too. They were given the same address to which they must deliver the cigarettes, that of a wholesale tobacco merchant in Manchester.

Gary came home pleased at the prospect of earning big money again. He told Hilda it was going to be a very well-organised operation. The date set was in early February, when daylight would be gone by five o'clock. They must show no lights so everything had to be finished before it was too dark to see what they were doing.

When the day came, Gary, feeling poised and on his

toes, was out and about in the morning looking for a suitable vehicle to steal. He intended to drive round industrial sites and had a Transit van in mind, but he'd hardly gone a mile from home when he noticed two men taking something heavy from the back of a white van slightly larger than a Transit. He pulled in to the kerb and gave it a second look. The van had no logo, nothing to make it stand out; it would be ideal for what he wanted. He saw the men disappear inside a guest house, and the door close behind them.

Gary drove his car round the corner, got out and hurried back, feeling his heart begin to beat faster. He was well practised in starting an engine without the key, but to his surprise the keys were still swinging in the ignition. This was too good to miss; it would save him precious minutes. All he had to do was jump into the driving seat, turn the key and go.

It was easier than taking sweets from a baby, though he took the first corner too fast and the squeal of tyres drew the attention of passers-by. All the same, he felt exhilarated and wanted to shout for joy. This was fun. He hadn't realised till now how much he'd been missing the thrill of breaking the law. For the first time, Gary reckoned it was good to be back home. He drove the van for a few miles to get the feel of it, then stopped at a garage to fill up with diesel ready for the evening's trip to Manchester.

This was his chance to open the back of the van and look inside. It was very roomy, just what he needed.

There were several rolls of new carpet inside, twelve feet wide and good quality stuff. They were well worth having: he knew where he could dispose of them and reap extra profit. He drove home and backed the van up to his garage.

He found the carpet rolls weighed a ton. Jason wasn't at home to help and the van was too high to get into the garage where it would be out of sight. He didn't want to keep a stolen vehicle here, where it could be seen from the road, for any longer than he had to.

He had to shell Hilda out from in front of the television to help, and even then the best they could do was roll the carpets out and drag them into the garage. Then he drove the van away and parked it on the dock road, reasonably handy for the job, but not too close.

Gary was satisfied he had everything in place now, and felt on a high because after four months at home at last he was going to earn some real money again. It was exciting, too, to pit his wits against the police. Sizzling with adrenalin, he took the bus back to where he'd left his car and then drove home.

Jason had begged to be included in the cigarette robbery. His dad reckoned it was impossible to earn a decent living without bending the law a bit. Jason didn't often agree with his father but he thought he was right about that.

During the morning, Jason rushed through his dry-cleaning drops without stopping for lunch. He'd gone home in the early afternoon having done most of what his employers expected him to do that day. He found his dad keyed up with excitement and waiting impatiently for the appointed starting time. After eating a sandwich, Jason drove him back to the stolen van on the dock road and went on to the disused dock where they were to meet.

It was deserted and his first feelings were that his father had got it all wrong, but then two more vans pulled up behind him and the drivers let him know they were on the same job. Within moments the articulated lorry drew on and pulled up close to some old buildings.

Seconds later the back of the vehicle was opened up and two men climbed up to toss out huge cartons of cigarettes. Two more men helped Jason load up as quickly as they could while other vans and more men arrived. He was the first to set off for Manchester.

Gary drove on to the dock in time to see him go. He'd had trouble starting the engine, but it was just that it was a strange vehicle and he wasn't used to anything of this size. There were three vans ahead of him in the queue to be loaded, but the gang were a good team. He could feel the excitement in the atmosphere. It was all hands to the plough and Gary did what he could to help, knowing his turn would soon come.

It seemed only moments before he was backing his van into position. He left the engine running while he went inside to arrange the cartons that were being tossed up into the back, so there'd be no waste of space, and he didn't at first notice the commotion outside. The van was half loaded when suddenly the men were no longer heaving the cartons on. Everything just stopped and brilliant lights were cutting through the gathering dusk. Gary went to the back door of the van and peered out to see why.

He went so cold with shock he couldn't get his breath. They'd been surrounded by police cars! His mouth was suddenly dry and his knees felt like rubber. They'd been caught red-handed. But Gary wasn't going to be trapped in the net if he could help it. He slid into the driving seat and set off with screaming tyres, heading for the space between two police cars, one of which was moving to block him. He put his foot down harder and raced for the gap. He hit the police car's bonnet and amid the most awful crunch of tearing metal he was jerked almost to a standstill.

Gary screamed as he was flung violently forward against the steering wheel, banging his forehead. It winded him but the engine hadn't stopped. The gear lever had jumped into neutral; he rammed it back into second, swerved round the other car, spun the steering wheel hard, and half blinded by blood and tears changed into third and headed to what he thought was an unguarded exit from the dock. He was accelerating hard when he turned a corner and hit a row of bollards. That stopped the van and the engine died, but

Gary wasn't finished. He almost fell out and started running.

One officer caught at his coat. Gary swung round and with his last ounce of strength brought his fist crashing into the man's face. But another officer was close on his heels and knocked Gary to the ground. Within seconds, several bodies were pinning him down.

Hilda Thorpe was on edge because she knew Gary and Jason were out on a job. It was the first big one Gary had done since their return home and it wasn't really his sort of thing. Kitty was restless too. Time had crawled since Gary and Jason had left. It was impossible to think of anything else and only too easy to let their nerves get the better of them.

When they heard Jason's van turn into the drive, they rushed to the back door to meet him. 'How did it go?'

'Without a hitch.' He was grinning triumphantly at them. 'A doddle, absolutely plain sailing, couldn't have been easier.'

'Marvellous,' Kitty sang out. 'So we're in funds again?'

'You bet. Give me a hand, Kit, bring that dry cleaning I left in the garage out for me. If I hang the stuff back in the van now, it'll save me time in the morning. Is there anything to eat? I'm starving.'

'Yes, hotpot. It's keeping warm for you in the oven.'

Hilda and Kitty had already eaten. Hilda was

dishing up his share when he came into the kitchen carrying cartons containing a thousand Senior Service cigarettes.

'What are those?'

He laughed. 'For my personal consumption – my private haul.' He stacked them beside his plate on the kitchen table, and gave them a more detailed account of what had happened while he ate.

'So where's your dad?' Hilda demanded. 'When will he be back?' She couldn't settle until he was safely home too.

'He shouldn't be far behind. Any minute now, I'd say.'

Another half-hour crawled past. Hilda couldn't relax, so she washed up Jason's supper dishes for something to do. She was growing more uneasy. 'Where can he be?'

'Perhaps he got lost,' Kitty suggested. 'Ma, does he know his way round Manchester?'

'I don't know.'

'I hope he's all right,' Jason said. 'He should be home by now.'

'Perhaps he couldn't find the wholesaler to make the drop off?'

'We were given maps,' Jason said. 'It wasn't hard to find and I've never been to Manchester before.'

While Kitty made tea for them all, Jason cut himself a large slice of cherry cake and bit into it. That finished, he opened one of his cartons and lit a Senior Service, inhaling deeply.

'Much better than the Woodies,' he said. 'Specially when they're free.' He offered the packet to Kitty. 'I wish Dad would come. Where could he have got to?'

'Don't you dare touch those things, Kitty,' her mother said firmly. 'You'll be sorry if you get hooked. Fags make your clothes and hair smell horrible. They put people off you.' Hilda had been a smoker once and it had been hell trying to give up. 'I do wish Gary would come home. You don't think something's gone wrong?'

She leaned over the sink to look out of the kitchen window. All was black outside except for a dim glow from the street lamp further down the road. At that moment she saw headlights turning into the drive.

'Here he is at last . . .' But was it? It was a car with a blue light on top. 'Hell, no. Jason, I think it's the police!'

He was beside her in an instant. 'Christ! It is!' With one swing of his arm, he posted his cigarette stub down the plug hole and turned on the tap.

'They must have caught him.' Hilda was holding on to the sink to keep herself upright.

'Kitty,' Jason spat, 'keep them waiting. Hold them up. I need a few minutes.'

Hilda couldn't move; she felt paralysed and panic-stricken and couldn't even think.

'Don't rush to let them in.' Jason was gathering up his cartons of cigarettes and running for the stairs. An instant later the silence was shattered by the peal of the front doorbell; it was pushed once, twice, three times. The sound echoed round the house.

Kitty swished the contents of Jason's ash tray down the sink and rinsed that too. Then, sliding an arm round her mother's waist, she hissed, 'Ma, come away from the window, they'll see you.'

Hilda felt herself being pushed into a chair at the table. The door knocker was being rattled violently, and the doorbell rang again. At the same time, a fist battered on the kitchen window, making it rattle, and a stentorian voice bellowed, 'Police. Open up.'

'Hadn't we better do it?' Hilda whispered to Kitty.

'Let the bastards wait.'

But Jason's shoes were pitpattering on the stairs. It was he who opened the door. 'Good evening,' he said. 'What's happened? Is something the matter?'

Hilda was in a fever of anxiety from the moment the police came into the house. Now they were checking on Gary, she was afraid they'd check into her past history too.

She'd be in big trouble if the thefts she'd been charged with two and a half years ago were raked up, and there was also the fact that she'd failed to attend when she'd been summoned to court. She felt sick with dread that everything might come out now. She could see them both being sent to prison.

Her mouth was dry and she was on tenterhooks. Their uniforms were enough to terrify her and there were four of them all firing questions at once.

'Does Gary Bolton live at this address? Is that his car outside? The Ford Cortina?'

'Yes.' Kitty smiled round at them.

'He went out, didn't he? Why wasn't he driving it?'

They were all looking her in the eye. Hilda managed, 'It's an old banger, isn't it? It was giving trouble.'

'Does he have a job?'

'No.'

'So he spends his time at home. What did he do today?'

That was easier. 'Work on his car.'

'But he went out this afternoon. What time would that be?'

'I can't remember exactly. It was mid-afternoon.'

'Who does that van on the drive belong to?'

Jason told them about his job at the dry-cleaning centre. 'I've been here since I came in from work at about five thirty.'

Hilda heard Kitty confirm that with wide innocent eyes, while she herself sat tongue-tied and silent. She had to admit that Jason was keeping his nerve under the awful barrage of questions. He seemed to know intuitively when he could hold forth and when to keep mum.

When they asked Kitty where she'd been this afternoon, she giggled and said, 'School.' That raised a few smiles.

Gary must also have kept his wits about him under

police questioning. They seemed to understand he lived with his wife, his son and her daughter. He'd told them her name was Gemma, his real wife's given name. She didn't know whether he'd done that to make everything seem legal and above board if they checked his marital status, or whether it was to protect her. Either way Hilda had good reason to go along with it.

When they asked if they could search the house, Jason said, 'Why not? We've nothing to hide here.'

Hilda's blood ran cold when she thought of the fags Jason had purloined for himself. The kitchen stank of fags; he'd smoked three since he'd come home. Three of the officers disappeared upstairs. The remaining man was opening and closing cupboard doors round the kitchen. He looked in the fridge and the cooker before asking Jason if he smoked Senior Service.

'I wish,' he said, standing up to fish an almost empty packet of Woodbines from his pocket. He lit up and left the packet in full view on the table before flinging himself back on a chair, 'Sorry, can I offer you one? Only Woodies, I'm afraid.'

'No thanks. Where did those rolls of carpet in the garage come from?'

Jason's innocent smile didn't waver, although Hilda knew he must have seen them when he'd stored the dry cleaning in the garage to make more room for fags in his small van. 'What rolls of carpet?'

Hilda's heart missed a beat. It had been a bad mistake to bring stolen property here, but they all shook their heads and said they knew nothing about any carpet.

'They'll be taken away as evidence,' they were informed. 'We're waiting for a van to come and collect them now.'

All the time Hilda could hear vague sounds as the three policemen searched through the other rooms, but the walls were so solidly built that she couldn't tell where they were, and in any case she didn't know where Jason had hidden his haul.

When they returned to the kitchen and had obviously found nothing, Hilda thought she was over her panic, but then all four of the officers seemed to focus their attention on her.

'And what did you do this afternoon?'

'I stayed in,' she choked.

'You were here all day?'

'I went shopping this morning, but otherwise, yes.'

'Where did you go shopping?'

'Somerfield's just down the road. We needed bacon.'

Slowly, from what they were saying, Hilda was able to piece together that Gary Bolton had been caught with a gang while the robbery was taking place. They were told he'd be held overnight in police custody and appear in court tomorrow.

CHAPTER FIVE

THE POLICE went at last. Hilda felt drained; she slumped back in the chair and closed her eyes. 'Those carpets! Why did Gary have to put them in our garage?'

Kitty said, 'He's dropped himself in the muck, hasn't he?'

'Oh, God, yes.'

Jason had appeared calm and collected throughout but now he was in a lather of sweat. 'They've got him! But it's his own fault, he should have had more sense.'

Hilda groaned. 'Should we be thinking about finding him a solicitor?'

'What's the point?' Jason asked. 'They'll give him a free one anyway. With evidence like he's provided, he won't get off. He might as well plead guilty.' He slid the last Woodbine out of his packet and lit up.

'What did you do with all the other fags?' Hilda asked. 'The Senior Service?'

Jason managed a wry smile. 'They didn't find them.

71

I tossed them up on top of that old wardrobe in the spare bedroom next to mine.'

'That huge Victorian thing?'

'It has a moulding standing up round the top, so nothing up there can be seen unless you climb up to look.'

'That was clever of you,' Kitty said. 'If they'd found those cigarettes . . .'

'Dad and I had a look round for hiding places. It's as well to have things like that clear in one's mind beforehand.'

Hilda said, 'When you told them they could search the house, I nearly died.'

'It's as well to look as though you've nothing to hide. If I'd said no, they'd have kept a watch on what we were doing while they got a search warrant. Then they'd come back and take the place apart believing there was something to find. Wasn't it lucky we'd put the dry cleaning back in the van?'

'If they'd seen it stacked in the garage they'd have wanted to know why,' Hilda said fearfully. 'And what if they'd called forensics out?'

'Would they have found traces from those cartons in your van?' Kitty wanted to know.

'How would I know? They'd probably have found traces of the right sort of mud and stuff to prove I'd driven on that dock. That's the sort of thing they do find. And lucky you washed up my plate and eating irons too.' Jason grinned at Hilda. 'Otherwise they might have asked where I was when you two ate your supper.'

'You've had the luck of the devil,' Hilda told him. 'So have I.'

Jason was triumphant. 'They found nothing to pin on us.'

Hilda had gone to Gary's court hearing the next morning, and because she felt the need of company, she'd taken Kitty with her. Jason took an hour or so off work to pop in too. It was only then that they heard he'd resisted arrest, assaulted a police officer and caused extensive damage both to a stolen van and to a police vehicle. He was released on police bail.

'That was daft,' Jason told him. 'They'll throw the book at you.'

Hilda almost told him she thought it typical of him and absolutely in character, but she held her tongue because Gary looked very down. It seemed he had more than that to worry about. While being interviewed by the police, he'd come to understand that it was his theft of the van in the morning that had alerted them. The other members of the gang would be looking for a fall guy and would want to believe it was his fault they'd been caught. He was afraid they'd give him a hard time.

It seemed that the men delivering the carpet had seen him drive their van away and had immediately notified the police. The neighbourhood force had been on the lookout for it and early in the afternoon had sighted it parked on the dock road. They'd kept it under surveillance after that and he'd been followed when he drove on to the dock. They'd then called for back-up, and when that arrived had caught the thieves in the act.

The few months waiting for the case to come up in court had been traumatic for Hilda. Gary was moody and his temper uncertain; he was always mouthing off about something or other and throwing dishes across the kitchen. He was right about being blamed by the rest of the gang, who beat him up one night when he was coming home from the pub. A passer-by phoned for an ambulance for him and he was taken to hospital.

Hilda was shocked when one of the hospital staff telephoned to let her know. Kitty was already in bed. Fortunately, Jason had just come home, and though he complained about turning out again when he was in the middle of frying egg and bacon for his supper, he drove her to the hospital. Gary was ready to be discharged. He'd had seventeen stitches put in his cuts and lacerations, many of them on his face. He'd also had his ribs strapped up, because he'd been kicked when he was lying on the ground and two had been broken.

He looked so ill and disheartened that Hilda bit back the acid comments she'd been about to make. Jason felt no such inhibition and said it all for her.

'You've been on the receiving end for once, Pa.

Doesn't feel so good, does it? It might teach you to keep your fists in your pockets in future.' He looked at him and smiled. 'You're going to have a black eye, too, by morning. A real shiner.'

Gary groaned. 'I feel terrible. I'm all aches and pains.'

Hilda said, 'I was too when you belted into me.' But she felt sufficient sympathy to make a cup of tea and find some paracetamol for him. It made up her mind. Gary was a violent man. She was going to ditch him before he hit her again.

She would find a gentle, law-abiding man she could respect. Someone who earned enough money by honest means to keep her and Kitty in comfort. She would like to share his home and his life, but if he was already married and wanted a mistress, that would be fine by her. It would be nice to imagine such a man as her husband, but marriage wasn't everything. She'd married Paul Thorpe and thought it was for life until he'd gone chasing after other women. Goodness knows what had happened to him. She hadn't seen him for years. He could be dead by now for all she knew.

She had something to thank Gary for: he'd named her as Gemma Bolton, his wife, which had saved her from being caught for her past offences. But he told her he'd only done that to score against the police, and scoring against authority was one thing Gary took great delight in.

When his case came up, the unthinkable happened.

He was given the heaviest sentence of them all, five years in prison. He was now inside and as he'd named her and Kitty as his dependents, she was able to claim social security. However, she'd had to do that in his wife's name, so now there was another crime to pin on her.

But with no job and Gary in prison, Hilda couldn't afford to pay the rent on the very substantial house. She was already in arrears and Gary had tied them to a long tenancy agreement. She'd had more than enough of Gary and his lawless ways, and didn't want to go on living on a knife edge, always looking back over her shoulder expecting trouble.

Jason, too, was up to his father's tricks and took even greater risks than Gary had. She thought it could only be a matter of time before he joined his father in prison. Since his success on the cigarette run he'd grown more confident. Over-confident, in Hilda's opinion. The dry-cleaning business dispensed with his services. They'd realised that while Jason wasn't working the hours for which he was being paid, the mileage he was putting on their van was astronomical.

'I'm glad,' he shrugged. 'They paid peanuts and it left me with no time to do anything else. And as Pa no longer needs his old banger I can use that.'

Hilda found him hard to cope with. If she asked him to do something, he did the opposite. He came home in the middle of the night and stayed in his bed until lunch time. He expected her to put meals in front of him and grumbled if they were not to his liking.

She counted herself lucky to have evaded the police when they'd come after Gary. If they were to come again after Jason, her luck might not hold. She knew he was beginning to earn money from fencing, and was spending it freely on luxuries. She needed his help with the rent, and other basic essentials, but found him reluctant to part with it to her.

He had bought Kitty a pair of shoes which she needed, and he often brought home cakes and chocolate that she liked. Hilda was afraid that if he stayed free and continued to develop his fencing contacts, the easy money would bind Kitty to him, as she'd been bound to his father. Moreover, he was a handsome virile young man, and they seemed closer than they used to be. She was afraid he'd persuade Kitty into his bed if they stayed much longer.

Hilda had decided a few weeks before Christmas that much the best thing for her to do was to cut and run from Jason. It had taken time, but she'd found herself and Kitty somewhere else to live at an affordable rent.

She'd said nothing to Kitty until the last minute in case she blabbed about it to Jason. This was to be the complete cut-off: they would go and leave no address. It was safer for them that way. She wasn't having Gary back when he came out of prison, and if Jason fell foul of the law in the meantime, she wasn't going to get involved. Most of all, she didn't want him coming round to see Kitty.

Hilda had quietly put her belongings together and packed some of Kitty's while she was at school. She arranged that moving day should be on a Saturday. Kitty was up by half past ten, and when Hilda heard Jason getting up she cooked a substantial brunch for them all. Jason went out shortly afterwards; usually he didn't return until after they'd gone to bed.

She knew then it was safe to tell Kitty; she presented it as an exciting event, an adventure. Together they fetched a taxi from the rank by the station, returned to collect their belongings, and moved to their new home. Kitty had howled with temper when she saw it.

'It's a dump! I hate it here. Why have we left a nice house for this? I want to go back.'

'We're never going back. We're cutting ourselves off from the Boltons. I don't want you dragged down into their criminal world. I want you to promise never to go near Jason again.'

'But he'll be worried when he finds we've gone. I think we should have told him.'

'Give me the front door key you had to that house.'

'I want to keep it.'

'No, give it to me,' Hilda screamed, knowing she had to get it. 'Come on, Kitty, I want it now.' Once she had it safely in her own handbag, she said, more calmly, 'I want you to promise that you won't go back to see him.'

'But Ma, I don't see—'

She'd gripped her daughter's arm and given it a twist. 'Promise. Promise me now.'

'All right,' Kitty had gasped. 'I promise.'

Kitty thought of their first days in the flatlet as hell on earth. She missed Jason. Without him all the fun had gone out of life. Ma was niggly, always on edge and keeping a close watch on her. She understood that her mother thought the move was for their own good, but it certainly wasn't what Kitty wanted. She loved Jason and he loved her. Despite Ma's wishes, she wasn't prepared to be parted from him. Within a week she'd made contact again.

She needed her key to Jason's house and went through her mother's handbag when Hilda wasn't looking. She found two keys in it. She slipped her own into her pocket and then, on further thought, took the other one too. One key would only remind Ma that there should be two.

The only time Ma allowed her out alone was to go to school. The next morning, instead of going there, she'd taken the bus back to Menlove Avenue to see Jason. She had left the flat at the usual time, which meant it was just after nine o'clock when she arrived, and she knew Jason was unlikely to be out of bed. She let herself in and rang the doorbell several times to wake him up before going upstairs. His bedroom was in semi-darkness, the curtains still drawn.

'Jason? Hello? Wake up, it's me.'

He stirred and an arm came out of the bedclothes. Slowly he sat up and laughed, his dark eyes still hazy with sleep. He was very good looking with large strong features and a square chin, his dark straight hair cut fashionably long, and just to see him again sent shivers down Kitty's spine. She threw herself on to the bed.

'Kitten! Am I glad to see you.' A warm arm came out of the bedclothes to pull her closer. He gave her a long lingering kiss. 'I thought you'd deserted me.'

'Not me. It's the last thing I'd do. It was Ma's idea.'

'I guessed it would be.' He was laughing, his pleasure at seeing her all too obvious. 'I was worried. I didn't know where you'd gone or how to find you.'

'You knew I'd come back?'

'I hoped you would,' he said. 'I need you. I love you. This house is as quiet as the grave now everybody's gone. You come back as often as you like. We won't let your mother keep us apart.'

Kitty beamed at him. 'Me and Ma are living in a rathole of a place just to get away from you. I can't bear it.'

'I've missed you terribly,' he told her. 'But I don't miss your mum. She was getting me down, nagging about everything, especially about you. She thinks I'm a bad lot, Kitten.'

She laughed. 'Don't I know it.'

'Now you've come back it doesn't matter.'

'But I can't stay. This is the first place she'd look for me, isn't it?'

'Probably, but if we went somewhere else things would be different. We could be together again. Just you and me.'

'Ma would have a fit.'

'Let her. Why not, if it's what we both want? Not just yet perhaps, but soon, and in the meantime there'll be advantages.' He nibbled her ear. 'When you visit me, we'll have the place to ourselves. I do love you, Kitten, it's marvellous to have you back. It did my head in, not knowing where you went.'

She pulled herself upright, slipping off her coat and letting it fall to the bedside mat. 'You're the tops. Shall I make you some breakfast? What would you like?'

He smiled and his eyes looked dreamy. 'I'd rather you got your kit off and got into bed with me for a bit.'

Kitty giggled. 'What a good idea.' She could see him struggling out of his clothes under the blankets.

Slowly, she began taking off her school uniform, waving each garment at him before tossing it on the floor. Jason lay back on his pillows with his hands behind his head, his dark eyes following every movement she made. She knew this was what he enjoyed. He called it 'a bit of strip tease' but it wasn't tease at all. It would be the real thing. Naked, she did a pirouette.

He was throwing back the bedclothes for her. She got in, pulling them over her and snuggling up against his warm and welcoming body.

'How much better life would be if Ma had let me stay with you.'

The thing was, Ma still treated her like a child and wanted to keep her that way for ever. Ma couldn't stay away from men herself, but she wanted to stop Kitty having any fun. Kitty was fed up with that. She gave herself up to Jason's lean firm body. To him, she was an adult and they did adult things.

Hilda had had to listen to Kitty moaning non-stop for days; about their new home and about leaving Jason to fend for himself.

'I like him,' she'd wept. 'He's good fun and gives me money for the pictures.'

That made Hilda glad they'd escaped. It sounded as though she'd only just got Kitty away in time.

'We've turned over a new leaf,' she told her daughter. 'We're going to be honest citizens from now on. You'll thank me for this when you're grown up.'

'Well, I certainly don't now. It's miles to get to school from here. I won't go any more.'

'Don't be silly, you have to go to school. We can change you to a nearer one, if you like.'

'It's all chop and change. I've only been at this one for a few months. Just long enough to make friends with Flossie, and now you want to move me again.

'Look, love, I know this flat is awful, but we'll find somewhere better. I'll get a job . . .'

'You've been trying to get a job for months. It isn't going to happen, is it?'

'I've got to find a job. I'll find a way.'

ALL THAT GLISTENS

When they went to bed on Christmas Eve, Hilda couldn't get to sleep. Kitty was taking more than her fair share of the mattress, so Hilda pulled her pillow closer and made herself think about just what she'd need to do to move herself and Kitty out of this dump. She had important decisions to make.

There were several things she had to do before it would be possible to get a job. The first problem was that as soon as she filled in any application form with the name Hilda Sarah Thorpe and her date of birth, she could be heading for trouble. Employers had only to check whether she had a police record and her application would be thrown out. Big employers probably did that routinely. She'd drawn a blank with the health service and the council, and though neither had told her why, she could guess. Even worse, her name and address might be brought to the attention of the police.

Hilda couldn't change her surname because then Kitty's name would not be the same as hers. She'd registered her in school under the name of Thorpe and she wanted everything about them to appear as ordinary and normal as possible.

But there was nothing to stop her changing her given name and her birth date. That would make it more difficult to pin that police record on her. She could knock a few years off, be younger . . . But no.

She remembered the men she'd seen coming out of that jewellery shop; men who could afford to buy their women diamonds. If she wanted to appeal to the older man who'd had time to make an honest fortune for himself, perhaps she should make herself a little older. Add five years or so?

But if she landed a job, would they ask for proof of her age? Yes, any employment in which she could earn a pension meant she'd be asked to produce her birth certificate. That would limit her choice of jobs.

And anyway, finding a job wouldn't solve their problems. She'd never earn enough to buy them a decent standard of living. She'd have to get a job but that would be just the start.

She'd call herself Honor Sarah Thorpe. There wasn't a more wholesome honest name than that. She'd say she was five years older; smarten herself up and find a better place to live. She'd take any job to start, she had to, and once she had that, the first thing she'd do would be to post that book back to Social Services. She didn't want to be caught drawing social security she wasn't legally entitled to. And life on state benefits didn't suit either her or Kitty.

She'd need to be fussy about where she looked for work. Men with money belonged to sailing clubs, tennis clubs or golf clubs. Some would employ catering staff. They patronised expensive hotels too; she could do reception work or bar work there. Perhaps even a shop that sold expensive clothes for men or a jewellery shop like the one they'd passed this afternoon. She needed to be where men with money went.

She had applied for a job with the benefits agency, and thank goodness she hadn't got it. To be surrounded by men looking for social security was where she'd been all her life: that had been her big problem. She had to break away.

She'd let herself go this last few months but she could still attract a man. She'd slept with quite a few in her time but always for love or comfort or just the hell of it. She wasn't queasy about doing it for money if that was what it took, and to be honest she couldn't think of any other way to earn the sort of money she'd need to turn over this new leaf. It was legal, wasn't it? Especially in her own home, in a middle-class suburb. At least, she wouldn't feel the police were watching her as she did now.

But she wasn't going to end up as a call girl, no thank you. That was not her goal. It would be just a temporary measure to get her and Kitty out of this hole. Her goal was to find someone who wanted her to share his life. She wanted to swing on the arm of a prosperous gentleman who could shower her with diamonds. She wasn't going to be put off that plan. She needed to get started.

The next morning, she was awake before Kitty. She touched her. 'Kitty, love, wake up. It's Christmas Day.'

Kitty would have turned over and gone back to sleep if she'd let her.

'Kitty, listen to me. From now on my name is Honor Sarah Thorpe. I'm going to call myself Honor.'

Kitty grunted. 'Give over, Ma. That's just as old-fashioned as Hilda.'

'I hate the name Hilda. Honor sounds honest and upright – it sounds middle class. I like it.'

She was going to think herself into being Honor Thorpe, like an actress thinking herself into a character she was going to play. She'd get it right. She'd get them out of this mess.

Kitty rated it her worst Christmas ever; she'd known it was going to be. What sort of Christmas could it be without Jason? She'd done her best to provide some cheer by having carols crashing through their room before Ma had the tea bags in the cups, but it hadn't really helped. The television was the only thing that had kept her sane. Jason had been furious when he'd missed that. She couldn't stop thinking about him and imagining the feel of his arms round her and the way he pulled her close.

But both Christmas Day and Boxing Day had been dire. She'd been cooped up with her mother in this miserable flat, and hadn't had one prezzy to unwrap. The only decent thing had been the ten pound note Mum had given her clipped inside a card.

When Kitty woke up on the twenty-eighth of December, she found herself alone in the sagging bed. A subdued drone told her the television was on in the room across the landing. But she was filled with relief and very glad the holiday was over. Normal life would return today. The shops would open, and that meant they could go out.

She'd been unable to get that white fur coat out of her mind. She'd looked fantastic in it. The sales would be starting now, so perhaps it would be reduced? But even her ten pounds wouldn't be enough for that.

By the time she was dressed, her mother had cleaned up the living room and was ready to leave.

'I'll be able to draw our social today,' she said. 'I'll get us something nice for dinner. Why don't you put your coat on and come to the shops with me? The walk will do you good.'

Kitty put the kettle on. 'Ma, I don't want to go round food shops. The sales will be starting. I want to go into town by myself.' Ma must have wanted to be on her own too, because for once she didn't insist on taking her. 'I'm going to spend my ten quid on a jumper.'

As the door closed behind her mother, she decided this was a good chance to go round and see Jason and they'd been few and far between. She'd drink her tea first, though, as there was no need to hurry: he was unlikely to get up for another hour.

She took the bus back to Menlove Avenue and found the old Ford parked on the drive and his bedroom curtains still drawn. She rang the bell twice to let him know who it was before she put her key in the lock and let herself in.

'Hello, Jason,' she called. 'Are you awake?'

He came out of the kitchen yawning, his thick dark hair uncombed, his father's heavy dressing gown swinging open to show the T-shirt and underpants he'd worn in bed.

'Hi, Kitten,' he said. 'Lovely to see you.' He kicked the door shut behind her and wrapped his arms round her in a bear hug, raining kisses on her face. 'Have you had a good Christmas?'

'Rotten. No prezzies, no parties, no turkey.'

'Poor you. I thought you might have come round on Christmas night. You knew I was having a few mates in. We had a great time.'

'I didn't dare. Ma would kill me if she knew I was here now. Where else could I say I was going on Christmas night? Everybody stays with their family, don't they?'

'Except us. We're on our own.' He pulled her into the kitchen. The sink was full of dirty dishes. 'D'you want some breakfast? I was thinking of bacon butties.'

'Yes, I'm starving.' Kitty knew her mother would be shocked at the state of this house now. She glimpsed the chaotic sitting room through the open door. Evidence of his party still remained; dirty glasses and plates stood on every surface, with bits of food and half-empty beer bottles. The house had looked neat and tidy when they'd lived here. Mum was fussy about such things.

'I've had a great Christmas. I went out with the boys again last night.' He rubbed his face and smiled sheepishly. 'I'm a bit hung over this morning.'

Kitty got out the frying pan. 'You can always go back to bed.'

'No, I've got a job.'

'A real job?'

'Yes, pukka. At the local off-licence. Start at three o'clock today. Three till nine.'

'I thought you were helping your dad's friends sell the stuff they'd pinched? You said you could make enough on the side and wouldn't have to bother with an ordinary job.'

His eyes still looked bleary, but he gave her a theatrical wink. 'I'll only do it for a week or so, though right now the wages will come in handy. What I'm really doing is a bit of research for a feller who wants to know about the shop's security. Who holds the keys, when they bank the takings and what day the stock comes in, that sort of stuff.'

'They won't be able to pin the job on you?'

'No. I'll leave before he does it, and I've made sure they won't be able to trace me from the details I filled in on their form.'

'This is why Ma thinks you're dangerous.'

'I know. But she cleared out with you, leaving me with rent arrears and a whole lot of bills to pay. You could say it's her fault I'm doing this job. Where else could I turn?'

Kitty laughed. 'She'd have a fit if she heard you say that.'

'We'll call this brunch,' Jason said as he helped Kitty

make bacon butties. They were good, though the bottle of brown sauce was empty. Afterwards, he cut two large slices of Christmas cake. When the hands of the kitchen clock stood at twelve thirty, he stood up.

'If you'll make a cup of tea for us, Kitten, I'll have a quick shower and then I'll take you out and buy you a prezzy before I go to work. What would you like?'

Kitty giggled with delight. 'Oh, Jason! I've seen a smashing white fur coat in town. I'd love that, if we could get to the shop before someone else buys it.'

'White fur coat! God, Kitten, that sounds expensive.'

She told him the story of how her mother hadn't had enough money to get it on Christmas Eve.

'They were marking things up for the sales then. They said thirty pounds but it'll be cheaper today. And Ma gave me ten pounds, so I'll throw that in.'

By the time Jason was ready to go out, he looked lovely in the new yellow sweater he'd treated himself to. Once he'd parked the Ford, Kitty hung on to his arm and led him towards the shop. As soon as they turned the corner of the street, she shrieked with delight. 'Oh, look! It's still in the window.'

'It's been reduced to twenty pounds,' Jason said when they drew near. 'If you really like it, that's not dear. Come on, try it on again and I'll see if I approve.'

Kitty knew he would. It gave her a real thrill to button it round her. She felt a queen in it, and had her anorak wrapped up so she could wear it to leave the shop.

'I've never wanted a coat more than this one,' she breathed. 'But Ma will want to know how I managed to get it. She knows I only have ten pounds.'

'Tell her your friend Flossie lent you a tenner,' Jason said. 'But that you'll have to pay her back.'

He dropped a kiss on her forehead and pulled her arm more tightly through his.

CHAPTER SIX

JANE HAD had a lovely Christmas, but what she was most looking forward to was going to the theatre with Nick. She hadn't been out with him on a date before. In fact, she'd never been out with any boyfriend, and she wasn't sure her father approved.

'But he is Sam's grandson,' he said to her, as though reassuring himself.

It was Nick's father who was Sam's son, and since his divorce he'd been away working in Africa in the oil industry. Nick had been taken on by her father six months ago, but he'd spent the first three of them working in the Crosby branch under the manager there.

'To knock the corners off him,' Sam had told her. 'Before he comes here where we're so much busier.'

'He's very good-looking,' Pam had reported, when Jane came home from school on his first day, 'and everybody seems to like him. He's young and I think he'll be fun to work with.'

Jane had taken to Nick straight away. According to

Miss Hadley he'd asked to change the time of his afternoon break so he could have it with her when she came home from school, and he seemed to take every opportunity to chat her up. All through Christmas, she sprayed herself with Coty L'Aimant and thought of him all the time.

Mrs McGrath cooked a meal for them every evening. She got everything ready and put it in the oven, and wrote a note to let them know at what time it must come out. Then she went home, leaving them to serve themselves.

There'd been much discussion about what should be on the menu when Nick and Sam came to supper. It was rare for anybody to be invited. Mrs McGrath advised a beef casserole because it could wait happily until they were ready to eat it, and it would be easy for Edwin to serve.

By lunch time, Jane couldn't sit still. She'd gone to great pains to look her best. She'd washed her dark straight hair last night and put it in curlers. She meant to wear her best green dress and her winter coat. Not that she had much choice, but he'd only ever seen her in school uniform or in a plain white blouse and skirt when she worked in the shop, so that didn't matter.

In the days before Christmas, she and Pam Kenny had gone to Boots in their lunch hour and had chosen bottles of foundation and lipsticks to suit what they judged to be their colouring. She'd taken Pam straight up to her bedroom to try them on. Jane had dark hair but fairish skin while Pam had light brown hair and a tanned skin tone.

'We've got it wrong,' Pam said. 'You look better in what I chose and I look better in yours. I wouldn't have believed it – I've been buying the wrong foundation shade for years.'

'But you don't wear it to work.'

'No, it saves time in the morning.' Pam still looked sixteen with her short straight hair and fringe.

'Let's swap.'

'Good idea. And if I were you, I'd be sparing with them to start with,' Pam advised. 'Especially the lippy.'

Jane had gone down to the rest room afterwards and Miss Hadley had said it made her look pretty, and the pale pink lipstick was very suitable for a young girl.

But Dad had said, 'Aren't you a bit young for that stuff?'

Jane wanted to look more grown up for Nick. He was twenty-two after all, and wouldn't want to be seen out with a schoolgirl.

She was ready when Nick and Sam arrived for supper. The meal was very good, but Dad wasn't used to having visitors in the flat, and was rather a stiff host. Things were better when she and Nick were on their own.

'You look different,' he told her, and his brown eyes gazed into hers. 'Really grown up.'

'You look different too,' she said quickly, to hide the

fact that she could feel herself blushing. He was wearing grey slacks and a sports jacket instead of the formal suit he wore to work.

She walked beside him, matching her steps to his. She wanted to hold on to his arm, but wondered whether that would be too familiar for a first outing. He took her hand in his, wrapped it round his arm and pushed both their hands into his pocket.

'Warmer this way,' he said, smiling. 'Aren't you cold? You've come without your gloves.'

'They're in my handbag,' she told him. 'I'm quite warm, actually.' She could feel her heart pumping, making her blood course round her body. She was thrilled to be out with him.

One of the nicest things about living in the centre of Liverpool as she did was that it was only a short walk to restaurants, theatres and cinemas and, of course, other shops. They were all within a stone's throw of Jardine's.

She'd been to the Empire before but this visit generated more of a thrill. It was lovely to be so close to Nick. She could see that even after the curtain went up, he kept looking at her instead of the stage. It was a wonderful play; she loved the costumes and the characters.

'Just the thing to see at Christmas,' Nick said. It was cold and dark when they came out and Tiny Tim's 'God bless us, every one' was still ringing in her head. When they reached the back doorway into the shop,

Nick took her into his arms and kissed her. Jane felt thrills running down her spine.

'I mightn't get another chance to do this when we're leaving,' he said. 'Not with Grandpa watching us. Not to mention your dad.'

They spent quite a long time in the back doorway. Jane knew she was falling in love.

The new year of 1972 came in. Jane spent as much time as she could working in the shop during her school holidays. It was what she enjoyed most and it meant she saw as much as possible of Nick.

They had a week together in the repair department and Sam taught them to replace watch straps and to put jewellery through the machine to clean it after he'd done small adjustments and repairs. A lot of the work involved packing and posting articles back to manufacturers for more complicated work. They helped with that.

When Jane went back to school, she looked forward to Saturdays when she could help out in the shop and be in the thick of things with her father and see more of Nick. He asked her out regularly, to see a film or a show or just to have a chat over a cup of coffee after the shop closed.

One Saturday morning, when she took a cup of tea to her father's office, he looked up from his ledgers and said, 'In June or July I'm going to move Nick to our Chester branch. He's here to be trained and I want him to have experience in several of our shops. As his mother's in Chester he'll have somewhere to live, and they probably want to see more of each other.'

Jane's spirits sank. 'How long will he be there?'

'Four months or so, but then I'd like him to go somewhere else. Perhaps to the Southport branch.'

'Couldn't he come back to one of the shops in Liverpool first? So we won't be parted for so long?'

'We'll have to see,' he told her. She knew her father thought she should spend more time on her schoolwork and less in the shop. 'I'd like you to stay on and perhaps go to university. I don't want to put pressure on you. It has to be your decision, but I'd like you to train for a profession.'

'Why?' she demanded. 'When you've got this glamorous business that I really want to work in?'

'There's nothing glamorous about the business, Jane. If you mean the gold and precious gems, I have to say that jewellery has no substance. It's all sparkle, froth and fairy stories.'

'Dad! Sam says you have a substantial business. You know you have.'

'In one sense. Anyway, you'd find working here humdrum in time.'

'Don't you want me here? I thought that's what most fathers wanted, someone to follow in their footsteps, build on what they'd started. Like you followed in Grandpa's.'

Her father said nothing for a few moments. She could see he was thinking about it.

'Really, that's what I do want,' he said at last. 'I love having you near me in the shop. It isn't that, but in business things can go wrong. If the profit went down and was no longer enough to support us . . .'

'Dad! I didn't know things were that bad?'

'No, no, love. I'd just like to think you could support yourself if you had to, as a teacher or lawyer or dentist or . . . well, whatever you like.'

'I don't want to train for anything like that. My heart wouldn't be in it, so it would be a waste of time. I want to be here with you. I want us to run this business together and I don't understand why you think it might not be able to support us both.'

Her father sighed. 'It's a long story and I've got things I have to see to now.'

'Right, you can tell me another time. But what I want to do is to leave school and work in the shop; make my career here.'

He said, 'If you're really serious about that, I'll train you to run the business properly. That means you'll have to learn to manage our other shops, and you can't expect to be near Nick all the time. It won't be possible. Also, you must be prepared to start at the bottom, so since you're spending so much of your spare time here now you can take over all the errand-running from Pam Kenny. That'll free her up to serve more customers.'

'That's fine by me.' Jane smiled. 'I'm glad I've persuaded you . . .'

Her father was frowning. 'Hang on a minute, there's another condition.'

'What's that?'

'That you take a course on bookkeeping at a secretarial college. In fact, it wouldn't hurt for you to learn to type as well. A big part of running a business like this is to be able to do every job in it and you'll certainly need a good grasp of our accounts. That's how I know which articles make a profit and which ones don't.'

'All right,' Jane agreed. It would be better than school.

'I'll ask Miss Pinfold which secretarial college she went to and book a place for you in September. And I'd better write to your school and let them know you'll be leaving at the end of the summer term.'

'Thank you, Dad. Thank you.' Jane dropped a kiss on his shiny bald patch.

Honor Thorpe knew she'd have a struggle to get her plans up and running, but in the middle of the January sales, Watson Prickard, a high class men's outfitters in Liverpool, were in difficulties. Two members of their staff were badly injured in an accident when the car bringing them to work skidded on a patch of ice.

Under her new name, Honor had already applied for a job there. She thought her luck had turned when she received a postcard asking her to come in and see the manager. In his kind and gentle manner, he explained about the accident and offered her a temporary job as a sales assistant.

'It's just for a few weeks,' he said. 'Until they can come back to work.'

She knew the wages were never going to solve her problem, but it was a start. She had her hair cut and bought herself some smarter clothes. On her first morning, she asked to be shown how the cash registers worked because she'd never seen that type before.

She'd thought the job would give her the chance to assess the customers with a view to picking up clients for her other service, but she soon discovered that men often brought their wives or girlfriends along to give an opinion before they bought a new suit. Even when they didn't, she quickly realised she couldn't spend enough time talking to them. They were all able to afford expensive suits, but they'd need more than that to afford her. She found it impossible to pick out with any certainty those who would suit her purpose.

She'd always been able to attract men; she smiled and smouldered at them and some responded, but in the time available with each customer she found it impossible to further her plans. She decided bar work would provide more opportunities for social chitchat.

Honor made up her mind to work hard and do her best to be honest, efficient and polite. She felt the staff accepted her and she quite enjoyed being there. Ten weeks later, when the injured assistants were ready to return to work, her employment was terminated. She asked the manager if she might give his name as a reference when she found another job, and he said he'd be pleased to recommend her.

Knowing her job was temporary, Honor had researched her next move. Only the week before, she'd clipped an advertisement from the *Liverpool Echo*. Woolton Park Golf Club was asking for applications from experienced catering staff, chefs, waitresses and barmen.

The golf course was some distance from where she lived so getting there and back would not be easy, but she applied immediately. She knew about catering, she was skilled in cooking and serving high quality meals, and she thought she might be the sort of person they were looking for. One difficulty was that she couldn't tell them where she'd gained her experience. She made up a story about setting up her own little catering business in Marbella, but having to return when her husband fell ill.

She was told the golf club had served meals for some time, but was ready to open a large extension to house a new dining room and kitchen. They were hoping to serve many more meals; dinner would be available every night, with lunch as well on Saturdays and Sundays. If the demand was there, they would provide lunch on a daily basis too.

They had a catering manager but he needed an assistant, capable of taking charge on two days each week. It was not an office job and it would mean split shifts at the weekends. Honor would be expected to fill in serving, cooking and helping in the bar as needed.

She saw other people waiting to be interviewed but a few days later she received a letter offering her the job. She felt it would suit her purpose down to the ground.

On the first evening she was asked to help serve at dinner. She'd done some waitressing before and was confident she could take and serve orders. They were not busy. She set out to be friendly to everybody. There were one or two men dining alone and she concentrated on them. A singleton always welcomed a bit of chitchat, and even if it didn't further her own plans, it usually meant a generous tip.

But within the first few weeks Barry Clarkson, a club member and a local builder, was showing interest in her. Honor had volunteered for a regular stint in charge of the bar at lunch time, and after several whiskies he told her his company was working on two sites; on one he was building small houses for sale and on the other two blocks of flats which he intended to rent out. They were going to provide him with an income when he retired. She felt a stirring of interest. He seemed to be a man of substance.

She judged him to be close on sixty; portly, with a florid complexion and hooded eyes. Not the type she would go for if she listened to her heart, nor the type likely to attract women, but he seemed pleasant enough.

He often ate in the club dining room, either alone or with another member. She found him receptive to her advances, and they became quite friendly. He'd often pop in for a drink and a chat over the bar. They started serving daily lunches and he was one of the regulars. She judged him to be a lavish spender.

One night he asked her if he could take her somewhere else for a drink, where she didn't have to keep breaking off to serve other customers. She met him in the bar of a hotel on her next night off. She'd sensed he was after more than a drink and when he suggested taking her up to one of the hotel bedrooms she wasn't surprised.

But she couldn't make up her mind whether she should ask for payment for her services, or rely on his generosity to provide goods in lieu. When he told her he loved her, she decided it was impossible to ask him for money, so instead she pretended to be in love with him. She found entertaining him entertained her at the same time. It was better than watching television with Kitty in the hovel they called home. He started taking her out to dinner every week, and he'd book a room in a hotel where they could go afterwards. He became fussy about being seen with her. It was all right in the golf club bar or the dining room but he didn't want her to be seen getting into his car in the car park. There was a small pub a short walk away. Honor would go down there on her night off, and find him in the bar waiting for her. Sometimes they spent the night together.

Honor had hoped he didn't have a wife, but although he didn't mention one from his air of secrecy she guessed he must have. She asked him.

'Yes, I'm married,' he said. 'I play a lot of golf but Mabel's given up playing, though she still acts as club treasurer.'

She heard all about Mabel then. They'd never had children, and she was more interested in wringing more profit from his business than she was in him. Her hobby was breeding Labradors. Their home was full of them; she judged at dog shows and had won several awards at Crufts.

Honor told him about Kitty and how they hated the uncomfortable flatlet they were renting. He actually offered to help her find somewhere better.

When she thanked him, he said, 'Well, it's my line of business, isn't it? I have a couple of empty flats to rent but I don't think I should become your landlord. It could say more about us than would be discreet.' He smiled knowingly and she knew exactly what he meant. The only link between them must be the golf club.

Honor said, 'I'll never be able to afford to buy.'

'Then I must temper the wind to the shorn lamb,' he said. 'Occasionally, I take a house in part exchange for a new and bigger one. If something suitable should come up, I'll see what I can do.'

ALL THAT GLISTENS

*

The summer holidays were about to start when Nick was moved to the Chester branch. Jane was sorry to see him go.

'It's not that far away,' he told her. 'I can come and see you often. If I come to Liverpool after the shop closes on a Saturday we can go out, and I can stay the night with Grandpa and spend most of Sunday with you too.' He did so as frequently as he could, and tried to tell her all about his life in Chester, but inevitably Jane wasn't able to see as much of him as she had, and he became involved with other things and other people she didn't know.

At the beginning of September Jane started at the Cavendish Secretarial College. The students were no longer treated like children and she felt quite grown up. To her surprise, she found she enjoyed the book-keeping lessons as well as learning to type and write shorthand.

One wet autumn Sunday, her father went down to his office after they'd had lunch, and when she'd tidied away and washed up, Jane followed. He'd lit the gas fire, and was settled in his big leather chair; she knew he found it comfortable. It was a good-sized room, but with the enormous partners' desk, the huge safe and a bank of filing cabinets, there wasn't much spare space. Ledgers, catalogues and papers were spread every-where, but Dad could always put his hand on what he wanted.

He always had his desk lamp on, because the small uncurtained window let in little light. It was covered in security mesh and the back of Church Street was very different from the front. The backs of the buildings were of soot-blackened brick, with a hotch-potch of extensions and alterations that had been added at various times through decades if not centuries. The buildings opposite, which fronted Leigh Street, still rose to five or six storeys, cutting off the sky, but they weren't so grand as those on Church Street. Here and there, half hidden, was a narrow alleyway between them, giving access to back doors. Every window visible, many rusting and all covered with city grime, was fitted with an iron grille to thwart burglars. It was a dismal scene.

Jane listened to the rain gusting round the building. 'Do you remember, ages ago, you were going to tell me why you don't think your business is big enough to support us both?' she reminded him.

'I can't say I do, but I think I know what I must have been talking about. It's nothing to do with the size of the business, Jane. It's the nature of the trade. It's all built on make-believe.'

'You mean those myths about certain pieces of jewellery, like the Sun Diamonds? Everybody takes stories like that with a pinch of salt, Dad. They have nothing to do with the everyday business of selling engagement rings.'

'No, that's not what I mean. I'm talking now about

true stories. Sam says I'm a fanciful old man and it'll never happen. Perhaps it won't in my time, but it could in yours.'

'What could?' Jane sat back expecting another fairy story.

'Years ago, at the end of the war, I had a friend called Bill Bowen. He owned a cinema, a big one. On Saturday nights there were queues waiting to go in for second house. I thought he had a wonderful business and so did he. It earned more profit than we did here. Then came television and the people who used to go to the pictures twice a week stayed at home watching their own set.'

'I still go to the pictures.'

'The young do, but it has to be a very special film to attract those with children or those set in their ways like me. Gradually, Bill found he couldn't fill his vast picture house, and his business produced less profit. The much reduced audience wanted smaller cinemas, with bigger, more comfortable seats and more choice of films. The ground floor of the old Rialto became a furniture showroom. Upstairs, in what used to be the balcony, he built a flat for himself. It had a very grand entrance and an imposing flight of stairs to reach it, but . . .'

'Dad, I can't see what that has to do with the jewellery trade. People will always want gemstones.'

'It was the advance in technology that ruined Bill's business. He had no control over that.'

'He must have seen it coming. It wouldn't have happened overnight.'

'You know Jack Williams with the photographic business up the road here? He's worried that advances in photography will put him out of business. He sees it coming and hopes it won't be in his time, but other than selling up if he can he doesn't know what to do about it.'

Jane could understand that. 'But not in the jewellery trade, surely?'

'Yes, very much in this trade. There've been huge advances in my time. Technical advances. Look what Mikimoto has done for the pearl necklace. Instead of fishing blindly for oysters and opening hundreds to find one wild pearl, the oysters are farmed and can be made to produce real pearls. Once, pearls were scarce and only the rich could afford them. Now they produce enough to glut the market and everybody can have them.'

'Is that a bad thing? The girls at college like pearls. So do I.'

'Not a bad thing for you or your friends, but for those of us trading in them . . . Well, it costs very little to produce pearls these days, and we're being undercut on price all the time. Some pearls are better than others, of course, and we sell only the best here, but the man in the street can't see much difference except in size. Sometimes I wonder how long it will be before women are given cultured pearls free when they buy a dress.'

Jane laughed. 'You're too fanciful, Dad, and there're still gemstones.'

'No there aren't. Synthetic rubies were being made by 1900, although they weren't as beautiful as the real stones. And it's been possible to grow emeralds of over ten carats since 1935, though I believe the process is still secret.'

Jane frowned. Of course she knew this, but she hadn't given it much thought. 'And sapphires?'

'Yes, about 1902. It's also possible to heat-treat badly flawed sapphires and make them into perfect gems. Right now, an expert can still tell the difference, but research is going on and scientists are improving them all the time. Soon, none of us will be able to differentiate between them. I believe they're working on a machine that'll be able to do that for us.'

'But not diamonds? We sell more diamonds than any other sort of stone.'

'Yes, I'm afraid diamonds too. By 1957 General Electric was marketing man-made industrial diamonds, so it's only a matter of time before they can turn out diamonds of gem quality.'

'But people will always prefer to have the real stones, won't they?'

'Yes, I'm sure you're right about that.'

'Well then, we'll always have a business.'

'That I'm not so sure about.'

'You mean there are other problems?'

'I'm afraid so. But I've talked long enough, it's your

turn now. I've got a collection of opals and another of sapphires. Some are real and some are man-made, and I want to see if you can sort out which are which. In this trade you mustn't buy man-made thinking they're real. Why don't you put the kettle on for a cup of tea while I open up the safe?'

CHAPTER SEVEN

FOR HONOR the months were rolling on. She was enjoying her new job and its wide variety of duties. Woolton Park Golf Club had begun holding dinner dances. For the first one, Mark Layton, the catering manager, was on duty; Honor was to work in the dining room. Among the tables she was allocated to serve was the top table where the club officials would sit. Mark had worked out the place settings.

He gave her the place cards. 'Write their names in your fanciest script,' he told her.

She ran her eye down the list. *Mr Barry Clarkson*, she read, then *Mrs Mabel Clarkson*.

She looked up and found Mark's dark eyes watching her from behind steel-rimmed spectacles. 'He's a past captain and she acts as club treasurer. She's an accountant, runs their company accounts too.'

'Millard & Clarkson,' Honor said. She'd looked up the name of his firm.

'She was a Millard,' Mark told her. 'Her father started the firm but he's passed on now. She took

Barry into the business when she married him.'

Honor bent her head over the desk and set about the task, her stomach churning. That altered things. It seemed the company didn't belong to Barry. She couldn't bank on him.

On the evening of the dinner, as the guests were being shown to their places, Honor was watching for Mrs Clarkson, burning with curiosity to see what she was like.

She led her party in. She was about Barry's age, a little taller than him and even more portly, her massive bare shoulders rising out of a too-tight bodice of black satin. She had grey hair and a severe expression, and altogether looked a formidable woman.

Joanna, one of the other waitresses, was standing beside her. 'I'm glad I'm not serving Mrs Clarkson tonight,' she said. 'She's a tartar. I accidentally slopped a spot of gravy on her dress once and she flew at me.'

'She can be a bit difficult?' Honor asked.

'She's used to ruling the roost. Barry makes out she does nothing but play with her dogs, but it isn't true. My boyfriend works in her business, and he says she's mustard. I think he's a bit scared of her.'

'But she's a good businesswoman?'

'Oh, yes. She'd make money from anything she did.'

Honor's spirits sank. So the business definitely did not belong to Barry. She went to serve the first course, asparagus soup. Barry ignored her.

Mrs Clarkson was wearing magnificent diamond

drop earrings and a matching necklace, and her hands glittered as she moved them. Her mouth was a slash of crimson lipstick which was spreading into the wrinkles round her lips. She was monopolising the conversation and her voice was strident. Honor had no difficulty believing it was Mabel who ran the company.

She went home that night and decided she'd been too optimistic. She mustn't let herself anticipate that Barry would do anything for her. She was afraid he was all mouth, and he must be spending more time at the club than he did at work.

The months continued to roll on. It was a hectic time for Honor, but she was seeing more of the club members and getting to know them. She was starting to feel on friendly terms with many of them and was thoroughly enjoying the social whirl. She went out with Stanley Byrne a few times, and when he suggested a hotel room she named her price. He paid up and they did it again. She chatted up other members in the bar, hoping to find more clients. Philip Marsden, a younger and more presentable man, took her up too. She bought herself some new black dresses, restrained in style and smart enough to show off her figure.

From time to time, she felt a little guilty about leaving her daughter alone so much, but Kitty seemed not to mind. 'Don't worry about me, Ma. I'm old enough to look after myself now,' she said, and occasionally she even had a meal prepared for Honor when she came home.

Christmas came round again and Honor was able to buy Kitty the fur boots she longed for, as well as all the seasonal delicacies they wanted. A couple of months later, just when she was getting used to juggling three men in her life, Barry told her he was taking over a 1930s three-bedroomed semi-detached as a part exchange and he thought it might suit her.

'That sounds wonderful.' Honor brightened at the thought.

'It's nothing special and it needs a bit of work on it.'

'It can't need as much as the place I'm living in now,' she told him.

'We'll wait for the present owner to move out and I'll take you round to see it. Do you have any furniture?'

'No.' She had nothing but a television set and a few pots and pans.

'I might be able to help there too,' he said. 'When we set up a show house, we put a bit of furniture in. The curtains and carpets are sold with the house, but there's some basic stuff in our store.'

'It would be marvellous if you could.' She smiled up at him and decided she'd start looking round and collecting bits and pieces herself.

'Three bedrooms!' She gloried in the thought of having a bedroom to herself. She wouldn't need hotel rooms once she'd got the new place fixed up. Honor could think of little else but moving house, and Kitty was even more excited about it than she was herself.

Barry had warned her that the house was shabby but

she wouldn't let herself be disappointed. It was on Queen's Drive, quite a busy thoroughfare, but a good address. The rooms were generous in size, and there was a garage as well as gardens to the front and back.

'I love it,' Honor told him. 'I can tidy up the garden and smarten it up a bit.'

'It needs a new bathroom,' Barry said. 'The firm can see to that, and I'll send my painters round to give the place a coat of paint, inside and out.'

'Can I choose the colours?'

'Of course. Usually, our customers come to the site office to choose what they want, but better if you don't. I'll bring the brochures for bathroom fittings and the colour cards for you tomorrow.'

Honor felt she'd reached a real milestone. She was well on the way to getting what she'd been aiming for. Barry was as good as his word. The house looked quite different by the time she had the key and could take Kitty inside.

'I came past a couple of times just to see what it was like,' Kitty admitted.

'D'you like it?'

'It's smashing.'

It was April 1973 when they moved in, and they had a fine old time deciding where to put the furniture that Barry sent round in a van. It was quite smart modern stuff that had had no wear. The place still looked a bit bare, but Barry promised more.

*

Dorothy Hadley enjoyed her job selling beautiful things at Jardine's. She was unpacking new stock today and that always gave her a thrill. Her job gave her every Sunday off, and, because all the staff were needed to work on Saturdays, also one day off in the middle of the week.

But she was not entirely content with her life. Her fiancé had gone down with his ship in 1943 during the Battle of the Atlantic. It had taken her a long time to get over that. She hadn't had a serious man friend since, and although she'd cherished hopes of finding love and getting married, they were fading as the years went by.

She was lucky that her sister Emily was in the same position and that they shared the home in which they'd been brought up. She felt they were settling into middle age now and her circumstances were unlikely to change. She told herself she had a lot to be grateful for and must be satisfied with what she had, and she'd always known that the best way to do that was to keep herself busy.

Cake decorating had been a hobby of hers since her teens, and she'd taken several courses to increase her skill. At one time, she'd made a little extra money by icing special occasion cakes for a baker. Now she made cakes only for her family and friends and had turned to teaching the art.

In term time she ran a class in cake decorating on Tuesday nights. As it was her job to draw up the rota of the girls' midweek days off, she usually arranged to have a Tuesday off herself. Most of the women she worked with had taken her course and praised it.

Over the years, Dorothy had grown fond of Edwin Jardine – perhaps more than fond. He was a lovely person. He had a way of looking at her sometimes that gave her hope he might feel the same. She wished there was some way she could give a hint of what she felt for him, but she'd be embarrassed.

One cold February week in 1967, Edwin had gone down with flu and Miss Hadley felt she got to know him better as a result. The staff had rallied round and seen to Jane, who was eleven years old at the time and fortunately able to take the bus to school on her own. They all made more than their usual fuss of her.

Miss Pinfold took the more important letters up to show him and he dictated the replies from his bed. Both she and Dorothy offered help with shopping and laundry but Mrs McGrath was determined to run his home without their help.

Until then, Dorothy had never even been upstairs to the flat. While he was ill, she went up every evening as soon as she'd closed the shop and cashed up. He always wanted to know what the takings were for the day.

Since that time, she'd been quietly imagining how it would be if he fell in love with her. She saw herself living with him and Jane, sleeping in his bed and running his home.

But nothing of a personal nature had developed.

Dorothy was afraid both she and Mr Jardine were too deeply embedded in habit and routine. Nevertheless, she continued to hope that if they could loosen up he'd begin to see her as a person in her own right and not just as his senior shop assistant.

Edwin Jardine was becoming concerned about his business because trade was falling off. Britain was being increasingly hit by recession. Factories were closing, and there was less cash about.

'We're at the luxury end of the market,' he told Jane. 'We're likely to feel the full force of any economic depression.'

He was also concerned about Miss Lewis, who hadn't been feeling well for some time. Edwin had sent her home from the shop more than once and told her to see her doctor. Last month, she'd rung Miss Pinfold to say she was being admitted to hospital, and the next thing they knew she'd been diagnosed as having bowel cancer. The operation had been a big one.

She came out of hospital and they hoped she was recovering, but then they heard she'd gone in again for a course of chemotherapy. She was still talking of coming back to work, but it seemed unlikely now that she would in the foreseeable future.

Hospital visiting was on Wednesday and Sunday afternoons. Miss Lewis lived with her brother, and as he had to be at work on Wednesday afternoons Edwin suggested that the girls take turns to go off then to see her and cheer her up. On Wednesday mornings, he sent Jane or Pam out to buy flowers or a few magazines to take with them.

Miss Pinfold's special friend was stout, grey-haired Miss Bundy, who had been telling them for months she was worried about her father. When her mother was dying she'd promised her she'd look after her dad, although she'd left the family home in Wigan twenty-two years earlier to find work in Liverpool, and was now comfortably settled in a one-bedroom flat. Her father was alone most of the week and when she visited him the neighbours told her his behaviour was becoming increasingly odd. Recently, she'd been taking the occasional day off every so often to take him on a round of doctor's and hospital appointments.

One morning at tea break, Alice Bundy had been in tears in the rest room. They were all upset to hear her father had Alzheimer's disease and she felt she had to give in her notice to return to Wigan to look after him.

'If you ever want your job back,' Jane heard her father say, 'do get in touch. If we're looking for more staff we'd all like it to be you.' Miss Pinfold had taken her to her own office to comfort her.

Miss Povey too was leaving. She'd finally given notice that she wanted to retire at the end of April. She was now sixty-four, having worked on past sixty so that she could retire at the same time as her younger sister. They'd bought a cottage together in the Lake District and planned an entirely different life.

Edwin was counting 1973 as a bad year before they'd reached May.

When the Cavendish Secretarial College broke up for the Easter holidays, Jane spent them working in the shop.

'You'll be finishing your secretarial course in June,' Edwin said, 'so I'll start paying you the starting wage for the hours you work in the shop. But you must start the day by helping Miss Pinfold open the morning post, and remember that Miss Hadley will be glad of a hand to keep the silverware gleaming.'

'Yes, Dad.'

Jane felt she wanted other changes in her life. With her first wages, she and Pam Kenny went out one lunch time and bought a pair of jeans and a pair of casual shoes each. Back at the shop, Jane changed into hers and then went to her father's office to show him.

'Trousers? And those awful shoes?'

'Don't you like them, Dad?'

'No. Where could you possibly wear them? Certainly not here in the shop.'

'When I go out with Nick.'

'I'm sure he'd rather you wore a pretty dress. That's what I want you to wear when I take you out.'

'Dad, I've only got that green dress.'

'You had a nice blue one . . .'

'It's too small for me, I'm bursting out of it. I've hardly got any clothes. This is just about the only cardigan I have.' It was the one Miss Pinfold had knitted for her the Christmas before last.

'I suppose you do need some warm sweaters. I'll have a word with Miss Hadley.'

Jane and her father were in agreement about most things, but her clothes could be a cause of contention. Dad had always asked Miss Hadley or Miss Pinfold to take her out to buy her clothes, and between them they had fitted her out in clothes that were more suited to a middle-aged woman than a teenager. She thought it wiser not to tell him Pam Kenny had helped her choose the jeans.

'Can't I go alone? Or with a friend from college? I'm perfectly capable, Dad.'

'Miss Hadley lets you choose, doesn't she?'

'She insists we go to the expensive shops. George Henry Lee's and Bon Marché. She says you tell her that's where you want us to go, but their stuff is what older people wear. My friends go to C & A.'

'You look very nice in what Miss Hadley gets you. I don't want you to wear jeans, Jane.'

'But twinsets are so old-fashioned. You said I need some warm sweaters. I'd like to go shopping for them by myself, or I'll ask Jazz. I went with her when she wanted to buy new shoes.'

'Jasmine's such a pretty name. I'm sure your friend's parents don't like you calling her Jazz.'

'Oh, Dad, they call her Jazz too. I'd like to take her with me to buy sweaters. Can I?'

But Dad was against it. He turned over a page in the ledger before him; she could see his mind was anywhere but on her wardrobe.

Jane brooded as she balanced on the corner of his desk. The atmosphere in the shop had always been one of contented unchanging routine, but now she sensed big changes were in the offing.

She said, 'I bet you're glad now you agreed to let me start work. You're really going to need me.'

'I certainly am. We aren't very busy just now, but with two girls going, and Miss Lewis still so poorly, we could be hard pushed. I think we'd better take on at least one more girl right away.'

'That's still only two to replace three,' Jane pointed out.

'Yes, but business is quiet generally. I could bring in one of the girls from Childwall, if we need it.'

'Isn't it time you brought Nick back? He must have learned all there is to learn about the Chester branch by now.'

'As a matter of fact, I was talking about that to Sam only an hour ago.' He smiled up at his daughter. 'We're short-handed at Aigburth with Miss Hurst off sick, and she could be away a month or so. I've decided Nick can go there to help out and get some experience of that branch at the same time. He'll come back to live with Sam, and after Aigburth he can go for a month or two to Childwall.'

'Good. What about Southport?'

'That's a bit far for him to travel daily from Sam's place. I thought he could go one Monday and I'd ask Eric Bannerman to put him up until Friday. That would give him a taster, which should be enough once he's been round everywhere else.'

'Even better.' Jane smiled. 'Now, I want us to make some decisions about what we're going to give Miss Povey and Miss Bundy for their leaving presents.' Edwin had given Jane and Pam the job of arranging a joint farewell party, and Jane was taking the responsibility very seriously.

'Right. You find Miss Hadley and we'll go to the gift department and pick out something now.' Edwin knew Miss Hadley liked to be consulted.

She came bustling up, smiling and helpful, and said, 'Probably not jewellery. I've heard the girls say they'd be afraid of being mugged if they wore anything expensive. Perhaps a piece of silver would suit them better.'

Edwin led her and Jane down to the gift department. 'We have a very good selection at the moment,' he said. 'Now, tell me, what d'you think Miss Povey would like?'

He watched Miss Hadley's eyes go to the most expensive items on display. 'The clock,' she said. 'She'd like that.'

'She'll love it,' Jane agreed. 'I know I would, anyway.'

Edwin picked it out and handed it to his daughter. It was a small bedroom clock in a pretty solid silver engraved case.

'An alarm clock for a retirement present?' he asked. 'Are you sure?'

'Yes,' Miss Hadley said. 'There are some mornings in every life when an alarm is needed.'

'Right then, what's it to be for Miss Bundy?' It would have to be a little cheaper, because if the girls didn't already know exactly what these things cost they'd be bound to check up, and Miss Povey had worked at Jardine's longer than Miss Bundy.

'A silver photograph frame,' Jane suggested.

'A good idea. You choose one, Miss Hadley. You'll know her taste.'

As he expected, she chose the most expensive out of loyalty to her colleague. It had a heavy plain frame.

'I like that one best too,' he said and handed it on to Jane. 'Take them up to Sam and ask him to engrave the clock with a suitable message for Miss Povey's thirty-two years' service and the photo frame for Miss Bundy's thirteen.'

Jane was back in his office within five minutes. 'About the party . . .'

'After hours,' he said. 'I don't want to close the shop early. We'll all be hungry by then, so not just cake.'

'What about a cheese and wine party?'

'Perhaps something more substantial? Sandwiches and pork pies, that sort of thing?'

'Most of the girls eat like sparrows,' Jane said. 'You should see what they bring to eat at lunch time.'

'You decide, then. I'll leave it to you. Go to Marks &

Spencer to see what they have; order it if necessary. You'd better ask Miss Hadley what she thinks.'

'She's collecting contributions from the staff so they can give little gifts too,' Jane said. 'I need some money, Dad. I want to start buying things.'

The Tuesday after Easter, Honor Thorpe caught the bus to Woolton Park Golf Club.

'Morning, Jill,' she sang out to one of the cleaners mopping the floor in the entrance.

The cleaner leaned on her mop. 'Mr Layton said to tell you you're wanted in the office right away.'

'Oh.' Honor sensed something ominous about that. 'Did he say why?'

'No.'

She breezed straight to the door with the sign 'Manager' on it, and found not only Mark Layton but also Mrs Clarkson, the club treasurer, waiting for her. Honor's spirits plummeted. One look at their faces told her she was in big trouble. She wasn't asked to sit down.

'We've been hearing rumours for some time,' Mrs Clarkson told her, 'but I didn't believe them.'

Honor felt a cold shiver run down her spine. 'What rumours?'

'That you're using club premises to solicit for sex.'

To have it spelled out so bluntly made her gasp. It felt like a slap in the face. 'Certainly not,' she managed.

'Members have complained that you've approached them, Mrs Thorpe. For the purpose of prostitution.'

'Absolutely not. A misunderstanding.'

'Would you like me to read out their names?'

Honor felt sick, her breakfast toast threatening to return. She should have been more careful. She met Mark's hostile gaze.

'I've worked hard. I've done my best to please,' she protested.

'You have, and we aren't complaining about your work,' he said. 'It's your behaviour.'

'Exactly,' Mrs Clarkson said through tight lips.

'I'm afraid we can't continue to employ you here after this,' Mark went on. 'We're dispensing with your services as of now. I'll pay any wages you're due into your bank account.'

Fear needled Honor. It would be a disaster if she lost this job. She protested, 'But I wasn't aware that—'

He was firm. 'You've used our premises to tout for clients for the purpose of prostitution.'

'I most certainly have not,' Honor denied hotly. She didn't want a reputation as a prostitute. It would turn off the men she most wanted to attract.

She'd already seen her employment cards on the desk in front of the club manager. Now he pushed them across to her, but Mrs Clarkson put her hand on them. 'Thank you, Mr Layton. There's another matter I'd like to discuss with Mrs Thorpe before she goes.'

There was a two-minute pause while Mark left. As she waited, Honor could feel her cheeks burning and her heart pounding like a machine. Mrs Clarkson stared frostily at her.

When the door closed behind him, she said, 'No doubt you found it easy to twist my husband round your finger. The silly fool thinks you're in love with him. He'll believe anything.'

Honor was struggling to get her breath. The bitch had found out about her house! If she were to lose that now . . .

What could she possibly say? 'I . . . I'm sorry . . . It just happened. I didn't mean to fall in love.'

'I think it's more likely you've set up some sort of sex ring, and you're preying on the vanity of silly old men.'

'No, absolutely not,' Honor protested. 'We fell in love.'

'Not love as the rest of the world understands it.' Mabel Clarkson raised her voice and threw out her ample bosom. 'I gather you've pillow-talked him into allowing you to move into a house owned by my company on the understanding you would live there rent free?'

Honor said nothing. The seconds dragged. Would that make her Barry's mistress?

'Yes or no?' Mrs Clarkson's voice had risen another octave.

'Yes, I've moved in, but I expect to pay.' What else could she say?

'Then either you move out or you arrange a mortgage to buy it at the market price. What is it to be?'

Honor lifted her eyes to meet Mabel Clarkson's. They were hard as nails and radiating hate and power and the need to take revenge. It was a struggle to get out the words. 'Rent . . . ? I'd like to rent it, please.'

'That's not an option. I want no permanent reminders of this. I'll give you two weeks to do one or the other, and if you don't you'll be squatting illegally and I'll get an eviction order.' She pushed a letter into Honor's hands. 'I've put it in writing so there can be no misunderstanding about what I'm saying.'

Honor tried to stand up to her. It took superhuman effort. 'The price – to buy the house?'

'It's in the letter. It's not negotiable.'

'I love Barry and I think he—'

'It's over, Mrs Thorpe. Barry has seen sense. He's promised me he'll make no move to see you again. Not ever. Now get out.'

Honor snatched up her cards, pushed them into the pocket of her coat and marched out with her dignity in tatters. Vomit was rising in her throat, and she only just managed to reach the staff cloakroom in time.

She went home on the bus shivering and fighting tears. Kitty was still on holiday, but she'd gone out and didn't return until late afternoon. By then Honor was feeling desperate. She had no job and therefore no wages. Her only contact with the clientele she'd built up with such care was through the golf club. If she couldn't meet them there, it meant no income at all. And without income, how could she keep this house?

She was glad to see Kitty come home. 'Where've you been?' she wailed.

'I went round the shops with some girls from school. I didn't buy anything.'

'You always seem to be out.' Honor recounted an edited version of what had happened at the golf club. 'I don't know what we're going to do,' she finished.

Kitty shrugged, 'Possession is nine-tenths of the law, isn't it?'

'Not in our case.'

'We could always go back to live with Jason.'

'No, absolutely not. Anyway, he's probably been evicted from there by now.'

Kitty gave a mirthless laugh. 'Don't even think of moving us to a bedsit. It's not on.'

'I want to stay here.' Honor looked round her new living room and felt the tears well into her eyes again. She'd worked so hard to get this lovely house and now she was afraid it was going to slip through her fingers. Her grand plan was in ruins. Mabel Clarkson had defeated her.

CHAPTER EIGHT

HONOR WAS at her wits' end. She'd asked her daughter to tidy the garden. The spring rains had made the weeds flourish in the borders and the grass had put on a spurt of growth, but Kitty had been quick to point out that if they couldn't stay in the house there was no point in knocking herself out trying to improve the garden.

'Ma,' she moaned, 'we're just getting the place as we want it. There's got to be something we can do. I could leave school and get a proper job.'

'No, I want you to stay on at school and then take some sort of training. I want you to get a decent job when you do start work.'

When they'd first returned to Liverpool, Kitty had been doing a newspaper round and working behind the counter of the same local newsagent on Saturdays to earn pocket money. When they'd left Menlove Avenue she'd given in her notice because the flat was too far away.

'Another newspaper round, then?'

'Yes, when we know whether we'll be staying here.'

'That's not going to help with a mortgage.'

'No.' Honor felt near despair. It was not a good time to be job hunting. The economic situation in Britain was on the decline, and businesses were laying off staff. 'I've got to find another job and I need to do it quickly.'

She collapsed in floods of tears. She couldn't get Mabel Clarkson's twisting face out of her mind. The hate and hostility she'd met in the office this morning was with her still. Even the tea Kitty made didn't help. She sent her out to buy the local newspaper in the hope there'd be something to suit her in the situations vacant columns and then went to lie on the bed in her lovely new bedroom. She needed to think this out. There had to be something she could do to get in touch with Barry.

Of course he knew where he could find her. He could just drive over here, but he'd promised that dragon of a wife to make no effort to contact her. But she had not been asked to give any such undertaking. She calmed down eventually and fell into a light doze. It was six o'clock when she woke up. She got up, took a bath and put on her new grey skirt and scarlet blouse. She had to look her best in case he came round.

It occurred to her that as she'd often met him in the small pub near the golf club, he might just go in there in the hope of seeing her. If Barry hadn't come to the house by mid-evening, she'd go and see if he was there.

She was hungry because she'd missed lunch. 'I'm going to cook egg and bacon for us,' she said to Kitty.

'Not for me, thanks.' Her daughter waved her offer away. 'I'm on my way out.'

'Where to?'

'To the pictures. You know I always go with Flossie on Tuesday nights.'

'I thought it was Thursdays.'

'That's Peggy.'

'You'll be hungry.'

'I had a big fry-up at lunch time, and we never stop stuffing popcorn and sweets in the pics.'

Honor cooked for herself and then caught a bus. It followed the route she'd taken to work but she went on another stop to the pub. She knew within two minutes that Barry wasn't there.

Feeling disappointed, she went to the bar and ordered herself a gin and tonic. She'd been here often enough to get to know Douggie the barman quite well. She liked him and tonight he was doing his best to chat her up. He might be fun, but she knew he wouldn't be able to help her get a mortgage. Tonight she wasn't in the mood for fun. She sat nursing her drink and watching the door.

When she saw Stanley Byrne standing in the doorway looking round, she brightened up and waved. He came over.

'I was hoping to find you here,' he said. 'You're the talk of the club. Everybody's up in arms. Some of us are for you and think you shouldn't have been sacked.'

'And the rest are against me, I suppose?'

He smiled. 'What about another drink?'

Honor decided Stanley was better than nobody. She had a pleasant evening with him; he took her to the usual hotel and she earned a little money. Not enough, but it was better than nothing.

She told him about her house and gave him the address, telling him she'd be glad to see him there in future. She pondered whether she should ask him to give her address to Philip, but decided against it. She didn't want him to think she sold her favours to every Tom, Dick and Harry. Better if each man thought he was her special favourite. Stanley referred to the money he paid over as a little present to get herself a new dress. He ran her home in his car, so he'd have no trouble finding the place in future.

She couldn't sleep. She had to try to save her house, but how? Barry might still be willing to help if only she could talk to him. Why didn't he come round?

By morning, she'd had an idea. She set about writing a note to Philip. She'd always gone out with him during her split shift on Thursday afternoons. She invited him to the house tomorrow afternoon, and drew him a little map to help him find the place.

Writing to Barry took her much longer, and she discarded several versions before she was satisfied. She told him that what they were saying about her at the club was a tissue of lies. She loved him and was missing him badly. *Please, please*, she wrote, *come round and see me*. She suggested Friday afternoon, feeling that if she didn't give him a definite day he might turn up while Philip or Stanley was with her and that would be so embarrassing she'd never see any of them again.

Then she paid a visit to the car park at the golf club, crossing her fingers in the hope that they'd both be playing this afternoon. Yes, she could see both Barry's rather staid black Wolseley and Philip's new green Renault; she slipped an envelope behind the windscreen wipers on both. She had to save what she could from this mess and she had no time to waste.

On the way home, she bought a matching set of wine glasses and another of whisky tumblers. Then she went to the off-licence and bought a bottle of whisky, one of gin and a couple of bottles of wine. She added a few packets of nuts and crisps. She'd need to entertain her men in future, welcome them, give them a good time to encourage them to come back.

Kitty was curled up on the sofa watching *The Benny Hill Show* on television, and giggling at his antics.

Honor said, 'If one of my men friends should come, you'll have to go straight to your bedroom and stay there out of the way.'

'Ma, no. I don't want to spend hours up there. I could act as receptionist, serve the drinks—'

'No, absolutely not. You stay away from all this. I don't want you involved in any way. And you're never to do this sort of thing yourself. This is an emergency. I have to, but not you. You're to be a good, clean-living girl.'

Kitty was rebellious. 'I'm not going to stay up in my bedroom. It would feel like prison if I couldn't come down. I'll go out more, stay out of your way. That would be better for both of us.'

'There's no need for you to do that.' Honor helped Kitty carry a small table to her bedroom. 'For you to do your homework on.'

To keep her happy, she agreed Kitty could take up the television set and even promised to buy another once the money started coming in. She was careful to make sure the lock on her bedroom door worked, to ensure Kitty didn't come in at the wrong moment.

She was delighted when Philip came on Thursday afternoon as she'd suggested. When he was leaving, he said he'd enjoyed himself, and thought it easier and pleasanter to be in her house than go to a hotel.

'Safer too, because I'm not likely to be seen here by anyone who knows me. Less fear that my wife will find out. But I'd feel safer still if you had curtains up in your windows,' he told her. 'It feels a bit like a goldfish bowl sitting here on your sofa.'

Honor went out the next day and bought heavy ready-made curtains for both the sitting room and her bedroom. Her guests must have privacy and feel safe while they were with her.

Kitty was delighted to be living in pleasant surroundings again, but fearful they'd have to move. Her mother was very tense and her attention was focused on how she could keep the house. Because of this Kitty felt she had more freedom. Ma was no longer on her back demanding to be told where she'd been and who with. She was able to come and go as she pleased.

She was spending more time with Jason. What they both appreciated was having the run of his house to themselves. They had total privacy and valued it highly.

There was a footpath behind the house and originally there'd been a back gate opening on to it from the garden. A previous owner had replaced the gate with a fencing panel, but Gary had restored it. The high hedges and trees made it impossible for nosy neighbours to see visitors coming that way. Of course, his customers had to telephone first so he could unlock the gate, and they had to come on foot, which meant that when they had goods to deliver they still had to come to the front. Nevertheless, it was an ideal house for Gary's purpose, as Jason was finding out for himself. He told Kitty he was beginning to make real money. He had learned how to fence different sorts of stolen property from his father, and with him out of the way, had taken over some of his contacts. Success brought him more work, and now he could boast of knowing half Liverpool's underworld.

When he wasn't casing a job for a client, Kitty spent whole days with him. She found playing house and sharing Jason's life very exciting and had almost given up going to school. What was the point? She'd be sixteen at Christmas and could leave. She'd find herself a job then, earn a bit of money. She said nothing to her mother, who was still getting her up early every weekday.

On Friday morning Kitty bounded up to the front door of Jason's house and let herself in with her key. With so much on her mind Ma had never missed the keys, or if she had she'd never mentioned it. Nowadays, Jason's house seemed quite scruffy. She usually tidied up a bit, put on his washing machine and made him change his bedclothes. Living with Ma had made her appreciate such niceties.

She crept upstairs and as she expected his bedroom was in deep gloom with the curtains drawn. Almost always, he was still in bed when she arrived; sometimes she had to prod him awake. She loved to see him like this, all drowsy with his tousled hair across the pillow.

'Wake up, come on, rise and shine,' she called. 'If you get up I'll make breakfast for you.'

Still bleary-eyed, he turned over and smiled up at her. 'Can't think about breakfast yet. Come on, get into bed with me for a bit.'

'You are naughty.' She was already easing her shoes off. 'I will if you'll make it up to me afterwards.'

He laughed. 'You know I will.'

Kitty let her clothes fall to the floor and climbed in beside him. All his drowsiness was gone in an instant and his lips came down hard on hers. He'd been her lover for over a year, and they'd had some marvellous times together.

On the way home with her new curtains, Honor called in at the job centre and applied for three of the jobs she saw there: catering assistant in a factory canteen, salesperson in a central Liverpool department store and booking clerk at the bus station.

She quite fancied the department store, and hoped that would come up. When she reached home she wrote two more job applications. She had to have a regular income, though she doubted whether any of these jobs would pay well enough to allow her to buy the house. What she earned from her men visitors was going to be a great help, but it was not an income she could declare when she applied for a mortgage.

Barry knocked on her door that afternoon. 'I'd like to put my car into the garage, Honor,' he said anxiously. 'I don't want it to be seen at your gate.'

She found the key and went out to unlock it for him. Kitty was in the kitchen when they went indoors. As she'd told him about Kitty, she introduced them, but then she banished her upstairs. She felt she needed her wits about her; she had to play this right if she was to keep the house. Barry was grey-faced and had a hang-dog expression. He asked for tea instead of whisky.

'I'm sorry,' he said, when she got him into the sitting room and shut the door. 'This must have come as a nasty shock to you. I've been worried about you.'

'I'm worried about everything. I've lost my job and I was afraid I'd lost you too.'

'No, you haven't lost me, but I have to be more careful. Mabel gave me an ultimatum. She made me promise never to see you again or she'd divorce me.'

'Would that be such a bad thing?' Honor asked tearfully. 'I could make you very comfortable here.'

'Here?' He looked round her sitting room as though the thought hadn't occurred to him. No doubt he was used to something grander than this.

She said, 'I can make it look smarter. I could do a lot here.'

'Yes, of course.' She saw his tongue come out to moisten his lips. 'Mabel said I must choose between her and you. It's her business, and if I choose you I won't be able to keep my job. She said she wouldn't want to face me every day.' His sigh was almost a groan. 'I don't even own half our house. Her parents bought it and left it to her.'

'I see.' Honor could feel a cold knot in her stomach. It was as she'd surmised. 'And so you've chosen her?'

He sighed. 'I'd rather it was you, Honor, and that's the truth, but how would we live?'

'What am I going to do? I hate to think of moving out of this house, we've hardly moved in. I'd do anything to keep it.'

She cried a little on his shoulder and told him she loved him. With his arms round her, she took him upstairs to her bedroom and locked the door. Barry was as eager as ever. Honor didn't rate him highly as a lover, but she did her best to make him believe she did.

In the aftermath of passion, she said, 'Please help me, Barry. I don't know which way to turn.'

'Of course I'll help you, but now Mabel knows, it isn't easy. She'll be watching me. I knocked a bit off the valuation of this house and I've collected some cash for you. It's the best I can do. I can't take a large sum out of my account just now.'

'How much?' she whispered.

'Five hundred.'

'Thank you, Barry.' She snuggled down into his arms. 'Thank you very much. That will help.'

'I can leak out about the same again in small amounts over the next month. That'll give you a thousand to put down as a deposit. If anyone asks, it's your life savings, all right?'

'Yes, of course.'

'And you must get yourself a mortgage.'

'I need a job first,' she said. 'I have to show some means of paying it off.'

'You'll get one, you'll be OK. But I don't think I can come here very often. I wouldn't put it past Mabel to have me followed. I'll have to think of something else.'

Honor had been going to the local job centre every day. Occasionally she went to a bigger job centre in town as well, and on the Monday after Barry's visit she went round the boards twice. A receptionist was needed at a doctor's surgery. She liked the sound of that, but didn't think she stood a chance of getting it. She scribbled down the details anyway, and moved on to the next card. Sales assistant required by E. H. Jardine & Son, Purveyors of Jewellery, Church Street, Liverpool.

She remembered passing the place one Christmas. Everybody had looked happy and prosperous. That would suit her even better. She'd love all their expensive jewellery and their customers would all have money. If she could get work there she might be back on track – except, of course, she wouldn't have much time to talk to the customers. Still, she fancied working amongst all that jewellery.

She went home and wrote a letter of application, describing her attainments in glowing terms. By the time she'd finished it was too late to catch the afternoon post. The next morning she polished it up, making herself sound the near perfect sales assistant before posting it.

But would that be enough? There was no way she could tell, but this was an opportunity she didn't want to miss. There had to be some way she could cinch it. She thought about it all day.

Edwin Jardine had asked Miss Pinfold to notify the job centre about the staff vacancy. 'Better advertise it in the *Echo* too,' he said. Applications were coming in, quite a lot of them; in the present recession he knew it wouldn't be hard to fill the vacancy. Jane was in his office, clipping the applications together.

'How do you know which one to choose?' she asked.

He sighed. 'I don't. The only thing to do is to pick out a few that sound all right and ask them to come in. When you see them and talk to them, you get a better idea of what they're like. I got Miss Hadley to sit in with me last time.'

'Last time? That must have been years ago.'

'Yes, when we employed Miss Kenny. We both liked the look of her; two heads are better than one.'

'Can I sit in with you this time?'

'Yes, or all three of us. Read through those applications and see what you think.'

'I will, Dad.'

At three o'clock that afternoon, Edwin was on the phone to the Birmingham jewellery centre when he heard a loud thumping on his office door. He tried to ignore it but it opened and Miss Kenny's agitated face looked round it at him.

'Please,' she implored. 'Come quickly.'

He excused himself and put the phone down. The look on Miss Kenny's face made his heart pound. Nothing like this had ever happened before.

'What's the matter?' he called. She was already running back to the stairs.

'A pickpocket,' she gasped; she was so excited she could hardly get the words out. 'A customer – on the ground floor.'

He was rushing down behind her flying heels. 'Has anyone been hurt?'

If she replied he didn't hear it above the commotion at the front of the shop, where a knot of customers and staff were all talking at once. He was relieved to find Miss Hadley had taken charge.

'It's all right,' she told him. 'There was a thief in the shop, a pickpocket, but he ran off without getting anything.'

'Thanks to this lady.' The man who spoke was beyond middle age and wearing a bespoke grey suit typical of Jardine's customers.

Edwin singled out the two people he took to be most involved. 'Perhaps you'd like to come somewhere quieter, where we can talk?' He led them away from the front counters to the alcove at the foot of the stairs.

Behind him, he heard Miss Hadley raise her voice. 'Sorry about that, ladies and gentlemen. We're ready to attend to your needs again. Miss Kenny, Miss Povey, behind the counters please.'

'I do apologise,' Edwin said to the man. 'Have you had your pocket picked in my shop? Do you want me to send for the police?'

'No, no, a storm in a teacup really. My wallet was picked out of my back pocket, but this lady saw her do it and raised the alarm.'

The woman too was in a state of excitement and spoke quickly. 'His jacket has a double vent at the back. I saw the boy's hand go under it.'

'Was it a boy?' Edwin asked. He'd understood the victim to say 'her'.

'It was a girl,' the man confirmed, but the woman was shaking her head.

'I think it was a lad,' she said.

'Well, no matter. The thief, male or female, dropped my wallet on the floor and ran.'

'Then there's no damage and nobody hurt?' Edwin felt as though a weight has been lifted off his shoulders.

'No harm done,' the man said, 'and I still have my wallet. I'm very grateful to you, young lady.'

For the first time, Edwin turned to look at her. 'Glad to be of help,' she said. Her face was surprisingly young and pretty. She wore a black suit, smart and well cut, with a froth of white lace at the throat. Very formal wear for one so young. 'It caused quite a panic.'

Edwin said, 'I'm sorry such a thing happened here. I don't want to frighten my customers off.'

'Not your fault,' said the man. 'I had a phone call to say my watch was ready and just popped in to collect it. But I paused over there to look at the Sun Diamonds. Magnificent gems. I didn't even realise what was happening until . . . But anyway, all's well. I'll be on my way. Thank you again.'

'Watch repairs are upstairs,' Edwin said, and then felt foolish. The man would know that if he'd brought his watch in. 'I must thank you too,' he said quickly, turning to the girl. 'There's nothing worse than to have customers robbed inside one's shop. I'm grateful you managed to prevent it.'

'It was nothing.'

'It meant a great deal to that gentleman: he still has his wallet. It means a great deal to me too.' He led her out on to the shop floor where the light was better. She was quite beautiful. 'Now, is there anything I can show you?'

'No, no, thank you.'

'You've already been attended to? Good.' He was about to escort her to the door.

'No. It's a little embarrassing, actually.' She smiled and looked shamefaced. He wondered why. 'The fact is I've applied for a job here.'

'Oh!'

'I saw the notice in the job centre, and came in to see what your shop was like.'

'Oh! Not much of a recommendation to find we get pickpockets in here.'

She smiled. 'It seems I can handle them. Your shop's lovely. I'd like to work here amongst all these beautiful things.'

He stood undecided, moving his weight from one foot to the other. He really liked the look of this girl and she certainly had her wits about her.

'Come upstairs to my office and let's have a little chat.'

She gave him such a dazzling smile that Edwin was immediately interested. Her stunning good looks lit up his office. 'I'd really love to work here.'

He found the folder of application letters in his desk drawer. 'Now, what is your name?'

'Honor Sarah Thorpe.'

'Yes, here we are, Mrs Thorpe. I see you're a widow?'

'Yes, and I have a daughter to support, that's why I need to work.'

He couldn't help but notice her age. Thirty-six. She looked younger. 'I see you've worked in a shop before. At Watson Prickard's.'

'Yes. I started during the January sales but it was only for a few weeks. I enjoyed working there and they were very kind, but I knew it was a temporary position before I started. They had staff off sick.'

'So that would be this January?'

'Yes, and February. I've been trying to get another job ever since. I've sent off dozens of applications, but it's very difficult just now.'

'Before then, where did you work?'

'When I was young I worked in Fortnum & Mason's in London for two years, and also at Heal's for a time.'

'Heal's, yes. So you've had good retail experience?'

She blinked hard, as though struggling to retain her composure. 'Sixteen years ago I married, and we came up to Liverpool to live. Crosby, actually. My husband was a solicitor. He didn't want me to work, and of course after our daughter was born there was no question of that. He died last November of a heart attack.'

Edwin had seen immediately that Mrs Thorpe was very middle class. Her address, her manners, her clothes all showed that. He was full of sympathy. 'You must find life on your own very hard.'

He knew what it was to lose a much loved spouse and be left with a daughter to support. He wanted to help her. He decided at that moment to take her on.

She was biting her lip now. 'I do miss him so. I feel so alone.' A tear ran down her cheek. 'Not that I am alone . . .'

He asked gently, 'How old is your daughter?'

'She's fifteen now.'

Edwin felt another rush of sympathy. She'd married very young just like Elena, had a baby daughter like her too, and been widowed at so young an age. 'Don't upset yourself,' he said in his kindly manner and pushed a box of tissues nearer to her.

'I'm sorry I have no other recent references to show you, but I adore jewellery and would love to have a job selling it. I think I could.'

She pushed a tissue into her pocket and swallowed hard. Her smile was brave but Edwin could see tears glistening in her lovely eyes.

'I'm sorry. I've had rather a difficult time since Leonard died. I've had to sell our home, I couldn't afford to run that now, but I've found something smaller. We're quite comfortable, so I mustn't complain. It's just that I need a job to support myself and my daughter.'

'Of course.' He saw another tear roll down her cheek. He'd have needed a heart of stone not to offer the post to her after that. He'd thought her black suit was smart business wear but now she'd told him she was a recent widow perhaps it was mourning? She looked chic and she had ease, self-possession and self-assurance. It sounded as though she'd had a terrible few months and she probably wasn't over the trauma yet, but he was sure she'd do very well in his shop.

'There's no problem. We can find a job for you here and now. What about a cup of tea while we talk about it?' He lifted the phone. 'Miss Pinfold, could I trouble you to find Jane and ask her to make us a cup of tea? For two, yes, thank you.'

Jane made the tea, still full of amazement at what she'd seen take place. The shop was heaving with excitement and the girls couldn't stop talking about it. She was eager to take another look at the woman who'd outwitted that thief.

She used the best china and added a plate of biscuits to the tray. Only the best was good enough for the heroine.

'I saw it all,' Jane assured her. 'It happened right in front of my counter. You were marvellous, tackling that pickpocket. So quick off the mark.'

'I only did what anyone would have done.' The woman seemed pleased to be praised. Dad beamed at her, though he'd been in the middle of saying something heavy. Jane went out and left them to it.

CHAPTER NINE

EDWIN FELT uneasy and couldn't settle down to work. For once he'd followed his instinct and done exactly what he wanted to and his reward had been Mrs Thorpe's swift, intimate smile and heartfelt thanks.

He was afraid that Miss Pinfold would question why he hadn't followed his own carefully laid down rules about hiring staff. He knew Jane and his girls would think it was out of character for him, but the sooner he broke the news to them the sooner he'd be able to relax.

He could hear the girls chattering in the rest room and went along to do it. Miss Pinfold wasn't there and nor was Jane, so he asked Miss Hadley to come to his office when she'd finished her tea. She came almost immediately as he knew she would.

'I've taken on a new sales assistant for this shop,' he told her. 'Mrs Thorpe is going to start on Monday. I think we'll all be very pleased with her work.'

He filled in a few details, knowing Miss Hadley would go along with anything he wanted, as she always did. To be on the safe side, he quickly changed the subject.

'Jane says she's short of clothes.' He handed her a list. 'Would you take her out and get her something suitable?'

Miss Hadley was blinking at him in indecision. 'Mr Jardine, I'm not sure I know what Jane would consider suitable.'

'She's been pleased with what you bought in the past. So have I.'

'Modern teenagers wear some very odd things. I don't understand clothes of that sort. There's a generation gap.'

He was frowning in concentration. 'Would you rather I asked Miss Pinfold if she'd oblige?'

'No, she's worse than I am. We're twenty years out of date.' Miss Hadley slid the list back on his desk. 'I think Jane would prefer to go alone.'

Edwin felt taken aback. She gave him a parting shot as she left. 'She's not a child any more.'

Honor couldn't stop smiling as she went home on the bus. She'd landed the job she wanted and she'd be starting next Monday. She felt on cloud nine. With an honest and regular wage she could declare to a building society, and the deposit Barry had promised her, she'd be able to buy the house.

As she opened the front door with her key, Kitty came running up the hall to meet her.

'Did I do all right?'

'You did wonderfully well. It worked a treat.' Honor threw her arms round Kitty in a triumphant hug. 'You were marvellous as a pickpocket. I hardly recognised you in those old clothes and with that hood up. Nobody realised it was a put-up job.'

'And now we'll be able to stay here?' Kitty asked.

'Yes, it's looking possible. I'll apply for a mortgage tomorrow and let Millard & Clarkson know I intend to buy it. That'll be one in the eye for Mabel Clarkson.'

'Good.' Kitty was all smiles.

'You know, I reckon Mabel's done us a favour. This way the house is in my name, and provided I keep paying the mortgage, nobody can put us out. We'll never have to live in a place like Churton House again.'

Kitty's eyes shone. 'Let's go out and celebrate. We could have a slap-up meal in a restaurant, or a trip to the theatre, or both.'

Honor hesitated. 'There'll be legal fees to pay and goodness knows what else. I'll need all the money I can get my hands on. So no big celebrations just yet, but if we're quick we've got time to nip down to that butcher in the village and get some fillet steak.'

'Great. And let's have fresh cream cakes to follow. I'll come with you to choose them. I did a good job getting that wallet out of that man's pocket, didn't I, Ma?'

Honor froze. Living on her wits as she did, the last thing she wanted was for Kitty to grow up doing the same. She meant to provide for her daughter. She should be an honest, clean-living young woman who could marry a rich man for love. Honor didn't want her to have the desperate problems she'd had. But she could see that by involving her in the pickpocket charade, she was encouraging Kitty to live her sort of life.

She put her arm round Kitty's shoulders and pulled her down beside her on the sofa. 'Yes, you did an excellent job, and I might not have got the job without your help. But you're never to do it again. Is that clear?'

'Ye-es, but . . .'

'I made a point of saying in the shop that I thought the pickpocket was a lad, so suspicion wouldn't fall on you.'

'But we got away with it, didn't we? There'll be no comeback from that.'

'Kitty, it's very important that you don't get a police record. Never do anything that could lead to one. If you're caught and get one, you'll be looking over your shoulder the whole time expecting trouble. And never again will anybody believe you are honest. Promise me, Kitty – you'll stay on the right side of the law from now on?'

She seemed reluctant but she said, 'I promise.'

'Right, and you know I have to bring men here from time to time? I want you to promise that you'll never do that.'

That made Kitty pull away from her. 'I'm to do what you say, not do what you do?'

'Don't be cheeky. This was an emergency and it called for desperate measures. We're both going to be honest from now on. I want you to have a happy life, a good life, and not have to go through what I've been through.'

Later, when they were eating their cream cakes, Kitty asked, 'Will you like working in that jeweller's, Ma?'

Honor was looking forward to it. 'Who wouldn't enjoy being surrounded with all those beautiful things? And Mr Jardine is a lovely man.'

She'd won his sympathy in that first interview, she'd seen it in his eyes. It had been a great idea. Her original plan was back on track. Yes, she had a few punters willing to pay for sex but that was to help her through what could be an expensive time. Once everything was up and running she could ditch Barry and the others.

She paused, thinking of another idea. Should she ask Barry to act as a guarantor for her mortgage first? If she had problems in the future, that might be a help.

Her long-term goal had always been to find a rich man who wanted her and Kitty to share his life. At last she thought she might have found him. Mr Jardine was very kind and very receptive to her. If she played her cards right, it might just work out. Yes, everything was in place. This was how she'd envisaged it during that first bleak Christmas in Churton House. She must go for it now, and even if it didn't work out, she could find herself another job in a club somewhere.

*

Dorothy Hadley had been surprised to hear that Mrs Thorpe was about to join the staff. In the days that followed, she heard a lot of whispered gossip about the whole incident. Jane and Miss Pinfold were equally surprised that Edwin had chosen Mrs Thorpe entirely on his own.

'That's not like him.' Miss Pinfold shook her head.

'But this is the woman who stopped a thief picking pockets in the shop on Thursday,' Miss Bundy pointed out. 'Clearly, that would impress him.'

'What's she like?' Miss Pinfold wanted to know.

'Mr Jardine spoke very highly of her,' Miss Hadley said. 'The rest of us have seen her, but in the commotion last Thursday . . .'

'We didn't take in much about her.' Miss Jessop shook her head.

They were all very curious and on Monday morning, first thing, they were watching out for her. Dorothy was taken aback to find she looked so young and elegant. She put her and the other girls to shame. Dorothy felt dowdy by comparison.

Mr Jardine came out of his office to welcome her to the staff and was very expansive. Her attitude to him seemed very different from theirs. That excited more gossip about her when she wasn't present, and the consensus was that she had plenty of confidence, but then she'd been married and knew how to handle men.

Miss Pinfold said she'd given an address in a high-class neighbourhood. She must be well-heeled to live in Queen's Drive, mustn't she? And be a customer in this shop? Not surprising really that she seemed to think herself a cut above them. She wasn't one of their sort.

Honor wore the same black suit to work on Monday morning and was determined to make a good impression on everybody. She'd be on her best behaviour, learn what the job entailed and get herself dug in. She must make friends with the shop staff and with his daughter.

She needed to find out if there was anybody in Edwin Jardine's life apart from Jane. It would be good news if there was no other woman. He could be a pushover.

On the first morning, Miss Hadley, the manageress, was friendly and took her under her wing. She was dark-haired, fat and forty. No, that was a bit hard. Plump rather than fat.

'I'll show you round the premises,' she said, 'and explain a few things.' Honor was introduced to the other workers, nearly all of whom seemed surprisingly old, and to have worked there for donkey's years. Miss Hadley told her she'd been here since she was seventeen and that Mr Jardine was a kind and considerate boss. Without even asking a direct question, she learned that he'd been a widower for many years.

Honor thought everything about the shop spoke of luxury and wealth. The displays of jewellery took her breath away. 'I'm going to love working here,' she said.

On Saturday evening, they had the farewell party. Miss Povey had stayed on for a couple of weeks so that she could leave on the same day as Miss Bundy, and Dorothy was sorry to see them go. She'd always got on well with both of them and counted them as friends.

Mr Jardine said some very nice things about them and when he presented Miss Povey with the silver clock, she said, 'I was very happy here, it's a lovely place to work. I shall miss you all.'

Her face really lit up when she saw the tea set the staff had clubbed together to buy her: a matching teapot, water jug, milk jug and sugar basin.

They all felt sorry for Miss Bundy, having to leave to look after a difficult ageing father. She wasn't far from tears when she saw the leather handbag and silver photograph frame. Mr Jardine told both ladies they must stop in to say hello whenever they came into town. He was a very kind man.

Miss Pinfold felt a bit down in the dumps. 'I shall miss Alice Bundy,' she said. 'We used to go to the pictures sometimes after I'd put Mother to bed.'

When Honor had worked at Jardine's for a few weeks, Edwin asked Dorothy how she was coping in the shop. In all honesty, she had to say Mrs Thorpe was quick to learn and very polite to the customers. She could see that pleased him.

She hadn't taken to Mrs Thorpe. She asked herself if it was envy she felt. Life seemed to have given Mrs Thorpe so much more than she and the other girls had. She was half their age but had done so much more. She even had a young daughter, quite near to Jane's age.

Jane was surprised when Dad handed her a folder containing job application letters. She'd thought all that was over and done with.

'One of the part-time girls at the Aigburth shop has given notice. I want you and Miss Pinfold to pick out two or three of the most suitable from here, and get them in for interviews. I'd like you both to sit in and help me choose.'

That made Jane more curious than ever as to why Mrs Thorpe had not been hired in the usual way. She was the first married woman her father had ever employed. 'A widow,' he'd told her. 'She's had a very hard time.'

Mrs Thorpe treated her like a friend and an equal, and having her in the shop made for a different atmosphere. Jane couldn't help but notice that she was more attractive than the other girls. Her skirts were smarter and always well pressed and the collar of her white blouses stood up to frame her face. She wore neat court shoes with a heel, while the others had broad feet and went for comfortable lace-ups or slip-ons because they were on their feet all day.

Jane found it hard to understand why Dad had chosen a person who was so different from the rest of the staff. Nothing had changed in E. H. Jardine & Son, Purveyors of High Class Jewellery since her grandfather's day. Dad had often told her Grandpa had had the winning formula. 'So there's nothing that needs changing,' he said.

He treated his girls with olde worlde respect just as Grandpa had, and they devoted themselves to selling his jewellery. Given names were not used except occasionally for Pam Kenny, who, he said, was little more than a child when she'd first come. He knew Jane saw her as a friend and he tended to treat her as an indulgent uncle would.

Most of the girls had been working in the shop since before Jane was born and they wanted to mother her. Dad had brought her up to treat them as a sort of extended family, and now she felt her father expected her to accept Mrs Thorpe as another member of it.

'Dad,' she said, 'I thought you wanted everything to go on in the shop year after year just as it always has, but you've made a big change.'

'What big change?'

It made her smile that he didn't recognise it as a change. 'Mrs Thorpe is not our usual sort of sales assistant.'

He turned to shuffle his papers about his desk. If she didn't know him better she'd have said he was embarrassed.

'I'm glad,' she told him, 'because everything should change in time. I'm grown up now, and I want changes. I'd like more freedom.'

That made him swing round to look at her. 'Freedom to do what? You already do exactly what you want. I treat you like a grown-up, don't I?'

'Well, sometimes . . .'

'If there's anything you do want, you talk me into it. Like letting you leave school and come to work here while you're still very young. I don't understand this talk of freedom. What else can you possibly want?'

'I need more clothes, Dad. Suitable clothes. I've only got schoolgirl stuff.' She was wearing the pleated navy skirt and white blouse she'd worn for school, with a small scarf round her neck instead of her school tie.

'Perhaps you do. We'll do something about that. I should give you a regular allowance . . .'

'That's really old-fashioned, Dad. Thanks, but I won't need an allowance once I'm working full time. We all expect to earn our own money these days and I'll buy my own things. And I don't want help from Miss Hadley or Miss Pinfold. Being sent out with them makes me feel ten years old. I want to go alone or with a friend.'

'Did she say something? Miss Hadley?'

'You mean you've already asked her?'

'I'm sorry. I don't understand the way young people

dress nowadays. You go out with Pam Kenny and come back with some very strange garments. That's not the way I want you to look.'

'That's what I mean by freedom, Dad. I don't want to dress like someone from my mother's generation. I want to look like girls now.'

Edwin sighed. 'Oh, dear. I am sorry. I do wish your mother was still with us. I suppose I want you to look as much like her as possible.'

'Dad! That makes me feel awful, as though I'm turning my back on her.'

'No, love. You're like Elena, but . . .' Jane certainly took after her Dutch mother. She was as tall as he was now. 'You're a different person. You must feel free to be yourself.' She was becoming more attractive as she grew up. There was a bloom about her, her hazel eyes had taken on a glow, her cheeks were pink and her dark hair shone.

'That's it exactly. Soon I'll be legally of age, an adult, and able to do what I want.'

'Oh, dear,' he teased. 'That sounds ominous.'

She laughed. 'Miss Hadley and Miss Pinfold are both very kind, but they've no eye for style. I want more independence about clothes. Apart from that I don't suppose you'll notice much difference.'

'Forgive me. I'm getting old too. I don't know why they had to drop the age of majority to eighteen. You'd have been twenty-one soon enough.'

'But they have.'

'Yes, but I think, my dear, you still need a little guidance when you go out to buy clothes.'

It was another cold Sunday afternoon. Edwin had been anxious all week since he'd noticed the price of rough diamonds was dropping. Of course, the country was sliding into recession and many prices were falling, but he knew there was another reason for the drop in the diamond price. Jane ought to know how he viewed the future prospects for his business.

'There's something I need to explain to you,' he said after lunch. 'Come on down to my office.'

'Is this another story about the jewellery trade?'

'Yes.' He lit his gas fire before sitting down. 'You've heard of the De Beers Mining Company?'

Jane nodded. 'They do diamonds, don't they?'

Edwin smiled. 'Do diamonds? Yes, I suppose you could put it that way. Cecil Rhodes set the company up about a hundred years ago. It owns the richest diamond mines in the Cape and made a fortune for him. He named his business the De Beers Mining Company after two Afrikaner brothers who had owned the land the mines were on. He made their name famous across the generations; it will always be associated with great wealth and diamonds, but the brothers remained poor. Unfortunately for them, they'd sold their land before the diamonds were found.'

Jane shook her head. 'I can't help feeling sorry for people who miss out like that.'

'Some lose and some win. Cecil Rhodes continued to buy up other mines and other claims and within a few years almost the entire world's supply of diamonds was in his hands. He was making a vast fortune and increasing his output. When the price for his diamonds went down, he realised it was because he was flooding the market. He immediately cut production from three million carats a year to two million carats and the price stabilised.'

'That's market forces, isn't it, Dad?'

'Yes, and it showed him he could control the world market in diamonds. Cecil Rhodes died long ago, and since then huge diamond deposits have been found in other parts of the world. Other diamond mining companies have come into being and the output could now be prodigious, but they'd learned their lesson from De Beers and formed a cartel to keep the price of diamonds artificially high.'

'You mean it's been artificially high ever since?'

'Well, it's crashed a few times, but so far they've always managed to get control again. When there's a war, when businesses are lost and buildings bombed, people put their money into gold and diamonds and hoard them. So do refugees, because diamonds are easy to carry, but when the war's over and they try to sell them they flood the market and the price goes down. They can't get back what they paid for them, if they can sell them at all. There's almost no second hand market for rough diamonds.'

He saw Jane straighten up. 'I find that unbelievable. I thought diamonds had an intrinsic value.'

Edwin smiled. 'We all thought that, but it's not so. Once they're made up into jewellery, each piece has a value based on artistic merit, and the work it took to make it, as well as the price of the raw materials.'

'But what about the price of diamonds now?'

'As I said, it's deliberately kept artificially high, and the number of diamonds coming on the market is restricted to keep it so. But even so, it is dropping.'

'Gosh, Dad, you mean it's going to crash?'

'I hope not, but it's quivering. Do you remember, back in August last year, Idi Amin expelled all the Asians from Uganda? They were given seventy-five days to get out. Many of them owned businesses and they were forced to abandon them as well as their homes. They weren't allowed to take cash out of the country either, so many converted it to rough diamonds and hid them about their bodies. I followed the story in the newspapers. They held British passports so most came here, and once in Britain they've tried to convert their diamonds to cash to have money to live on. That brought extra diamonds on to the market and now it's affecting the price.'

'But it won't crash?'

'Hopefully not. What the Ugandan Asians could buy didn't amount to all that much, and I understand some are setting up as dealers. They will need to keep their diamonds as stock.'

'If there was a crash now, Dad, what would happen?' Jane was sitting upright, anxious and eager.

Edwin stretched out in his chair. 'It doesn't bear thinking about, but it hasn't crashed since the war.'

'But it did then?'

'Many small businesses ground to a halt then.'

'What happened to ours?'

'I was called up and so were many of our staff. Your grandfather closed most of his branches, since no jewellery was being made so no new stock was available. We had to move quickly when the war was over to open new premises. When you think about it, Jane, what we sell are pretty baubles but they're no use to anybody.'

She was indignant. 'Of course they are.'

'If your house had been bombed and you were cold and short of food, you wouldn't concern yourself with jewellery.'

'This isn't a war, Dad.'

'No, and it's only a hiccup in the diamond price. But all the same, don't you think it strange that people want to decorate themselves with minerals? Stuff that's been dug up out of the ground?'

'No. They're pretty and we all love jewellery. Diamonds are a girl's best friend.'

'And d'you know why diamonds are a girl's best friend? It's because jewellery was all a married woman could own. A hundred years ago, a woman's money went to her husband when she married. But if a woman owned diamonds, she had something to fall back on in time of need.'

Jane smiled. 'Is that where the saying comes from?'

'Indeed it is. And diamonds also give an aura of wealth, power and status to the wearer, or in many cases to her husband. That's why people want them. And don't forget the garnets, opals, peridots and lots more. They're equally pretty, one could say, but not so prized.'

'They don't cost as much.'

'Exactly, and therefore don't provide the same aura. Think of Cleopatra and her flashing emeralds; think of our own Queen when she goes to open Parliament.'

'Visible wealth, power and status.' Jane nodded. 'It's traditional to wear jewellery.'

'Diamonds are only traditional because De Beers employed an advertising agency in New York to make them so. In the early years of this century, coloured stones were thought to be prettier, but what De Beers had in plenty, and wanted to sell, were small colourless diamonds. They made it traditional for a young man to buy his fiancée a diamond ring when they became engaged. Isn't that what we sell most of?'

'It's a romantic idea.'

'Only since De Beers spent a fortune on advertising to tell us that, like marriage, a diamond is for ever. Diamonds are a marketing miracle, Jane. There are huge stockpiles of them in the world today. Their value is an invention, but people pay a lot for them and so believe them to be an exclusive luxury.'

'You're being cynical.'

'Perhaps I am,' he sighed. 'But it's all so much froth. Sometimes I wonder when it'll collapse.'

CHAPTER TEN

HONOR WAS very pleased with her house. Even the finishing touches were in place now and she had it furnished as she wanted it. She hadn't seen Barry over recent weeks and she'd been unable to persuade him to guarantee her mortgage, but she was managing. She now had four regular gentlemen clients, two of whom met her in a local hotel for drinks or a meal before she brought them home.

'I even like working in the shop,' she told Kitty as they relaxed on her pink velour sofa one evening. 'What men will pay for jewellery is a real eye-opener. I sold two necklaces today, one for four hundred pounds and the other for nearly a thousand. It's to please their womenfolk, of course.'

'But it pleases you too?'

'Yes, I'm a successful saleswoman. I can do it as well as anybody.'

'So this is it then?'

'What d'you mean?'

'I thought the job was just a means to an end, that

167

you were going to hitch yourself to a rich man and be able to forget all these punters.'

Honor sighed. 'I am, but it all takes time. Aren't you happy here?'

'Ma, it's marvellous compared to Churton House. My stomach turns over when I think about that place. I'm very happy you got us out of there.'

'Good. I don't want to rush the next step because I want the boss to approve of me. I have to show him I'm a good and honest worker.' She smiled. 'Now we're both enjoying life more I can afford to take my time.'

'Do you still think the owner would do? As a husband, I mean.'

'He'd make an excellent husband but I'm already married to a deadbeat, aren't I? I'd be very happy to become his mistress.' She reckoned he hadn't been with a woman since his wife died, and thought he must be desperate for it. 'I'd settle for that and ditch all the others. He might even be willing to set me up in a nice house where he'd feel free to visit me often.'

'But you like it here, Ma,' Kitty protested. 'You don't want to move.'

'I know. But then we'd have two houses, wouldn't we? You're growing up; you might want a place of your own one day. Anyway, I'd be a woman of property and I rather fancy that.'

Kitty giggled. 'You are clever.'

'The likes of us have to look out for ourselves. Since

I've been doing that, things have improved, haven't they?'

'You bet. What's this man like?'

'You've seen him at the shop.'

'I didn't notice.'

'He's bald and he's got a face like a benign horse.' Kitty laughed outright. 'But he's quite sweet really, very kind and polite to everybody. He'll do, yes, I think he'll suit. He's generous, too. I might have found a real sugar daddy.'

'And what about his daughter?'

'She's naive. Very innocent, but so is her father in some ways. He's a good businessman but he'll believe anything. Jane's two years older than you, but she's a child by comparison. He still treats her like one.'

'I thought you said she had a boyfriend?'

'Yes, she has, Nick Collins. He expects to be made a manager in the business before much longer.'

Kitty asked, 'Will that make him rich?'

'It'll give him a reasonable salary, but no. He's got no more money than we have.'

'She'll own that business one day. That's enough to attract a man, isn't it?'

'Yes, Kitty, but I'm aiming to take some of that business for myself.'

'She'll still be rich.'

'It depends how much of it I manage to get.'

'Aim higher, Mum. All you have to do is marry him. If you did that you'd have it all. After all, Paul Thorpe isn't likely to come back, is he? I rather fancy Edwin Jardine as a stepfather.'

Ten minutes later, Kitty ran out to meet Jason. He'd agreed to pick her up and take her for a meal. She could see him waiting for her two or three doors further down the road. He couldn't stop right in front of the house, of course, because Ma would recognise the car. And she'd told her she was going to the pictures with Flossie.

Since his father had gone to prison, Jason had commandeered Gary's old Ford Cortina. Its previous owner had described it as a good runner and it was, but it was shabby and Jason longed to have a car with more style.

'Hi there.' Kitty snatched open the door and flung herself on to the passenger seat. 'This beats waiting around for a bus. I'm jolly glad you've got a car.'

'It's a shed,' he complained. 'I'd really like something sporty, something that makes people turn round when they see it and say, "Wow!" '

'What sort's that?'

'I'd quite like a little MG Midget.'

'And you could afford that?'

'Yep, reckon I could stretch to one that's been done up.' He turned to smile at her.

'Not new?'

'They don't make them any more, not the sort I fancy. It's by way of being a classic.'

'It sounds lovely.'

'I know someone who runs a garage. I've asked him to look out for one for me.'

'That's marvellous.'

Three weeks later, he came to meet her driving a scarlet two-seater MG Midget.

'It's gorgeous,' Kitty said.

'I'm thrilled with it.' She could see he was. He was laughing and smiling at the same time. 'It seems to belong to a bygone age, doesn't it? It's easy to drive too.'

Kitty sat back in the passenger seat, the wind tossing and pulling at her hair. 'I feel we're almost flying,' she said. 'I wish I could learn to drive.'

He laughed. 'You're not even sixteen yet.'

'I could do it.' Kitty was sure of that. 'Let me have a go, please.'

'OK. I know a place where you can start – my dad took me there. It's a big overspill car park, but when it's empty there'll be nothing you can hit. You'll be able to get the feel of the MG there.'

In August 1973 when Jane started working full time in the business, her father took her into his office and showed her a training schedule he'd drawn up for her.

'To start with, three or four months sitting in Miss Pinfold's office. I want you to get a good grip on the accounts. Nothing is more important in business. I know you're fresh from college with a book-keeping qualification, but Miss Pinfold can explain exactly how our system works.'

Jane knew it was what she needed. 'I can do shorthand and typing too, Dad.'

'I'll dictate some of my letters to you, so you can practise your shorthand and typing too.'

Jane helped Miss Pinfold generally with the paper-work and felt she was learning a lot about running her father's business. On Saturdays when the shop tended to be busier she worked as she'd always done under Miss Hadley's supervision behind the counters.

Dad had always visited his other shops on a regular basis, and now he took Jane with him. While the Church Street shop was much the grandest, and she'd seen all the other shops before, she now understood the extent of the business.

He'd taken her to the Birmingham Jewellery Quarter before when he'd gone to see their new designs and order new stock. But she was no longer left sitting in a quiet corner to watch. Now he was trying to teach her the finer points of what he did, and why he chose certain designs above others. Jane found it exhilarating.

That autumn, she and Pam Kenny enrolled in Miss Hadley's cake decorating class on Tuesday evenings and enjoyed it. The Kenny family ran a small café which was not far from the school and on some Tuesdays Pam took her there to have a meal before the class.

For the last three years the Crosby branch of E. H. Jardine & Son had been managed by Miss Moira Simpson, who unexpectedly announced her engagement to an old family friend living in London. She gave three months' notice of her wedding, after which she meant to leave Liverpool for good.

'When do you next expect to see Nick?' Edwin asked his daughter.

'Tonight. We're going to the pictures.'

'Good. When he comes to collect you, I want to talk to him.'

'What about?'

'I knew you'd be interested.'

'Come on, Dad, don't tease me.'

'Miss Simpson is getting married and going to live in London. Crosby's our smallest branch, I know, but it does good trade. A good place for Nick to cut his teeth as manager.'

'Wow, Dad, he'll be delighted. Be jolly handy for him too, living upstairs.'

'Please don't say anything to him. I want to tell him myself.'

On the morning Nick took over the shop, Edwin took Jane with him when he went to give him the keys and talk him through the figures in the account books. After that they took him out to lunch.

Jane studied him across the table. He was twenty-four now and six foot two, noticeably taller than she was. He was thin and gangly but beginning to broaden across the shoulders; his dark intense eyes kept meeting hers, full of love for her. It was hard to drag her gaze from his and keep her mind on the work. It must be obvious that they were in love. They couldn't hide it if they'd wanted to.

Dad drove her back to Church Street. She wasn't expecting to see Nick again that day but they were just finishing supper when he rang and asked if she'd like to go out for a drink.

'My mother's staying the night in Liverpool and it would be great if you could meet her,' he said. 'Would you like to? She's at the Exchange Hotel.'

'I'd love to.'

'I'll call for you in about half an hour.'

Jane rushed to change into her best dress and put on a bit of lipstick. She was on the way downstairs when she heard the back doorbell ring. She ran down the last flight to open the door.

He pulled her into his arms and his lips fluttered all over her face. She could feel his passion and her own longing reaching out for him. He groaned. 'We've got to go. Mum will be waiting for us.'

He pulled her arm through his for the short walk to the Exchange Hotel. Liverpool was all bright lights and bustle as people made their way to theatres, cinemas and restaurants.

'Mum asked if I had a girlfriend and I told her about you,' he said.

Jane was fizzing inside. It sounded as though he was

as serious about her as she was about him. She was familiar with the Victorian splendour of the Exchange Hotel. They found his mother in the lounge. She was tall, thin and rather elegant.

She got to her feet. 'I'm very pleased to meet you, Jane.' She put out a hand in greeting and it felt cold. 'Tell me about yourself.'

Jane did her best. 'You must know about our shop, because Sam has worked for us for decades.'

'Yes. It's the best jeweller's in Liverpool.'

'We like to think so.'

'Now Nick's left home he has a completely new life, and it's quite difficult for me to keep up with what he's doing.'

She said little more as she sipped at a very dry sherry. Jane decided Nick must take after his father's side of the family. Both he and Sam had plenty of social chitchat.

She was glad to have met his mother. It made her feel that Nick wanted her to be part of his family.

Jane's eighteenth birthday was on the fifteenth of November. Beforehand, her father had asked her what she'd like to do to celebrate. Usually on her birthdays he took her out for a meal.

'I'd like you and me to go out at lunch time,' she said. 'Could we?'

'All right. For once a longish lunch won't matter.' His eyes were twinkling. 'I suppose Nick wants to arrange something for the evening?' Jane knew he already had.

She was making her own preparations for coming of age too. Throughout her childhood, Miss Hadley had taken her to have her hair cut by Alma at Snips, who was about Miss Hadley's age. Pam Kenny said her mother went to Alma, and after a shampoo and set most of her elderly clients came out looking like the Queen Mother.

She'd always cut Jane's dark straight hair into a plain ordinary bob, which at ten years of age she'd held back with hair slides. At secondary school, ponytails had been popular and she'd let her bob grow a bit, but the cut had never changed and a new appointment was always made for her six weeks later. Jane had insisted on going alone over recent years and last time she'd told Alma she didn't want another appointment. She wanted to grow her hair long.

Well, it had grown and it was now an untidy mess. She planned to go to a fashionable hairdresser and have it restyled. She'd been saving her shop earnings for weeks for this.

'I'd go to that new shop in Bold Street,' Pam Kenny said when she asked her advice. 'Not that I've been, I can't afford their prices, but I've heard they're very good. Up to the minute styles.'

Jane told her father and asked for time off to go. She made an appointment for the day before her birthday. It happened that Princess Anne was marrying Captain Mark Phillips on that day and it was to be the first royal wedding to be shown on television. Everywhere, there was an air of excitement and festivity. The girls could talk of nothing else.

The salon was very smart and the service slick. The clientele was able to listen to a radio commentary on the wedding. Jane had to tear her attention away when she found herself trapped between a huge mirror and the stylist's penetrating gaze.

'You want something different? I think your hair needs to be combed forward instead of back. You have a high forehead and a fringe would reduce that. Yes, definitely, a fringe would suit you. How much do you want off the length? I'll layer it for you and not take off too much.'

Jane closed her eyes so she couldn't see it coming off in what felt like swaths. When it was finished she looked at her reflection in the mirror and saw herself transformed. Her features now seemed to be better balanced and her nose smaller. She thought it a great improvement.

When she returned to the shop the girls cooed their approval and even Dad had to admit it made her look prettier.

The air of festivity seemed to carry on into the next day. She received a two-strand cultured pearl necklace from her father and a shoal of birthday cards and small gifts from the staff. Dorothy had made her a birthday cake festooned in jewellery made by colouring the icing.

Dad had booked a table for the two of them at a small restaurant in Dale Street. To celebrate a birthday, they usually bought cream cakes for the girls to have with their afternoon tea. This year, Edwin said a few congratulatory words and turned Jane's cutting of her birthday cake into a little ceremony.

When Nick met her that evening, he told her that her new haircut had turned her into a real beauty, and he was proud to have her on his arm. He presented her with a smart handbag and took her to a supper club they'd been to before. Jane reckoned she had a magnificent coming of age.

Jane knew that trade had been slack all year, not just for her father's business but for all retailers throughout the country. By now the recession was biting hard. The weeks running up to Christmas were usually their busiest and they were all hoping trade would pick up.

'There isn't much profit to spend on decorations this year,' said Edwin. 'Do your best with what we have and spend no more than fifteen pounds adding to them.' Jane and Pam got out last year's shop decorations and tried to shake life back into the silver Christmas trees.

Mrs Thorpe took an interest. 'Why don't you use real holly? I have a tree in my garden with plenty of berries on it. Shall I bring some in?'

'Yes, please,' Jane said.

The following day, Mrs Thorpe brought in a great armload of foliage and berries, and together they broke it up into small sprays. They combined them with the best of last year's silver streamers and placed them round the shop.

Dorothy said, 'It looks very effective.'

Dad said the shop looked magnificent. 'You've got real artistic taste,' he told Mrs Thorpe. 'I've never seen it look better.'

When the holly dried out in the warm shop and began to look tired, she brought in a fresh supply.

The days were darker and colder now but the customers were coming in. Jane knew her father was pleased that they were doing better than he'd expected. She loved the festive season and all the Christmas traditions in the shop that they'd followed since her grandfather's day.

With some time still to go, Nick said, 'Let's make Christmas Eve special. Let me take you for a big night out.' Jane would need to break with one family tradition.

'Dad, d'you mind if I don't come to midnight service with you this year?' she asked. She told him what Nick was planning.

'I suppose I should expect you young ones to live it up,' Edwin said. 'You go with Nick, Jane, if that's what you want.'

Later, he raised the subject again. 'What about Miss Hadley?' he asked. 'She always comes to church with us on Christmas Eve.'

'You can take her just the same, can't you?'

'Yes, I suppose so.' He seemed less than eager. 'Hadn't you better tell her you won't be coming?'

'I already have.'

'What did she say?'

'Well, nothing really.' Dorothy had looked a little dismayed, but she wasn't going to tell him that.

'What about the present you usually give her?'

'*We* usually give her. You could do that too, couldn't you?'

He was frowning. 'What did we decide she should have?'

'Dad!'

They both knew Miss Hadley had very much admired the silver alarm clock they'd presented to Miss Povey. It was Dad who'd suggested they give her one for Christmas.

They'd reordered one exactly the same and two more in similar but slightly updated designs that Dorothy wouldn't have seen yet. When the order was delivered, Jane unpacked it and took out the clock she liked best to gift-wrap for Dorothy.

It was late afternoon and Dorothy was feeling tired. The run-up to Christmas had been quite hectic and she was glad there was only one more day to go. She and Emily had everything ready; she was looking forward to the festivities and having a few days off work to sit back.

The shop had gone quiet. Only Jane on the far

counter was still serving. Dorothy was fond of Jane. She watched her for a few moments, thinking that she was now a competent and attractive young lady. She'd really grown up in this last year and that would mean changes – big changes. One day she'd be running this shop. She already had a boyfriend. Dorothy wondered if Jane and Nick would eventually marry. He certainly seemed keen on her.

Nick had started coming to church on Sunday mornings to sit next to Jane. Back at work, Dorothy had commented on it to Miss Jessop, who said, 'Perhaps he's taken up churchgoing to make himself more eligible in Mr Jardine's eyes.'

'Well, I don't know about that. He might have been a regular churchgoer when he lived at home with his mother.'

Miss Jessop shrugged. 'Perhaps he just wants to spend more time with Jane.'

Whatever the reason, it drove home to Dorothy that Jane no longer needed her supervision in church. The next time he came to sit on the other side of Jane, she smiled and said, 'I'm beginning to feel a bit of a gooseberry.'

They'd both looked contrite. 'Oh, Dorothy, I'm sorry,' Jane had said. 'We've made you feel uncomfortable.'

At that moment Miss Pinfold rang down. 'Mr Jardine would like you to come up to see him.' Dorothy almost ran upstairs.

Edwin stood up to greet her. 'Have a seat, Miss Hadley,' he said. He went through a few minor details to do with the business and then said, 'I understand Jane has told you she won't be coming to the midnight service. I'll be glad to come and collect you as usual.'

'That's very kind of you, Mr Jardine.' Dorothy had had time to think about what she should say to him. 'But if I'm not needed I can't drag you out to pick me up and then let you take me home.'

'It's no bother, you know that.'

He'd have to leave her to play the organ, and the journey only took six or seven minutes.

'No, it would be a trouble to you. I'll go to church with Emily on Christmas morning instead.'

'Are you sure? Goodness, it'll be the first time in years that you haven't come.'

Was he glad she'd refused? He seemed suddenly more relaxed, more jovial, and he certainly wasn't trying to persuade her to change her mind. She stood up and made for the door. Tears were stinging her eyes and she wanted to get away, worried now that she'd done the wrong thing.

'Oh, Miss Hadley,' he said, and that made her pause. Edwin was on his feet, taking a gift from the bottom drawer of his desk. 'What am I thinking of? Jane would be so cross with me. I'm very grateful for all you've done for us over the years. Grateful for all you still do.' He pushed it into her hands. 'Have a good Christmas. All the best to you.'

He bent and kissed her cheek. Just a peck really, but it took her by surprise. 'Thank you,' she said and fled.

It was Christmas Eve, and Jane gloried in providing all the festive traditions. They all enjoyed the rich fruit cake and sweet sherry in the rest room. Gifts were given and accepted, and once the stock was locked safely away they were closing early. The girls were leaving for the holiday, all jollity and excited smiles. Jane and her father went to the door to see them out amidst a flurry of good wishes.

Within moments only Mrs Thorpe remained. Now with her hat and coat on, she stood smiling at them.

'I was wondering, Mr Jardine, if you and Jane would like to come to tea at my house on Boxing Day?'

Jane knew her father was as unprepared for the invitation as she was.

Mrs Thorpe gulped, and using an embroidered handkerchief delicately wiped a glistening drop from the corner of each eye. 'And since we are now on our own, it would be such a help to us to have your company.'

Jane knew that was an appeal her father would not be able to resist, though he hesitated and seemed somewhat at a loss.

'It's very kind of you to think of us.' None of his other girls had ever asked them to their homes, not even Miss Hadley. 'Well, Jane, would you like to go?'

'Yes, please.' She was keen. She was always happy to

spend time with Dad, and never bored with his company, but it was the season for being out and about, and would give them something new to do on Boxing Day.

Her father said, 'Quite a treat for us. Thank you.'

'I have a daughter very near to your age, Jane. Kitty is almost sixteen. She's looking forward to meeting you.'

'I'm two years older than her,' Jane said.

'Two years means little when you get to my age.' Her father was all joviality now.

'About four o'clock, then. You know my address? It's Queen's Drive.'

'Yes, I have it in my records. Have a good Christmas.'

They watched her until she disappeared into the crowd of last-minute shoppers.

Her father smiled at Jane. 'How nice of her to ask us.'

Jane rushed upstairs to change. She'd saved up to buy a new red party dress to wear to the supper dance and Nick would be round to collect her soon. He was taking her to see a revival of Dickens's *A Christmas Carol*, which she'd enjoyed so much two years before, and afterwards to a restaurant for a supper dance.

He held her hand all through the performance, and to have his arms round her on the tiny dance floor sent thrills down Jane's spine. She loved the play and the food was delicious but the part she enjoyed most was when he took her home. It was very late and bitterly cold, and she took him inside to say good night.

'You're very beautiful, Jane,' he said. 'I love you very much. I have for a long time.'

It seemed no time at all before she heard her father's steps approaching, and Nick beat a hasty retreat.

Jane went upstairs to bed with her head in a whirl. Tomorrow would be wonderful too. She'd be seeing Nick again, when he and Sam had lunch with her and Dad at the Adelphi. After that, Nick was going to Chester to spend the rest of the holiday with his mother.

CHAPTER ELEVEN

JANE WOKE up on Boxing Day morning looking forward to visiting Mrs Thorpe's house, and thought her father was too. At half past three, he said, 'I'll just pop down to my office to confirm Mrs Thorpe's address and pick up my street map.'

It was a cold grey afternoon of freezing fog and slippery pavements. 'Wrap up warm,' he said, as he reached for the white wool scarf Jane had given him for Christmas. They had a five-minute walk to the lock-up garage.

Jane didn't have much to wrap up in. Her new red party dress was not meant to keep her warm and it was too dressy for afternoon tea. She had only the blue wool skirt and twinset she'd worn for lunch at the Adelphi. This year's gift from Miss Pinfold was a cardigan in blue two-ply knitting wool. For once, it fitted well and she liked it. She tried it on over several everyday blouses but decided she must buy a new one to suit it. Until then, her twinset would be better.

Today the streets were almost deserted, and once

outside she shivered. Her coat didn't feel warm enough. The sales would be starting tomorrow, and she meant to go out and buy herself some more clothes. Her favourite shop, C & A Modes, was closed, but as they passed it she paused to look at the fashions displayed in the windows.

'There's a nice blouse that might suit my new cardigan. I'll come here tomorrow and see what they look like together. And just look at those yellow pullovers. I might get one of those.'

Her father turned to scrutinise them. 'D'you really like them? They're very cheap.'

'I'd like a warm winter coat and some boots as well. While the sales are on, Dad, I'll get twice as much for my money.'

'It's not a question of money, Jane. I'll be happy to buy you more clothes if you think you need them.'

'I do,' she said firmly.

'Right. What I'm trying to say is, I think it's better to go for quality, even if you get less. They'll last longer.'

'Dad,' she wailed, 'it's the styles I'm interested in. I want to look fashionable. I don't want my clothes to last.'

She heard him sigh. 'Things have changed since my day.' He blew his nose, and added, 'How very kind of Honor Thorpe to ask us to her house.'

Jane found that unsettling. Honor Thorpe? Dad never referred to Miss Pinfold as Marjorie, or Miss

Hadley as Dorothy, nor was she encouraged to. Dad was afraid his staff would think they were being over-familiar.

Mrs Thorpe's house in Queen's Drive turned out to be a smartly painted semi-detached in a small garden, which was neat but bare at this time of year. It was four o'clock precisely when Dad pulled on to her drive. The front door opened straight away, as though she'd been watching for them. She came out to greet them looking very pretty in a smart paisley printed winter dress with her fair hair curling round her face.

'Very good of you to come. My daughter Kitty's looking forward to meeting you, Jane. Come inside.'

It was already dusk and the lights were on in the house, which looked welcoming and felt warm. Their coats were being hung in the hall as Kitty came downstairs. She was smiling and pretty, and had the same fair curly hair and blue eyes as her mother. She was wearing tight denim jeans and the most gorgeous fluffy sweater in rainbow colours. Jane thought her clothes were out of this world.

It surprised her to find the house more comfortable than their own quarters over the shop, and the spread on the tea table more luxurious than what they enjoyed at home. It was beautifully set out. They talked of the weather and of the season. Jane asked Kitty which school she went to.

Her mother answered for her. 'Rather a sore point, I'm afraid. She was very happy at St Margaret's, but since her father died I've not been able to afford that. Kitty now goes to the local comprehensive.'

'Are you not happy at your new school?' Edwin asked.

'It's all right.' She smiled at him. 'I'm not grumbling.'

'Very brave of you,' he said. 'That's the right attitude.'

'I'll be sixteen soon so I won't be at any school for much longer.'

'Kitty's getting very good grades,' her mother said. 'I'm proud of her.'

Then Mrs Thorpe turned the conversation to the shop. It surprised Jane to hear Dad telling her details about their successful run-up to Christmas. She'd understood he talked of such things only to her and Miss Pinfold.

When they'd eaten all they could of the dainty sandwiches, chocolate yule log, hot mince pies, and Christmas cake, Mrs Thorpe suggested Kitty might like to show Jane her Christmas presents.

Jane followed Kitty up the white-painted stairs, which were carpeted in red, to a bedroom so beautiful it took her breath away. It was decorated in cream and pastel pink and Kitty was allowed to put posters on her walls.

Mostly, it appeared, she'd been given clothes for Christmas. A pink coat, fur-lined boots, a full-length party dress. It was enough to make Jane gasp in wonder. She saw a whole row of jeans hanging in the wardrobe and was shown drawers full of sweaters. Far more clothes than she possessed herself.

Jane opened up and told her she had no mother and that Miss Hadley or Miss Pinfold had always taken her to buy clothes. Kitty gave her twinset and skirt a pitying look.

'You're eighteen, aren't you? Tell them to get lost. If you don't, you'll end up looking fusty like them. I'll come with you. I could help you get some really good stuff.'

Jane smiled. 'Nothing I'd like better, but Dad's got a hang-up about what I wear. He likes what old people choose for me, not what I like myself.'

'That's awful.'

'I know. He'd think you were too young, and would just encourage me to buy all the wrong things.'

'My mum could come with us. She's good with clothes, though sometimes she has funny ideas about what's suitable. But I can talk her round – you'd get what you wanted. And she works for your dad too, so why not?'

Jane warmed to her. 'That sounds good. I'll put it to him.'

'Now,' Kitty said. 'Right now is the time to ask him, while we're together. Your dad won't be able to refuse, will he, if Mum hears you ask?'

Jane smiled. Kitty was right, though Dad probably wouldn't refuse in any case. He must have noticed that

Mrs Thorpe had excellent taste, not only in decorating the shop but in clothes, home furnishings, food and just about everything else.

Moments later she and Kitty faced them with the request. Her father said diffidently, 'I don't want to impose on you, Honor.'

But she beamed at them both. 'I'll be glad to help. Just make a list of the clothes you want Jane to have, and I'll have a lovely time helping her choose them.'

'I want to come too,' Kitty reminded them.

'It's a good time to shop for clothes,' Mrs Thorpe assured Edwin. 'The sales will be on. We should go as soon as possible.'

'But the shops will be crowded during the sales. It would make it easier if you waited until they were over.'

'It's more fun when they're on,' Kitty assured him. 'What about tomorrow?'

'No, you must go on a working day,' he protested. Following Grandpa's tradition, Dad never opened the shop on the 27th. 'I wouldn't want you to go on your day off. That would be taking advantage of you.'

'Not at all.' Mrs Thorpe's face shone with anticipation. 'Tomorrow would be an excellent time to go.'

'We can't put it off,' Kitty explained to him. 'All the best things will be sold if we do.'

When they returned home Jane started making a list of what she wanted. Always it had been like this, clothes for a whole season bought in one session. She wanted to be like other girls: go shopping on her own, buy clothes more often, a few at a time, so she could give each garment more attention.

Her father said, 'I'll pay for what's on this list. You don't need to use the money I'm paying you for working in the shop.'

'Are you sure? That's very generous of you.'

Her list was growing. A winter coat, a warm dress for going out, boots, sober blouses and skirts to wear in the shop. Two pretty blouses, three pullovers, and a cardigan. Nightdresses, underwear, gloves.

Mrs Thorpe and Kitty arrived early the next morning. Before they set out Jane asked, 'Can I buy another pair of jeans, Dad? I'd like a dark blue pair with wide legs.'

She knew her father thought trousers unladylike for girls. He was about to shake his head and suggest another skirt instead, but Mrs Thorpe smiled sweetly at him.

'Almost all women wear trousers these days. I do myself. Kitty loves jeans and they're very practical. Young girls like to keep up with the current fashions. I think you should let her have them.'

As Edwin saw them out of the back door of the shop, Jane gave him a hug and a kiss on his cheek. 'Thanks for everything, Dad,' she said. Edwin watched her walk away with the Thorpes, and saw there was a little skip in her step.

He went back upstairs to his office. Usually he felt

just as happy attending to the affairs of the shop as he did when seeking outside pleasures, but today he couldn't concentrate. His head buzzed with excitement. He felt unsettled and couldn't keep still. Suddenly, it seemed, what he'd been deliberating on for so long had happened this Christmas, without any effort from him.

Seeing so much of Honor, going to her house, understanding how she lived, meeting her daughter, had changed everything. He had only to close his eyes now to see her face again. When he was with her he couldn't take his eyes away. He'd never seen a more beautiful woman. Just to look at her wide blue eyes and see her slow smile brought him immense pleasure.

His life had centred round Jane for years; they had a satisfying and close relationship, but she was no longer a child and he felt out of his depth dealing with a young woman. Bringing up a daughter without much help was not easy. Miss Hadley and Miss Pinfold did their best but they were spinsters well on in life, and knew no more about teenage girls than he did. He'd known Jane's clothes didn't please her and he was grateful for Honor's help.

He jerked to his feet to get her personal file from the drawer. It was beginning to look well thumbed; he'd been getting it out quite often over the few months she'd worked for him. He read once more the form she'd filled in giving her personal details.

Honor Sarah Thorpe, aged thirty-six. Would she consider his fifty-three years made him too old for her? Too old for what? He didn't really know, he couldn't make up his mind. Of course he hadn't mentioned anything to her. He didn't even know how to approach the subject, and felt very wary of doing so. But all the same, the future suddenly looked rosy.

Jane had never enjoyed a shopping expedition so much. Mrs Thorpe took her to all the shops she and Kitty patronised and though they were busy she had a way of getting the assistants to serve them.

She and Kitty picked out the styles they liked while an assistant helped Mrs Thorpe find them in the right sizes. Occasionally, she'd add something she thought the girls would like and brought everything to the changing rooms draped over her arm. Some shops had individual changing rooms but they were so busy that Kitty would push into the one Jane was using to try something on. Both she and her mother gave their opinion on style and fit, but mostly Jane made up her own mind about what she wanted. She was thrilled with the two pairs of jeans they helped her choose, one pale blue and one dark.

'You have to sit in the bath with them on,' Kitty advised her. 'With the water as hot as you can stand. You try to shrink them to your shape. That way, they're more flattering.'

Mrs Thorpe advised on a skirt for more formal

occasions and brought Jane a selection of blouses and tops to try on with it.

'Oh, Mum.' Kitty snatched one up. 'This blouse is gorgeous. I really like it.'

It was an embroidered peasant style with a drawstring neckline. She pulled it on, preening in front of the mirrors, and they all agreed it really suited her. 'I've got to have this,' she said. 'It's lovely.'

Jane hesitated over a similar one but decided she preferred a more tailored shirt style. 'You're trying on almost as many things as I am,' she giggled.

'I love clothes,' Kitty told her. 'I don't want to miss out on the fun.'

Jane found Kitty's underwear a revelation. It made hers look like that of a primary school child. Kitty looked more grown up in every way; she had a plump rounded figure and a well-developed bust. She laughed at Jane who was a very different shape, much taller and reed slim, and told her, 'Your boobs are just little buds.'

It made Jane feel inadequate, but at least she did have a bra. Two years ago, when Miss Hadley had taken her shopping, she'd wanted to try some on.

'You don't need one yet,' Miss Hadley had told her. 'I didn't have them when I was your age and they're not on the list your father's given me.' Miss Hadley's bust had become very ample and she certainly wore one now.

So Jane had saved up her pocket money and Pam had taken her to the shop where she bought hers. Jane studied those displayed on the counter and picked out what she thought would fit her. She took it home and tried it on, but it was too tight across her back. Pam went with her to take it back and get a larger size. When that proved comfortable she'd bought another.

Mrs Thorpe shook her head when she saw the one she was wearing. 'It's not a good fit,' she said. 'You need to be properly measured.'

She took Jane to the lingerie department in Lewis's, a store that Dad approved of, and after a consultation bought her four bras, though there were none on her list. Jane loved the knickers and underskirts and a reasonable number of those were bought too. They were the pretty things she'd longed for, lacy, skimpy and almost see-through. If she'd suggested anything like these to Miss Hadley she'd have been told, 'Your father won't want you to wear things like that. Anyway, what use are those flimsy things to you? There's no warmth in them.'

Jane was tired when they returned to the shop with her new clothes. She let them in through the back door with her key and led the way upstairs. Dad was working in his office and he invited Mrs Thorpe in while Kitty helped her carry the packages up to her bedroom and lay them out on her bed.

'This is your home?' There was no mistaking the surprise in Kitty's voice or her disdain, as her eyes probed into every corner. 'I thought you'd have a big house somewhere near.'

'No,' Jane told her flatly. It was almost one o'clock and she was hungry. On holidays like this, she and Dad usually went to the kitchen together and made a light lunch, poached eggs or something like that. She wished Mrs Thorpe would take Kitty home. She was looking forward to showing her father what she'd bought, though perhaps she wouldn't display all the underwear. But Dad called them down, and surprised her by insisting they all go out to lunch at the Adelphi.

'After the time and trouble you've taken outfitting Jane,' he told Honor, 'it's the least I can do.'

Both the Thorpes seemed pleased. The Adelphi Hotel was only a short walk away and they set off, Edwin leading the way with Mrs Thorpe, while Jane and Kitty followed behind. Jane was uneasy. While she was thrilled with her new clothes, she didn't know what to make of their new friends, or of her father's sudden enthusiasm for their company.

They'd barely turned the corner when Kitty whispered, 'I think your dad fancies my mum.'

Jane jerked to a full stop. She felt the blood rush into her cheeks. Surely not! They hardly knew each other. 'What makes you say that?' she demanded.

'Have you noticed how he looks at her? As if she was chocolate and he could eat her.'

Jane hadn't.

'It would be spiffing, wouldn't it? If my mum and your dad fell in love and got married?'

Jane couldn't get her breath, she was so shocked. She

knew it would be good for her father to marry again. She would be happier if he had someone of his own now she was spending so much time with Nick. But Mrs Thorpe? She was too young for Dad, too energetic, too modern in her ways. She didn't think it would happen. Anyway, Dad would need time to make up his mind. He never did anything on the spur of the moment.

'He's a lovely father,' Kitty went on. 'He lets you have everything you want, doesn't he?'

'No,' she choked. 'I don't think he does.'

Lunch was served with great formality at the Adelphi. Black-suited waiters moved silently to bring dishes from the extensive menu. The tables were set with crisp white damask and sparkling cutlery and crystal.

Dad was in good form, quite the life and soul of the party. Mrs Thorpe chatted away nineteen to the dozen and he seemed happy to cap each of her anecdotes. He even tried to bring Kitty into the conversation by asking her what she intended to do when she left school.

'Kitty can't make up her mind.' Her mother smiled indulgently at her daughter. 'I was just the same at her age, I didn't know what I wanted, and I made the mistake of drifting. I'd like to put Kitty's feet on a career path.'

Dad suggested a variety of careers but Kitty shook her head and said they'd be beyond her.

'You could do worse than go to the secretarial school Jane went to,' Edwin advised. 'It would give you a basic training. You enjoyed it there, didn't you, Jane?'

'I'm afraid it might be too expensive for me.' Mrs Thorpe smiled gently. 'It takes me all my time to pay the household expenses on my salary.'

Jane found herself watching her father. He was all sympathy for Mrs Thorpe and was probably going to give her a rise after that. Did he really fancy her? She was very pretty and not old-looking at all. She had delicate table manners and an engaging way of fluttering her hands about, and she was definitely holding Dad's attention.

She wondered whether by inviting them to her house yesterday Mrs Thorpe had been trying to worm her way into Dad's good books.

But Dad was old. He was set in his ways, wasn't he? He had nothing in common with the heroes in the books she read and the films she watched with Nick. All the same, she was horribly afraid Kitty might be right.

The lunch should have been a treat, but Jane didn't enjoy it.

Outside the Adelphi, Edwin had been reluctant to say goodbye to Honor, but he'd noticed Jane watching them from across the table and knew she wasn't pleased with what she saw. He mustn't rush things. Give Jane time to get used to the idea and she'd be all right. Once home, Jane rushed to unpack her new clothes and he settled at his office desk, feeling the day had gone flat.

He'd seen so much of Honor over the last two days, it seemed like a reawakening. He felt young again. There was a spring in his step. He was beginning to think that what he felt for Honor was love.

He took out the large bundle of bills Honor had given him together with the list he and Jane had drawn up of the clothes she'd wanted to buy. After a lifetime in business, it was second nature for him to check all his expenditure. He soon discovered they'd bought many more items than were on the list, which was not something that had happened when Miss Hadley had been in charge. He added the bills up on his calculator and checked the figure against the amount they'd spent. It was exact to the penny.

Jane was right, there was a huge number of garments yet the total was not massive. He hoped they wouldn't look cheap, but if they were what she wanted, what did it matter?

'Dad.' Jane ran down from the flat and did a twirl in front of him. 'How d'you like this skirt and sweater?'

He smiled. 'Very much. Quite a transformation. You look very smart.'

'I knew you'd like them. They're much the same sort of thing Miss Hadley would have chosen for me. Come upstairs. I've got a lot more to show you.'

'I can see you must have.' He pointed towards the bundle of bills.

'Have I bought too much?'

'No. You were right, you needed new clothes.'

'And wasn't it cheaper to go to the sales?'

'Yes, you've not been extravagant.' He gave her the bundle of bills. 'See for yourself.'

'I love everything I've got, Dad. Come and see.'

He followed her and saw she'd spread them out all over her bed and her chest of drawers. There were other piles on her chairs. She was holding them up one by one for his approval.

'Very pretty, yes.' But he wasn't sure. That pullover was such a garish green.

'I've a whole lot of new undies.' She didn't hold these up, but merely waved her hand towards the neat piles. But they looked more skimpy than he'd expected and all of flimsy lace. Quite sexy, in fact, which rather shocked him. Surely she was too young for this sort of thing? It didn't seem long since Miss Hadley had been buying her Chilpruf vests.

But no, he was being silly, of course Jane would want underwear like this. She was eighteen and an adult and working in the business. She even had a boyfriend. Her mother had been only nineteen when they'd married, and it had never occurred to him that she was too young.

'What about the jeans you wanted so much? When am I to see those?'

She took them out of her wardrobe. 'I got two pairs, not just one. I'm afraid Mrs Thorpe encouraged me to be greedy.' She looked a little shamefaced.

'No matter,' he said. 'I'll go and read in my armchair and you dress yourself up in your new finery for me to see.'

She came out a few minutes later wearing the dark blue pair with the lighter pair over her arm. 'I love them, Dad. Thank you very much. You've been wonderfully generous.'

'You have Mrs Thorpe to thank,' he said. 'You should tell her how pleased you are with everything.' Should he refer to her as Honor now? Not to do so might seem a bit odd when Jane must have heard him call her Honor over lunch.

'I know. I've thanked both her and Kitty but I'll do so again.'

Jane began putting her new clothes away. She was thrilled with them. Never again would she feel she had nothing to wear. Then she noticed the bundle of bills; she picked them up and flicked through them. Dad was very keen on accounting for every penny spent, but even he said she hadn't been extravagant.

She stopped at the bill from Eddington's and read it twice. Two poplin blouses – she'd bought them to wear when she worked in the shop – but also an embroidered peasant blouse at £3.99? She hadn't bought a peasant blouse. She remembered trying one on; it didn't suit her, and she hadn't liked it. But Kitty had loved it. She started hunting through the piles of clothes looking for the peasant blouse. It wasn't here.

Kitty had bought two or three things. She'd said she'd been given money for Christmas. It must have been put on her bill by mistake. Jane began checking all the bills against her new clothes in the way Dad and Miss Pinfold had taught her to check them against the shop merchandise.

A dozen pairs of tights from Lewis's? Mrs Thorpe had said she'd need tights and suggested she buy some, even advised on what sort. Jane remembered deciding to buy six pairs. She found them hidden under a pile of sweaters, still in their packets. She counted them and there were only six and she could find no more. She was shocked. She'd bought two filmy waist slips with matching knickers but the bill was for four. She carried on checking every bill carefully, but everything else was as it should be.

She flopped down on her bed and tried to think. If it had been just the blouse, there would have been nothing to prove it wasn't an accident. Mrs Thorpe had taken charge of the money but the tills had been busy, the shops full and they'd bought a lot of stuff. But with the tights and the undies as well? Would she be likely to make the same mistake three times?

She could feel anger welling up inside her, as she remembered how Dad had given Mrs Thorpe a job after that strange happening in the shop. Had it been a put-up job? And now she thought about it, could that pickpocket have been Kitty?

The blood rushed to her cheeks, making them burn.

Of course not. Mrs Thorpe wouldn't do anything like that. Jane felt she was being unfair and overly suspicious.

Why would anyone go to all that trouble? To get Dad's ear and his approval and make sure she got the job? Jobs weren't so easy to find these days. She'd certainly got his sympathy.

Jane was angry because Kitty had said Dad fancied her mother. And angry with him because she was afraid Kitty might be right.

Chapter Twelve

Edwin had settled at his piano in the living room and was playing a romantic piece by Rachmaninov. He could see Honor Thorpe's beautiful face before him and was reliving what she'd told him over lunch. He saw himself offering to pay her daughter's fees at the secretarial college. Kitty had had a hard time too since her father had died, and he wanted to give her a good start in life. Honor was murmuring her thanks, her face full of gratitude, when the door burst open and Jane was standing before him.

'Dad,' she said, 'I've been checking the bills Mrs Thorpe paid for my clothes.' She put them on the keys in front of him. 'There're a few things that aren't right.'

'What's that?'

'She bought a blouse for Kitty and put it on the bill with my things so you've paid for it.'

'It must be a mistake.'

'I don't think so because I've got six pairs of tights, but you've been billed for a dozen pairs. Then there's the undies . . .'

He was taken aback. 'Mrs Thorpe would never do such a thing! No, Jane, you must be mistaken.'

He was outraged at the suggestion and spoke too sharply, as though he didn't want to hear any ill of Honor. He saw his daughter's face fall.

That wrung him out. Jane seemed to be jealous of Honor Thorpe! He could see it in her hot cheeks and glittering eyes. He understood why only too well. They'd been all in all to each other for years and now . . .

Jane didn't realise how he felt about Nick Collins. He found it hurtful to see her greet him with such pleasure and wanting to spend her time with him, but Edwin knew he couldn't be all in all to Jane for ever. She was growing up. It was in the nature of things that she'd find her own friends and, hopefully, one day a man she'd want to marry.

The last thing he wanted was to stand in the way of that. He wanted her to have a full and happy life. He must be grateful she was so wholehearted, not only about Nick but also about wanting to work in the business.

Jane said, 'Kitty says you fancy her mother. She hopes you're going to marry her.' That took his breath away. 'Is it true?'

Edwin swallowed hard. How could he admit to it when he'd said nothing to Honor yet? It was too soon; he hadn't had time to decide what he meant to do. He didn't really know how he felt.

'She's a beautiful woman, Jane,' was the best he

could manage. 'She attracts attention. Other people were looking at her in the restaurant.'

Poor Jane was too young to understand how he felt. He loved her very much and it pained him to see such bitter feelings. The last thing he wanted was to hurt her. He must be more careful.

He searched for words that would make her feel better and said, 'I told Honor to get something for Kitty, a little gift.'

It wasn't true, but there was no need for her to be jealous of Kitty.

'Oh! I didn't realise that.' It had certainly taken the wind out of her sails. Her eyes levelled with his, and she said calmly and with dignity, 'I feel there's something strange about the Thorpes. Kitty watches her mother carefully and takes her lead from her.'

'Why shouldn't she?'

Jane swung on her heel and headed back to her bedroom, but Edwin couldn't get what she'd said out of his mind. After a few minutes he went down to his office to put more distance between them. Jane must be mistaken. He must attach no importance to what she'd told him. She'd accused Honor of fraud to blacken her in his eyes.

It would be too embarrassing to question Honor about such a thing. He had to give her the benefit of the doubt. Either Jane was mistaken or they were genuine mistakes on Honor's part. It would be better if he never mentioned it to either of them again.

*

Honor and Kitty rode home on the bus well pleased with their morning's work.

'Lunch at the Adelphi.' Kitty hugged herself with satisfaction. 'Wasn't it posh? I couldn't believe it when the waiter spread our serviettes on our knees.'

'Table napkins, dear.'

'How the rich live, able to take people to places like that at the drop of a hat. He likes you, Ma, he likes you very much.'

'I think I've made good progress with him over Christmas.' Honor was very satisfied with the way things were working out. 'And we've got to know Jane too.'

'She was thrilled with what we bought for her.'

'So she should be, but for us both to be invited to have lunch at the Adelphi . . .'

'They went there on Christmas Day too.'

'It shows he thinks we're socially acceptable. In fact, it makes us part of his social life. A big step forward for us.'

'He's eating out of your hand, that's what it shows. I told Jane he was falling for you.'

'What?' Honor was unnerved. 'I'm not sure that was wise. What exactly did you say?'

'Oh, something like – wouldn't it be wonderful if your dad and my mum got married?'

'Oh, God, Kitty! You shouldn't have. It's too soon for that sort of thing. What did she say?'

'She sort of agreed.'

'Honestly?'

'Well, she didn't say much of anything. I took it she agreed.'

Honor wouldn't have mentioned the word marriage in the Jardines' hearing so soon. She felt she had a sixth sense that told her when she should hold back in a relationship; she thought Edwin wasn't ready to push ahead just yet. He was the sort of man who took everything slowly. 'I don't think I should rush things, not with him.'

'Ah, Ma, don't back off now. He fancies you, he really does. Go for it.'

'No. To land a man you have to play with him as a fisherman plays with a fish. I'm going to give him time to think about me.'

At eight thirty the next morning, Jane and her father went downstairs to take the more valuable stock from the safe in his office and set it out in the shop. They met Mrs McGrath, their cleaning lady, on the stairs on her way up to the flat.

On the ground floor behind the shop was the back door used by the staff, and in the tiny room where they hung their coats was another safe set into the concrete floor. Dad's insurance policy laid down that all stock must be locked in a safe overnight. Stock of lesser value was stored here to save their legs on the stairs. Some of it was already out on the shelves. Miss Hadley kept a key and she and Miss Lewis were already in.

Jane could hear them chattering about what they'd done over Christmas; who they'd seen, what they'd eaten and what they'd been given.

'Have you had a good Christmas, Jane?' Miss Hadley asked.

'Yes, lovely, thanks.' Dad's reaction to her doubts about Mrs Thorpe had been hurtful, but she'd made up her mind to say no more about it. After all, she was grateful for her help. 'Mrs Thorpe asked us to her house on Boxing Day for afternoon tea.'

She was half aware that both ladies had stopped what they were doing. 'Yesterday she took me shopping and helped me buy a lovely lot of clothes.'

It took Jane a moment to realise she'd dropped a bombshell. Miss Hadley was astonished. 'Mrs Thorpe asked you both to her house?'

'Yes. I'm thrilled with my new outfits. She even persuaded Dad to let me have two pairs of jeans.'

Pam Kenny had come in and heard that. 'I'd love to see your new clothes,' she said.

'I'll take you up to my room at morning break,' Jane told her, 'so you can have a peek.'

Miss Hadley pushed a tray of stock into Pam's arms. 'Let's get on with the job,' she said tersely, her usual bonhomie completely wiped out.

'What's the matter?' Jane was quite shocked to see the effect her news had had on Miss Hadley. She'd known her all her life and rarely seen her in a bad mood. She was one of those perennially cheerful people, always friendly and kind.

'Nothing,' Miss Hadley said.

Twenty minutes later, the stock was all sparkling in the windows and Mr Jardine was on his way down to unlock the front door and open the shop.

Miss Hadley was re-locking the empty ground floor safe when Miss Lewis took it upon herself to have a quick word. 'I knew that woman would be trouble,' she whispered.

'Mrs Thorpe takes too much on herself.' Dorothy Hadley was indignant. 'Asking the boss round to her house when she's only been working here for a few months.' She felt Honor Thorpe had stolen a march on her. She hadn't taken to her.

'A bit on the sly side.' Miss Lewis's lips were straight and condemning. 'She said nothing to us beforehand about doing that, or we'd have told her it wasn't done.'

Miss Hadley agreed. 'There's something about her I don't trust.' But even worse, it seemed that on the spur of the moment she was able to make up her mind and do the things that Dorothy had been weighing up for years, and still hadn't done. She was also young and good-looking. Dorothy felt outclassed.

What a dull life she'd had by comparison. A spinster, who'd worked in the same shop for nearly twenty-eight years. Living with her older sister Emily, also a spinster, who'd worked in the local bank for over thirty years.

On many evenings she'd gone home to the house in which they'd both been brought up and tried to imagine how things would be if Edwin Jardine were to fall in love with her. She'd been fantasising about him for years. Now she sometimes told her sister things she wished had happened but had not. She'd even allowed herself to tell Emily little anecdotes of Edwin's doings as examples of his affection. Dorothy had talked of his motherless daughter too, and how she helped him care for her. Nowadays, Emily sometimes smiled enviously as she asked after her sister's boss.

To Dorothy, it looked as though Honor Thorpe was elbowing her way into Edwin's affections and she was going to be pushed aside. Nobody in the shop liked Mrs Thorpe, and none of them thought she'd be good for Edwin. She was a sly one, out to feather her own nest.

Dorothy wished she knew what she could do about it.

Over the following weeks, Honor grew to love the scented warmth of the shop on cold mornings and the feel of her heels sinking into the deep carpet with every step she took. Most of all, she enjoyed being able to feast her eyes on the dazzling jewellery she'd only been able to admire from a distance before. She asked countless questions about gemstones and was learning fast, but though the air of luxury and wealth delighted her what she really longed to do was to try on the most expensive pieces. And not just try them on: she dreamed of owning some of these glittering jewels soon.

She knew that she was expected to keep the security of the stock in mind at all times, but other than that it seemed all she needed to do was to show infinite patience and politeness to their customers, find out what they wanted and then show them everything they had in that line.

This morning business was slack, until an elderly couple came in and headed towards her. Miss Hadley came leaping across the shop to support what she considered to be an inexperienced assistant.

'Good morning, Mrs Carruthers, Mr Carruthers.'

'Good morning. It's our ruby wedding on Sunday,' chirruped the woman.

The gentleman smiled. 'I need to buy a little something to mark the occasion.'

'Rubies, Mrs Thorpe,' Miss Hadley shot at her as she escorted the customers to chairs in front of the counter. 'What would you like to see? Rings, or brooches, or . . .'

'Rings, I think.'

As Honor brought out two black velvet pads of ruby rings, she studied the man. He was bald and corpulent and had clearly enjoyed high living for many years. His matronly wife threw open her coat. She was bulging out of her dress but had the remnants of a pretty face. Expensive jewellery glittered on her fingers; more swung from her wrist and round her neck.

Miss Hadley said, 'I'll let Mr Jardine know you're here. He likes to say hello when you come in.' She was off upstairs at the double. Honor decided they must be Edwin's personal friends or very good customers.

Mrs Carruthers put on her glasses and pulled two or three rings from the pad for a closer look, but pushed them back. She had a diamond brooch in her lapel and was wearing a three-strand baroque pearl necklace. She touched it and smiled at Honor.

'Miles bought this here for me quite recently. It's much admired and I really love it. He bought my engagement ring here too, forty-one years ago.'

Edwin Jardine was down in time to hear her say that. 'My father would have owned the shop then,' he told them. 'Mr and Mrs Carruthers, how nice to see you again. I hope you're both keeping well?'

'Yes indeed, and you too, I hope? I'd like to get Marcia a nice ruby to mark our anniversary.'

'Get out tray number eighteen, Mrs Thorpe. There are some specially nice gems on that. Yes, this is one of the rings I was thinking of. Do you fancy it?'

Honor certainly did.

'I do like it.' Mrs Carruthers held it up to the light. 'Yes, the stone's very pretty, but isn't the shank a little small?'

Honor thought it was Mrs Carruthers's fingers that were podgy, but Edwin Jardine gave a buzz of sympathy.

'I'm afraid it is rather, but we can make any of these rings fit you. You choose the design you like and Sam Collins will make it fit. You remember Sam?'

'Why yes. Is he still with you?'

'Still going strong.'

Mrs Carruthers picked out the biggest and most fiery stone on the tray. It was encircled with small diamonds. She pushed it on her finger but it wouldn't pass over her knuckle, which was swollen and mis-shapen. She was bothered with arthritis and very much overweight, but full of smiles and vitality. 'I do like this one. What d'you think, Miles?'

'Very nice, dear. If that's the one you fancy, you must have it.'

Honor approved of her choice, and noticed that neither seemed bothered about what it was going to cost.

Edwin said, 'Pass me the ring sizer, Mrs Thorpe. Now, Mrs Carruthers, I'll need to measure your finger. Is this the one you want to wear it on?'

'Yes.' She tugged and twisted at the pretty emerald ring she was already wearing on it.

He measured both her finger and the ring. 'Could I just suggest that you have this made a little larger too? Half a size would do it.'

'And perhaps your engagement ring too, dear, while the others are being done,' her husband suggested. She wrestled off the large solitaire diamond ring, and Edwin examined it through his loupe.

'I'm afraid it needs work on the claws. One is broken, and have you noticed the gold has worn down where it's rubbed against your wedding ring?'

'Then I'd better have it repaired, hadn't I?'

'It isn't safe to go on wearing it like this. You could lose the stone.'

Her husband said, 'Right, how long will it take to do all that? We're giving a little party on Sunday and Marcia will want them all back by then.'

'Yes, of course. I'm sure we'll be able to manage that. Today's Thursday; we'll have everything ready to be collected on Saturday. Have you time to come upstairs for a cup of coffee in my office?'

Mr Carruthers consulted his Rolex watch. 'That's kind of you, but we're on our way to lunch now.'

'Well, never mind. Next time you come in.'

Honor watched Edwin Jardine escort the couple towards the door and thought the last thing that woman needed was more jewellery. She was glittering like the fairy on top of a Christmas tree. Another customer was coming to the counter when Honor saw them stop to admire the Sun Diamonds.

'They're very beautiful,' Mrs Carruthers said. 'I'd love to have them.'

Her husband smiled indulgently. 'Perhaps for our diamond wedding.'

Honor told herself that if only she'd focused on getting the right man when she was young, she might be in Mrs Carruthers's position now. But she hadn't.

She'd believed all that nonsense about love ruling the world.

On Saturday, Honor was serving and enjoying the feeling of being on top of the job when she saw Mrs Carruthers return to the shop alone to collect her jewellery. She was heading straight for the stairs when Miss Hadley intercepted her with polite small talk.

Some time later, Honor was leaving the staff rest room on the third floor, having had her mid-morning break, when she saw Edwin escorting the lady across the landing towards the stairs. The telephone in his office rang at that moment, making him hesitate.

'Don't bother about me, Mr Jardine,' Mrs Carruthers said. 'You've been very kind and I've taken up a lot of your time already.'

Honor saw Edwin's eyes settle on her. 'Mrs Thorpe, will you show Mrs Carruthers the gifts we have for men? She'd particularly like to see the silver letter openers.' He turned back to the customer. 'I'll catch up with you before you go,' he said, and hurried back to pick up his phone.

'Of course, Mrs Carruthers,' Honor said. 'It's one floor down.'

She stood back to allow the customer to go down the stairs first. Mrs Carruthers was wearing a smart suit with a tight skirt, and Honor could see rolls of fat rising and falling on her backside as she descended. Now Honor was above her, she could see a lot of grey hair on the crown of her head though the rest of her hair was coloured blonde.

How had a woman who had let herself go to seed like this kept a man eager to shower her with expensive jewellery? It seemed he would give her everything she fancied. Even now she was eyeing the display of gifts over the banister as she went down to the floor beneath. They had some very pretty silver and cut glass hip flasks on show.

Honor too was engrossed in the silverware and didn't actually see Mrs Carruthers fall. She went down with a crash that shook the floor. They all heard that, as well as her cry of agony. Alarmed, Honor ran down the last few steps expecting to help her up.

But Mrs Carruthers was a crumpled mound on the carpet. Her tight skirt had split and ridden up and she was showing her stocking tops, her massive thighs and some pink silk underwear. Honor knelt beside her and tugged at her skirt to preserve her modesty.

'My ankle,' she moaned. 'It hurts. Oh. Oh.'

The last vestige of natural colour was draining from Mrs Carruthers's cheeks, leaving rouged circles as prominent as those on a painted doll. She groaned again and seemed to be losing consciousness with the pain.

How could she help her? Honor had no idea. There was no way she could get her to her feet, which seemed to be twisted under her. She couldn't drag her eyes away from the handbag. It was a smart lizard one with a gilt clasp on top which had burst open. Honor could see the small manila packet into which Sam Collins put jewellery after he'd repaired it. Dare she? It seemed a heaven-sent opportunity.

An agitated Jane was the first to reach her. 'She's fainted,' Honor said. 'Get your father. I think she's hurt herself.'

She moistened her lips and looked again at that manila packet. She knew what was in it and was tempted. Her heart was pounding as her hand snaked out to slide the package out of the lizard handbag and into her pocket. Then she leaned on the bag to click the clasp shut. She was only just in time. Honor felt the heat rush up her cheeks as Miss Hadley came up at the double, closely followed by Miss Jessop.

Mrs Carruthers was stirring. 'My ankle. Oh, my goodness. It really hurts.'

'I'm a doctor,' a voice said behind them. 'Can I help?' Honor and the others moved back out of the way and the doctor was freeing Mrs Carruthers's foot from beneath her as a worried Edwin came rushing down in front of his daughter.

'She'll need to go to hospital,' the doctor said. 'This ankle could be broken.'

Honor gasped. 'Shall I ring for an ambulance?'

Edwin said, 'Jane, get Miss Pinfold to do it.'

Honor followed Jane as she raced up the stairs. She was desperate to put distance between herself and that lizard handbag. She'd not intended to take anything in this shop. She wanted her life with Edwin to be honest and above board. It had been a close call, but she'd been in the right place at the right moment and it had been an opportunity she hadn't been able to resist. She was very conscious of the small packet in her pocket.

She watched Jane from the office doorway, feeling like a spare part. As soon as Miss Pinfold reached for her phone Jane headed back. Honor followed, telling herself she had to keep a clear head. The shop seemed to be in an uproar, and quite a knot of customers and staff had gathered. Everybody was talking at once.

Miss Hadley clapped her hands for attention. 'Girls, please go back to your counters. Let's get things back to normal.' Honor heard her whisper to Jane to make a pot of fresh tea, 'for those who need to calm their nerves'.

Slowly the crowd began to disperse. Edwin was talking to Mrs Carruthers in soothing tones, telling her the ambulance would soon be here. She was still groaning with pain. Honor knelt beside her and rubbed her wrists. She didn't know whether she did any good, but she was showing sympathy, wasn't she?

She couldn't take her eyes away from Mrs Carruthers's hands. She was wearing both her emerald dress ring and the diamond solitaire engagement ring. Both were sparkling like new. That must mean that the packet Honor had picked up contained only the new ruby ring. Still, that was a cracker and she knew exactly how much Mr Carruthers had paid for it. To Honor, it seemed an age before the patient was stretchered off to hospital.

Edwin stood up and dusted the knees of his trousers. 'Come up to my office,' he said to her.

She felt the blood rush to her cheeks again. Did he suspect? Her head was reeling, and she could see that he was agitated too.

'What happened, did you see?' he asked on the way upstairs. 'Did she miss her step or something? You were on the landing when she was leaving. You must have been the nearest to her when it happened.'

Honor breathed again. 'Yes, I was following her down. I noticed her looking over the banister at the display of silver on the second floor. She wasn't concentrating on where she put her feet. I think she must have thought she'd reached the bottom and stepped off one stair up. That would disorient her and make her fall, wouldn't it? She went down with a tremendous crash as though from a height.'

He looked worried. 'I wish it hadn't happened in my shop. You did well: thank you.'

Honor said, 'She carries quite a lot of weight. I hope she hasn't done herself too much damage.'

'I'd better ring her husband and let him know. Oh, dear.'

At the first possible opportunity, Honor went to the cloakroom and was relieved to find it empty. She took the packet from her skirt and slipped it into her coat pocket, pushing a handkerchief down on top.

Her heart was in her throat all Saturday afternoon. She expected any minute to see an agitated Edwin rushing down to say he'd had a phone call to say Mrs Carruthers's ruby ring had been stolen. She was dreading the questions and the full scale search that would surely follow. Would he search her coat? The staff were still agog with excitement about the accident. Honor counted the minutes to closing time, desperate to escape with her coat and get away.

CHAPTER THIRTEEN

O N THE BUS going home, Honor's fingers played with the small packet but she didn't take it out of her pocket until she reached the privacy of her own bedroom.

Inside the manila envelope was a small box gift-wrapped in gold paper. She tore it off. The tooled leather box was familiar: there were lots of them under the counters. Every ring was put inside one when it was sold.

She opened it and the two-carat blood-red ruby surrounded by small diamonds glittered up at her. It was dazzling. She tried it on. It was too big for her, but to see it flashing and winking on her own finger made her feel she was rich. Only a wealthy woman could afford a ring like this. She kept lifting her hand to admire it and couldn't bear to take it off.

She couldn't keep it, of course. Edwin would be bound to recognise it, but she could wear it for an hour or so here in her own home. It felt too loose, so she pulled off her wedding ring and slid it on the same finger to anchor the ruby. It wouldn't do to lose it.

The best thing for her to do would be to hide it safely away and forget about it for a while. She'd need to let any hullaballoo die down and the ring be forgotten before any fence could sell it on. He'd only get a fraction of the original price anyway, and it would be hot property over the coming weeks.

She had to get rid of the leather box straight away. That was too dangerous to keep. On the white satin lining was the name E. H. Jardine & Son, Purveyors of High Class Jewellery printed in gold, together with the Church Street address. It was proof of where it had come from.

She pushed the box in her pocket and went downstairs to light the fire in the living-room grate. Then she started preparing an evening meal for herself and Kitty. Half an hour later the back door burst open and her daughter came in all smiles.

'Where've you been, Kit? Have you had a good day?'

'I went round the shops with Flossie. Didn't have any money to buy anything, though. Is that spaghetti? It smells heavenly, Ma. I'm starving.'

Suddenly she caught at Honor's wrist. 'Gosh, that's a smashing ring. Did he give you that – your new feller?'

Honor snatched her hand back, cross with herself for letting Kitty see it. She was too tired to think and hadn't kept her wits about her.

'It's just imitation,' she said lightly.

'It never is.' Kitty was trying to hold her hand still. 'That's a valuable stone and you know it. Gary showed us plenty before he flogged them on. Where did you get it?'

Honor remembered the ring box she'd put in her pocket. She strode into the living room and flung the box on to the fire, which was now burning up well. The less Kitty knew about this the better.

She was back at the stove stirring the spaghetti sauce when Kitty came to the kitchen door with the box impaled on the end of the poker. 'You've pinched it from Jardine's,' she crowed.

'Put that back on the fire this minute,' Honor screamed. 'It's half burned – it'll mark the carpet if you drop it.'

Kitty did so and was back moments later. 'Good lord, Ma. I thought you were going to keep your nose clean and be a model employee? Wasn't the plan to make the boss fall for you and then let him persuade you to shack up with him?'

'It still is.'

Kitty was frowning. 'I don't understand. You thought you were making good progress, so why are you helping yourself to his stuff now? Aren't you expecting him to be giving it to you soon?'

'Yes, with luck.' The ring sparkled up at her. Honor sighed. 'I saw the opportunity and just grabbed it. It was a split-second decision.'

'Wow! If you'd had time to think, would you have done it?'

'I don't know.' Probably not. 'But it's a magnificent ring and it's mine now.'

Kitty had a wide smile. 'What a pity you can't ask Gary to get rid of it for you.'

'It's not a good idea at the moment. Lists of stolen property are circulated round jewellers' shops so we assistants can keep an eye out for it. Better if I keep the ring for a while until the hue and cry dies down.'

Honor had had a trying day and felt exhausted. After they'd eaten, she said, 'I'm going to have a hot bath and flop down in front of the telly. If you'll make our usual cup of tea I'll have it afterwards.'

Kitty said, 'I don't want any tea, I haven't got time. I'm going to the pics with Flossie tonight, but I'll make a cup for you.'

Honor went upstairs and started to run her bath. In the bedroom, she took off her rings and looked round for a safe place to hide the ruby. Her dressing table had three small drawers on each side of a kneehole; it stood against a wall. She dragged one end of it three inches forward, so she could see what the back of it was like. The backs of the drawers were solid wood – ideal.

She went to have her bath. It was bliss to lie back and steam in the hot water. She heard Kitty shout, 'I've put your tea in your bedroom, Ma. I'm going now, bye-bye.'

'Don't be late,' Honor called as she dried herself. She quite enjoyed an evening by herself, but Kitty was going out too much, several nights a week. Honor wondered uneasily where she was getting the money to pay for all these cinema trips, because she hadn't got round to finding herself another paper round or a Saturday job. It would be better if she stayed home and devoted more time and energy to her homework, or what had been the point in persuading her to stay on at school?

She found her cup of tea cooling on the end of her dressing table and drank it while she put on her night clothes. She was having second thoughts about this ruby. It was no longer making her feel good about herself. She should have remained upright and honest and not succumbed to temptation. When Edwin had given her this job, she'd told herself she'd turn over a new leaf and she had, except for that shopping expedition. But what she'd added to his bill had been only peanuts and Edwin hadn't suspected. He'd view the loss of the ruby ring more seriously, but he need never know she'd had anything to do with it.

She found a plain envelope and a roll of sellotape, then taped it to the back of her dressing table and lifted it back against the wall. She was pleased with her hiding place. It would be much safer there than hidden in one of the drawers. Who would find it now?

Honor went downstairs, taking with her the manila envelope and gift wrapping. She made up the fire and threw them on to it. The ring box had already burned completely away. Then, feeling absolutely shattered, she turned on the television and dropped down in front of it.

*

In order to avoid trouble and not upset her mother, Kitty had told her she was going to the pictures with Flossie tonight, whereas in fact Jason had arranged to come and collect her. At the appointed time she went out to find his MG Midget parked further down the road with Jason sitting in the passenger seat. Kitty got into the driving seat and started the engine. Jason had given her a few lessons and she'd found she had a real bent for driving.

As she was too young to apply for a licence, Jason had given her one. It was a full driving licence in the name of Helen Swift, who was aged eighteen and lived at an address in Maghull. One of his friends had found it inside a handbag he'd stolen and Jason had commandeered it.

'Memorise this girl's details first, and if you're ever stopped by the police, just show it,' he told her. 'It's pukka, they'll believe you're Helen Swift. If they've caught you doing something illegal you can sling it afterwards, and they'll never catch up with you.'

Kitty carried it in her handbag but so far nobody had asked to see it. She drove to Menlove Avenue where Jason had earlier lit the fire and bought cream cakes for them. He made coffee too and afterwards he undressed Kitty on the hearth rug. It was more fun than going to the pictures.

Later, they lay together in the glow of the fire. Usually they were relaxed and content at times like this, but today Jason had been to see his father in prison and it was on his mind.

'Pa's always sounding off about something. He had a go at me because I didn't go to see him last month. He was angry and said he's only allowed one visit a month and if nobody turns up it's wasted. "What sort of a family are you when you know I need you? Where's Hilda? Why doesn't she come?" ' he mimicked.

'The last time I went, I told him she'd scarpered and taken you with her. He made such a fuss then, dancing with rage and kicking and thumping the table. I thought the warders were going to take him back to his cell there and then.'

'He's accepted it now?'

'No, he's still angry, and he doesn't believe I don't know where you've gone.'

'You could have told him now.'

'Well I didn't. I don't want him going round and knocking you about.'

'If he knocks anybody about it'll be Ma.'

'Yes, you can tell her she's got me to thank for keeping my mouth shut.'

'I bet he's looking forward to getting out,' Kitty said. 'But it'll put a stop to evenings like this for you and me.'

'I know, it'll be no fun living here with him. He'll boss me around, treat me like a kid.' Jason sighed. 'Pa can't wait to get out. He can't believe I'm surviving without him and keeps asking if I'm paying the rent and the bills. He thanked me though, said he was grateful he'd have a home to come back to. But I'll be gone before then. I couldn't stand it.'

'Cheer up,' she said. 'Let's do something nice tomorrow.'

'Let's go on a shopping spree,' he said lazily. 'I'll buy something special for you.'

Kitty always enjoyed shopping with him. Sometimes they bought food and came home to cook it together. Sometimes she helped him buy clothes for himself and sometimes interesting things for his house. Often Jason indulged her own hankering for new clothes. She already had a wardrobe full, but she had to keep most of them here where Ma wouldn't see them. She'd kill her if she knew what she was doing.

'Ma thinks she's the only one making big plans for the future,' she said. 'All she can think about is finding a man to take care of her.' Kitty resented what she saw as her mother's attempts to keep her in the background, away from all the fun. 'She wants to keep me honest and pure and far from all men, especially you.'

'Fat chance,' he said.

'I haven't told her that you and I are making big plans too.' In the grey cold of Liverpool, Spain had begun to seem more and more like the promised land.

'Why don't we go there?' she had suggested a week or so ago. 'Why don't we do what my ma and your pa did?'

'That's a spiffing idea.' Jason had jumped at it. 'We'll get right away from all this.'

'We could stay for good. We'd be fine. We could find jobs there because we can get by in Spanish, which they couldn't.'

Jason was really keen. 'We'll get a camper van and tour the country, have a bit of a holiday before we settle down. We'll really enjoy ourselves.'

Kitty beamed with satisfaction. 'That would be marvellous. I haven't seen much of Spain yet apart from Marbella.' She felt nostalgic, remembering the wonderful times they'd had. 'I hanker for the endless sunny days.' They'd spent many of them on the beaches, where they'd both been taught to sail a dinghy and to waterski behind a motor boat. Jason was obsessional about all water sports and particularly keen on surfing.

'I'd like a job in a sailing school,' Kitty said now. 'Or doing something on the beach. Ma didn't like working in a bar there. It stayed open half the night and she said they didn't pay enough.'

'It's not jobs we want.' Jason was lying with his hands cradled behind his head, mulling over his plans. 'What I'd like to do is set up a business – or buy one when we get to Spain. You're right about working on the beach. Water sports, that's the thing. We could rent out equipment to holidaymakers; or take them on boating trips round the bay; teach them surfing or waterskiing, something like that. We'd have a wonderful time.'

Kitty smiled. 'That sounds more like it.'

'We aren't going to make the same mistakes our parents made,' Jason said. 'Their problems started because they ran out of cash and had to come back here. Pa spent too much time in the bars living it up every night. He forgot about work and he lost his touch.'

'All this time he's spending in prison will have the same effect.'

'That depends whether he's learning new tricks while he's locked up with the experts.' Jason laughed. 'But he'll have his work cut out to get going again; when he went down he took part of the Liverpool underworld with him. They won't forgive him. I tried to tell him they'll never work with him again, that he's bad news to them, but he takes no notice of what I say.'

'Parents never do. We want a business that'll earn enough to live on, then we need never come back at all.' Kitty was frowning. 'But it'll cost a lot to set up, won't it?'

'We've got to make sure we have enough of the readies before we go. First, we want a holiday and a good look up and down the coast to pick the best place for our business. Then we'll have to buy boats and goodness knows what else.'

'We'd better start saving.'

'Earning more here before we go is the answer,' Jason said. 'I need to get my head round the best way to do that.'

'This new feller of my mother's,' Kitty said. 'He owns a big jewellery business. We might be able to get a big haul from there.'

'If we can get in.'

Kitty told him about taking Jane on a shopping trip. 'You should have seen all the stuff she was allowed to buy. Her dad's filthy rich. Ma pushed a blouse for me and some tights and stuff for herself on their bill and they didn't even notice.'

Jason chuckled, and Kitty smiled. 'Her dad was so pleased with what we'd done, he stood us a slap-up lunch at the Adelphi.'

'Did you go inside their place?'

'Yes. I helped Jane carry up her clothes after the shopping trip, but the shop was shut.' Kitty tried to describe the five floors. 'Mostly, I saw flight after flight of stairs and her bedroom on the top floor. It was awful.'

'That's not the only time, I remember you telling me.'

'Yes. Ma wanted to make sure of getting a job there. We went in to do a bit of play-acting and it worked like a charm.'

'That's when you pretended to pick a customer's pocket?'

'That's right. But I was so intent on what I had to do then that I didn't notice anything about the shop.'

'See if you can get in again, at closing time might be best. If you could find out where the safe is and where

233

the keys are kept, and anything you can about their security.'

'If I get half a chance I will.' Kitty smiled. 'They've got some lovely stuff there.'

Later, she drove back to Queen's Drive. 'You're not a bad driver now,' Jason praised her. 'It didn't take you long to learn.'

Kitty slept late on Sunday morning, and woke to find the weather had turned warm and spring-like. By midday she could hear her mother hoovering downstairs. She slid out of bed and tiptoed to her mother's bedroom. The sun was shining in, the curtains were fluttering at the open window and the bed was neatly made.

Yesterday, when she brought up the tea, she'd noticed Ma had moved one end of her dressing table a few inches away from the wall. Now it was back in its original position. Kitty could guess the reason. She lifted it to where it had been last night, causing a lipstick to roll and drop on to the carpet. She groped for it and looked behind the furniture in one swift movement.

Yes! As she'd suspected, an envelope had been freshly taped there. She ran her fingers over it and could feel the ring inside. Good, she now knew where it was and could take it if she needed more funds to escape to Spain. It would be months before Ma missed it.

The buzz of the hoover suddenly stopped. Kitty's heart raced; she mustn't be found here. Hurriedly she moved the dressing table back and replaced the lipstick on top. Seconds later she was back in her own room and listening for her mother's footsteps, but she didn't come upstairs.

That afternoon, Kitty let herself out of the front door and was just in time to see Jason's red MG swish past their gate. As she expected, it pulled in to the kerb three doors down. She got into the driving seat.

'Hello, Kitten. How are you, love?' He tugged her closer and gave her a smacking kiss. The hood was up and inside the car the air was heavy with a strong fresh scent.

'You smell lovely,' Kitty told him. 'What is it?'

'Aftershave and cologne. I've been slaving in that garage all morning. I'd hate to work full time there, it's a killer. I had to go home and have a shower to revive myself.'

'You've lit the fire?'

'Yes, even cleaned up a bit. We'll stop at the pub for a drink, then we'll go and stretch ourselves out on the rug. What's new with you?'

Kitty told him about her mother helping herself to a ruby ring from Jardine's.

'She seemed half sorry she'd taken it, because she meant to be straight and honest with the boss. She said she'd snatched it on the spur of the moment; it had been too easy.'

'I could help her sell it on.'

'I know, but I couldn't tell her that, could I? Anyway, she's planning to hang on to it for a while. Did you know the police send out lists of stolen stuff to jewellery shops so they can keep an eye out for it?'

'Yes.'

Kitty giggled. 'I know where she's stashed it. I noticed she'd pulled her dressing table away from the wall, so I checked this morning when she was downstairs. It's in an envelope taped to the back.'

Jason laughed. 'Not a bad hiding place.'

'We could use it towards our trip to Spain,' Kitty said, pulling into the car park of the Dog and Duck.

'We'll need a lot more than that,' Jason said. 'This new feller of your mother's – he owns a big business. The other day, I walked past the shop where she works and had a good look at the place. There's a lot of good stuff in the windows.'

'It doesn't stay there when the shop's closed. The expensive stuff is put in the safe every night.'

'Oh! If we could get in, we could pick up a big haul from there.'

'That's what I said. And get more than just commission when you sell it on.'

They'd reached the pub lounge. Kitty found a table for them in a dark and quiet corner while Jason got the drinks. She stayed away from bright light in pubs, because she didn't want the landlords to ask how old she was. Jason said nobody would believe she was only sixteen: with make-up on she could be in her twenties. She opened her bag and put on a thicker layer of lipstick, studying herself in the mirror opposite, though gold letters advertising beer partly obscured her reflection. Yes, in her red high-heeled court shoes, she looked at least twenty.

As Jason slid a brimming glass of lager in front of her, she preened into the mirror.

'This is what Ma bought for me when we went shopping with Jane Jardine,' she giggled as she loosened the drawstring round the neckline of the peasant blouse to show a bit more bosom. 'As I said, neither of them even noticed. They must be filthy rich.'

'What are they like?'

'Jane's two years older than me, but you'd never know it. She's as innocent as a babe in arms, naive really. No oil painting either. According to Ma, her dad's innocent too.'

'He must be to let your mother get her claws in him. When you were inside the shop, I don't suppose you saw the safe?'

'No. Mr Jardine has an office on the floor below the flat but I didn't go in there.'

'Your mother would know where the safe is and where the keys are kept.'

'I'm not asking her,' Kitty burst out. 'She might guess what we're planning . . . She'd be dead against us burgling the place anyway. The owner is her boyfriend.'

'He won't lose out, he'll have everything insured. No need to worry about him.'

'Well, you won't be able to get a job there, not with Ma already well dug in.'

'No, though I could go in and buy something, or even just for a look round.'

'You'd make Ma suspicious.'

'Kitty, if she starts talking about work listen hard. You might pick up something useful. Where the safe is, for instance. Just be interested, you know the sort of thing.'

'It might work if she had a couple of drinks first.'

'Or better still, see if you can get in again and have a proper look round.'

'I might get the chance,' she said. 'Come on, let's go. It's nicer at your place where we can do what we like.'

Once in front of the fire, Jason untied the gathering string round the neck of her peasant blouse and let it drop back off her shoulders. He had her bra undone in moments and buried his face in her breasts.

On Monday morning, Honor's stomach was churning as she set out for work. When she arrived, she found Edwin and Jane already down on the ground floor, looking worried and upset. They were talking to the staff as they came in. Honor was bracing herself to cope with what she knew was coming, when Pam Kenny whispered, 'Mrs Carruthers has lost her ruby ring.'

'Good heavens! How did that happen?'

'When she looked for the package, it wasn't in her handbag.'

Edwin said, 'I've already spoken to Sam about it. We're all very shocked.'

'And trying to work out exactly what happened,' Jane said.

'We all know Mrs Carruthers fell on the stairs on Saturday morning,' he went on. 'When she came in to collect the ring her husband had bought for her. It had been left with Sam for resizing.'

Sam had arrived and was taking off his mackintosh. Edwin said, 'On Saturday, you buzzed through to let me know she'd come in.'

'Yes,' Sam said. 'She tried all three of her rings on and when she was satisfied they fitted, she paid for the work and decided to wear the diamond solitaire and the emerald. She asked to have the ruby gift-wrapped, so her husband could present it to her. I rang down to Miss Hadley . . .'

Dorothy said, 'Yes, I went up and got it and took it down to wrap.'

Edwin said, 'I took Mrs Carruthers up to my office to wait for that to be done. She was pleased with her rings and held out her hands so I could see she was wearing them and admire them. She said they were more comfortable and looked much brighter now they'd been cleaned.'

Miss Hadley said, 'I took the ruby ring up to your

office and gave it to her. What happened to it after that?'

'We both saw her put it in her handbag. So we know she had it with her.'

Honor saw him close his eyes for a moment and sigh. 'As if having an accident in the shop wasn't bad enough. She thinks it must have been taken from her when she fainted.'

'No!' the girls chorused.

'Stolen, you mean?' Honor asked, trying to sound horrified.

'Yes, I suppose so. You reached her first, Mrs Thorpe, and were with her most of the time. Did you notice anything?'

She shook her head. 'Nothing like that.'

'Did you notice her handbag while you were with her?'

'Erm . . .' Honor rubbed her forehead. 'Let me think. Yes, I remember now. I saw it beside her, a lizard handbag. Yes, the clasp had opened . . .'

'It was open, you say?'

'I thought it must have burst open when she fell. I clicked the clasp shut and made sure she had it when the ambulance men took her away.'

'But you saw it open?'

'Yes.'

'Did anything fall out?'

'I don't know. I didn't see any gift-wrapped package.'

Miss Hadley said, 'I gift-wrapped the ring box but

then I put it in one of our manila envelopes. You'd have recognised that.'

'I didn't see anything.' Honor's heart was banging away. She felt hot and wished this would end. She was afraid a red tide might be spreading up her cheeks.

'But only the doctor and members of staff went near her before the ambulance men arrived,' Miss Hadley pointed out.

'Who was this doctor?' Edwin asked. 'Did any of you know him?'

They all shook their heads. 'He just happened to be in the shop.'

'He was very helpful,' Honor assured them. 'He knew what he was doing.'

'It could have happened at the hospital,' Miss Pinfold said. 'There's no proof it happened here.'

Honor tried to change the subject. Looking as worried as she could, she asked, 'How is Mrs Carruthers? Did she break her ankle?'

'She hurt both her ankles,' Edwin said. 'She had an operation on one on Saturday evening – a plate was put in, I believe – and both are in plaster. Apparently, her ring wasn't missed until Sunday morning.'

'The shop was quite full when it happened.' Miss Hadley put the discussion back on track. 'It could have been jerked out of her handbag when it opened, and anybody could have picked it up.'

Jane said, 'Dad, normally you see her out, but on Saturday you didn't.'

'No. This wouldn't have happened if I had.' Edwin looked serious. 'She said she'd like to get a little gift for her husband and asked my advice. I told her about that silver letter opener we have, the one set with garnets, and she seemed interested. I was taking her down to see it when the phone rang and I turned back.'

'She'd have fallen just the same,' Jane pointed out. 'Even if you had been behind her.'

'Yes, I suppose so. But she might still have her ruby. I'm afraid a policeman will be coming to take statements from us all this morning.'

As Honor helped take the valuables out of the safes and build up the displays, she felt she'd acquitted herself reasonably well. She could be sure now that nobody had seen her take the package, otherwise they'd have said so. She shouldn't have taken it; it wasn't part of her big plan. She'd been tempted and she'd done what came naturally, but no matter, she'd got away with it.

For once the shop was a little late opening, and all morning the staff were chattering about what had happened. Honor heard most of them say several times over that the ring must have been taken either in the ambulance or at the hospital.

It was Jane who said, 'Poor Mrs Carruthers. I'm afraid she won't have enjoyed her ruby wedding anniversary.'

CHAPTER FOURTEEN

IT TOOK A full week before the girls at the shop relaxed and no longer talked of the missing ring at every tea break. It took Honor even longer to get over it. She heard Miss Pinfold say that their most expensive items came with a year's free insurance to give the new owners time to take out their own policies. And that, for the first time ever, Edwin had claimed on the shop insurance and ordered a replacement ring from their supplier for Mrs Carruthers.

Honor hadn't meant to steal from him or cause trouble for him, and regretted that she had. She was feeling at ease behind the counters now and apart from smiling at Edwin whenever he came near, she made no effort to seek him out.

She'd made the first approach to him on Boxing Day, and it was now his turn. She fully expected that sooner or later he'd ask her to do another little job for him and then he'd invite her out to repay her kindness. Jane wasn't going to need more clothes for a long time but he'd think of something else. He'd find some move he could make to further their relationship.

A month passed and he did nothing. Honor was afraid he was forgetting how much he'd enjoyed coming to her house and taking her and Kitty out for lunch. The shop continued quiet and routine work occupied her. It looked as though she'd have to do something to draw him closer. But what? She needed to put her mind to this.

Honor quite enjoyed working in the shop when they were busy, but when the customers didn't come she found time hung heavily. The girls chatted together but she felt they excluded her. She resented the close eye Miss Hadley kept on her; the older woman clearly believed it was necessary for people to work here for twenty years before they could be counted as proficient. But Miss Hadley kept a close eye on the rest of the staff and the customers as well.

It was mid-April, and the customers had still not returned in any number; it was another quiet Monday morning in the shop. Since Miss Pinfold had whispered in the tea room that the takings were down again, Miss Hadley was afraid Edwin must be worrying about his business.

In slack times like this, Dorothy tried to keep the staff busy repolishing the silverware and getting them to try out new ways of displaying the goods. They'd been quiet for so long, they'd even dusted out the safes and tidied up odd corners of the shop.

The staff took their tea breaks in turn, so there was always someone behind the counters. This morning, Dorothy told them to take breaks of half an hour instead of the usual twenty minutes.

She came back from her own break to find the shop still empty of customers. Jane and Mrs Thorpe were behind a counter with their backs to it. She could see them both reflected in the mirror between the display shelves and thought at first they were studying their own reflections, but the empty stand on the counter told a different story.

'Please don't try things on,' Jane was saying. 'It's not something we do. Dad doesn't like it.'

'What difference does it make?' Mrs Thorpe continued to preen, turning her blond head this way and that. 'They'll still look new. Anyway, they can always be cleaned and polished again.'

Dorothy felt her face flush with annoyance. She was in charge here and she wasn't having this.

'Jane is right,' she said firmly from the other side of the shop. 'Staff are not allowed to try on stock.'

Mrs Thorpe unhooked the diamond pendant with one quick movement and had it back on the black display stand within seconds. She half smiled. 'It's so tempting . . .'

'It's meant to tempt paying customers, not us.'

'Sorry.'

All Dorothy's previous dislike of this woman was welling up. 'I don't think that earring is your property either.'

There was a pair of faux pearl studs on the counter together with one pendant earring of five diamonds. Its partner was hanging from Mrs Thorpe's ear.

'No.' It took her a little longer to return that to the stand.

'Now lock it all back in the cabinet. Diamond jewellery is very expensive.' Dorothy's tone was severe. 'It's not here to be played with and left lying about on the counter. Like Mrs Carruthers's ring, it could easily get lost or stolen. On top of that, we sell it as new. Customers expect it to look new, not show signs of being handled and tried on.'

'As if it would . . .'

'Our fingers have traces of grease that can leave a film on precious metals and gems.'

'I've just washed mine.'

'Don't try to justify what you've done. Mr Jardine expects us to take great care of the stock and does not like us trying it on. If I catch you doing it again I'll have to tell him.'

Mrs Thorpe's blue eyes looked straight into hers, rebutting her authority. 'I shall tell Edwin myself,' she retorted. 'Straight away. I'm sure he won't mind me trying on some of his things.'

At that moment Dorothy noticed the brooch of jet pinned on Mrs Thorpe's white blouse and felt a rush of fury.

'Mrs Thorpe, take that brooch off this minute. You're here to sell jewellery, not wear it.'

Mrs Thorpe smiled insolently. 'The Victorians thought of jet as mourning jewellery. It looks good, doesn't it? I might buy it myself, to wear in memory of my husband. Jet is not worth any great fortune.' She scooped up her pearl studs from the counter. 'Shall I take my morning break? Now you're back I think it's my turn.'

Dorothy watched her go, feeling as though she'd been kicked. Mrs Thorpe had shown only too clearly what she thought of her authority as shop manager. She'd also demonstrated her intimacy with the boss, calling him Edwin while she'd referred to him as Mr Jardine.

That Jane had seen it all made it seem worse. She was standing transfixed. Her mouth had fallen open.

Edwin Jardine was working at his desk on the third floor studying catalogues from his suppliers. He usually ordered new stock at the beginning of the year, but as business had been so slack he hadn't needed to until now. He was about to send for Jane to include her in the choice when there was a tap on his door and Honor Thorpe burst in. She looked so distressed that he leaped to his feet.

'Whatever has happened?'

There were tears in her eyes, and her lip was quivering. He put his arm round her heaving shoulders to escort her to the visitor's chair, but she twisted round and buried her face against his chest. His other arm seemed to go round her automatically, and before he knew what was happening she was sliding her arms round his neck. He'd not meant to hold her in his arms. He'd known that to have her this close would inflame his very being, and that he must not kiss her lovely lips.

She'd left his office door open and Jane and other members of his staff were coming and going to the rest room close by. What would they think if they were to see him doing this? It would compromise Mrs Thorpe's good name. He felt totally inhibited. He gave Honor a reassuring hug and backed her towards the chair.

'My dear, what has upset you? You mustn't take on like this.'

Honor swallowed hard and gave a little shake of her head. 'Miss Hadley is very cross with me. I didn't mean to upset her but I have.'

'Miss Hadley?' Edwin was surprised. 'What happened?'

'I decided I'd like to buy this little jet brooch. In memory of my husband, you know? I do miss him so, and feel so alone without him, but Miss Hadley shouted at me and said staff were not allowed to try the stock on; that I'd get into trouble with you. I didn't want that, not after you've been so kind to me.'

'That's not like Miss Hadley. She must have misunderstood. If you intended to buy . . .'

'I tried to explain that to her.'

'Of course, but please don't cry. There's no need to upset yourself.'

'I'm sorry to make such a fuss.' Tears hung on her long lashes like tiny diamonds. 'I shouldn't have troubled you.'

There seemed to be no way of stemming her distress. She unpinned the brooch and tried to put it in his hand.

'No.' He gave it back to her. 'You must keep it – a little gift.'

'No, I can't, you're too kind.'

He folded her fingers round it. 'To wear it as a mourning brooch for your late husband is a lovely idea. Old-fashioned like me.'

His head was swimming. He had to cool this down before he took her in his arms again. He went to the door and shouted across to the tea room.

'Miss Kenny, are you there?'

'Yes, Mr Jardine.'

'Make two cups of tea, would you? Bring them to my office as soon as you can.'

Mrs Thorpe was patting her eyes dry when he turned round.

'That's better,' he told her. She was trying to smile up at him, but it was a sad brave smile that made him feel another rush of sympathy.

'You're very generous,' she said. 'Thank you so much. I shall always treasure it. I didn't know jet would sparkle like this.'

He was explaining that there were specks of pyrite in the jet when Miss Kenny brought in a tray of tea and biscuits.

*

Two hours later, when there were customers in his shop, and everything seemed to have settled back to normal, Edwin was still thinking about Honor Thorpe. She'd thrown her arms round his neck and the warm thrill it had brought was still with him.

Jane came into his room and slid into his visitor's chair. She didn't often come without invitation when he was working. He remembered then he'd been about to consult her about the choice of new stock. When he looked up at her, he was surprised to see her eyes burning with fierce intensity.

'What is it, love?'

'Dad,' she said, 'have you really given that brooch to Mrs Thorpe?'

'Well . . .' He hadn't given any thought as to how Jane would feel. He should have known she wouldn't like it. 'Yes, I did. She was upset.'

'You've made a terrible mistake.' He could see she was cross with him.

'What makes you think that?' he asked mildly.

'She's got it pinned on her blouse and she's telling everybody it's a gift from you. She's triumphant. She's won and she's rubbing Miss Hadley's nose in it.'

That made him think about the wider repercussions of what he'd done. 'Rubbing her nose in what?'

'How d'you think Miss Hadley feels? You've taken Mrs Thorpe's side against her.'

'It wasn't like that,' he protested. 'Not a question of sides.'

'It is to everybody else. You've got your girls up in arms. All of them are supporting Miss Hadley.'

Edwin caught his breath. He should have known Miss Hadley wouldn't like it either. With Honor Thorpe in his arms he'd not been able to think of anybody else.

Jane said, 'Did she tell you what happened?'

'Yes, of course. Miss Hadley told her off because she thought she was trying on stock, but really she wanted to buy that brooch.'

'My eye! She didn't tell you that I came down after my break to find her trying on diamonds? She'd unlocked one of the cabinets and had some of the stock out on top of the counter. She was trying it on. That pendant necklace and the five-stone dangling earrings. I told her the staff didn't do that sort of thing, but she thumbed her nose at me. Miss Hadley came to support me—'

'I don't want you to exaggerate, Jane.'

'I'm not exaggerating, Dad.'

'You seem biased against Mrs Thorpe and I don't understand why. You're building this up into far more than it was.'

He saw Jane's patience snap. 'Dad, I'm not. You mustn't believe all her stories. Mrs Thorpe isn't as perfect as she tries to make out. The girls think she knows how to turn on the waterworks to get sympathy, and with you it works every time.'

251

Waterworks! Edwin leaped out of his chair and paced the few yards that he could.

'There're two sides to this, Jane. She's a young and lonely widow – quite a recent widow. The other girls are much older and they've never known a loss such as that. I think all of you should be more patient with her, and kinder . . .'

'Dad.' Jane was showing her exasperation with him now. 'By giving that brooch to her, you've built a skirmish into a full-scale war. You've shown the rest of the staff you take her part.'

'But I don't want any of you to—'

Jane had gone, shutting the door behind her with some force. He sank back on his chair and groaned. He'd built a skirmish into a full-scale war? The thought scared him. He had no experience of placating his staff: he'd never needed to. They supported each other and they'd got on with their work quietly and efficiently. He blamed this slack spell. They hadn't enough to do, and were looking for something else to fill their day. For decades, he'd prided himself on running a business where everybody was happy to pull together. But now this.

Edwin dropped his head on his hands. He was sorry Miss Hadley had been involved. She'd managed his shop and his staff very well over the years. He liked her and would have supported her against anyone else.

He wished this hadn't happened. It was showing him how strongly he was attracted to Honor Thorpe. He must do something. Perhaps if he apologised to Miss Hadley, and tried to explain the misunderstanding? But how was he to bring Jane round? He couldn't stand being at odds with her.

Jane shot across the landing to the rest room, feeling she couldn't go back to work until she'd calmed down. She'd never before sounded off like that at her father. She hated being at loggerheads with him; they were usually happy together. Yes, they'd had the odd tiff, but who didn't? And Dad had always been quick to make it up with her, but this was different. They'd been having repeated spats about Mrs Thorpe; this was a big one.

She'd forgotten the staff on early lunch break would be starting to come up. Pam and Miss Hadley already had their heads together at one end of the table. Jane poured herself a cup and joined them.

'I'm brassed off,' she whispered, and told them why. They were both quick to condemn Mrs Thorpe. Jane had never seen Miss Hadley so vehement.

'The shop hasn't been the same since she came to work here. It's no longer the happy place it used to be.'

Jane couldn't have agreed more. She resented Mrs Thorpe too. She'd seen herself as Dad's right hand; they were running this business together. Now Mrs Thorpe was pushing her way in and ousting her.

To start with, Jane had admired her elegance and liked her. She'd been grateful for her help with buying clothes at Christmas; she now had outfits for every occasion. It had upset her to find Mrs Thorpe trying on their diamonds and being openly rude about it, but perhaps it should not have done. Miss Hadley and Miss Pinfold had forced her to stick rigidly to Dad's shopping lists, but Mrs Thorpe had encouraged her to buy whatever caught her fancy. It seemed she didn't understand rules.

'She's having an unstabilising effect on everything.' Dorothy Hadley's lips were straight and severe. 'I've never known such rows and upset.'

Pam Kenny sniffed. 'We all used to be such friends.'

'She's got us at each other's throats. Even Dad is worked up because of her.'

'I wish we could do something about it,' Dorothy Hadley said. 'Sort her out.'

'How can we do that?' Pam was asking when Mrs Thorpe came in. Jane stood up quickly.

'I'd better get back to work. It's not my lunch break yet and they'll be short-handed downstairs now.'

She felt torn apart as she went down to serve on the ground floor. After years of peace and friendly cooperation in the shop, this morning's events were like an explosion.

Even as Jane showed her customers glittering jewels, slid valuable rings on chubby fingers and named prices, she couldn't get the problem of Mrs Thorpe out of her mind.

She felt a stirring of sympathy for Miss Hadley.

Dorothy had mothered her for as long as she could remember, but now she was grown up Dorothy stood back and treated her like any other new assistant in the shop. She'd never cause any trouble for any of them.

It was ridiculous that Dad still called her Miss Hadley when she'd been working for him for decades. And not just working for him – going out of her way to help him in other ways She had the feeling that Dorothy Hadley nursed a soft spot for her father and would be very pleased to be more than just his senior assistant. And in his own odd fashion, she felt Dad was drawn to her.

She'd been truly shocked when Kitty had suggested Dad was falling in love with her mother and might want to marry her. If he was looking for a wife then Jane felt Dorothy Hadley would be far more suitable than Mrs Thorpe. The trouble was, Dorothy needed a bit of encouragement too. She wasn't one for pressing her own ends, otherwise she'd have sorted things out between them long ago.

The more Jane pondered on it, the better pleased she was with the thought of having Dorothy as a stepmother. Dad had more in common with her than with Mrs Thorpe. She'd have to find some way of bringing them closer – somewhere away from the shop. She needed to think about this.

It was not a plan Jane could talk about to anybody, certainly not to Dad, and she mustn't try to sound out the other girls for ideas on what to do. No, this must be entirely off her own bat. If she could come up with something, it might baulk Mrs Thorpe's plans.

Honor sat apart from the tight clique at the other end of the rest room table, eating the sandwich she'd brought for her lunch. She couldn't fail to notice the way the other girls excluded her; they turned their backs and chatted softly together. Their hostility made her feel uncomfortable.

She'd been foolish to be caught trying on those diamonds. It had been a little charade she'd set up to get her own back on Miss Hadley, who had been getting on her nerves for a long time. Whenever she looked up Miss Hadley was watching her and her gaze was anything but friendly. Heaven knows, trying on diamonds was a harmless way to fritter away a dull half-hour, but it broke the shop rules and Honor had known that would rile her. It had been very bad luck that Jane had come down early from her tea break and had played a part in the little scene.

Honor knew she needed to stay in Jane's good books, so from that angle it had been a disaster. Jane was disapproving and the others all had long faces. She could see that her ruse to turn on the tears and get Edwin on her side had backfired. Miss Hadley's gaze was now vicious and she was turning the others against her.

She must try to break down this wall of hostility, and do it quickly. She unpinned the jet brooch from her blouse and slipped it in her pocket. She had to recoup her losses if she could.

Edwin had proved to be more set in his ways than she'd supposed. He'd been slow to respond when she'd thrown her arms round his neck. But he would if she worked on him; it would just take him longer than the average man.

Honor had found seducing her clients easy. She made all the running; they were expecting advances from her and were prepared to respond and enjoy themselves. Edwin, she thought, wanted that too, but he didn't think of her as a call girl and must never do so, if she was to get what she wanted from him. He had to believe he was in charge and things happened because of what he did. She had to work out how to set him up and then become passive. It would be a challenge, but the rewards would be all the greater.

For the first part of the afternoon the shop was busier than it had been for a while, and Honor needed a slack moment to get the full attention not only of Miss Hadley, but of at least one of the other girls as a witness.

She returned from her afternoon tea break to find Miss Hadley and Miss Jessop conversing by one of the showcases with Miss Kenny behind a nearby counter. Now was the moment.

Trying to look remorseful, Honor went up to Miss Hadley, and said, 'I'm very sorry for the trouble I caused this morning. It was very wrong of me.' She took out the jet brooch and pushed it across the counter towards Miss Hadley. 'I don't feel I should keep this. It won't remind me of Leonard but of how rude I was to you. I do hope you'll forgive me?'

Dorothy Hadley looked almost as taken aback by her apology as she had this morning at the height of their spat. Honor was afraid she'd overdone it.

'I hope the brooch can still be sold?'

Miss Hadley was frowning. 'Didn't you say Mr Jardine had given it to you?'

'I did, but I can't accept it. I don't want to upset any of you and I'm afraid I have.'

'Hadn't you better tell him what you're doing?'

'Yes, but can it go back into stock?'

Miss Hadley found one of their special cleaning tissues below the counter. 'Yes.' Her face was still severe as she polished hard, though the damn thing looked none the worse for being worn for a couple of hours.

Honor said, 'I hope you'll accept my apology?'

'Yes, this time.' With a final flourish of the tissue, Miss Hadley returned the brooch to the tray from which Honor had taken it.

'Thank you. It won't happen again.'

She did her best to look contrite, then sucked in her lips and let a tear run down her cheek. She'd spent a long time perfecting the art of crying prettily. It was a skill that had bent many a man to her will. With a gulp, she said, 'I'll let Mr Jardine know now.'

She shut herself in the lavatory for a few minutes to

psych herself up for it. She had to get it right this time. She forced a few more tears to run down her face before she tapped on his door. Above all else, she needed his sympathy and concern. He called to her to come in, and half blinded by her tears she closed the door and advanced to his desk.

'I've come to say I'm sorry.' She gulped, and then let the words come out too fast. 'I've already apologised to Miss Hadley and I've given her the brooch to put back into stock. I couldn't possibly accept it. You only gave it to me because you were sorry for me.'

He was on his feet and backing her to his visitor's chair. 'No, no, my dear. You're more than welcome to it.'

Honor gave a sniffle. 'I'm so terribly sorry. I've upset everybody, including you. I didn't mean to.'

'No, of course not.' He took a tissue from the box on his desk and pushed it into her hand. 'Please don't distress yourself.'

'It was all a misunderstanding,' Honor said, 'and my fault entirely.'

'I'm sure it was six of one and half a dozen of the other.'

'No, it was my fault. I haven't felt too well today.'

'Then you should have rested at home.'

'It's really nothing . . .' For a moment, she covered her face with both hands. 'I think the problem is that I'm not yet over Leonard's death. I can't put it behind me. I feel knocked off course, out of kilter . . .'

'My dear, I know exactly how you feel. Of course you didn't mean to upset anybody.'

'Very remiss of me.' Honor let the tears flow faster and rubbed at her eyes to make them red. 'I caused mayhem amongst your staff. Can you forgive me?'

'There's nothing to forgive, Honor. Things have just been too much for you. You mustn't be so hard on yourself.'

CHAPTER FIFTEEN

EDWIN COULDN'T take his eyes away from Honor's tearstained face. He wanted to throw his arms round her and comfort her, but he backed away and sat down on his side of the desk, gripping the arms of his chair.

He said slowly, 'You should have stayed at home today, if you didn't feel well.' She was clearly not up to working in the shop at the moment.

'I'll be all right. I just feel a bit under the weather.'

He felt a surge of sympathy. How many times had he sat in this chair feeling tired and out of sorts himself? 'Would you like to go home now?'

'I just need a minute to pull myself together. My head's throbbing. I'm just having a bad day.'

He didn't know how to cope with an emotional woman. Should he send for Miss Hadley? No, it might make matters worse, as the original confrontation seemed to have been with her.

Unfortunately, he'd told Miss Pinfold to take the afternoon off. She'd gone home at lunch time to find her mother unwell, and had telephoned to say she wanted to send for her doctor. He'd said immediately that she mustn't think of coming back to work today.

Honor was crying quite openly. It would be cruel to send her back downstairs to the shop and they wouldn't need her while business was slack. He'd meant to go out this afternoon anyway. He'd told Eric Bannerman he'd come out to the Southport branch to see him.

'I'll run you home,' he told her. What would the customers think if they saw her looking like this?

'It's very kind of you, but I can easily take the bus. I mustn't trouble you.'

'It's no trouble. Really it isn't.'

'Oh! I've just remembered.' She held her hand against her mouth. 'Kitty was coming in to meet me when the shop closed. We planned to go to the Odeon to see *The Sting*. Would you mind if I rang her to stop her coming? In truth I don't feel like the cinema tonight.'

'Of course not.'

She had to ask: she couldn't let him hear any of this. 'Can I use the phone in Miss Pinfold's office, so as not to disturb you further? There must be things you need to do first.'

'Just put my papers together and get ready. And perhaps have a word with Jane.'

Honor let herself quietly into Miss Pinfold's room and closed the door carefully. She dialled her home number, hoping Kitty would be back from school. The phone was picked up and, relieved, she said in an urgent whisper, 'I want you to come and meet me outside the shop at half past five. Have you got that?'

'Yes, Ma. Why? Are you going to take me somewhere nice?'

'No, but I want you to spin a story to Jane.'

'What story?'

'That I asked you to come and meet me because I'm taking you to the Odeon to see *The Sting*.'

'But where will you be? What are you up to?'

'Edwin's going to bring me home and I want the house to myself. OK? Don't come home till late. This is important, Kitty. Don't foul up on me.'

'I won't, Ma. I quite fancy going to the shop and seeing Jane again. What d'you mean by late?'

'After ten, and go straight to bed so he doesn't see you. Make sure you're in by midnight at the latest.'

Honor put the phone down, hoping her plan would work out. She meant to invite Edwin inside, and if Kitty was there he'd be so inhibited she wouldn't stand a chance of getting him to do anything. Now she had to organise Edwin.

She went back to his office and said, 'I'll get my coat, shall I, and wait outside?'

'If you would. I'll only be a minute or two.'

Edwin had taken out his file for the Southport branch, slid it into his briefcase and put on his coat. Just the thought of taking Honor home made the blood rush to his face as though he were a schoolboy. Thank goodness Honor was still thinking straight. It wouldn't be wise for them to walk through the shop together. He didn't want to upset Miss Hadley further.

He found his daughter serving in Men's Gifts. 'I'm off to Southport,' he said.

She looked up from the bill she was making out. 'Isn't it a bit late for that, Dad?'

'Yes. It's been one thing after another this afternoon.' He waited until she had given the customer his change and he had her full attention.

'My car was nearly out of petrol, but Sam took it out and queued for me, so the tank's full again. He managed to park it round the corner so I won't have to walk to the garage.'

'Right.' Her smile was contrite. 'I want to make my peace with you. I'm sorry, Dad, I lost my rag over the bother with Mrs Thorpe this morning. I was rude and I said more than I should.'

Edwin felt he was on dangerous ground. 'You did get a bit hot under the collar, but I want you to tell me what's going on in the shop. I need to know these things. It's all been settled now. Mrs Thorpe has apologised to Miss Hadley and the brooch has been put back in stock. She was upset after that, and a bit tearful, so I've sent her home.'

What was he saying? Edwin prided himself on being truthful and honest with everybody, but that was stretching it a bit. 'A storm in a teacup, you could say.'

His cheeks were burning again. It was not the whole truth but he'd said it to spare Jane and the rest of the girls. The sooner they forget their differences with Honor Thorpe the better.

He pulled himself together and said, 'Will you see that everything's locked away if I'm not back in time?'

'Of course. If you're going to Southport now, you won't be back. D'you want me to cash up too?'

'Yes. Good practice for you.'

'How late will you be?'

He was impatient to get away now. 'Don't wait supper for me. I'll take Eric out for a pub meal.' The manager of the Southport branch was a young bachelor who was always ready for a trip to the pub.

Jane's eyes were searching his face. It was making him feel guilty, so he said, 'Why don't you ask Nick round to eat my share tonight?'

'I will, thanks. We were going to the pictures anyway. I'll give him a ring now. It's stew and dumplings tonight, isn't it?'

'Yes, I think so.'

As Edwin went down the remaining flight of stairs he met Miss Hadley coming up. 'Goodbye,' he said. 'I'm leaving early tonight.' He must stay calm, not show the quivering excitement he felt. He quickened his pace.

Honor had found his car and was waiting beside it. He rushed to unlock the door for her. As soon as he got in beside her, he caught a slight whiff of perfume. It made him very conscious of the shapely nylon-covered legs stretched out in front of her. He would drive her home and then go straight on to Southport. It was just a kindness to an employee who didn't feel well.

He remembered then getting Miss Pinfold to call a taxi to take Miss Lewis home when she'd felt ill. It brought the guilt thudding back. Honor Thorpe's melodious voice was apologising again for the trouble she'd caused. She talked about her daughter, told him she'd been out when she'd tried to phone her and that she was afraid Kitty planned to come straight into town from school. 'She's going to end up waiting for me outside the shop.'

'She'll ask, won't she, when you don't come out? Jane will be there. Here we are.'

He drew up outside her house. He wouldn't turn the engine off. He'd just wait to see her safely indoors. He leaned across her to open the passenger door and could feel her trembling. 'You're all right?'

'Yes, yes, thank you.'

At the front door he saw her ring the bell. He wound down the window and called, 'Don't come in tomorrow unless you feel better.'

She smiled and burrowed in her handbag, then dropped her keys on the step. She bent stiffly to pick them up, and he thought she didn't look at all well. As she tried to insert a key into the lock, she dropped them again.

Edwin switched off the engine, locked his car and

went to help her. He got the door to swing open
without difficulty, but he could feel her swaying against
him and thought she was about to faint. He put an arm
round her waist to support her.

'Let's get you to a seat.' He guided her into her
sitting room and on to her pink Dralon sofa. She
slumped down and somehow that made him lose his
balance and sink down beside her. He was excited and
alarmed.

'You're not all right, Honor. Can I get you
something? A drink of water?'

Her voice was faint. 'I do feel a bit strange. Perhaps
a little brandy would help.'

Edwin was glad to be told to pour a little for himself
at the same time. He felt in need of it too.

Jane found they were quite busy in the shop during
the late afternoon, and without Mrs Thorpe they were
one person short. Fortunately, Miss Lewis had returned
to work in the new year, after a long convalescence.
She'd been told officially that her cancer was in
remission, and the girls had welcomed her back with
open arms.

Dad had told her that to start with she needn't come
to work before ten in the morning and she should leave
at four, so she didn't tire herself out. But today she'd
stayed on because they were busy, and she was still here
now though it was well after half past five.

Mrs McGrath was up in the flat cooking stew

and dumplings for Jane's supper, and her married daughter Nona had arrived and was hoovering through the shop.

'Do go home,' Jane urged Miss Lewis. 'Dad will be cross if he thinks we're working you too hard.'

'I'm going to see her home,' Miss Hadley said. 'She lives in the next road to me.'

As it seemed to be taking longer than usual to lock everything safely away for the night, they made Miss Lewis sit down in the rest room. Some of the staff left; Miss Hadley stayed on to help Jane cash up. It was no small task because there was a cash register on each floor. They added up the contents of each and took the money up to her father's office. Usually, he walked up to the bank with it and dropped it into the night safe, but he'd told her to lock it in the safe for tonight.

That done, Jane insisted that Miss Hadley and Miss Lewis should go home while she finished off alone. She was tired but she worked on, knowing Nick would soon be with her. The Crosby branch was much smaller and took less time to close down for the night. When she heard the back doorbell, she ran to let him in.

'Hello, Nick.'

She was surprised to find it was raining hard and that Kitty Thorpe was on the doorstep too, huddling close to Nick as they both tried to keep out of the downpour.

'Come on in,' she said, opening the door wider. She couldn't do anything else, though she was not over-pleased to see Kitty. She couldn't help but regard her in the same light as her mother, thinking they were tarred with the same brush. She pulled herself up. Perhaps that was unfair; she'd liked Kitty well enough to start with.

'Hello.' Kitty was shaking herself like a puppy. 'Is my mother still working? She asked me to meet her here when the shop closed.'

'No, everybody's gone long ago. It's nearly six.'

'She said half past five, but I couldn't get a bus.'

'Dad sent her home early, about half past three.'

'What?' Kitty looked taken aback. 'She was going to take me out for a bite to eat and then to the pictures.'

'Wasn't she at home before you left? She'd have had time.'

'I came straight from school. Why did she leave early?'

Kitty looked so dismayed that Jane brushed over the problems with her mother. 'She was upset by something that happened in the shop.'

'Is she all right?' Kitty looked at a loss.

'Yes . . . What will you do now?'

'Go back, I suppose, and eat at home.'

'Look,' Jane said, 'Nick and I were about to have a bite of supper. Why don't you come up and share it? It's only stew and dumplings.'

'Are you sure? Thanks, I love dumplings. That's very kind.'

'It was meant just for Dad and me, but Mrs McGrath usually makes plenty.'

Jane led the way to the stairs. Kitty followed slowly, looking round. 'Mummy's told me so much about the lovely things you sell here. I'd love to have a peek at the Sun Diamonds. She says she's never seen anything like them before.'

'We lock them away in a safe every night. Why don't you pop in some time when the shop's open?'

'I'd like that.'

'Any time.'

On the first floor, they found Mrs McGrath polishing the counters. 'Isn't it time you left?' Jane asked. 'You've been here all day.'

The housekeeper looked up and tightened the strings on her overall. 'I'm helping Nona clean through tonight, so we can go to the pictures together. *The Sting* is on at the Odeon.'

Kitty said, 'That's where Mummy was going to take me.'

'It's supposed to be a good film.' Nick paused on the stairs. 'Jane and I are going there tonight too.'

That made them laugh. 'That's all of us going,' Jane said. 'Hope it is good.'

'See you there,' Mrs McGrath called after them as they continued up the stairs.

When they reached the top floor flat, Jane said, 'Let

me take your coat, Kitty. Gosh, that's a smashing outfit. You look lovely.'

Her tight jeans were pale blue and she was wearing the rainbow sweater Jane had admired.

'My favourite outfit.' Kitty smiled.

Jane thought the impromptu supper turned into quite a party. Kitty was chatty and good company; she kept flashing smiles between her and Nick. While Jane was dishing up in the kitchen, she heard Nick talking about being brought up in a one-parent family, and how much time he'd spent at home alone because his mother was at work.

When she took the plates to the table, Kitty was saying laughingly, 'Me too. In the school holidays my mother expected me to go shopping for food as well as get the evening meal started. And heaven help me if I made any mess in the house.'

That made Jane pull up short. 'I thought your father died quite recently and your mother didn't work?' She was sure that's what Mrs Thorpe had told them.

'Yes . . . yes! That's right.'

'Were you left alone much as a child?'

'I was actually.' Kitty hastened to retrieve her slip. 'Mummy had quite a busy social life, the tennis club and all that. She did a lot of charity work too. What I meant was, we three are in one-parent families now.'

'Oh.' Jane couldn't help but notice that Kitty was suddenly much less relaxed. As though she'd let her tongue run away with her. 'You must miss your father very much.'

'Yes, I do,' Kitty was forking up her dumplings as though there was no tomorrow.

'Kitty's father died suddenly of a heart attack,' Jane explained to Nick.

'Must have been a terrible shock to you and your mother,' he said sympathetically.

'Yes.' She was blinking hard.

Nick said, 'It takes a while to get over a shock like that, doesn't it? Was it very recent?'

'Yes.'

The pause lengthened. Jane was surprised and curious. Why had Kitty suddenly gone quiet? She usually talked non-stop. Surely she couldn't have forgotten when her father died?

'Eighteen months ago, wasn't it?' she asked.

'Yes. I'm trying to put it behind me, forget all about it.'

Nick started talking about his father, who had worked abroad in the oil industry for many years. 'At least I still get letters from him,' he said. 'And he takes me out and gives me a good time when he comes home.'

Kitty and Nick washed up afterwards while Jane changed. She could hear them laughing together as they worked, so it seemed Kitty had managed to put her father's death behind her again.

Then, as they were going down through the empty

shop, she heard Kitty say that she'd like to work here when she left school. 'It's such a jolly place. My mum loves it.'

Jane didn't want her here. She'd have to talk to Dad about that before the Thorpes did.

'But I thought you were going to secretarial college?' she said. 'The same place I went to. I'm sure your mother told me you were.'

'Oh, yes. I'm starting there in September. I meant after that.'

While Jane was locking up she heard Nick say, 'D'you want to come to the pictures with us?'

'I'd love to, but I'd better go home and see if Mummy's all right.'

Jane was relieved. She'd enjoyed the film, but what she'd heard Kitty Thorpe say niggled at her. As they walked home, she said, 'There's something odd about both mother and daughter. What they tell us doesn't quite add up.'

'Such as what?' Nick asked.

'Did you notice, Kitty said that as a child she'd spent a lot of time alone at home because her mother worked?'

'She said her mother had had a full social life.'

'Yes, I can see her enjoying that, but charity work? And in the school holidays? Surely all that would come to a halt when she had Kitty to look after?'

'Perhaps she didn't quite catch what I was talking about.'

'I did and I was dishing up. It's only working mothers who can't stop, and Mrs Thorpe said she didn't work while her husband was alive. He was a solicitor in Crosby.'

Nick said, 'We all get mixed up from time to time. Perhaps we were talking at cross purposes. I mean, why would anybody want to say something like that if it wasn't true? There'd be no point, would there?'

Jane said dryly, 'As a recent widow, Honor Thorpe milked a lot of sympathy and help from Dad. I think Kitty forgot the story she was supposed to tell.'

'Surely not! You mean you think she told a pack of lies?'

'Dad's bowled over by Honor. He thinks I'm jealous, but it isn't just me. All the girls in the shop think she's after Dad.'

'What d'you mean, after him?'

'Kitty's looking forward to seeing them married.'

'Your dad? My God!'

'I'm serious, Nick. He'll not hear a word against the Thorpes. He's infatuated with Honor, and she's got him right where she wants him. I wish there was some way I could check on her.'

Once indoors, she pulled him into Miss Pinfold's office and used her key to take Honor's file from the cabinet. Together they studied it.

Nick said, 'She describes herself as a widow, but there's nothing here to say her husband was a solicitor.'

'Dad told me he was. He must have asked.'

'He could have got mixed up too, couldn't he?'

'His head's pretty clear, Nick. I wish there was some way . . . You're based in Crosby. Do you know any solicitors there?'

'There's a small firm practising a few doors along the road from the shop, but I don't know them. There's no mention of her husband's name here.'

'She often talks about her beloved Leonard, mopping at her eyes.'

'Acting the grieving widow, you mean?'

'Could be.' Jane had a moment of doubt. 'Am I being too hard on her? She'd have to be a good actress to manage it. Have I got a bee in my bonnet about the Thorpes?'

'Possibly,' Nick said, squeezing her arm. 'Or perhaps you or your dad got things wrong? Or again, perhaps it was just a slip of the tongue on Kitty's part. When she's a couple of years older and she's lost her puppy fat, she'll be a cracker of a girl.'

'Like her mother,' Jane said.

As soon as she parted from Jane and Nick, Kitty looked for a telephone box and rang Jason.

'Can you come and pick me up?' she asked. 'Ma wants me out of the house tonight.'

'You bet,' he said, and when she told him where she was he added, 'I'll be there in ten minutes.'

He was as good as his word and Kitty was eager to tell him her news.

'I've been inside Jardine's again. Ma asked me to meet her outside the shop after work today. It was too good a chance to miss.'

'Great. What did you find out?'

'Quite a lot.'

'Enough to break in and get your hands on the diamonds?'

'No, course not.' Kitty laughed. 'Not half enough for anything like that. Jane took me straight up to their flat on the top floor, so yet again it was only what I could see on the way up and the way down.'

'Go on, then. What's to stop us breaking in?'

'They have metal grilles on the main shop door and windows that they pull down when it's closed. So there's no way in from the front.'

'I had noticed that.'

'Jane uses a door at the back. The staff do too.'

'Are there windows at the back?'

'Yes. I had a good look at them, and they have permanent iron grilles fixed on them. There's no way in there either.'

'What about the windows higher up? Did you notice?'

'I couldn't see the shop windows, but there's nothing on the windows of their flat.'

'That's five floors up. You'd need to be a bird to get up there. What about keys?'

'Jane had a great bunch of them.'

'Does your mother have a key to the back door?'

'No, but she told me some of the staff do.'

'Right. We also need to know where the safe is.'

'It could be in the office.'

'And whether it works on a security code or is opened with a key.'

Kitty shook her head. 'I've no idea. That isn't something I could ask.'

'We need to get our hands on the main shop keys then.'

'While it was fresh in my mind, I drew a rough map of each floor, the layout and that, but there's a lot of blank spaces.'

'For starters, Kitten, you did quite well.'

'I'm not so sure. I think I might have dropped a clanger.'

Jason's gaze shot up to meet hers. 'In what way?'

Kitty was annoyed with herself for doing it. 'I was so busy keeping my eyes peeled, I forgot the story about Ma being a recent widow and her husband not wanting her to work. Well, she had to tell them that to get round having no references.'

'So what was the clanger?'

'Jane's boyfriend was banging on about his mother working when he was a kid and him being left alone at home. I said I was too.'

'I was with you quite a lot.'

'And quite a lot of the time you weren't.'

'Did they notice your gaffe?'

'Yes, Jane did. She was suspicious – she's not dumb.

But I think I talked my way out of it all right.'

'Will it alter things for us?' Jason asked.

'I dunno. It's more likely to foul up Ma's plans.'

Edwin woke up slowly. It took him a moment to realise he was in Honor's bed, not his own. A nearby church clock began to strike, and he counted the chimes. Midnight! He jerked himself up against the pillows, feeling profoundly shocked at what he'd done.

Honor hadn't drawn the curtains and the room was flooded with soft silvery moonlight. She was asleep beside him, her bare arms outstretched; with her fair curls tumbling about her face she looked utterly beautiful. His heart was thudding, but the only sound was her light and steady breathing, until, in the distance, a dog barked.

He couldn't stay here. Edwin slid out from under the bedding and groped for his clothes. He'd had sex with her, the first with anyone since his wife died. At the time it had been wonderful, even better than he remembered, rejuvenating. He glanced again at Honor. She looked younger than ever and very innocent. The sudden weight of guilt on his shoulders made him sink back on the edge of the bed.

Honor stirred but she settled back to sleep. Yes, he loved her; no point in pretending otherwise now. He'd been obsessed with her for months. He felt committed to her and so he should after tonight.

He'd taken advantage of her and Edwin knew that

it was very wrong of him. He must offer her marriage, nothing less would do, but that was what he wanted more than anything else anyway. He tore a page from the back of his diary and went to the window sill to scribble a quick note of thanks to Honor. He told her he loved her but couldn't stay any longer, and put the piece of paper on her bedside table. He could buy a pleasant house out here in the suburbs, away from the rush and bustle of the shop. Honor could take care of it, make it a proper home. With her daughter and Jane they'd have a real family life.

Jane! What was he doing here after midnight? She'd be worried that he hadn't returned home. He finished dressing quickly and crept out of the house with his shoes in his hand. What would Jane say? He'd have to give her some sort of explanation, but what?

He was in a near frenzy of worry. Had she locked up properly? He'd never left her to do it before. He drove fast, thankful there was very little traffic in the streets at this time of night. He wouldn't take the car back to the garage. It would be easy to find somewhere to park it at this hour.

Everything was as it should be in the shop, the security lights switched on. He crept up the creaking stairs feeling like a criminal. He'd never noticed how much noise they made before.

Jane's bedroom door was ajar. Was that intentional? Had she been listening for his return? He nudged it further open; she was fast asleep and breathing deeply.

He crept to his own room and got into bed as quickly as he could, but he couldn't get to sleep again. His feet were cold and he was worried about what he'd allowed himself to do with Honor.

CHAPTER SIXTEEN

EDWIN HARDLY knew how to face Jane the next morning, he was so guilt-ridden. He'd told her he was going to do one thing and had done something very different. What was she going to think if she ever found out?

Breakfast was usually toast or cereal. Recently Jane had been making it. He found her in the kitchen preparing a grapefruit.

'That'll be a nice change,' he told her.

'Is everything all right at Southport?'

'Yes. I'm afraid I was very late getting home last night.'

'I had a late night too. I went to the pictures with Nick. By the way, Kitty came here. I shared the stew and dumplings between the three of us.'

'Kitty?' That redoubled the guilt Edwin was feeling.

'She came looking for her mother; said she'd arranged to meet her when the shop closed.'

Jane took the grapefruit to the table. Edwin followed and sat down feeling awful. 'Mrs Thorpe tried to phone her to stop her coming.'

'She came straight from school.' Jane was digging into her grapefruit, her face screwing with thought. 'You did say Mrs Thorpe was a recent widow, didn't you?'

'Yes, that's what she told me when she started.' He paused, but he had to ask. 'Why?'

'Just something Kitty said.'

He was afraid it concerned her mother. 'What about?'

'About spending a lot of time alone at home when she was young because her mother was at work.' Her eyes met his momentarily. 'While Honor says she didn't work.'

He couldn't help saying, 'Jane love, you sound so suspicious.'

'About Kitty? No, she's the chatty sort. She lets it all flow out without stopping to think what she's saying.'

Edwin felt overcome. 'Let's drop this.' He knew of course that her suspicions concerned Honor. He'd had the feeling before that Jane was jealous of the Thorpes. He must be very careful of what he said about Honor and what his future plans were. He went down to unlock the safes and greet his staff. Some were already in and had started work, others were still taking off their coats.

'Good morning,' he said, assuming his usual jovial manner. 'Good morning.'

He was looking round for Mrs Thorpe, and it bothered him that she wasn't here. But she came fifteen minutes late, looking pale and even a little agitated, which gave him another rush of guilt. He should never have allowed himself to get into her bed. She was trying to smile at him, but it seemed to take great effort. He wanted to ask her to come upstairs to see if a cup of tea would help, but he knew he mustn't.

Feeling somewhat at a loss, he went up to his office and shut the door. The other girls had seemed unusually subdued, he thought. Were they, like Jane, showing lack of trust and liking for Honor? It appeared they hadn't forgotten yesterday's dispute with her, or the jet brooch. The happy atmosphere wasn't there this morning, but his staff would settle down and forgive; they always did. They'd realise how hard life was for the recently bereaved.

Edwin gave himself up to daydreaming about Honor. He was in love with her. His life and Jane's would have to change. Whatever happened, he couldn't turn his back on what Honor offered now. Not after all these years of celibacy. It was his second chance for love and marriage and he wanted to snatch it with both hands.

But he'd have to be careful not to upset Jane. He knew exactly how she'd feel. Hadn't he felt the same when he'd seen her blossom in Nick Collins's company? The problem was, Jane might not be mature enough yet to want him to find someone else. Then there were the girls. They'd all got the wrong idea about Honor. He'd need to go slowly, give them all time to get used to the idea.

*

Honor woke up as a milk cart rattled up the road. It was daylight and she was alone in her bed, but she could see the hollow Edwin's head had made in the pillows on the other side. She lay back to enjoy the moment; triumph was flooding through her. She'd done it! She'd seduced him, taken a big step forward in her plans. And she'd turned the tables on those spiteful old spinsters in the shop.

Edwin was a real softy with a jelly centre; a sugar daddy to everybody. All she'd need to do now was consolidate. Give him regular sex and he'd be so grateful, she'd be able to milk him dry. He was that sort. Eventually, she'd be able to give her other punters the push and enjoy the good life as Edwin Jardine's mistress. He'd already shown he was more than happy to give Kitty a leg up in the world too.

In the meantime, she had to get up and go to work. On the way to the bathroom she hammered on Kitty's bedroom door. On the way back, she called, 'Kitty, it's time to get up,' and getting no response she threw open the door.

Kitty wasn't there. She heard her own startled gasp. Her bed had not been slept in. She'd been out all night!

Honor was overcome with panic. She hurled herself at Kitty's wardrobe. All her clothes were hanging there. She yanked a drawer open, and then another. Yes, lots of underwear, pyjamas and pullovers. She might have taken something with her, but not much. It didn't look as though she intended to stay away. But where was she? She should be here getting ready for school.

She couldn't think, her head was reeling, but she'd have to go to work. She got dressed, went downstairs, made a slice of toast and some tea and walked round eating with the mug in her hand. Should she phone the police and report Kitty missing? Had she been mugged and left unconscious in a ditch somewhere?

Honor heard what she thought was the key turn in the front door and shot into the hall.

'Kitty, where've you been? I've been almost out of my mind with worry!'

Kitty tried to pass her and go upstairs. 'Sorry, Ma. I've got to get changed for school.'

'Where've you been all night? I was thinking of phoning round the hospitals.'

'You told me to stay out of your way,' she said. 'You wanted the house to yourself.'

'I thought you'd go to see *The Sting* and come home late. You said you wanted to.'

'Jane and Nick were going, and they asked me if I wanted to go with them, but I pretended I was anxious about you and wanted to come home. I couldn't risk them seeing me there after that. It would have ruined the whole story.'

'There are plenty of other cinemas and theatres you could have gone to,' Honor wailed.

'Ma, don't nag me.'

'Kitty, where've you been all night?'

'OK. Well, if you must know, I gave Jason Bolton a bell and went to see him.'

'Jason? You spent the night with him?'

'Yes.' She was defiant.

'Kitty, you fool! He's a fence, a criminal. He's going to end up in prison like his father.'

'He's taking good care that won't happen.'

'Oh, my God, Kitty! Why d'you think I wanted to get away from them? They have an awful life. I wanted something better for us. Have nothing more to do with Jason, he'll drag you down.'

She watched Kitty slump against the newel post and yawn. That cleared Honor's head. 'It's more than two years since we walked out on Jason. You didn't just ring him out of the blue, did you? You must have been seeing him without telling me.'

'What if I have?'

Honor's stomach muscles contracted painfully. This was awful news. 'I suppose that means you've been having sex with him?'

'It's what you do if you fancy a feller, isn't it? Why shouldn't I have some fun?'

Honor couldn't get her breath. She felt as though Kitty had cut away the ground beneath her feet. It made a nonsense of everything she was trying to do for her.

'You're too young to be having sex. You'll get yourself in trouble.'

There was an insolent smirk on Kitty's face. 'Like you did?'

In a flush of anger, Honor put weight behind the slap she gave her daughter's cheek. It made Kitty run to the sitting room and collapse on the sofa in a fit of noisy tears. Honor sank down beside her, suffused with guilt. She shouldn't have hit her.

'You've got to take care of yourself. Have you been down to the family planning clinic?'

'Jason takes care of all that.' It was an angry shriek.

'Kitty! Don't trust him! Haven't I explained it all to you? If you're going to have sex, you've got to get yourself on the pill before it's too late.'

'I can trust him,' she shouted. 'He's managed it all right over the last two years.'

'Two years? Ever since we left?'

Kitty straightened up, full of hostility, her face wet with tears. 'Since before we left.'

Honor couldn't believe it had gone on without her knowing about it. The thought of Kitty spending so much time with Jason Bolton gave her the shivers. 'I wanted to get you away from him, keep you safe.'

'Jason's lovely, Ma. He knows how to have a good time.'

'He's a headstrong lad and a fence like his dad. I tried to keep you away from people who break the law. I wanted you to be an honest citizen. I didn't want you to be worried about the police coming to your door.'

'I'm not.'

'Don't be silly, Kitty. You know what I mean. You will be if you throw in your lot with the Boltons.'

Kitty's lips were straight and determined. It was obvious she meant to carry on seeing him. Honor was prickling with apprehension. Jason was dangerous.

'Is he fencing still?'

'He does a bit. He's in with all his dad's contacts. He'd get you a good price for that ruby.'

'No thanks. I don't want anything to do with him.'

'Suit yourself,' Kitty said.

'What would suit me is for you to give Jason the push. I don't like what you're doing. I mean it, Kitty. I'm afraid you'll get hurt.'

'Give over, Ma. I know how to look after myself.'

'We might as well have stayed in Menlove Avenue with him,' Honor choked.

'I told you that at the time,' Kitty said. 'But you wouldn't listen.'

'I suppose all those trips to the pictures and the shops with Flossie and Peggy were with him?'

'What if they were? You'd have nagged at me and it would have worried you.'

'You told lies!'

'And you never do?' Kitty flounced upstairs and her bedroom door slammed.

Honor was really upset. She collapsed against the cushions wanting to scream. What was the point of trying to give her daughter a better life? Kitty was going to make a bigger mess of it than she had herself. Damn Kitty for going behind her back; why couldn't she have found herself a decent boyfriend?

ALL THAT GLISTENS

It hadn't been easy to get her away from Jason. They'd endured hell in that rathole of a flatlet she'd found, and all for what? She'd not wanted Jason to know where they lived; he had Gary's car and could pick Kitty up and spin her off goodness knows where. And no doubt he'd tell Gary when he came out, or Kitty would, and she'd have Gary to contend with too before much longer.

Jason was just like him, the same good looks, the same sexy charm, the same sort of criminal underneath. And it seemed Kitty was just like her. Honor had been a fool to think her daughter was too young to be interested in boys at fourteen. Why hadn't it occurred to her that her daughter might use her as a role model?

Just when Honor thought their lot was improving, here she was gripped in another crisis and feeling incapable of dealing with it.

It was a relief to think of Edwin Jardine. If only men like him had come her way when she was young. Not that she was in love with him, but he was rich enough to provide her with a permanent meal ticket. He'd look after Kitty too. Hadn't he already offered to pay her fees at the secretarial college? He was the sort who looked after everybody else.

She mustn't leave it too long, mustn't let him forget the thrill of going to bed with her. She could ask him here for dinner; lay on the full trimmings, get him into bed again. But when? Friday would be a good night, Kitty always went out then. What did it matter if she was with Jason? She was going to go her own way and wouldn't take advice from her. Edwin would expect a few days' notice when he received invitations; he couldn't just drop things and come the same night. If she got half a chance, she'd ask him this week for next.

Kitty wasn't sure she'd done the right thing by telling Ma how things stood between her and Jason. It had been a dark secret for so long she'd got fed up with making excuses, and pussyfooting round it all the time. She was cross with her mother for wanting her out of the house last night, and not very pleased with Jason because he'd had a job organised for today as well as for tonight.

They had much more exciting lives than she had and both were keeping her at arm's length from the fun. She was spending more and more time with Jason, but when he expected his accomplices to come round to the house, or had a job planned, he wanted her to go home to Ma.

'Safer for both you and us if you know nothing,' he told her. 'If we have a slip-up, the police won't be able to get any info from you, and neither will they be able to charge you with anything.'

What Kitty really wanted was to move back and live permanently with Jason. It was high time for her to forget all this nonsense about going to college.

'We'll be together all the time soon,' Jason said comfortingly. 'I've got to work hard now so we can get away from here. I've been to see Pa again. I hate those visits. Walton jail looks a dismal place – threatening in a way, because if things ever go wrong for me as they did for him, I might well get locked up in there myself.'

'You're careful,' Kitty said. 'You won't make the mistakes he made.'

'He was quite upbeat, said he'll be released soon. Can't wait, of course.'

'How soon?'

'He doesn't know exactly,' Jason said. 'He's had his parole reduced for bad behaviour, fighting and that. Pa never learns, does he? He reckons it'll be late August. If we're going to get out of here by then, it doesn't give us much longer to get organised.'

'They don't have them in my size,' Pam Kenny wailed. She'd asked Jane to go with her to British Home Stores in their lunch hour to buy a pair of pyjamas. She had a week's holiday coming up and was going to spend a few days with an aunt in Penzance.

Jane fingered them. 'I love satin jimjams, but no, I shouldn't, I've got plenty already.'

'Have we got time to go to Marks?' Pam asked.

'Yes, just about. We could see what they've got, anyway.'

They were rushing past the racks of bathing suits when Jane almost bumped into Kitty Thorpe.

'Hello, Jane. Fancy seeing you.'

Jane pulled up short. She was wary of Kitty now.

Kitty smiled. 'This is my boyfriend, Jason Bolton.'

'Hi, Jane.' He was handsome and friendly.

Jane knew she needed to relax. 'I've heard a lot about you,' she said to him. 'All good.' Kitty was just a kid; she mustn't equate her with her mother.

'Clothes shopping again?' Kitty asked.

'Not for me this time. For my friend Pam. This is Pam, she works in the shop.'

'I keep meaning to pop in and see your Sun Diamonds,' Kitty said.

'Come now.'

'Jason's with me. Is it all right if he comes too?'

'Of course, why not?'

'My mother says we mustn't come gawping round your shop when everybody knows we can't afford to buy.'

Jane laughed. 'She won't know. It's her day off, remember?'

'Oh, goody. I'll just pay for this swim suit.'

'Our lunch time is up, I need to go back. You come when you're ready.'

'Right. I'll see you shortly.'

'Pam, you go and cast your eye over the nightwear. I'll tell Miss Hadley you're on your way.'

'No, I'd better come with you. I don't want her to think I'm taking advantage.'

Jane went up to the office to finish a job she'd started before lunch. It was half an hour later when Pam rang up from the ground floor to let her know that Kitty and

Jason had arrived. When she ran down, she saw Kitty standing by herself, admiring the general stock.

'You've got some absolutely gorgeous jewellery here,' she enthused.

'Yes, everybody says so. Have you seen the Sun Diamonds?'

'No.'

'They're just here.' They were in a display cabinet in the most prominent part of the shop. Jane led the way. 'You must have walked past them.'

'They're magnificent,' Kitty breathed. 'I've never seen coloured diamonds before.' She sighed with delight. 'They'll be yours one day, won't they?'

'If we've still got them when I'm twenty-one.'

'How can you bear to see them up for sale?'

Jane hesitated. She wouldn't tell Kitty there was a jinx on them, and that was why. Dad said it was just a myth and there was no truth in it, but he half believed it because of what had happened to her mother. He'd asked her not to spread the stories as nobody else would want them if they knew.

'They're very ornate. You know – dressy.'

'D'you think so?'

'It's such a fancy necklace, the sort to wear to a grand ball. I doubt I'd get much chance to show it off.'

Kitty laughed. 'I'd wear it all the time. It'd look great on a black jumper, one with a roll neck. I'd just love to own them.'

'They are rather magnificent.' Jason had joined them.

'Don't let us keep you if you're busy, Jane,' Kitty said. There were quite a few customers now. 'But if you don't mind, I'd like to look round every corner of your shop while we're here.'

'Of course.'

'I'm interested because Mummy works here and I've heard so much about it. You have such lovely things.'

It only occurred to Jane when she was back at the typewriter that Kitty Thorpe should have been at school. Her boyfriend hadn't been at work either. And surely she must have known her mother wasn't in today?

She shivered. Once she'd liked Kitty; liked her mother, too, and thought she'd be like a breath of fresh air through the shop. So why had she turned against them?

She sighed. It was just suspicion. Just a gut feeling that things didn't seem right. Suspicion wasn't enough; what she needed was concrete facts. Some proof they were either innocent or guilty.

This year, St Cuthbert's church was to celebrate its centenary. The actual date of its consecration fell at the end of November, a time of year when the congregation was busy with preparations for Christmas. The rector, the curate and the church dignitaries decided therefore to hold a series of functions, stretching from late summer to early December when the highlight of the programme would be a performance of Handel's *Messiah*.

Like many Liverpool churches built in the nineteenth century, St Cuthbert's was a building with little architectural merit and much in need of repair and refurbishment. A centenary committee was formed so that its hundred years could be celebrated with as much style as could be combined with the urgent need for fund-raising. Several appeals were made to the congregation for new ideas and suggestions.

Nick had started coming to church on Sunday mornings too, and in order to do their bit to help he and Jane had volunteered to take paying members of the public up the church tower to admire the view and see the great bells, not all of which could be rung these days because of their need for repair. Some in the congregation did not like the idea because of the dangerously steep winding stairs and lack of a hand-rail. The wardens too were afraid there might be accidents.

Jane's father said, 'I'm not entirely in favour of it either. The summer fete will be held on a Saturday, our busiest day – we can't all be spared to help.'

Another young couple volunteered to take on Jane and Nick's idea.

Fortunately, money had already been spent on maintaining the organ, and it was in good condition. Edwin Jardine had promised to give two recitals, one in September and one in November. In addition, he would help with the music for the *Messiah*. The rector hoped to be able to organise a small orchestra for this with professional singers for the solo parts from amongst those recently qualified from schools of music. All were determined to make it the event of the year.

Like the rest of the congregation, Dorothy Hadley had already circled 24 August on her calendar. They'd always held a bring-and-buy sale known as the Summer Fete in the grounds in August. There was to be the usual white elephant stall and others selling home-made cakes and jams, plants and flowers, books and handicrafts. Games would be organised for the children, and cups of tea for their parents.

Today, business was slack in the hour before the shop closed. Jane was chatting with Miss Lewis on the ground floor when the elderly lady who delivered the monthly church magazine came in and handed it to Jane. She glanced at it and an announcement caught her eye. St Cuthbert's was seeking new members for its choir. Those interested were invited to contact the choirmaster, Mr Smith, for further information, and his telephone number was given.

Jane immediately thought of Dorothy, who had a good voice and had once told her she'd be interested in joining a choir. Perhaps the time for her to do it had come. It would give her something different to do during Sunday morning services. In addition, if the choir was practising the music for the *Messiah*, it was more than likely that she and Edwin would see more of each other. After all, if the rector succeeded in getting a small orchestra together Dad would surely play the organ in it, and if not, he would still accompany them on his own.

Jane knew Dorothy would receive her own copy of the church magazine, but she went to the other side of the shop, where she was serving, and slid the magazine across the counter to her.

'How about this?' she asked. 'It seems the choir would be glad to have a voice like yours.'

CHAPTER SEVENTEEN

DOROTHY STUDIED the announcement in the church magazine without much enthusiasm. She'd been feeling low in spirits over the last few weeks.

It had become only too obvious that Mrs Thorpe was succeeding in getting Mr Jardine's attention. Dorothy tried not to think of her as a rival, but that was really what she was. A rival, who not only looked more attractive but had the personality to put herself forward to get what she wanted. Dorothy felt she was being pushed aside. It was sapping her confidence and it made her do what she always had. She tried to forget her disappointment and look instead for a new interest to fill the void.

She thought about the church choir. Yes, once she'd really fancied joining it. She knew she had a good voice. Her taste ran more to Gilbert & Sullivan than to church music, but the *Messiah*? She thought she might enjoy taking part in that.

It would be something different to do and she already knew the choirmaster and most of the choir members. She scribbled down the telephone number in case her copy of the magazine had not yet been delivered.

When she went to catch the bus home that evening, she found she had fifteen minutes to wait and she could see an empty public phone box. She decided to ring straight away. Mr Smith, the choirmaster, answered the phone himself.

'Miss Hadley, hello. You're a contralto? Excellent, we're particularly in need of contraltos. We're meeting tomorrow night in the church hall. It's rather short notice, I'm afraid, but could you come along and let us hear you sing?'

Dorothy was pleased. 'Yes. Thank you, I'll do that.'

It was only after she'd put the phone down that she wished she'd asked what he'd expect her to sing. Should she be choosing a song or would he? She decided she'd better have something ready and went home to practise Schubert's 'Ave Maria', accompanying herself on Emily's piano.

After half an hour, her sister burst out, 'I'm sick of hearing that same thing over and over. For heaven's sake stop, I want to watch television.'

By the following evening, Dorothy was feeling nervous. Mr Smith greeted her and she found she wasn't the only person applying to join the choir.

He told them all that the Liverpool Choral Society had agreed to join them to put on the *Messiah* and that there would be a performance in the Philharmonic

Hall as well as one in St Cuthbert's.

'Also, a small orchestra is being arranged to accompany the performances. We will be holding regular rehearsals on Thursday evenings starting next week, and Mr Jardine will be coming to help get us all in shape.' Dorothy thought it sounded quite exciting.

Then he wanted to hear the new voices. 'Miss Hadley, as we all know you, could we ask you to sing first?'

She hoped her voice would be considered adequate, and was glad Mr Jardine was not with them to hear her first attempt at a solo in public. The choirmaster's wife came forward to accompany her and with her heart racing, Dorothy gave her the music and watched her open it on the piano.

To her own ears her voice sounded out of condition but she managed to hit the high notes and Mr Smith told her she had a lovely strong clear voice. 'You've been hiding your light under a bushel for years,' he told her. 'I wish I'd known.'

Dorothy was thrilled to be invited to join the choir. The next morning, she told everybody at the shop. Jane said, 'I'm pleased – you'll enjoy it. You have the sort of voice that could lift the roof if you let rip.'

'I won't be sitting next to you on Sunday mornings any more,' Dorothy said.

'I'll miss you.'

'I doubt it.' She smiled. 'You have Nick to keep you company now.'

'You're going to be busy, what with *Messiah* practice,

and learning all the harmonies to hymns and things. When will you do that?'

'Sunday morning before the service starts. I'm quite looking forward to it all.'

When Edwin asked Dorothy to come up to his office to discuss some new items of stock, she mentioned it to him.

He was enthusiastic. 'I shall be accompanying the choir at practices,' he told her.

Dorothy was delighted to find she'd be seeing more of him. 'I'm surprised you can find the time to play for church services, and manage all this as well.'

'When Jane was small, morning service was all I could do, but last year I felt I needed to try different things, get myself out more.'

'That's exactly why I've joined the choir,' she said.

'I really enjoy working at a production like this. You will too. We all do, though it's hard to find the time for it when it gets near to Christmas.'

The next day, Jane was put in a taxi by her father with a box of expensive jewellery for the Crosby shop. This month, Nick had sold more than had been expected.

'Dad's pleased with you,' she said as she watched him do the necessary paperwork and then put the pieces out on display. 'He thinks you're working very hard.'

'I am.' He flashed a smile in her direction, but she thought he seemed a little distracted.

Jane was still worrying about the effect Honor Thorpe was having at the Church Street shop. 'I want to ask at that solicitor's practice further along the parade if they ever knew a Leonard Thorpe. I think it might be worth a try.'

'I'll come with you if you like.'

'Yes, do.'

It wasn't something Jane felt entirely comfortable about doing, but she had those horrible suspicions about Honor that she needed to prove one way or the other.

It was raining as they hurried along the parade of small shops. The solicitors' practice was only six doors away. The big shop window was partially masked with a net curtain, though Jane could see it was a small office rather than a shop inside. She took a deep breath and went in.

A youth in a formal suit got up from his desk and came to the counter by the door. 'Good morning. Can I help you?'

'My name's Jane Jardine,' she said. 'My father has a branch of his jewellery business further along this parade of shops.'

He smiled. 'Yes, I pass it every time I go out.'

'We're making a few enquiries. Would you be kind enough to help?'

'If we can.'

'Do you know of a solicitor who practised in Crosby until recently, by the name of Leonard Thorpe?'

'Can't say I do.'

'We think he died in November 1972 of a heart attack.'

He turned to the occupant of the other desk, who was much older. 'George, do you know?'

Jane could see the man was mystified. 'Leonard Thorpe? No, I don't know the name. Where was his office? D'you know the address?'

Jane shook her head.

'Did he work single-handed or have partners?' Clearly the man couldn't help her. 'I've practised in this district for the last thirty years,' he said. 'But I don't think I've ever heard that name.'

'Thank you.' Jane was retreating.

'I thought I knew all the solicitors practising round here,' he said. 'Sorry I can't help.'

Once outside, with the door shut behind them, Jane clung to Nick's arm. 'If they've never heard of Leonard Thorpe, perhaps he only exists in Honor's imagination.'

Nick said, 'I don't think you can assume that. His office could have been some distance away.'

'Crosby's like a village. I'd think solicitors practising here would know each other – at least by name.'

'It proves nothing either way,' Nick said firmly. 'You'd be better off quizzing Honor directly.'

She sighed. 'But how to do that without letting her know that we're suspicious about her?'

Jane couldn't let it drop. Back in their shop she

consulted the Yellow Pages to see if any solicitors' practice had Thorpe in its name.

'There's none, and this is for the whole of Liverpool and the surrounding area.'

'If he died in 1972, wouldn't his name be removed from the firm?'

'If he owned the practice it might not be. It could have been sold as a going concern.'

'You told me Honor reckons she's hard up, so the chances are he didn't own it.'

'The next thing is to consult the electoral roll,' Jane said. 'I'll walk down to the local library and do that now. Are you coming?'

'I'd better stay here,' Nick told her. 'John's the only one in this morning.' John was a recent school leaver. 'Look, Jane, none of this proves anything, you know. Don't let your imagination run away with you, will you?' He kissed her – perfunctorily, she thought – and waved her on her way.

Jane enlisted the help of one of the librarians but found that without knowing where the Thorpes had lived, or where he had practised, it was virtually impossible to pinpoint them. There seemed to be no Leonard Thorpe on the electoral roll, or any variant on the spelling of that name; and, even more mystifying, there was no Honor Sarah Thorpe either.

'If he was a solicitor,' the librarian said, 'the Law Society might be able to help you find him. Professional associations usually keep a list of all their members.'

'I don't suppose you have that list here?'

'No, and I'm not sure whether the Liverpool Central Library would. It might be better if you wrote direct to the Law Society. I can give you their London address.'

'Thank you,' Jane said. 'I'll do that.'

On the bus going back to Church Street, she thought of what Nick had said about asking Honor directly and set about formulating a few questions to put to her, questions that hopefully would tell Honor nothing.

At the afternoon tea break, there was the usual group round the table. Jane helped herself to tea and sat down next to Honor. 'Dad said you used to live in Crosby,' she said. 'I went out to our shop there this morning.'

'Yes, I did.' Honor smiled at her.

'I suppose you knew our shop?'

'Yes, bang in the middle of the shopping area.'

'Did you live far from there?'

Did she imagine it, or did Honor hesitate for a few seconds? She added, 'Crosby's a nice part of the city.'

'Quite some distance.' Honor didn't look rattled, but perhaps not quite at her usual ease.

Jane had not arranged for any of the other girls to support her, but out of the blue Pam Kenny said, 'There's some lovely big houses round there. I have an aunt who lives near Adelaide Gardens and she has smashing views of the river. A lovely house as well.'

They both smiled at Honor, who said, 'I know Adelaide Gardens, but I lived in Glenriver Drive, the first house on the right as you turn in. Do you know it?'

'No,' they chorused, but Jane was thrilled that she now had an address.

Honor was getting to her feet, smiling from her to Pam. 'It's time I went back to work,' she said, rinsing her cup at the sink.

The moment she went, Jane jerked to her feet and went straight to Miss Pinfold's office. 'Do you know Glenriver Drive?' she asked, taking the Liverpool A to Z from its place on her shelf.

'No. Whereabouts is it?'

Five minutes later Jane said, 'I don't know,' and pushed the book in front of Miss Pinfold. 'Can you see it? Glenriver Drive? There's Glen this and Glen that, but I can't see any Glenriver.'

'Neither can I,' Miss Pinfold confirmed.

It settled several things for Jane. Honor had proved she could think on her feet; that she could lie on the spur of the moment and be totally believable. It told her she was right to assume Honor wasn't entirely honest, but it didn't prove she wasn't in love with her father.

She must have some reason to lie about such a thing, but if Jane told Dad about it, would he see it as grounds for supposing Honor was out to do him down? Or would it give him another reason to think she was jealous of Honor?

She'd write to the Law Society. If Leonard Thorpe's name had never appeared on their list of solicitors, then he'd have to believe her.

ALL THAT GLISTENS

But exactly how did she word such a request? What reason could she give for wanting information like that? She'd ask Miss Hadley's help, or Miss Pinfold's, or possibly both.

On the face of it, it seemed neither Honor nor Leonard had ever lived in Crosby. She had to get to the bottom of this for all their sakes.

Jane was thinking about Nick as she ran down to the ground floor to relieve Mrs Thorpe for her morning tea break. Suddenly she stopped, gripped by what was taking place before her eyes.

Honor Thorpe was behind the counter ready to serve and a couple had just come into the shop and were heading towards her. They were middle-aged and prosperous-looking, like most of their customers, and Jane could see nothing out of the ordinary there, but as soon as Honor saw them her jaw dropped open and she took to her heels, almost cannoning into Jane.

'Tea break,' Honor murmured as she veered for the stairs. She was out of sight in seconds.

Jane slid behind the counter and greeted the couple. 'Good morning. Can I help you?' She decided Honor must have recognised them. There was no other explanation.

The woman looked rather severe. She raised her eyebrows and said, 'Somebody's trying to avoid us,' which confirmed Jane's impression.

Her companion said, 'We're looking for a trophy. Do you have silver cups or shields?'

'Yes, we have a display up on the next floor,' Jane said. 'Both cups and shields and several other things you might like to consider. I'll take you up to see them.'

'We're looking for something suitable to present as a prize in a golf club tournament.'

'Do you want silver or plate?'

'Solid silver,' the woman said. 'But nothing grand. It's to be a new prize for our junior players.'

'Here we are,' Jane said. 'This was the sort of thing I was thinking of.' She took a little statuette of a golfer from the display case and put it on the counter.

'No, we have one very similar to this. I think a cup. Not that we haven't got several cups already, but they don't all look the same, do they?'

Jane set two cups on the counter before them. The woman inspected them closely.

'Very nice, but perhaps too nice. I don't want it to outclass our main trophies.'

'We have this very plain one, which comes in two sizes, and in plate too. Or there are shields if you prefer.' She was setting out samples as she spoke. 'But if these are not what you're looking for, we have catalogues from our suppliers. We can order something specially for you.'

As they studied the catalogues Jane wondered why Honor had run to escape them. She wished she'd had the presence of mind to ask when the woman had made her comment.

'I think the smaller of these plain cups.'

'Solid silver,' Jane said, showing them the hallmark. 'On an ebony plinth.'

'Very plain, very tasteful,' the woman agreed. 'I'll want to have it engraved. Do you do that here?'

'Yes, our Mr Collins does engraving up on the next floor.'

'I've written down what I want to put on it.' She pushed a piece of paper in front of Jane. It seemed to be a longish inscription and the cup wasn't all that big.

'I think the best thing would be for me to take you up to see Mr Collins. He'll be able to tell you how many words he can get on, and when he'll have it done. I'm afraid I have to ask you to pay first.'

'No problem,' the woman told her. 'I've decided my company will donate this prize. Will you accept a cheque from them?'

'We'll be glad to.'

When she handed the cheque to Jane, she saw the company's name printed on it: Millard & Clarkson. She couldn't let this chance go as she had the last. She asked, 'Did our Mrs Thorpe once work for you?'

The woman had a spiteful twist to her mouth and Jane thought for a second she was about to open up, but the man took her arm and whispered to her. 'Leave it, Mabel.' Then he turned to Jane and said, 'She helped to manage the catering in the clubhouse at one time. Do you mind if we hurry? I'm afraid we're running late.'

Jane ran them up the next flight of stairs to see Sam Collins, hoping they'd meet Mrs Thorpe coming down thinking that by now the coast would be clear, but they met nobody.

Seeing Mrs Thorpe on a daily basis and hearing the other girls talk about her meant Dorothy Hadley couldn't shut Honor out of her mind.

She could feel herself burning with dislike for her and was finding it hard to forgive her for slighting her authority. Yes, Honor had said she was sorry. Really, she'd apologised magnanimously, and done it in front of the others, but it hadn't helped.

In particular she didn't like the way Mrs Thorpe had referred to Edwin by his given name, when she herself never did. It implied greater intimacy with him, and one-upmanship. Mrs Thorpe pretended to be the perfect lady, a social class above the rest of them, but Dorothy thought she wasn't as refined as she tried to make out.

From the moment she'd heard that Mrs Thorpe had invited Edwin to her house, Dorothy had been afraid she meant to worm her way into his affections, and furthermore felt she herself was being pushed out. As time had passed, she'd grown more certain that this was the case. Honor was in and out of his office by the minute and Dorothy had noticed that Edwin treated her differently from the rest of them. Also, Honor was putting on airs with the other girls.

She was growing more confident about her position here.

Dorothy ached to do something about it. She longed for Mr Jardine to give Honor the sack, but she knew he wouldn't. Like most of the girls, she feared and distrusted Honor and what she was doing to Edwin. He believed the best of everybody and would never see that he was being manipulated.

She and Jane had mulled over a letter to the Law Society asking whether Leonard Thorpe's name was on their list of solicitors. If they knew definitely it wasn't, even Mr Jardine must believe she'd lied. But they'd only just posted it, so it was too soon to expect a reply. Dorothy wished they'd been quicker off the mark and that there was something else they could do, but she couldn't think of anything.

Seeing Honor flee from those customers had made her boil with curiosity. Honor was usually intent on making every situation work for her, but this morning she'd completely lost control. Dorothy had been looking for a chance to ask Jane who the customers were ever since, but as usual she and her father had gone upstairs to eat in their flat at lunch time.

When Dorothy went up to the rest room for her afternoon tea break, she was glad to see Jane and Miss Pinfold at one end of the table. She joined them and found that Jane's curiosity matched hers. At least she had some of the answers.

'I had to screw myself up to ask if they knew her,'

she said. 'It seemed a bit forward, you know?'

'And did they?'

'Yes. I'd have found out more, I'm sure, if the woman had been on her own.'

'Who were they?' Dorothy was on the edge of her chair.

'The cheque was signed by a Mabel Clarkson, managing director of a building firm called Millard & Clarkson. Have you heard of them?'

Dorothy had to shake her head.

'They bought a trophy for a golf club. They said Honor had managed the catering in the clubhouse.'

'Catering?' Miss Pinfold asked. 'She's a sales assistant.'

'Which golf club?' Dorothy wanted to know. 'If we knew that we might be able to find out more.'

'We could look in her file,' Miss Pinfold said. 'She filled in a CV when she applied to come here, but I don't remember anything about catering.'

'Come on, let's make sure,' Jane said. 'I had a look not so long ago to see what details she'd given about her husband, but there's nothing about him in it.'

'There wouldn't be,' Miss Pinfold said.

Moments later, with the office door shut fast behind them, they were poring over Honor's file. There was no mention of her having worked in catering, or at any golf club. There was nothing since she'd worked in London years ago except Watson Prickard's, temporarily, for a few weeks.

'Did they give her a reference?' Jane asked.

'No, we never took it up, since Mr Jardine offered her the job on the spot. I understand she lived in London when she was young and worked in Heal's and other posh shops.' Miss Pinfold was biting her lip. 'Mr Jardine said they'd be unlikely to have records after all this time and it wasn't worth writing for references.'

'So he took her on without references?' Dorothy marvelled. Jane met her thoughtful gaze.

'Mrs Thorpe knew this couple,' she pointed out. 'And they knew her, so she must have worked in the golf clubhouse.'

'If she didn't put it in her CV,' Miss Pinfold said, 'there must be something she wants to hide. But if we don't know which golf club . . .'

'Hang on,' Jane said. 'They left the trophy to be engraved. They'd want the name on that, wouldn't they?'

'Nip up and take a look,' Dorothy suggested. 'We can't all trail up there. It'll be less noticeable if you do it.'

She waited in Miss Pinfold's office, hoping Jane would find out something useful. As soon as she came back, Dorothy knew from her smile of success that she had.

'Sam was talking to a customer at the counter,' she told them. 'I found the trophy lined up on the shelf behind his work bench amongst the other jobs waiting to be done. The message they wanted engraved was taped to it. It's the Woolton Park Golf Club, but I've never heard of it. Have you?'

'Yes,' Dorothy said. 'I know where it is.'

Jane asked urgently, 'Do you know any of the members? Anybody you could ask?'

Dorothy had to say no. 'I don't know anybody who plays golf.'

Miss Pinfold was shaking her head. 'Neither do I, so it doesn't get us any further.'

'It does,' Jane said. 'Honor Thorpe *must* have worked there. She recognised that couple and ran before they spoke to her. She's hiding that, and there's only one reason why she would. She was caught doing something she doesn't want us to know about.'

Miss Pinfold was deep in thought. 'We could ask the other girls. Miss Lewis has a brother, hasn't she? Did she say he plays golf ?'

Dorothy saw Jane shake her head and did so too. 'All the same,' she said, 'it's the best lead we've had so far.'

She couldn't sleep that night and spent wakeful hours asking herself what she could do to show Mrs Thorpe up for what she was. By morning she had no answer. Honor was clever, always one step ahead of her and Jane. As she got dressed, Dorothy shivered. She was a little scared of her too.

It was only when she reached the shop and saw Honor giving Mr Jardine her special smile and radiating sweetness and light in his direction that it came to her.

The couple who'd come in to buy that trophy yesterday had all the answers, they must have. In the first free moment she had, Dorothy nipped upstairs to see Sam. He was busy engraving the trophy.

'Will you let me know when they come back to collect it?' she asked. Sam raised his eyebrows. She knew he kept himself aloof from what he called girls' gossip.

'It's important,' she said. 'I need to talk to that woman.'

'All right.'

In her tea break she mentioned it to Jane, who agreed it was a good idea.

CHAPTER EIGHTEEN

IN THE days that followed, Jane noticed that the atmosphere in the shop was growing even colder, but she had something more pressing on her mind. Usually, Nick rang her up regularly to chat about the events of the day. She'd not heard from him since the day she'd been to Crosby.

Saturday came. They always went out on Saturday nights, and if he wasn't planning to go to church the next morning they'd make arrangements to meet after lunch. At twelve o'clock, when Miss Pinfold went home for her lunch, Jane went to her office to ring him.

'Shall I try to get tickets for the Playhouse tonight?' she asked.

He sounded less than keen. 'What's on?'

'It's a Noel Coward play called *Blithe Spirit*. Dad saw it years ago; he says it's very good.'

'All right. What time d'you want me to come over for you?'

Jane enjoyed the play, but Nick didn't seem his usual self. He said he didn't feel too well. The following afternoon, they went to the Maritime Museum, and afterwards she took him home to have a supper of cold meat and salad with Dad. Even he remarked that Nick had been quieter than usual.

She and Nick had always taken great pleasure in the hugs and kisses in the privacy of the backyard before they said good night, but he seemed half-hearted about that on both occasions. Jane put it down to his not feeling well, but he wasn't able to tell her what was wrong.

She didn't see him during the week, which was unusual, but she spoke to him twice on the phone on business matters. He said he was having early nights and that the next weekend he was going to Chester to spend some time with his mother.

The following week, he made no effort to speak to her. She rang him, expecting him to suggest the pictures, and when he didn't she was afraid he'd put the phone down without making any date.

'What about a walk? I love finding my way through all those Georgian streets up near the cathedral,' she said. 'It'll blow the cobwebs away after being in the shop all day.'

'It looks a bit like rain.'

'If it does, we could find somewhere to have a cup of coffee.' For the first time she wondered if he was trying to avoid her.

They went for the walk and had the coffee, though it didn't rain. The outing was not a success. Jane remembered the night she'd introduced him to Kitty

Thorpe. It was only after that that Nick had seemed to change.

He'd got on well with Kitty. They'd laughed and chatted together while Jane had been getting ready to go out. Kitty was a pretty girl, and although she was two years younger than Jane, she didn't seem so. She was chatty and good company, perhaps more lively than Jane was herself. Jane wondered if Nick had decided he preferred her.

Now she was seeing less of him, Jane felt lost. She loved Nick and had thought he loved her. She'd been fool enough to think he wanted to marry her. It was painful having to accept that he was cooling off.

The following morning, Jane was opening the morning post in Miss Pinfold's office.

'It's a good thing for you to do,' her father had told her last year. 'You'll see all the letters coming in and know what's going on in the business.'

Jane slit open an envelope that looked familiar and pulled out a bill. She was about to place it on top of other accounts when she gave it a second glance. It was for a term's fees at the Cavendish Secretarial College, and it was addressed to her father.

'Look at this.' She laughed. 'I can't believe it. They kept banging on about how we students must be efficient, and yet their office makes a mistake like this. It's over a year since I left.'

Miss Pinfold stopped typing and looked at the bill.

Her mouth dropped open. 'These are fees for Kitty Thorpe, not you,' she said.

Jane felt the strength drain from her legs and sank back on a chair. 'Kitty Thorpe? Oh, my goodness! Honor did tell me she was going to start there in September.'

She snatched up the bill to study it, then ran to her father's office and banged it down on his desk. 'Dad, why are you paying Kitty Thorpe's college fees?'

'Oh!' He slid the bill nearer to look at it, then swept it into his desk drawer and rammed it closed. 'Everybody needs help to get a start in life. A skill will make all the difference to Kitty when she begins to look for a job.'

Jane was cross with him. 'She told me she'd love to come and work in our shop, but you can expect more trouble if you agree to that. A lot more.'

'I wouldn't . . .'

'But why do you have to help?'

'She has no father, Jane.'

'Dad, you're doing this for her mother, but you don't help the rest of the staff.'

'I do my best for them all.'

'But it's noticeable that you do more for Mrs Thorpe. You didn't want me to know, did you? You didn't tell me.'

'I was afraid you'd be . . . And I didn't want that.' Her father looked embarrassed.

'I'm not jealous of her, Dad. It's you I'm worried about.'

She couldn't stop herself telling him about the nonexistent address in Crosby Honor had given them, and that she'd recently worked as a catering manager for a golf club.

Her father looked flushed, his hands covering his mouth. 'I think you might be exaggerating what Mrs Thorpe says and does. Weaving fanciful stories about her.'

That he didn't believe what she was trying to tell him made her even more cross. She burst out, 'She can talk you into doing anything. She's using you.'

'No, Jane,' Edwin sighed. Jane was right, he'd do anything for Honor, but she wasn't using him. He loved her; he couldn't stop thinking about her. He knew his shop was no longer the peaceful place it once had been, and he was afraid there'd be more discord, quarrels and waves of discontent amongst his staff. He just wished he knew how to handle it.

Jane rushed back to Miss Pinfold's office, furious with her father. 'He's offered to pay Kitty Thorpe's college fees,' she told her. 'I can't believe it.'

Miss Pinfold's face was stern. 'She makes him feel sorry for her. He wants to help her, but he's like that with all of us.'

'No, much more so with her. She's taking over here.'

'You don't think . . . Mrs Thorpe and your father, they're walking out? I mean . . .'

At any other time, Jane would have laughed at her old-maidish way of putting it.

'Walking out? I think she means to marry him.'

'Good gracious me!'

'And even worse, I think it's what Dad wants too.'

Miss Pinfold was shocked. 'What? No.'

'Kitty Thorpe is all for it.'

'And you?'

'I think it's a terrible idea.'

'So do I. Oh, my goodness!' Miss Pinfold had to sit down. 'If she was Mrs Jardine, Honor Thorpe would be made up, wouldn't she? She'd be lording it over the rest of us.'

'It's as though he's blind. She can do no wrong. He won't hear a word against her.'

'Love is said to be blind.'

Love? It wasn't easy to think of Dad being in love with anybody. And certainly not with *her*.

'By the way,' Miss Pinfold said, 'Miss Hadley's rung to say they're busy on the ground floor and would you go down?'

'Oh, dear, then I mustn't hang about here wasting your time too.' Jane ran down and served behind the counter for the rest of the morning, fulminating in quiet moments about Honor Thorpe.

She'd rubbed everybody but Dad up the wrong way. Well, with the exception of Sam who was sitting on the fence. All the girls couldn't be wrong about her, could they?

Jane ran through all her misdemeanours to herself.

First, there was the drama of the pickpocket in the shop. Had Honor set that up to get Dad's gratitude and hopefully ensure a job? Then on that shopping spree, she'd pushed a blouse and tights and some undies on the bill for Dad to pay.

And when Mrs Carruthers had fallen on the stairs, nobody had pointed out that Mrs Thorpe had been the first to reach her. But Jane had seen it happen. She knew Honor had had the opportunity to steal that ring when Mrs Carruthers had fainted.

Suspicions about Honor were crowding in on her the whole time, but was she really justified in thinking Honor was a thief?

She'd fled from that couple who'd come in to choose a golf club trophy, hadn't she?

Then there was what Kitty had said over supper the other night. That she'd been left alone at home while her mother worked. Jane suspected that all Honor had told Dad about her recent widowhood was lies and the purpose was to play on his sympathy, but she didn't really know.

She'd certainly used that to get other things she wanted, the jet brooch and now Kitty's college fees. Jane sucked in her breath at the thought of how much more she might winkle from him.

Mrs Thorpe was a manipulative woman, and they all wanted to get him out of her clutches. Jane was convinced Dad needed to be saved.

*

Jane knew that the rehearsals for the *Messiah* were taking place regularly on Thursday evenings, and that her father was running Miss Hadley home afterwards. But she didn't want to talk to either of them about it.

Dorothy was now taking Thursday as her day off. Choir practice started at seven, and since she rarely left work before five thirty it didn't give her much time to get home, eat a meal and get back to the church hall.

Today, when Jane went up for her morning tea break, she found a discussion going on. It seemed Pam Kenny had especially asked for Thursday off this week because it was her boyfriend's birthday, and Miss Jessop wanted that day too, to go to her niece's wedding.

'I'll take Wednesday instead this week,' Dorothy said. 'No problem. You two must have Thursday.'

'I'm afraid it'll be an awful rush for you,' Miss Jessop said.

'We can let you go a little earlier for once,' Jane told her.

'No, that means more work for you. I'll not go home. I'll bring a sandwich with me and eat it here. If I go straight to choir practice I'll have plenty of time.'

Jane suddenly had a good idea. 'Don't bring sandwiches,' she said. 'No, come and have a bite of supper upstairs with us on Thursday. Then you can go to your practice with Dad. That's the answer. I'll go and talk to him now.'

She pushed her chair back and stood up. She couldn't help but notice that Mrs Thorpe had looked a little dismayed to hear Dorothy being invited to eat with them. As Jane went into her father's office, he looked up from the accounts he was working on.

'Miss Hadley to have supper with us?' he asked. 'You know we don't entertain at home. Should I book a restaurant?'

'Dad! No, it's just Miss Hadley. She's hardly a guest and she's talking of bringing a sandwich and eating it alone in the rest room.' She explained the need. 'That's not on, Dad. We can't let her do that.'

'No, perhaps not.'

'I'll get Mrs McGrath to provide something better than usual.'

Edwin forgot about it until he heard Jane talking to Mrs McGrath about having lamb chops followed by bread and butter pudding for supper on Thursday. He looked round the kitchen, which also served as their dining room. It looked worn and shabby. He ought to get something done about it. Having seen how Honor lived, he was afraid Miss Hadley would also be used to better accommodation.

He went upstairs and found that Jane had taken her up and they were both in the kitchen before him. Miss Hadley seemed more at ease than he did.

He'd never stopped to consider how she and Jane got on together, and their air of intimacy and companionship surprised him. She helped Jane dish up and seemed quite at home in their kitchen. She had them both laughing over an anecdote about a customer who'd come in that afternoon.

He thought Miss Hadley was good company, and she seemed equally relaxed when alone with him. When he dropped her outside her house at the end of the evening, Edwin surprised himself by saying, 'We must do this again next Thursday. There's no need for you to rush home and back. Not if you don't have to.'

Dorothy Hadley felt up on cloud nine and much encouraged. She'd thoroughly enjoyed having supper with Edwin and Jane and felt closer to them both as a result. She was very grateful to Jane for arranging it. It made her feel she was sharing their domestic life.

A few days later, early in the morning when the shop had only just opened, Miss Hadley was still arranging the stock when the internal phone behind the front counter buzzed.

She picked it up. It was Sam. 'You wanted me to tell you,' he said. 'There's somebody here to collect that trophy.'

Dorothy felt excitement fizz in her stomach. She crossed her fingers that it was Mrs Clarkson who had come. Jane had said she'd get more information out of her than her husband. She'd had the name on the tip of her tongue for days.

After a quick look round for Honor Thorpe, Dorothy ran to the stairs. This was her chance to find out more about her. If possible, she meant to make Honor face the people from whom she'd fled the other day.

She saw her with Pam Kenny on the first floor, polishing up the silver. Right, now she knew where she was. Dorothy was breathless by the time she reached Sam's department. It took all the wind out of her sails to see a slim young man waiting for her.

'Oh!' She could feel herself sagging with disappointment and had to pull herself together. 'I was hoping to see Mrs Clarkson.'

'No, she sent me in to get this.' He held up the bag.

Dorothy was trying to think on her feet. 'Do you work at the golf club?'

'No, for Millard & Clarkson, the builders.'

'Oh! I don't suppose . . . Do you know the people who work at the golf club?'

'No, I've never set foot in the place.'

Dorothy knew she'd drawn a blank. Why hadn't it occurred to her that this might happen?

'D'you want me to give Mrs Clarkson a message?' The youth was waiting.

'No. No, thank you.'

Dorothy followed slowly behind him as he went downstairs. She'd been so sure she'd find out what it was that Mrs Thorpe wanted to keep hidden. Now she felt crushed.

As she went lower, she heard Mrs Thorpe's silvery voice drifting across the first floor, polite and respectful.

She was showing an array of silver and cut glass hip flasks to an elderly gentleman

Jane was missing Nick's frequent phone calls and her social life felt flat. The atmosphere in the shop seemed a little flat too, though she still enjoyed her work. At morning break today, Mrs Thorpe had looked anything but happy. She was sitting by herself, some distance from the gossiping cluster at the other end of the table.

Jane poured herself a cup of tea and feeling she should include her, asked, 'How's Kitty?'

'She's fine.' Mrs Thorpe was frowning. 'She's out all the time, so I don't see so much of her. She's got herself a boyfriend.'

Jane gave a start which made her slop her tea. 'A new one?' Did she mean Nick? They'd got on very well together over her stew and dumplings the other night.

'No, she's known him a long time, it's just that they seem suddenly engrossed with each other.'

Jane took a sip of her tea. 'Jason something . . . ?'

'That's him.'

So Nick hadn't taken up with Kitty Thorpe. Jane felt she had to snap out of this. She had no reason to be suspicious of Kitty. If Nick had lost interest in her there was nothing she could do about it.

But yes, there was. He seemed to be avoiding her, but he couldn't do that for ever when they both worked for the same company. She could ask him if she'd upset him, if there was something the matter. She hated to think she might have to accept she was losing him, but at least she'd know where she stood.

She turned hurriedly to Miss Pinfold and enquired after her mother. It wasn't good news there either: the old lady was failing now and not at all well.

Jane had tried to fill her leisure hours with other things. When the cake decorating course had finished at the end of May, she and Pam had started going to the pictures on Tuesdays instead, but Pam had a serious boyfriend now and her weekends were taken up with him. Jane met her old college friend Jazz once or twice, although somehow they didn't hit it off as well as they used to, and sometimes Dad took her out on Saturday nights.

Nothing quite did the trick, and she found herself longing for Nick Collins. So she was part apprehensive, part excited when, the next morning, Dad said, 'Would you mind doing a stock inventory at Crosby? I know I usually help Nick do it, but it might be good practice for you.'

Jane wondered if he was giving her the chance to sort things out with Nick.

'It's easier when the shop is closed and most of the stuff is in the safe, but I'm falling behind and still have to stock-take at Aigburth and Southport.'

'Of course I'll do it, Dad.'

'Next Sunday, then. I pay overtime.'

*

The rain was pouring down on Sunday morning when she took the train to Crosby. She walked from the station huddled under an umbrella, but her shoes and stockings were wet through by the time she arrived. The sight of Nick, looking shy and embarrassed but ready to help her off with her mac, made her long for them to be back on their old friendly terms. As far as she was concerned, the chemistry was still there between them.

It was Sam who put her wet shoes in his airing cupboard and provided an enormous pair of his own slippers for her to shuffle around in. He also made them a cup of coffee before they began. He even followed them down to the shop to help them get started, but Jane told him they could manage.

At midday, he set off to his local for a beer and a sandwich and she was alone with Nick at last. He was concentrating hard on the job in hand and saying little. She was counting too and together they filled in the boxes on the forms Dad had supplied. She let the work roll on; they'd have to do it anyway. By one o'clock she was feeling hungry. Dad had told her to take Nick out for a snack.

When she suggested it, he said, 'I made a salad for us, so we don't have to waste time by going out.'

Sam had set it out beautifully on the table upstairs in the flat. Chicken salad with fresh rolls and cake. She sat down facing Nick across the table and her heart began to beat harder. She knew the moment was on her.

'What have I done, Nick,' she asked, looking him straight in the eyes, 'to deserve the cold shoulder like this?'

The chicken on his fork paused halfway to his mouth but he said nothing.

'Don't tell me this isn't the cold shoulder,' she went on, 'and that you aren't behaving differently.'

A red flush was spreading up his cheeks. 'No, no. I'm sorry.'

'It's very hurtful, Nick.'

He seemed shocked. 'I didn't mean to hurt you. That's the last thing I want to do.'

'What am I supposed to think? You said you loved me, we were seeing each other two or three nights a week, then suddenly without a word of explanation you bring everything to a halt.'

His face was troubled, and he didn't know where to look. 'I'm sorry. I didn't think of it from your point of view.'

'Well, why? Are you fed up with me?'

'Of course not!'

'You've found someone else you like better? Until I had a word with her mother, I was afraid it was Kitty Thorpe?'

'For heaven's sake! No.' He gave a travesty of a laugh. 'Never.'

'You seemed to like her well enough on the night she had supper with us. You two were laughing all the time. You asked her to come to the pictures with us.'

'I was only being polite,' he said. 'I thought that was what you wanted. Kitty isn't my style.'

'Too young, you mean? But she's pretty, isn't she?'

'She seems older than you with her scarlet nail varnish and pierced ears. Kitty's streetwise,' Nick said. 'She looks a bit of a tart.'

'A tart? Really? Then what is it?'

He pushed back his chair and swept round to her side of the table and took her in his arms. 'Oh, Jane, I'm sorry. I love you. I've given us both a horrible time this last month or so, haven't I?'

'Yes. I thought you'd gone off me. So what is it?'

He found it hard to get the words out. 'You're an heiress and I have nothing.'

She pushed him far enough away to be able to see his face. He looked embarrassed. 'Why on earth should that matter?'

'It does. It worries me. I thought I should give you the opportunity to find someone else. Someone of your own class.'

'You are my class.'

'No, I'm not.'

'Nick, you're what I want.' She rested her forehead against his shoulder and felt as though she'd come home. He lifted her chin to kiss her. 'What put that silly idea in your head? Was it Kitty?'

'Yes, in a way.'

'What did she say?'

'That I was on to a good thing with you. I could

marry you and set myself up for life. But it wasn't just her. My mother, too, on that night I took you to meet her – she said it would make my fortune to marry you.'

'Why didn't you tell me?'

'It's not the sort of thing I wanted you to hear. But I should have done, shouldn't I?'

'Yes, and I'd have asked where you expected me to find someone to suit me better. You suit me, we suit each other, I thought we'd decided that? I mean, Dad likes you . . .'

'He likes everybody, Jane. I work for him; he likes me well enough as an employee, but would he welcome me as a son-in-law?'

'Of course he would. He believes some things are more important than money.'

Nick drew away again. 'Only the rich say things like that. The rest of us know just how important it is.'

'Dad wants me to be happy. If we love each other, that's all he'd ask.'

'Are you sure?'

'I'm certain. On a couple of Saturdays, when you weren't offering, he took me to the theatre. He could see I was upset. He asked if you were all right, but I was uptight and I couldn't explain.' Nick hugged her closer. 'And I think he might have set up this stock-taking to give us the chance to sort things out.'

His lips came down on hers again. 'Well, we have, and I've found out what a fool I've been. I've been pretty miserable. Forgive me, Jane.'

ALL THAT GLISTENS

*

On Friday evening, Jane had agreed to go to the pictures to see *Ryan's Daughter* with Nick, but when he arrived at the shop he said, 'D'you mind if we put that off to another night? I'd like to talk things through with you. I've learned my lesson, and I want things to be clearly understood between you and me from now on. What about a walk to the Pier Head?'

'All right, though it's going to be blowy down there tonight.'

Even in town, the stiff breeze was gusting dust and litter along the pavements, and away from the high buildings the wind off the estuary buffeted them. Now it was dark the river looked pretty, with lights twinkling on the boats and on the far bank. They stood for a moment watching a Mersey ferry pull away from the landing stage.

'What did you want to talk about?' she asked.

He slid an arm round her waist. 'You and me. I'd like to get some things settled.' He pulled her closer and kissed her.

'Such as?'

'I want you to marry me. Will you?' He straightened up so he could see her face.

Jane felt she'd been given the world. She couldn't stop smiling. 'Yes,' she said. 'Yes!'

He laughed. 'I prepared a little speech to tell you how much I loved you, and now I've made a mess of it.'

'That doesn't matter.' She nestled into his arms. 'The message is clear.'

'Are you sure?' he asked. 'After last month . . .'

'I'm sure.'

'You don't need more time to think it over? It's a big step and I don't want to rush you.'

'I've been thinking a great deal about it recently.' She smiled. 'I'm quite sure.'

'And I'm absolutely certain, so can we be engaged and tell everybody? Make it public?'

'Yes, let's do that.'

'I know I'm no great catch.'

That made Jane smile. He was a good-looking young man of twenty-four who worked hard.

'You're what I want. I love you, Nick.'

'And I love you. I want you to know I'd work my guts out for you, if I had to.'

She laughed out loud. 'I don't think you'll have to do that.'

'I'd like us to ask your father tonight. Then we can talk about when we're going to be married. We'll have to get him to agree, won't we?'

'I'm eighteen and of age. I can do it anyway.'

'Yes, but I'll ask just the same. He's your father and my boss.'

'Yes, you must. He'll probably expect you to ask for my hand. It's the old-fashioned way, isn't it?'

'He's going to say you're too young, and want us to wait.'

'I don't know.' Jane put her arm through his as they turned to stroll back to the shop. 'Life's strange, isn't it? Everything stands still for years and then suddenly it's all on the move.'

'Yes. And now we're engaged and soon I hope we'll be married.' He dropped a kiss on her forehead.

Jane could feel little swirls of pleasure running down her back. 'But things are changing between me and Dad too,' she said dreamily. 'Only a few months ago, I think he saw himself as totally responsible for me. He took care of me, made all decisions on my behalf and looked after me in every way. Now, suddenly, I feel I need to look after him.'

'You've grown up.'

'But he's managed without any help from me up till now. Why should I suddenly feel I have to look after him?'

Even as she asked, she knew the answer to that. 'It's because of Mrs Thorpe.'

CHAPTER NINETEEN

EDWIN WAS relaxing in his armchair with a newspaper, but his attention kept wandering. He was thinking of Honor making supper in her comfortable house, watching television with her daughter and then going to bed in her pretty bedroom.

A footfall on the stairs brought him back with a jerk. Was this Jane? Yes, and that was Nick's laugh. They'd come back earlier than usual. The sitting room door burst open. Jane's smile was radiant.

'Dad,' she said, crossing the room to their Victorian sofa. 'Can we have a little talk?'

'Yes, of course.' He folded away his newspaper. 'Come and sit down, Nick.'

Nick remained standing near the door looking oddly awkward, not his usual self. 'Mr Jardine,' he said, sounding very formal, 'I'd like to ask your permission to marry Jane.'

'Oh!' He looked from one to the other. 'You want to get married, Jane?' It shouldn't have come as any great shock. He'd seen it on the cards for some time, but

336

recently he'd been thinking . . . 'Are you sure?' But she was sparkling; it was obvious she was.

'Yes, Dad. Quite sure. It's what we both want. More than anything else in the world.'

Nick said, 'I hope you don't think Jane is too young.'

Edwin said dryly, 'She is young, but she usually knows what she wants and rarely changes her mind.'

'Then we can, Dad?'

He smiled. 'I'm sure you realise there's nothing I could do to stop you. Didn't we have a conversation not so long ago about you doing exactly what you wanted now you were of age?'

'Mm, something like that. But we want your approval, Dad.'

'You have it, love.' That brought her across the room to fling her arms round him in a hug.

Nick said, 'Thank you, sir.' He felt able to sit down on the sofa now. 'I was afraid you'd want a rich man as a son-in-law. Someone older and more sophisticated.'

'Well,' Edwin said, 'I didn't expect to be given much choice in the matter. Jane generally gets her own way.'

Jane was laughing. 'Nick was worried stiff you'd say I was too young, and you'd want us to wait.'

'Your mother was just nineteen when we got married. She wasn't too young. When did you have in mind for the wedding?'

'We haven't had time to talk about that yet,' Nick said, 'but we won't want a long engagement.'

'Months rather than years,' Jane added, smiling at

him. 'In the autumn? Would that be all right?'

'The autumn?' Edwin sat up straighter. 'Quite soon, then.'

'And a quiet wedding, I think.'

Nick was nodding his agreement. 'We'd like everybody to know we're engaged, though.'

'Jane can announce it to the girls in the shop tomorrow morning,' Edwin said. 'Nothing interests them more than a romance. They'll love the whole idea and talk of nothing else for weeks.'

Jane laughed. In her present mood she'd laugh at anything. 'Now we know you're happy with the idea, we're going out for a drink and we'll decide on the next step.'

'Don't be late,' he said before he could stop himself.

Once they'd gone, Edwin lay back in his chair. He should have wished them well for the future, and offered to provide the engagement ring. He had hundreds down in the shop. There was little point in Nick paying out for one on his salary.

Yes, Jane was young, but Elena had been too, and she'd been very happy in their first years of marriage. If it had suited her, why not Jane? Nick was a good lad; his heart was in the right place. He was quick to learn, too. Jane could have done a lot worse.

But Edwin knew nothing would have made him object or ask them to wait. Once Jane was married, he'd be free to marry Honor. All the jealousy Jane felt, all the sniping and getting worked up because he was paying college fees for Kitty, would stop. It would clear the air and she'd accept Honor in his life.

Probably the first thing Jane would want to talk about when she came home again was where they would live. He still owned the house he and Elena had shared. He'd rented it out for years, but he'd have no trouble getting vacant possession. He wouldn't want to live there with Honor; somehow it was Elena's house. Perhaps Jane and Nick would like it?

But at last Edwin thought he could see his own way forward with Honor. It would be July next week; what did she mean by autumn? September or October? It could be only three months or so off. He was almost as thrilled as Jane was.

He was cleaning his teeth, getting ready for bed when Jane came home. He went to the bathroom door. He'd never seen her with such wide smiles. She came along the landing as though she was dancing on air.

'We rang Nick's mother to tell her we were engaged,' she said, 'and she invited us over tomorrow when the shops close. She's going to cook a celebration dinner for us. I'm to stay the night, Dad, and we'll come back after Sunday lunch.'

That news gave him a real lift. It was an immediate opportunity to spend some time with Honor. He'd be able to stay overnight with her. The thought of it made him tingle.

'Have you made any decisions about the wedding?' he asked. 'When it's to be?'

'We've talked about it, but it's difficult. What would be the best day of the week? We'd like to ask everybody in the shop, but how can we when we open six days a week?'

'I don't know . . . unless . . . yes, that's it. Wednesday used to be early closing day here, before all the city shops were kept open for six days. We could close all our Liverpool shops on one Wednesday afternoon, couldn't we? Closed for your wedding.'

'That's a lovely idea, Dad! Thank you.'

'We can invite all the staff then. We have to. It would be too difficult to decide who must be excluded to run the shops.'

'We thought perhaps in September. If we both took our summer holiday then, we could go to the Greek islands for our honeymoon.'

September? That was excellent. Edwin was happy to say yes to everything.

The next morning, Jane was on a high as she met the girls coming into work. From the moment she announced her engagement to Nick, they were all in a state of incandescent excitement. When she told them she'd be married within a few months, it lifted them all on to their toes. They were leaping to serve customers with wide smiles on their faces.

Jane was very conscious of the excitement centring on her. The girls asked what sort of wedding dress she was going to choose, where she wanted to be married, where the reception would be held, and where she and Nick would live.

She got round it all by saying Nick had swept her off her feet and they hadn't had time to talk about what they wanted; she really didn't know. 'That's all for the future,' she'd said.

'But what about an engagement ring?' Dorothy Hadley asked. 'You need to think about that now.'

'Nick only asked me last night,' she protested, but she found herself looking at the rings in the shop with new eyes. Her father had said they must look at rings on Sunday when they came home. He probably meant to tell her and Nick to choose one from stock. He paid Nick's wages, so he knew that without his help it wouldn't be possible for Nick to give her an expensive ring. But Dad knew everything there was to know about gemstones and wouldn't want her to wear anything but the best. She needed to find out how Nick felt about that.

Really she'd be just as pleased with one of the rings that had belonged to Elena and would be hers when she was twenty-one. The idea of wearing the ring that Dad had given her mother to mark their engagement appealed to her very much. Elena's engagement ring was a sapphire with a diamond on each side of it. Jane decided to suggest it to Nick and Dad. More than likely they'd both be happy to agree.

Dad was brimming with smiles too. He told her that after the carping and backbiting of recent weeks it was lovely to see the staff so happy and full of goodwill again. He sent Pam out to Marks & Spencer to buy cream cakes to have with their afternoon tea by way of celebration.

Even Sam Collins said he noticed the difference in the shop atmosphere. 'The way the old girls are carrying on, you'd think they were all about to get married.' He kissed Jane's forehead. 'Nick's a lucky fellow, and I'm delighted you're joining my family.'

Happy voices and joyful laughter rang in Edwin's ears all morning. Just as he'd expected, the girls were thrilled with Jane's news; a tide of excitement seemed to wash through the shop. He heard Miss Pinfold starting a collection among the staff for a wedding present and there were many discussions about what they should give.

Later, he overheard Honor wishing Jane every happiness and asking if he approved. It gave him the opportunity to tell the girls he was very pleased, and that he thought Jane would be happy with Nick. Honor gave him a beaming smile; it made him feel both full of love and full of guilt.

She'd invited him back to her house and even back to her bed, but he hadn't yet found the words to tell her all that was in his mind. Twice he'd taken her to a restaurant for dinner with the express intention of discussing their future. He felt it was his duty to propose marriage; it was what he wanted, what he needed, but he was afraid she might turn him down. Why would a young woman so beautiful and vibrant want to tie herself to a man like him? He was so much older and slower and dull.

During her tea break, Honor knocked on his office door and came in, closing it behind her and leaning back against it. The dark paintwork was a foil for her bright hair and dancing eyes. She looked full of life.

'Jane's been swept off her feet,' she said. 'As she's deserting you to be with Nick's mother tonight, I'd like you to come to dinner at my house. You don't want to spend the evening here on your own, do you?'

'No,' he said. 'I'd like that. Thank you. I can't invite you here to eat Jane's share of our supper. Mrs McGrath would be sure to let the girls in the shop know you'd been. News like that would travel like wildfire.'

'Would it matter?' Her face lit up with another smile before she left him. 'Seven o'clock then?'

Edwin gasped. Honor didn't see things in the way he did. That underlined how old-fashioned she must think him. He really had to talk to her about the future and find out if she wanted to spend it with him.

At lunch time, Jane packed an overnight bag with a smart dress for the celebration dinner, and laid out her jeans and pullover for the journey. As soon as the shop closed, Dad sent her up to get herself ready. After the bustle of the day, the flat seemed suddenly quiet. Tonight, even Mrs McGrath wasn't in the kitchen stirring pots on the stove. Dad was still downstairs; it looked as though he meant to go out to dinner and carry on celebrating.

Nick phoned her when he was on the point of leaving the Crosby shop, so she could time their meeting outside James Street station. On the way out, she shot into her father's office to say goodbye to him.

As she ran down to the station she could see Nick already waiting for her. He wrapped his arms round her in a big bear hug before leading her towards the train with an arm round her waist. After what seemed like years of mundane routine, Jane felt as though she was suddenly being whirled along at breakneck speed.

She'd been looking forward to seeing his home. He'd told her he'd been brought up in a flat, but she found that compared to hers and Dad's it was quite a sumptuous one. Like theirs, it was in the centre of the shopping district with all the shops, restaurants and theatres of the city close to hand. But it was in a beautiful black and white building, very much larger than theirs and furnished with antiques on a sophisticated and quite grand scale.

Nick's mother seemed excited too. Her face was flushed and for the first time Jane saw that Nick had inherited her straight nose and dark eyes. She'd thought her rather stiff and cold on the only other occasion they'd met, but tonight she seemed much friendlier and more relaxed. She produced a bottle of champagne for Nick to open.

'I see you haven't bought Jane an engagement ring yet,' she said. Then, turning to Jane, she went on, 'I'd like to provide one for Nick to give you, if I may? I have several rings that would be suitable.'

Jane didn't know where to look. 'Oh! That's so kind of you . . . I'm a bit embarrassed by everybody's generosity.'

'Jane, it's just that it's an expensive item for Nick to buy at this stage in his life, and I thought it might help.'

Nick put in hastily, 'I'd be happy to buy Jane's ring. In fact I was looking forward to it. I've cash saved for it.'

Jane couldn't help smiling. 'Nick and I talked about this on the way here. My dad has offered to give us a ring too. Engagement rings are his stock in trade, after all. He wanted us to choose it tomorrow when we get back. Nothing is decided yet, but I have my own ideas about it. I think I'd like to wear my mother's engagement ring. It would be mine anyway when I'm twenty-one but I think Dad might let me have it now.'

'That's a lovely idea,' Madeleine Collins said. 'With so much offered to you I stand back. Right, let's drink to your future happiness.'

Nick pushed a glass of champagne into Jane's hand. The bubbles went up her nose as she sipped. The celebration dinner turned out to be a starter of smoked trout, roast pheasant for the main course and profiteroles Madeleine had made herself. It was served in style.

'A wonderful meal,' Jane told her. 'You're an excellent cook. I'm afraid I've a lot to learn!'

Honor saw Jane's forthcoming marriage as a wonderful stroke of luck, and one she hadn't even thought of as a possibility. It would separate Jane from Edwin. Not entirely, of course, but far enough for him to feel the need to have someone else in his life. And Honor was ready waiting to step in.

On her way home from work she called at her local supermarket and bought steak and a few other things she'd need to give Edwin a good dinner. When she reached home with her shopping bag, Kitty was drinking tea at the kitchen table. 'D'you want a cup, Ma?' she asked. 'The kettle's just boiled.'

'I'd love one. Thanks.'

She started to unpack her bag and Kitty saw the steak. 'Goody,' she said. 'I see we're in for a treat tonight.'

Honor felt a rush of guilt. She'd decided Kitty could make do with eggs. 'Sorry, it's not for you. I've got Edwin coming for dinner tonight. Do you think you could make yourself scarce?'

'You're pushing me out again?'

Honor could see her daughter wasn't pleased. 'No, love, it's just that I need space to work on him. You do understand? In the long run, you'll benefit too.' She went to the dining room to set the table. Kitty's books were spread across one end. 'You're benefiting now, aren't you? He's organised everything and paid your fees so you can go to secretarial college in September.'

'Nobody asked me if I wanted to go.'

'Don't be silly, dear. You know it'll make a world of difference when you start job-hunting. Could you move your things, please?'

Kitty was mutinous and swept them away with bad grace.

'When you come home, you will come in quietly and go straight to your room? It would be better if you were neither seen nor heard, and be sure to shut your door before you get into bed.'

Kitty's ill temper flashed out. 'I won't come home at all. I know when I'm not wanted.'

'Wait, Kitty,' Honor cried, but her daughter had flounced out to the hall and a moment later she heard her speaking on the phone.

'Jason, could you come and get me? Mum wants me out of here. You'll need to feed me too.'

Honor felt deflated. It was the first time Kitty had rung Jason in her hearing. It seemed she wanted their relationship out in the open and that filled Honor with apprehension. Jason would give Kitty the sort of life his father had given her. They'd have their good times, yes, but they'd also have their bad ones. Gary would be out of prison soon and Honor wasn't having him coming round here wanting to take up with her again.

She realised then that Kitty was pleading. Jason seemed to be less than eager to fall in with her request.

Honor went to the door as her daughter put the phone down.

'You could always go to the pictures,' she suggested.

Kitty looked anything but pleased. 'He's coming to collect me and we're going out for a meal, but he's got something else arranged for later on. I'll be coming back here to sleep.' She went noisily upstairs.

Honor set about preparing dinner. Twenty minutes later Kitty came down from her bedroom wearing high heels and a scarlet coat Honor had never seen before. It looked expensive.

'Isn't it lovely, Mum?' She did a twirl, her good humour apparently restored.

'When did you get that?'

'Jason bought it for me. This dress, too. He's taking me to a posh restaurant.'

Honor heard a car hoot outside.

'Got to go,' Kitty said, opening the door.

Honor sank down on the bottom stair feeling miserable enough to cry. If it wasn't for Kitty she wouldn't be doing any of this. She'd so wanted her to have a better life and not get mixed up with criminals. But it sounded as though it was too late, and all the effort she'd made to look after her had come to naught. She sighed and went back to the kitchen. She had to forget her daughter and get on, or she wouldn't be ready for Edwin.

By seven o'clock when she heard his car pull up on the drive, appetising scents were filling the house.

Honor had had a bath and made up her face and was wearing a smart blue dress. She'd set the table with great care. All she had to do was light the candles and dish up the meal, but first they'd have a drink and she'd psych herself into the right mood.

She shot to the door to welcome him. Edwin had changed out of the black striped suit he wore in the shop but looked hardly less formal in his grey worsted three-piece with grey silk tie. His cheeks were flushed.

'You look hot,' she said. 'Why don't you make yourself comfortable?' She persuaded him to take off his tie and jacket, then, seeing his waistcoat, got him to remove that too, and hung them on the hallstand. His manners belonged to an earlier age. He seemed to think it improper to divest himself of his tie in a woman's presence.

It took him for ever to open the bottle of wine he'd brought. She could have done it in half the time. She told herself they both needed to relax.

'Such good news about Jane.' Honor didn't have to force her enthusiasm. 'I do hope she'll be very happy with Nick.'

'I think she will; he's a good lad. Where's Kitty tonight?'

'I packed her off to spend the evening with a friend, so we could have some time by ourselves.'

That went down well. He smiled and took a few gulps from his glass. She immediately topped it up. To talk of engagements, love and marriage, even Jane's, seemed to

Honor to be a good way to start the evening.

She wasted no time pulling his arm through hers and leading him to the dining room. She was hungry and didn't want the steak to be overcooked. Jane had told her that at home they ate their dinner as soon as they closed the shop, so he should be hungry too.

But when she saw him feasting his eyes on her face she knew he was more interested in her than he was in the food, and felt better. She'd got him where she wanted him. She kept his glass filled and offered brandy with the coffee she served in the sitting room.

She was glad she'd chosen to have two sofas and no armchairs. Even her window seat would accommodate two or three people. It gave her space to sit close to her guests. She'd always found that touching a man helped to soften him up. She held his hand and he bent to kiss her cheek.

It surprised her to find Edwin was apologetic. 'I've been feeling very guilty about you,' he told her. 'I should never have allowed myself to compromise you in the way I have.'

Honor was at a loss. She wasn't sure how to deal with this.

'You must forgive me.'

'No, no, Edwin. There's nothing to forgive.'

'There is. What must you think of me?'

She thought him a real gentleman, though he seemed to think he was the worst sort of cad.

He went on, 'I've taken all the privileges of a

husband and offered you nothing in return. I love you very much, but I've given you no promises, nothing. I've taken advantage of you.'

'I don't feel that. Don't upset yourself.'

'I need to explain, my dear, and try to put things right. Everything has been at sixes and sevens recently. Jane has been cross with me, and the girls in the shop – well, you must have felt how worked up they've been against me and you. There's been such an atmosphere of turmoil and strife, but Jane's engagement seems to have spread oil on troubled waters. So now I think I should make my intentions clear to you.'

Honor snuggled closer. 'Bless you,' she said.

'I very much want you to be my wife,' he told her.

Honor straightened up. 'Edwin, that's lovely.'

It was the successful end to all her plans and it had come much sooner and more easily than she'd expected. He was surveying her seriously.

'Would you be willing to marry me? Would you want to? I'm fifty-three, so much older than you.'

She threw her arms round him. 'Yes, Edwin. Of course I will. I'm thrilled. There's nothing I want more.' She pulled him closer and kissed his lips, reawakening his passion.

'My dear, I feel honoured. I'd like our wedding to take place as soon as possible, but I'm worried it may seem rushed to Jane, and I don't want to upset her. So I must ask you to please be patient with me.'

'Of course, Edwin. Take all the time you need, but I

hope we can see more of each other.' She felt the sooner she got them upstairs to her bed the better. That, too, took less time than before, and once upstairs there was no holding him back. She hadn't expected such passion from Edwin. She'd felt that was one of the things she'd be trading against having more money.

Afterwards, she lay in his arms and he talked again of their future. 'I'd like us to be engaged. Secretly engaged, if you don't mind. I'd like to wait until Jane is married before we say anything. Even now I'm afraid she'd be upset if we were to announce our intentions and marry quickly. I feel that she's being very unfair to you. The girls will be against it too.'

'Too true, I'm afraid, but I'm quite happy to wait a little longer. What I really wanted was to know how you feel about me.'

'Honor darling, that's very sweet of you. I love you and I always will. We have an understanding now. I want us to feel engaged and know that we'll be married before very long. I'm going to take you to the shop in the morning and want you to choose your engagement ring.'

There was just one flaw marring Honor's satisfaction. She was still married to Paul Thorpe. She hadn't seen him or heard of him for eight years: could she legally presume him to be dead? Dare she marry again, or would it be bigamy? And would it matter? Who would be likely to find out?

CHAPTER TWENTY

At eleven thirty, when Kitty brought Jason's MG to a halt in Queen's Drive, the house was in total darkness. She could see Edwin Jardine's large black saloon pulled up on the drive.

'The two lovebirds are tucked up in bed,' Jason sniggered.

'I don't know about lovebirds. It's more a business proposition to Ma.' Kitty got out and Jason slid over into the driving seat. 'Best of luck with tonight's job.'

'It'll go well, it has for the last six weeks.'

'You make it sound like routine work.'

'It is. I'm just taking a consignment of electrical goods to a wholesaler in Birmingham. Don't you worry, nothing can go wrong. I'll see you tomorrow.'

Kitty knew the goods had been stolen. 'I'll be round about tea time. Bye-bye.'

She eased her way past Mr Jardine's car and felt for the lock to insert her key. It was warmer inside, as silent as the grave and just as black. She put on the light to see her way to the kitchen to get a drink of water.

The grey worsted jacket hanging on the hallstand caught her attention. Impossible to miss it. It was his, of course. She touched it and saw the silk tie behind. Something bulky in his pocket made the coat swing. She slid her hand inside to see what it was. A bunch of keys – a large and heavy bunch of keys.

She let them fall back to check his other pockets. His wallet wasn't here, just spectacles, a handkerchief and some loose change. She transferred some of that to her own pocket. He'd be unlikely to know exactly how much he had.

Then she fished the keys out again and looked at them more closely. She could feel her heart beating faster. This was an important find. Jason and she had discussed the possibility of breaking into Edwin's shop and helping themselves to his precious stones. Jason knew jewellers who'd be glad to buy them off him. These must be the keys to the shop and probably the keys to the safe as well!

Kitty was tingling all over. All trace of tiredness was gone on the instant. If only Jason were still outside – he knew a locksmith who ran a little business and was prepared to copy any key at any time of day or night. But she'd seen Jason's tail lights disappear down the road, and anyway he had other things on tonight and no time to deal with anything else.

She couldn't just take them. The car key was easy to pick out and without that Edwin Jardine couldn't leave. What could she do?

Soap! That was it. Kitty had heard somewhere that a key could be pressed into a tablet of soap to make an impression and a locksmith could make a copy of the key from that. She took the key ring to the downstairs loo and looked at it again. There was a Yale key and one for a deadlock and . . . Gosh! There were two keys with the name Chubb on them. They must be the keys to his safe. The keys were not the same – were there two safes in his shop? Her heart was racing now. This was a gift from the gods, if only she could get good impressions.

She started on what seemed to be the door keys. After all, they had to get inside before they could do anything. They were easy to press into the soap but how deep did the impression have to be? Not all that easy: she smudged an impression when she took the first key off the bar. She tried again more gently and got three keys done, but she couldn't turn the soap over to use the other side without spoiling what she'd done.

She went to the kitchen and found an unopened packet of six Lux toilet soap tablets under the sink. But they were too hard: she couldn't make any impression at all on them. She put three tablets to soak in some water and crept upstairs to get undressed while they softened up. The third stair creaked with a noise that shattered the silence and made her freeze. She should have remembered and stepped close to the wall. Her mother's bedroom door was shut, and she hoped they were both fast asleep.

Down again for another try. She mustn't give up, she might not get another chance like this. The Chubb keys now. She found there was a narrow margin between the soap's being soft enough and being too soft. She blurred her next attempts and ruined one tablet. There were a whole lot more keys for which she couldn't guess a purpose, but they might turn out to be crucial to their success. Kitty worked doggedly on until she'd got an impression of each of them.

She took them upstairs on a tray and slid them under her bed to harden off. Then she had to tidy up. The sitting room fire had gone out, so she struck a match to burn the soap wrappers in the grate; then she dug the charred remains into the ashes.

She must be careful not to leave traces of Lux on the keys. She picked bits off with her nails and then polished the keys well on the towel. They'd be covered with her fingerprints but Mr Jardine would never know, he wasn't the police. All she needed to do was arouse no suspicion. She'd spoiled one new tablet of Lux with useless impressions, and she washed her hands vigorously with it in hot water to smooth them out and make it look half used. She left it on the washbasin. It replaced a tablet of Imperial Leather, and she hoped her mother wouldn't notice.

She was creeping upstairs again to go to bed when her mother's bedroom door opened and Honor came out on to the landing. 'What are you doing, Kitty?'

It made her jump and almost trip. She was

floundering for a believable reply. 'I couldn't sleep and I was hungry. I went down to get a biscuit.'

'You woke me up walking round in the middle of the night. Put these lights off and go back to bed.'

'Sorry, Ma.'

Kitty saw her head towards the bathroom. She shot to her own room and leaped into bed. That was a close one, and the shock had given her a bad dose of jitters. She was stone cold too. She pulled the bedclothes over her head and hoped she'd made a passable job of the impressions, and that she'd not wasted such a heaven-sent chance. The smell of toilet soap hung in a heavy wholesome cloud round her bed. She got up again to open the window and push her tray of impressions closer to the wall where Ma would be less likely to notice them.

The next morning, knowing Edwin was watching her, Honor dressed slowly and posed once or twice in the new lacy underwear she'd bought specially for occasions like this. Edwin was sitting on the end of her bed in his underpants.

His underwear made her smile. She thought herself an expert on men's underwear but she'd not seen any quite so old-fashioned as his. They looked hot and woolly for this time of the year and he wore too many layers. If they ever did get married, she'd have to take his whole wardrobe in hand. He needed informal pullovers and slacks.

'What if I meet Kitty on the landing?' he asked.

'It's Sunday. She won't be up for a couple of hours yet,' Honor assured him, but he asked her to check first to make sure the coast was clear.

When he had been safely escorted to the bathroom, she went downstairs to make them tea and toast. He was more relaxed when he came down dressed and shaved and no longer needed much encouragement to pet and kiss her.

'Honor, you've made me so very happy,' he told her. 'It's as though life has taken a new turn for us all. The future looks so much brighter. I can hardly believe you've agreed to be my wife.'

'I have, and I'm thrilled that you want us to be married,' she told him. 'I love you very much.'

He smiled. 'You make me feel twenty years old again. This morning, I'd like you to come and choose your engagement ring. We can't do it while the shop's open: everybody would be watching and speculating about us.'

'Yes,' Honor said. 'This morning's a good time, because Jane's away too. We'll have the place to ourselves.'

They were almost ready to leave when Kitty came downstairs in her dressing gown and slippers. As she knew he was here, Honor had not expected her to put in an appearance.

'Good morning,' Kitty said to him as though it was the most natural thing in the world to see a strange man at the breakfast table. Edwin, poor lamb, looked a little embarrassed, but he made a big effort to seem at ease.

'Hello, Kitty. Are you looking forward to starting at commercial college?'

'Very much. I know I'm going to love it. I can't wait for September.' She pushed two slices of bread in the toaster and switched it on.

'Good. Get those exams under your belt and I think you'll find it helps when you start job-hunting.'

'I'm sure it will.' After a slight pause she looked up and smiled at him. 'Thank you for making it possible. I'm very grateful.'

Honor was glad to see her daughter on her best behaviour. She was afraid Kitty hadn't been going to school recently. She'd denied she was truanting, but Honor wasn't sure she was telling the truth. She hoped Kitty would find the college more to her liking.

On the journey into town, Edwin remarked on Kitty's good manners while Honor sat back and enjoyed the ride. It was a treat when usually she had to travel by bus. She wondered if one day she might learn to drive and persuade him to buy her a car of her own.

They entered through the back door as she did every morning when she arrived for work, but today the shop wasn't going to open. Something much more exciting was about to happen. She followed him up to his office. Honor had been here many times, but this was very different. She was tingling with anticipation as she watched him take out his bunch of keys and unlock the great safe. She craned to see inside it. She was about to get her reward for all the effort she'd made to improve her lot. She was going to choose her first piece of expensive jewellery.

'What sort of ring would you like?' He turned to smile at her. 'Have you given it any thought?'

'You haven't allowed me much time for thought.' She laughed, though in fact she'd been turning it over in her mind since she'd stood outside with Kitty on that bleak Christmas Eve two and a half years ago.

'I've rushed you?'

She shook her head and let her eyes flirt with his. It had taken a good bit of push on her part.

'I think you proposed in a very romantic way.' Honor knew she'd be given more if she didn't appear grasping. 'I shall be proud to wear whichever ring you give me.' She believed him to be generous and knew his stock was all of high quality. She knew it was safe to say that.

'I've brought you to choose. I want you to have a ring you really like.' It was what she'd hoped he would say. 'You must be familiar with my stock by now. Do you not have a favourite? You must have a preference for one gemstone over another?'

'Yes,' Honor admitted. 'I do, but I couldn't possibly . . . No, that would be over-extravagant. Far too expensive.'

He dropped a kiss on her nose. 'I want you to have

the best,' he said. 'I deal in engagement rings, after all. Don't forget they all come to me at wholesale prices.'

Honor decided to go for it. 'Then what I've admired beyond any other I've ever seen are those deep yellow diamonds you keep locked in that display case on the end of the counter.'

'Do you mean the Sun Diamonds? Oh, my dear!'

Honor could see from his face that he was shocked. The girls spoke of the Sun Diamonds with bated breath, but Honor was in the habit of asking for what she wanted and very often she got it.

He took the large shagreen case from his safe and opened it up on the end of his desk. The rich orange-yellow diamonds sparkled up at her. Honor put out her hand to bring them nearer, but he caught it between both his own and caressed it.

'I don't want you to touch them,' he said, and he told her all the stories about the Sun Diamonds. 'I don't want them to bring you bad luck,' he finished.

Honor felt she'd had more than her share of bad luck already and she didn't believe in myths and fairy tales. They were tantalisingly close and she'd have loved to try them on.

'I'd forgotten there was a matching necklace and earrings and not just a ring,' she murmured. 'Of course, the set mustn't be broken.' She hadn't, of course, she'd hoped to get them all.

'Actually, they belonged to Jane's mother and one day they'll be Jane's. But because they're very ornate for modern tastes and because of the stories about ill luck, I decided it would be wiser to sell them and give her the money instead.'

Jane was richer than Honor had supposed. 'And that's why they're on show in the shop?'

'Yes, but they've proved difficult to sell. I thought I had a customer for them last month. He opened negotiations on the price, but they dragged on and collapsed only yesterday. They're too expensive for Liverpool. I should consider sending them down to Sotheby's.' He closed the lid and snapped the catch on. 'I'm afraid I have no other fancy vivid yellows here. The demand is for clear transparent stones. I could perhaps see what the wholesalers have, and order a ring with a coloured diamond for you.'

'No, Edwin, thank you.' Honor put her hand on top of his. She wanted to have her ring now. 'I'm very fond of transparent diamonds too.'

He took a black velvet cloth from his desk drawer and started bringing out trays of sparkling rings from his safe.

'I'm almost overcome,' Honor murmured. 'They're so beautiful.'

'Let's have your hand.' He slid a large diamond solitaire on her third finger. 'This is a nice ring. It's a three point two carat brilliant-cut. Do you like it?'

It was scintillating light rays in all directions. 'It's gorgeous.'

'The band is eighteen-carat gold with platinum

shoulders. I have a very similar one that's all platinum, if you prefer that.' He put it on the black cloth in front of her. 'Or you could have three stones.'

'No.' She'd gathered that one large stone cost more than three smaller ones even if the total carat size was greater. 'No thank you. I'd prefer a solitaire.'

'Or I have stones cut in fancy shapes. Here's a pear-shaped one.'

'I think I like this one you've put on my finger.'

'The brilliant-cut on a gold band?'

'It's truly beautiful.' The sort of ring only a rich man could afford for his fiancée, even if it didn't have the life, colour and sparkle of the Sun Diamonds.

'A wise choice, my dear. Will you wear it now?'

'I think I ought to take my wedding ring off when I wear your diamond.' She slid it into her handbag. 'But I won't wear your ring to work just yet. It will attract too much attention.'

He caught both her hands in his. 'I was about to ask you not to.'

'Aren't we a pair of . . .'

'Only to save the feelings of others, my dear. I'd really like you to choose something else. I see you have pierced ears. I have some very nice diamond earrings that would go very well with that ring.'

'You are so generous . . .'

He put the rings away and brought out a tray of earrings. 'Do you prefer studs or drops?'

'They're all so beautiful it takes my breath away.'

'Studs,' he said. 'Then you can wear them every day. The danglers are for parties and special occasions.'

Honor smiled and removed her imitation pearls. 'Studs then, please. I won't want to leave them at home in a drawer.'

He kissed her ears and fixed the diamonds in for her. 'You have such pretty ears.'

On the way downstairs she showed interest in a lizard handbag on the shelf on the first floor, and he gave her that too. He cut off the price tag, but she knew to a penny how much it cost – she'd admired it only yesterday. She removed the tissue paper inside and hung the bag on her arm. He was giving her these lovely things gladly, almost encouraging her to ask for more. She'd got Edwin Jardine exactly where she wanted him.

'Perhaps a spot of lunch now?' he suggested. 'We'll go to the Exchange Hotel and have a bottle of champagne to celebrate. We're not likely to see anybody we know there.'

Not like the Adelphi, Honor thought. She'd have preferred to go there, but at the Exchange they had an elaborate and long-drawn-out meal that she very much enjoyed.

She felt triumphant when at five o'clock he drove her home. She knew he was expecting Jane and Nick back that evening.

*

From the sitting room window, Kitty watched Edwin Jardine drive off, with her mother waving from the passenger seat. Then she threw herself down on the sofa to have the tea and toast she'd made. She knew Jason had been working last night and would spend most of today catching up on his sleep. She meant to enjoy a lazy day at home by herself.

She tidied up her bedroom and had a long bath, then put her washing in the machine and settled down in front of the television. At four o'clock, she packed the soap impressions she'd made in a box and took the bus over to Jason's house.

She found him up and dressed when she arrived. 'How did you get on last night?'

'Fine. It went like clockwork, just as I said it would. That's a bit more to add to our getaway fund.'

'Enough for us to go?'

'No, not yet. Only enough to last for a year or so,' he said. 'Maybe a bit longer, especially as we'll get a camper to live in to start with, but then it'll run out just as it did for the parents.'

'Heaven forbid. That was an awful comedown.' Kitty giggled. 'I've got something to show you.' She brought out the soap impressions and told him how she'd come to make them. He studied them carefully.

'Good thinking on my part, wasn't it?' Kitty felt she deserved a pat on the back.

'Yes, you did well, but . . .'

'But what?'

'Some look perfect, but not all of them. This one has collapsed inwards. I'm a bit worried that keys cut from these may not turn in the locks. It's risky enough copying the key – doing it through soap makes it twice as dicey.'

'You mean they're no good?' Some of the wind was taken out of Kitty's sails. 'After all the trouble I took? I numbered them and wrote down what I thought each key would open.'

'I'll have them made up, of course, but I'd like the chance to try them before we do the job. To see if they'll work.'

'How are we going to do that?' Kitty could see no possibility.

'I don't know.' He smiled at her. 'Unless you ask your mother to—'

'No! She wouldn't anyway. She wants to butter the owner up, not see him robbed. I don't want her to know we're even thinking of it.'

Jason sighed. 'If only you could get hold of his key ring again so I could have another set made up direct from that. Otherwise . . . He's bound to have a spare set somewhere.'

'Yes, but how do we get our hands on that? If we can get inside his shop and take enough to survive on in Spain, then I think we should have a go,' Kitty said.

Jason was biting his lip in thought, but she could see he felt the same excitement she did. 'I could sell some of the jewellery and hide the rest in the camper to flog off later.'

'It would be like having money in the bank.' Kitty laughed. It would be marvellous to have the funds they needed but just to plan a job like this gave her a thrill. She knew Jason was even more hooked on thrills of this sort than she was.

'But we don't know if we can get into their safe,' he objected. 'It might be one that opens with a combination, and if it is we'd never get into it.'

'It opens with a key, I'm sure. I copied two keys with the name Chubb stamped on them. They make safes, don't they?'

'Yes, but some safes need both a combination and a key to open them.'

'Oh!'

'Your ma will probably know how the safe is opened. She works there, she's bound to.'

'I'm not going to ask her.'

'No, but you might be able to find out without asking direct questions. Get her to talk about her job.'

'She does sometimes,' Kitty said. 'Perhaps I'll try.'

'Good girl,' Jason said. 'Next time I take you home and we see Jardine's car on your drive, I'll wait outside to see if you can get hold of his keys again.'

But when he dropped her outside her house at ten o'clock that night, there was no car parked outside. The front-room light was showing round the curtains so Kitty knew her mother was still up. She went straight to the sitting room. Honor was relaxed on the pink Dralon sofa sipping a drink. She was slanting her left hand into the light to make her diamond flash fire.

'Ma! He's given you a ring!'

Kitty took hold of her hand to see it better. 'It's gorgeous.'

'A three point two carat diamond.'

'It's fantastic. Can I try it on?'

'No. He gave me these earrings too.' Honor lifted her blond hair away from the side of her head. 'Diamond studs, and each weighs one point six carats.'

Kitty laughed. 'Success at last! Congratulations. You said you could do it and you have. I'm thrilled for you.'

Honor laughed too. 'Really, he's a pushover, a real sugar daddy. He let me choose the ring I wanted, so I chose the biggest.'

'Lucky you.' Kitty knew this was the chance Jason had spoken of. Could she keep her talking? 'You went round the shop trying them all on?'

'No, he took me up to his office. Most of the stuff's put away in the safes when the shop's shut.'

'You mean there's more than one safe?'

'Yes, there're two. I told you, I have to help pack the stuff away every night and get it out again the next morning. The really expensive stuff is kept in the safe in his office.'

Kitty couldn't believe the ease with which she had her mother talking about the safes. 'Where's the other one?'

'In the ground-floor cloakroom, where we hang our coats, but it's hidden in a cupboard. The jewellery kept there is his less expensive range but it's still good stuff.'

Kitty could feel her cheeks burning. She'd never felt so alive, but she must be careful. She must ask the right questions and not let Ma suspect what she was doing.

'How exciting. I bet your mouth was watering as you watched him twiddle the knob on his safe putting in the combination. You have to listen for the clicks or something, don't you?'

'Oh, his safes aren't like that. They just lock with a key. They look like strong metal cupboards, though somebody told me they're bolted to the floor or the wall or something.'

'So his safes are not like the ones I've seen on telly? Not so exciting?'

'Exciting enough when he got his trays of rings out on his desk. He told me to pick the one I liked best. He wanted me to have an expensive one.'

'It's lovely. So you're engaged now?'

'Yes.'

'When will you be getting married?'

'Not yet. Our engagement is to be a secret for the moment. Edwin doesn't want to announce it until after Jane's wedding. The old girls at the shop are a gang of bitches. They'll be after my blood when they find out, and Jane will take their side.' Honor smiled. 'He wants her out of the way first.'

'Probably just as well for you. He's been jolly generous. Earrings as well.'

'Oh, that's not all, he gave me this lizard handbag too. It was priced at a hundred and thirty pounds. I sold one not very different the other day. It's not as though he has to buy it for me, is it? I don't suppose it means as much to him, when it's stock from his shop.'

Kitty went to bed well pleased with what she'd found out.

Earlier in the evening, Jane had taken Nick home with her. By then, they'd discussed their future from every angle, much of it with Nick's mother. As Jane and her father went most Sunday mornings to the service in St Cuthbert's, she wanted to be married there on a date in mid-September.

They found Edwin reading in his favourite armchair. After greeting them, he asked, 'How did the visit go?'

'Nick's mum made a real fuss of us,' Jane told him. 'She cooked us a lovely dinner.' She was filled with the joy of being engaged, and knew Nick was even more thrilled. 'We had roast pheasant and a bottle of champagne.'

Nick said, smiling at Jane, 'Mother's glad I'm ready to settle down and she very much approves of my bride to be.'

Her father was beaming at them. Jane could feel him simmering with pleasure.

'Everybody seems so pleased for us,' she said.

'Madeleine wanted to provide my engagement ring, but . . .'

He laughed. 'You told her that providing the ring was going to be my pleasure?'

'No, I didn't. I told her I was being offered an embarrassing number of engagement rings. I hope I didn't upset her.'

'You didn't,' said Nick. 'You're all being kind and trying to save me the expense.'

Jane said, 'I've been thinking, Dad. I'd like to wear the ring you gave my mother when you got engaged.'

She could see he was pleased. 'That will be yours when you're twenty-one anyway.'

'Yes, you told me. But it seems right somehow, doesn't it? To wear it as my engagement ring?'

'It's a lovely thought, Jane. Why don't we go downstairs and get it now?' She could see emotional tears brimming in her dad's eyes.

CHAPTER TWENTY-ONE

THE NEXT morning Jane was down in the shop before her father, showing off her sapphire and diamond engagement ring to the girls as they came in to work. They went into raptures when they saw it and heard that it had been her mother's. Nowadays, her father trusted her to open up the safes in the mornings. She and Dorothy Hadley went to his office together and carried the stock down to the shop to set it out. Jane was giving a tray of sumptuous diamond engagement rings pride of place in the main window when she heard Dorothy's gasp of horror.

'What's the matter?'

'There's a ring missing from this tray.' It was one of Edwin's rules that when they sold a ring from a display tray they immediately withdrew another from stock to replace it.

'Oh, heck!' Jane's mouth went suddenly dry as she stared at the empty slot in the black velvet. 'Those are our most expensive ones.'

Dorothy's voice was shocked. 'Have I dropped it? Is it here? Can you see it?'

Jane looked minutely over every inch of the window. They walked back to the counter together to where they'd rested the trays. 'It shouldn't be difficult to see against this dark carpet.'

'Could it have fallen out of the slot? It's never happened before.'

'We'd better go back and take a look in the safe.'

'And on the stairs.' Dorothy sounded frantic.

Jane ran upstairs, raking every step with panic-stricken eyes, Dorothy panting behind her. When they reached the office her father was at his desk, calm and benign.

'Good morning, Miss Hadley.' He smiled at them.

Dorothy went directly to the safe. 'It's not here,' she said after a moment, straightening up.

Jane said, 'Dad, there's a ring missing.' She pushed the black velvet display tray with its empty slot in front of him. 'It can't have been stolen,' she said, 'but where could it have gone?'

The expression on his face changed before her eyes. 'It's all right, don't worry.' He looked flushed. 'You must blame me. I took a ring out and forgot to replace it with another.'

'You intended to give it to me? And then I said I'd prefer Mother's ring.'

He didn't answer, and the scarlet tide rushing up his neck and cheeks was deepening to crimson.

'No.' He was painfully embarrassed, and having difficulty getting the words out. 'Well, you'll have to know now, I suppose. I've given it to Mrs Thorpe.'

Jane felt paralysed. She knew her mouth had fallen open.

Dorothy gave another of her shocked and very audible gasps. 'It was a traditional engagement ring,' she said.

'Miss Hadley.' Edwin sounded breathless. 'I'd be obliged . . . Please be good enough to make sure the stock is being set out properly down below.'

'Yes. I'm sorry, Mr Jardine.' Dorothy's face was as red as his as she stumbled out of the room.

Jane was still trying to pull herself together when he said, 'We meant to keep it quiet so as not to steal your thunder. I'm sorry it had to come out like that. Oh, dear, now Miss Hadley knows. It'll be all round the shop in no time.'

Jane was appalled. 'You're engaged to Mrs Thorpe? You asked her to marry you?'

'Yes.' His dark eyes struggled to meet hers. 'I was afraid you wouldn't approve.'

Jane stood sucking her lip. There was a lot she wanted to say but she knew it could only make matters worse. The news certainly racheted up the pressure. It was now urgent to find out more about Honor Thorpe.

He said gently, 'I'm going to lose you soon. It's only right that you get married but then I'll be on my own and lonely. Can't you understand, Jane, that I need somebody too?'

'Yes, but I don't think Mrs Thorpe is the right person to make you happy.'

'Jane! I allow you to make your own choice of a spouse. You must allow me the same freedom.'

'I'm sorry, Dad.'

'Being older and wiser, I'd say I was better qualified than you to choose the right person. I know you love Nick. Don't you believe I have the same feelings for Mrs Thorpe?'

His eyes met hers again, begging for understanding, but she had to tell him honestly what she felt.

'I know Nick loves me, Dad, but I'm worried about what Mrs Thorpe's feelings are. I'm afraid she only pretends to love you.'

'Now, Jane.' She could hear the vexation in his voice. 'You've taken against her for no reason I can see. This isn't like—'

'Hear me out, Dad. I'm suspicious of her, yes. So are all the girls in the shop. She doesn't act in the way they do; she's really quite odd. I told you, didn't I, that she ran and hid when a couple came in the shop to buy a trophy for a golf club? I'm sure she knew them and they her, and she didn't want to talk to them.'

'Yes, you told me at the time, but I can't see that it has anything to do with me.'

'I believe it does. I wanted you to ring them and ask about her. How they knew her.'

'I can't just ring up people I don't know and ask questions like that.' She could tell he was getting impatient with her.

'Dad, you employed her without taking up any references. Surely it wouldn't be improper to write and ask for one now?'

'It would look as though I'm not satisfied with her work. She's been here for over a year and everybody agrees she's efficient and courteous and a good worker.'

'Then let me do it. I could write to the manager of that golf club on behalf of the firm, and ask if he knows her . . .'

He sat down. She knew he was losing patience with her. 'No, Jane. It would look as though I don't trust her.'

Jane felt rebellious, and wondered if she should write to the golf club anyway. 'But do you trust her?'

'Yes, of course I do.'

'Well I don't.'

She couldn't believe Honor Thorpe had fallen madly in love with her father. He needed to be protected from her, unless . . .

Jane was overcome with misgivings. Could she and the girls be getting it wrong? That was the awful part: she couldn't be sure she wasn't making a fuss about nothing. People could be a bit odd and still be honest citizens. And everybody could fall in love.

By morning break, all the staff knew Honor Thorpe had ensnared Mr Jardine. Everybody had looked to see if she was wearing the ring and had to agree that she was not. Nobody mentioned it to her, let alone congratulated her, but they were up in arms and had plenty to say about it to each other.

Miss Pinfold said, 'Mr Jardine's too kind and gentlemanly for his own good. We only have to ask for a day off or a longer lunch hour and he lets us have it.'

Miss Jessop said, 'Honor Thorpe's a seductress. She's out to feather her own nest. It's money she's after.' They couldn't stop speculating about when the marriage would take place. They were all dreading it; the shop would never be the same once she became Mrs Jardine.

'She'll want to run the place,' Pam Kenny said. 'It'll give her the upper hand and she'll lord it over us.'

'And my dad too,' Jane put in.

'She'll suck him dry.'

One by one they brought up the sins they'd known Mrs Thorpe to commit, the fact that she was obsessional about trying items on, and the matter of the jet brooch.

While Mrs Thorpe was still serving down on the ground floor at first break, Miss Jessop was particularly vocal about the way she'd ingratiated herself with Mr Jardine.

'And look what it's doing now,' Dorothy Hadley exclaimed. 'We should all be glad for Jane and congratulating her, and instead here we are sounding off because Mrs Thorpe has got herself engaged to the boss. We really are delighted for you and Nick, Jane. We're sure you'll be very happy, but we're worried about your father.'

Jane told them about trying to discover if the late Mr Thorpe had ever existed, and finding no proof that he had. 'But as Nick said, it doesn't prove that he didn't.'

Miss Hadley said, 'I wish the Law Society would reply to our letter. If only we knew for sure whether she'd lied about her husband being a solicitor.'

'I wasted time,' Jane lamented. 'I should have got down to it sooner.'

'How long d'you think it'll take them?'

'There's no way of knowing, is there? Or even if they'll tell us what we want to know.'

Miss Pinfold said, 'There must be something else we can do.'

It was a comfort to Jane to have them all in solid agreement with her.

They all remembered the couple who'd come in to choose a golf trophy. Jane said she'd suggested to her father that she should write to the Woolton Park Golf Club to ask if Mrs Thorpe was known there, but he'd told her not to.

'I'm wondering if I should do it anyway,' she said. But they sucked in their cheeks and said better not if her father had said no.

Only Pam Kenny came up with a helpful idea. Her boyfriend was in the Liverpool police.

'If you think she could have been pilfering from the

golf club, I could ask Wayne to find out if she's got a criminal record.'

They all urged her to do that. 'That would be a good thing to check on,' Miss Pinfold said firmly. 'I'll copy her full name, present address and date of birth from her file. Now she's officially engaged to Mr Jardine, we've got to find out if she's hiding anything.'

Kitty had not been near her school for two weeks. Now it had broken up for the summer holidays, and she need never darken its doors again. It was good riddance to bad rubbish. Ma had taken her to see the principal of the secretarial college. She'd been told a place had been reserved for her starting at the beginning of the new term on 9 September, but she wouldn't bother to go. She hoped to be on her way to Spain before then or, if not, at least shortly afterwards.

It was late evening, and Kitty and Jason were upstairs lying on his bed when the phone rang in the hall.

'Let it wait,' he said, but it rang and rang through the house, distracting him. He gave up and pushed himself away from Kitty just as it stopped.

'Could that have been your father?'

'No. Everything runs to a strict timetable in prison. It's too late for him.' Gary was now allowed limited phone calls which he had to make between six and seven thirty in the evening. Jason pulled Kitty closer and bent to kiss her, and the phone started ringing again.

'Hell! Who can this be?' He rolled off the bed, pulled the counterpane with him, and wrapped it round his naked body as he ran for the stairs.

Kitty lay back and listened, but she was too far away to hear what Jason said. He'd been relaxed and amorous moments ago, but now his voice was suddenly angry. She knew he worked with a circle of accomplices, and was in constant touch both with them and with the people who wanted his services. She was afraid a job might have gone wrong.

He came back looking very put out. Jason didn't often swear, but he let out a string of expletives. She raised herself up on her elbow.

'What's that for?'

'Pa's got his discharge date. It's August the nineteenth.'

'That's not far off.'

'Too damn close for comfort.'

Kitty was dreading Gary's release from prison, because they'd no longer have this house to themselves and their comfortable way of life would have to change. She knew that bothered Jason too, but he had other reasons for wishing the day would never come.

He'd told her that before Gary went to prison he'd been saving money from the jobs he was doing without telling Hilda. He'd wanted to keep control of it as he thought she spent extravagantly on things for herself. So he'd hidden his little haul under the corner of the carpet in a spare bedroom and doled it out sparingly for household necessities.

Jason had seen him add to his hoard one night, and once his father was in prison he'd used some of it to buy his MG and keep himself afloat. He could pay it back now and had intended to, but if he was going to leave for Spain quite soon he'd need to take everything he had for himself and Kitty.

'When we've set up our water sports business and start raking in the cash, I'll think about repaying him. But that won't please Pa. He'll want his money now, if he's coming out of prison.'

'He can't complain,' Kitty assured him. 'You've kept this house on so he'll have a home to come back to, and you're leaving him the MG. He'll get the car if he doesn't get his money.'

'He sees the house as his anyway – it's his name on the rent book – and since he left me his Ford the car will only be tit for tat. We've got to get away before Pa realises his little hoard has gone, and we don't want him to know we're off to Spain. Anyway, he'll expect to rule the roost here again.'

'Is that why you're in a rage?'

'He was in a rage. He couldn't get me earlier and had to ask for special permission to ring now.'

'We were out.' They'd had a meal at the Horse and Hounds. They often did; it was less trouble than cooking at home.

'Damn Pa. He was cross because I didn't visit

yesterday. I know it's only once a month but I had something I had to do and I hate going there anyway. Walton jail gives me the jitters.'

'It's meant to. You can't expect the place to look like a hotel.'

'Gosh, Kitten, he'll be out before we know it. Where's the calendar?'

Pulling the counterpane closer, he went downstairs to look at it.

On his return he was aghast. 'It's five weeks on Monday. He said, in his bossy way, "They let us out early in the morning. I want you to come and collect me." I had to say I would.'

'I bet he's dying to get out.'

'It doesn't give us much time, Kitten. I mean, we've talked about our plans but we've done nothing. We'd better get started. We need to be out of here as soon as we can.'

Kitty was not displeased. At last things were about to happen for her.

'Just to think of him coming out gives me the willies. He'll expect to be cut in on all my deals, but my mates are against it. They don't want to work with him. After the debacle that landed him and some of the gang in jail what else can he expect? They see him as trouble. We've got to get away.'

'Have you saved enough cash?'

'I'd like more, but there's still five more working weeks. It'll have to be enough then.'

They'd been talking of buying a camper van for months, and had pored over camping magazines and brochures studying the layout of different models.

'Tomorrow, we'll go and look at the real thing,' Jason said. 'There's a big company out on the East Lancs Road that sells both new and second-hand. We don't want it to be too big. The roads through most Spanish villages are very narrow.'

'Not too small either,' Kitty said. 'We'll be living in it.' She was excited. 'It'll be our first little home together. I'm really looking forward to this.'

'I want you to come with me to choose it,' Jason said. She laughed. 'Try and stop me. It'll be fun.'

They saw three or four nearly new campers and made their choice. Kitty was thrilled with the dinky bathroom and the tiny fridge and cooker, and most of all with the idea that they could drive away from here and find a new life touring the Continent. They took delivery ten days later. Jason arranged to park it behind a nearby petrol station which belonged to a man with whom he sometimes did business.

'There's plenty of space for it alongside your garage,' Kitty pointed out. 'It would be more convenient there. We'll need to pack our stuff in and fit it up with pots and pans and bedding and things.'

'I want it out of sight and it's too high to get under the garage door,' he said. 'We don't want the whole world to know we're about to take off, do we?'

They needed lots of things to equip it. They went

round the house collecting together bedding and kitchen utensils, and stored them ready in their garage. They made lists and bought basic tinned foods.

'Only three and a half more weeks till we go,' Kitty marvelled. She'd decided on the clothes she wanted to take and made up her mind to pinch her mother's ruby on the day they were leaving. She felt ready to set off now.

'There's still a lot to get ready,' Jason told her, poring over the books of maps he'd bought. 'I need to get a route worked out and book a Channel crossing. And really, we've never tried out this camper and we should.'

'Yes, so we can test the shower and the fire and the cooker and make sure we've got everything we need,' Kitty said.

'How about a night or two in the Lake District?'

'Marvellous.'

'I'd like to drive it to get the feel of the thing before we set off.'

'Next weekend?'

'No, I've got a job on. I can't put that off. The following weekend too. To be honest, we could do with more cash than we're going to get.'

'Are we going to do Jardine's? That would give us plenty.' Kitty was keen. She would be in on it, and it would allow her to sample Jason's more exciting life.

'I'd love to, but the keys are a bit iffy. If only you could get your hands on the originals again.'

'Yes, but time's getting short.'

'If your ma would just try our keys in the locks we'd know one way or the other. I mean, she's working there every day.'

'No,' Kitty said. 'I can't ask her. She wouldn't anyway.'

He bit at his lip. 'OK, then let's go to Windermere in the middle of next week. Tuesday and Wednesday, is that all right with you?'

'Any time will suit me.' She giggled. 'This is going to be great.'

'We'll buy the food to take with us on Monday and take off first thing on Tuesday morning. Can you stay with me on Monday night?'

'You bet. Now Ma knows she's failed to part us, I shall just tell her I'm staying with you. She won't like it, but it doesn't matter any longer, does it?'

He was anxious. 'You haven't told her about the camper and that we're going back to Spain?'

'No, course not. Not a word.'

'Good. Let's keep our plans secret.' Jason smiled. 'If things go wrong they won't know where we've gone, and they certainly won't be watching campsites.'

'You think of everything.'

'To be safe we have to think ahead.'

Kitty was scared. She'd been telling herself not to panic for the last week and trying not to think about it. She was overdue. This had never happened before – well, a day or two perhaps, but never a whole week.

She had to face the facts. Building up within her like a stone wall with glass embedded on the top was the fear that she was pregnant. She knew it was more than possible and it was no good trying to kid herself she wasn't.

Ma had warned her it could happen. Jason had sworn he'd always be careful but it looked as though he'd slipped up somewhere. She told him when he came to pick her up the following Monday that she was overdue.

'Christ!' he said. 'That's all we need right now. Just when we're getting ready to scarper. Are you sure?'

'No, I'm not sure. It's too soon to be sure.'

'So what do we do?'

'What can we do but wait and see?'

He said through gritted teeth, 'Keep our fingers crossed and hope it's a false alarm.'

'Don't you want a baby?'

'Not right now, no. Do you?'

'Oh gosh, Jason, no, course I don't.'

'You could have an abortion, couldn't you?' Jason was staring straight ahead through the windscreen.

Kitty could feel her stomach beginning to churn. Yes, she'd had her dream for the future: living in a large villa overlooking the sea in Spain, married to Jason who was making a huge success of his boating business, having two small children and a nanny. But now was totally the wrong time to be pregnant. Just thinking she could be was enough to bring her out in a cold sweat.

'Fixing up to have an abortion will take time. And I can't even think about that until I'm sure, can I?'

'And after that you'd have to wait to see the doctor, then wait for an appointment at the clinic, wait for this and wait for that.' Jason sounded impatient. 'We can't wait. We've got the camper van ready and I've booked our Channel crossing.'

'But what if I am pregnant?'

'Babies can be born in Spain, and anyway that's way off in the future. What if you're not pregnant? We'll have let a marvellous chance slip away and Pa will be giving me stick.'

'If I am, Ma will play hell with me.'

'Kitten, you've got to make up your mind whether you're coming or not.'

She swallowed hard. 'I'm coming,' she said. 'I've had enough of Liverpool, and Ma too.'

'Good. We've both got good reasons to get away, then. Don't worry about it now.'

Instead, Kitty made herself think about what she saw as a mini-holiday in the Lake District. They watched the weather forecast on television that night and learned that rain would spread in from the west the next day. Tuesday turned out to be a dry but grey morning, and they were both in good spirits as they set off.

Jason was thrilled with the van. 'Handles well,' he said. 'I'll have no trouble driving this.'

'I want to have a go,' Kitty said.

'When we get there.'

It was not a long drive to Lake Windermere but the day was growing darker. It was raining before they arrived and they could see little of the fine scenery because the hills were shrouded in heavy mist. Nor was it easy to find the campsite where they'd intended to stay. After driving around fruitlessly for a while, they saw a road sign advertising a nearby site and booked into that instead. It was in a rather muddy field behind a country pub and there were half a dozen other campers and caravans already there.

'Handy,' Jason said. 'We can have a drink in the bar tonight.'

A very elderly man from the next caravan showed them how to open their gas bottle and attach it to the piping in order to light the stove. Kitty fried sausage and eggs in the new frying pan for their lunch. By then the rain was coming down in sheets and the field was being churned into a muddy morass.

Afterwards, Kitty said, 'I want to go out to see the sights and try driving this camper.' Jason had his feet up and looked as though he wanted a nap, but he agreed.

Kitty could feel the van sliding in the mud but she managed to get it out on to the road and into a car park in the town. The vehicle seemed enormous after the little MG.

Jason said, 'It isn't much fun walking round in the wet. Come on, let's cheer ourselves up with tea and cream cakes.' He led her into a little café. Afterwards, they could have had a boat trip on the lake. Kitty suggested they do it but in the driving rain it didn't appeal to Jason.

They went back to their site and spent the evening in the bar drinking and having a pub meal. The rain never did stop, and it was still wet the next morning. They decided to go straight home.

'Not a huge success as a holiday,' Jason said, 'but the camper van will be fine in hot weather.'

'When we get used to it,' Kitty added. 'And we now know we really do need a hundred and one more things.'

Jason started to recite the list he'd made: waterproofs, a book of continental campsites, a decent torch, a tin opener . . .

CHAPTER TWENTY-TWO

JASON DROPPED Kitty in Queen's Drive on Wednesday afternoon. He had arranged to do a job that night, and another with a different partner on Thursday night. 'Also, I need to take some stuff to a man in Manchester. I'll go Friday lunch time, and then I've got another job on Friday night.'

'You're doing a lot,' Kitty told him.

'I need to. Only two more weeks and Pa'll be out. Two weeks next Monday.'

'Will we have enough cash by then?'

'Not as much as I'd hoped, but we won't be hanging about after that.'

'If we did Jardine's, we would have.'

Kitty knew her mother wouldn't yet be home from work. She'd been cross at breakfast time on Monday when Kitty had told her she was going to spend a couple of nights with Jason. But Ma could like it or lump it because she and Jason would soon be together for good. She looked in the fridge, thinking she might butter her mother up by cooking a meal. She found four small lamb chops there and hesitated. Had Ma planned to cook supper for Edwin Jardine?

No, surely not. Kitty had told her she'd be back this afternoon. Ma must have bought them as a peace offering, because she'd been so nasty to her on Monday morning. Kitty set about preparing the meal and tried not to think about having a baby. She was worried stiff; every passing day was making it more certain. No way could she tell her mother: she'd have a fit. Hadn't she warned her and told her to take precautions? Kitty was scared, and wished now she'd taken more heed.

Honor came in, hung up her coat and sang out cheerfully, 'Hello, Kitty. Something smells nice.' She went into the sitting room and flopped down on the sofa.

'Hello, Ma. I'm cooking the chops.' She'd found a bottle of wine in the kitchen cupboard and opened it; she took a glass in to her mother, slid an arm round her neck and kissed her cheek. Ma was wearing her 3.2 carat diamond solitaire. 'How are things? The engagement's still on, I see.'

'The news is out at the shop.' Honor was all smiles as she wafted her hand backwards and forwards, making the diamond flash with life. 'The cats hate me. They'd like to claw me to death, but now of course they daren't. They know it would upset Edwin.' She laughed triumphantly. 'I've got them all where I want them.'

'Does Jane know too?'

'Yes.' Honor took a deep drink from her glass. 'This is by way of being a celebration. There's an ice cream cake in the freezer to follow.'

'So there's nothing to stop you getting married now?'

'I'm afraid there is. Jane loathes me even more than the girls do and Edwin wants to wait until she's out of the way. But he says we'll not have to wait long. Jane's wedding is fixed for September the eighteenth. All the Jardine shops are to be closed for the afternoon so the staff can go to the wedding.'

'Big deal. Are you really going to marry him?'

'I haven't made up my mind. I wish I knew whether Paul was dead or not.'

'Why would he be dead? He isn't all that old.'

'No, but it's eight years since he ran off with that barmaid and I've heard nothing of him since. He could be dead.'

'Or you could be a bigamist.'

'That's what bothers me.'

'Can't you get a divorce on the grounds of desertion?'

'I think I've read somewhere that I can go to a solicitor and have him legally presumed dead after seven years, but what if I'm wrong? And I'm scared to ask. It would ruin everything if Edwin heard of it. I might just keep my mouth shut and risk it. Why would Paul come back after all this time?'

'He won't be able to find you, Ma. You've moved enough times, haven't you? I'd forget him. D'you want more wine? I'm going to get myself a glass and help you celebrate. Now you and Edwin are engaged and Jane knows, he can come here whenever he likes.'

Her mother laughed. 'He came last night, because I knew you'd not be here.'

Kitty smiled. So that's why Ma was no longer mad with her for being away for two nights.

Honor said, 'He's invited me out to dinner tomorrow. It'll be somewhere posh.'

'Lucky you.'

'Will you be staying out all night?'

'No, Ma, I'll be in. Jason's got a job on.'

'Oh, God, Kitty, that feller's going to end up in trouble sooner or later. I wish you'd give him the push.'

'Jason's very careful and I like him. Don't you worry about us.'

'I have to. Look, there's something coming up – I want to ask Edwin to stay the night and give him a good time. Cook him a fancy meal first, and all that. I'd like you to stay out of the way; knowing you're in the next bedroom puts him off.'

'When's this to be?'

'It's two weeks on Saturday, the seventeenth of August. He says Jane has been invited to stay overnight with Nick's mother.'

'Again?'

'Yes. It's to meet Nick's relatives, an aunt and uncle,

who live in St Anne's. They're going on holiday to Minorca and flying from Manchester. When they do that, they usually spend a few days in Chester with Nick's mother. It's her older sister.'

Kitty felt a tremor of excitement. 'OK, if that's what you want, I'll stay out all that night.'

When they'd eaten, they settled down in front of the television, but Kitty couldn't concentrate. Her head was buzzing with the news that both Jane and her father would be out of their flat on the night of 17 August. As Gary would be out of prison the following Monday morning, it was all going to fit in very nicely. It thrilled her to picture herself and Jason creeping up those stairs in the dark. She couldn't wait to tell him but had to hang on until Saturday came round. She was in a fever of anticipation by then.

At lunch time, when she reached Menlove Avenue, he was still in bed asleep, and he wasn't easy to wake up. Kitty prodded him until he stirred.

'Ugh. It was four o'clock before I got to bed,' he said, rubbing his eyes. 'I was whacked. We had a busy night.'

Kitty lay down beside him fully dressed and pulled his eiderdown over her. 'But everything went all right?'

'Like clockwork.' He yawned.

'Well done. I've got some good news.' She told him that neither Jane nor her father would be at home on the night of the 17th. 'So we'll have a chance to get into Jardine's while there's nobody in the building.'

He was fully awake now. 'I'd decided to give Jardine's a miss.'

'Why?' She was affronted. 'After all the effort I put into those soap impressions?'

'I've got a lot of other jobs planned. Too many, really.'

'But if we do Jardine's it'll give us loads more cash, and you've already had my soap keys made up.'

Kitty felt exasperated. She wanted to help but felt she was being kept away from the action, as usual. She went on, 'I know you wanted a chance to try them first, but if there's nobody there . . . Didn't the fellow who made the keys say he thought they'd probably be all right?'

'He said they might be, but they're iffy. What if we can't open the safes?'

'From what Ma says, there's lots of expensive stuff that isn't locked away every night, silver and leather and that. And if there's nobody in the building we'll be able to take our time.'

He lay back in silence.

'Jason, either we get in and open the safes or we don't, but it's worth a try.'

'I suppose it is,' he said.

'Of course it is. If our luck's in, it'll give us loads of extra money. Enough to last for years.'

'Things are getting on top of me.' Jason sighed. 'Time's getting short now.'

'Yes, only two more weeks. The pressure's building

up. Make Jardine's your last job. We'll have a rest and a good holiday once we get away.'

'All right. We'll give it a go,' he said.

It was Honor's mid-week day off and she liked to relax and take things easy. She got up late, took a bath and got dressed ready to go out. She'd decided to spend the day in town and treat herself to some new clothes. She was boiling an egg and making toast in the kitchen when she heard a news flash on the local radio station. There'd been a murder in the Tuebrook area of Liverpool last night. It sounded a particularly gruesome one, and she stopped to listen.

'A woman was found lying on the floor of her flat having received horrific injuries. With her was the body of her eighteen-month-old baby girl who had been battered to death. The woman's cries were heard in the next flat and a young couple had rung the police before going to see if they could help. By that time, they found the front door ajar and the attacker gone. The woman is now in hospital fighting for her life.'

Honor had seen violence at first hand during her life and hated to think of it. She went to switch off but the news was over and Abba had started belting out 'Waterloo' which was very much to her taste. Later on, walking round town in the afternoon, she saw the story featured on newspaper placards. On the way home she bought a *Liverpool Echo* and the story appeared prominently on the front page.

She took it home and spread the paper out on her worktops to read more about the case.

The mother, Sharon Burke, aged 26, has not yet recovered consciousness. She is suffering from head injuries and several other fractures, having been kicked after she'd fallen to the floor.

There was a photograph of her taken some weeks earlier, in which she was laughing up at Millie, her baby girl. Honor studied it. She didn't know them or even the part of the city in which they'd lived, but gruesome though they were she found the new details compelling. She read on.

Her boyfriend, Paul Thorpe, aged 38, an unemployed barman, had been living with them at the same address. He is being asked to come forward to help the police with their inquiries.

Honor broke off, feeling suddenly sick. Paul Thorpe? Oh, my goodness! Could this be her husband, the man she'd married to give Kitty a father? He could have battered her to death! She counted up on her fingers . . . yes, he'd be thirty-eight now. She was shaking as she read it all through again and wished there was a photograph of the man so she could be sure. Now she thought about it, even in her day he'd been rough with Kitty at times, and very ready to put his fists up and brawl. Not that he'd been a barman then; he'd mostly been unemployed.

Honor poured herself a gin and tonic to calm her nerves. How was this going to affect her? Well, if it was the same man, she wasn't a widow, not yet. But this Paul Thorpe wasn't going to be on the loose for much longer by the sound of things. Could this harm her standing with Edwin Jardine?

No. She told herself she was worrying for nothing, but it didn't ease her raw nerves. The man she'd married was called Paul Leonard Thorpe, but she'd referred to him only as Leonard to Edwin and the girls. Thorpe was not a common name but it was not that rare either – there must be hundreds of Thorpes living in Liverpool. There'd been no hint that he had a wife, and he was living with this woman as her boyfriend. Surely she must be safe from being linked with him?

After all these years, it was a shock to find out he was still in Liverpool and probably a murderer. She wished the police would hurry up and find him, then lock him up so she'd never come face to face with him. But at the moment he was on the run. It was a comfort to know half Liverpool would be at his heels.

On Saturday morning, Jane was down in the shop setting out the jewellery when Pam Kenny came in looking glum. She took Jane aside.

'No luck,' she whispered. 'Wayne has looked through the files and he's found nothing. He says Honor Sarah Thorpe appears to be an honest citizen.'

And if that wasn't bad enough, there was a reply from the Law Society in the morning's post.

We are sorry, but a name without other particulars is not sufficient to enable us to pinpoint a member on our professional lists.

As a minimum, we would need to know his qualifications and the date on which he became qualified to practise.

We very much regret that we are unable to help you.

Jane was depressed. It was beginning to seem impossible to turn up any proof that Mrs Thorpe was anything but what she claimed. By morning tea break all the girls knew, and were commiserating with her. Mrs Thorpe sat on her own at the end of the table. She was now wearing her engagement ring and the magnificent diamond flashed sparks of light round the room, showing them all her growing power here. Dorothy Hadley had pinned her hopes on Pam Kenny's boyfriend's turning something up and was very cast down.

'Everything's going her way,' she said. 'There must be something we can do to stop her.'

'But what?' everyone asked.

The arrangements for her own wedding were also occupying Jane's attention, particularly the question of where she and Nick would live afterwards. When she tried to talk to Dad about it, he couldn't decide on anything. His mind seemed to be more on Honor, possibly on where *they* would live when they were married. Of course, that did complicate things, but no date had been set for them, whereas for her and Nick time was getting short. They'd talked the subject through inside out and back to front.

There were several options. Nick could just move in with them – there was enough space in her room for a double bed and that would be all that was needed, but it was the option they liked least. She and Nick wanted a place of their own. Perhaps Sam could move in with Dad for a few weeks? They'd always been good friends, and it would free up the Crosby flat for her and Nick. Or did Dad expect to move in with Honor?

Nick felt they should start looking for a flat for themselves, but they could only afford to rent. Jane wanted to know what Dad's plans were before they did anything, but she was finding it difficult to pin him down.

The girls were keen to hear every detail of her wedding plans and had their own ideas about how they could help.

'We are going to make your wedding cake,' Dorothy told her. 'It's to be a joint project. I'm organising it.'

Jane smiled. 'Can I help? You taught me cake decorating too.'

'No, you've enough to do. I know what each of the girls is capable of.'

'Dare I ask? Is it to be a three-tier cake? That would be lovely.'

'Better than that. It's going to be the largest and most ambitious wedding cake I've ever worked on. Five tiers.'

'Wow, it'll be magnificent!'

'We hope so. We've got the five tins in related sizes and we're baking the cakes this Sunday. Rich fruit cake would improve if it was kept longer, but that can't be helped. Five of us will be baking them, each to her own recipe. We all swear by our own.'

'Of course.'

'I'm designing the decorations so it'll look like one cake when it's finished. I've got the stand and the pillars to build the tiers up one on the other.'

'It's going to be lovely.'

'What about the colour scheme? Have you decided what colour your bridesmaid's dresses will be?'

'Not yet. I'm only having one, Pam Kenny. I'll be taking her out to choose it next week.'

'We're all getting quite excited about it,' Dorothy said.

Jane knew she was too.

Honor was aware that over the next few days the hunt for baby Millie Burke's killer had gripped the nation. The story had made the national newspapers and was being reported in news broadcasts.

She held her cup of tea in an iron grip as she watched the television news. It was bringing her out in a cold sweat. Others as well as the young couple from the flat next door confirmed they'd seen Paul Thorpe at home the night of the murder. A full-scale search for him was going on and the public were warned he could be dangerous and must not be approached should they see him.

Honor had seen several photographs of the wanted man now and there was no doubt in her mind that he was her husband. Sightings of him were reported in Liverpool, Manchester, Birmingham and London but so far he'd managed to evade capture. Theories about what might have happened were discussed – he'd struck the child and when the mother tried to protect her he'd assaulted her too.

At the shop, the girls talked about it all the time, and Honor lived in dread that one of them might suggest the wanted man could be a relative or even her husband. She felt driven to buy a daily newspaper, and in one his name was given as Paul Leonard Thorpe. That brought a lump the size of a golf ball into her throat. She could think of nothing else. She felt sick and totally stressed out.

Jane was woken up just before midnight on Saturday night, by a commotion below in the street. Her bedroom was at the front and as it was a warm night her window was open. She was scared stiff when she heard a crash and the splintering of glass. It was followed by raucous laughs and yells of delight from late pub-crawlers. She leaped out of bed and looked out to see a small but noisy crowd gathering on the pavement five floors down. Hastily pulling on her dressing gown and slippers, she rushed to wake her father. She found he already had his light on and was out of bed.

Heading for the stairs, she called, 'Dad, I'm going to see—'

'No,' he shouted. 'No, don't go down there. It sounds as though they're drunk and I don't want you hurt. Just put on all the lights, so they know we're up and about, and hopefully they'll do no more damage. I'm going to ring the police.'

As Jane ran round switching on all their lights, there was another crash, more breaking glass and more excited yelling and screaming, but then the noise outside died down. Once downstairs, she could no longer see out on to the pavement. Her father sent her back upstairs and asked her to make some tea.

'We'll wait until the police get here,' he said. The police were ringing the outside bell five minutes later. In their opinion, it was the work of drunks. They found a brick and some empty beer bottles that had been thrown through one of the shop's main windows on Church Street. The plate glass was shattered but the grille had stopped them from getting into the showroom. Nothing had been stolen because the window had been cleared of stock, though some of the glass shelves had been damaged. Jane knew the insurance would cover the repairs.

The police gave them an all-hours emergency phone number for a firm who would come round and board up the window. Jane went to ring them.

When she returned, one of the police officers told them a fellow officer had been trained in measures to prevent thieves from breaking in. He suggested they have him assess the premises and make recommendations about their security. Her father jumped at the offer.

'How long is it since these grilles were installed?' he was asked.

'I can't remember, but it's many years. I think they date from when my father first handed the business over to me.'

'They did what they were meant to do tonight,' the officer told them. 'They prevented access to the shop, but nowadays there are more effective measures you can take. There are new and stronger locks, and they make electric shutters now that come down on the outside and hide all your windows and doors. If your plate glass can't be seen, you won't have drunks hurling their beer bottles at it.'

'Well, I certainly don't want a repeat of what happened tonight.'

'In a city centre area like this,' Jane said, 'I think we should update all our security measures. We often hear drunks singing outside, don't we?'

'I'd discuss it with your insurance company,' the officer said. 'You might well find your premiums are reduced if you have state of the art security.'

'Dad, would that also mean we don't have to strip out all the valuables from our windows? It would save such a lot of work.'

'Possibly, if it made the shop that much more secure. We'll look into it. You go back to bed,' Edwin said. 'I'll see the officers out.'

As he led the way down the stairs, he said, 'Two weeks tonight there'll be nobody in the building. Both my daughter and I will be away.' He hadn't told Jane that when she went to Chester, he meant to spend the night with Honor. 'I wonder, would you be kind enough to keep an eye on the place that night?'

'Yes, sir. I'll put your request to the night patrol. That's Saturday – what date will that be?'

'Saturday the seventeenth, just for one night.'

Early on Sunday morning, Honor went out to her nearest newsagent and found that almost all the newspapers featured the murder story on their front pages. Never before had she bought three different newspapers on one day, but she was desperate for news of her husband. The story had developed.

Paul Leonard Thorpe has been arrested and will appear in court tomorrow morning charged with the murder of his eighteen-month-old daughter, Millie, and with the attempted murder of the child's mother, Sharon Burke, aged 26, who is currently in intensive care fighting for her life.

Honor felt thoroughly shaken up. The news had really thrown her off balance. But Paul Thorpe would surely be detained in police custody now, and he had more to worry about than a wife he hadn't seen in eight years. She felt safer. She and Kitty had had a lucky escape. She'd been badly frightened but this hiccup need not affect her plans. If anybody asked her now if Paul Leonard Thorpe was her husband she'd deny it.

But she was worried too about what Kitty was up to. She'd hardly seen her in days.

CHAPTER TWENTY-THREE

B Y LUNCH TIME on Monday, Jardine's shop looked much as it always had. The plate glass had been replaced and a reduced amount of stock was being displayed on new shelves.

That morning, Jane had opened the post in the secretary's office and taken the letters she thought her father would want to see to his office.

'Miss Pinfold isn't in yet,' she said. Last week, she'd come in late once or twice.

Her father was sympathetic. 'Oh, dear, I'm afraid her mother is a big worry to her. Quite a burden for her to carry on her own. Fetch your pad, Jane. We can answer these letters now.'

Jane had written only one page of shorthand when the phone on his desk rang. Her father picked it up. 'Oh, Miss Pinfold, hello. Good morning.'

She knew from his face that he was hearing bad news. He said, 'You must take all the time off you need. Don't worry about us. Now you've trained Jane to do your job we can manage without you for a little while.'

Another silence during which her father bit his lip. 'It's a difficult time for you. I'll let the girls know, Miss Pinfold. We'll keep in touch, and if there's anything we can do to help, you must let me know.' He put the phone down with a heavy sigh.

'Her mother's ill again?' Jane asked.

'The doctor thinks she won't last much longer.'

'Poor Miss Pinfold.'

'Yes. It's the lot of the spinster daughter, isn't it? Her mother's ninety-eight now and has been quite a burden to her for the last few years, and there's no other family to help. Can you arrange to send her some flowers . . . No, don't, not yet. Tell the girls. Perhaps one of them would like to take her some from us all. She might welcome a chat with a friend.'

By morning tea break Pam Kenny had offered to buy the flowers in her lunch hour and most of the other girls had volunteered to take them. Miss Hadley decided she'd go. 'I'll call on my way home,' she said.

'Leave at four o'clock,' Edwin told her, 'so you have time to spend with her. Give her our good wishes.'

When she arrived on Miss Pinfold's doorstep, Dorothy had to ring the bell twice. She was reaching for the knocker when the door was suddenly opened and a pale and red-eyed Miss Pinfold appeared.

'Oh, my dear!' Dorothy could see she was very upset. 'Marjorie! Are you all right?'

'Come in,' her friend choked and burst into tears.

Dorothy followed her into the living room, put the

flowers on a chair and wrapped her arms round Miss Pinfold.

'My mother died at lunch time.'

'Oh, I'm so sorry . . .' Dorothy was glad she'd come.

Miss Pinfold was drying her eyes. 'I know it's for the best. Mother had lost interest in everything. She was a shadow of her former self. She didn't want to eat, didn't want to get up, just wanted to be left in peace.'

'All the same, it's a difficult and sad time for you.'

'I've been dreading it.'

It was Dorothy who put the kettle on and made them tea. Then she took her home to have a meal with her and Emily. 'It's not a night you'll want to be alone,' she said.

The next morning, she told Mr Jardine and Jane that after looking after her mother for so long Miss Pinfold had gone to pieces. 'Emily and I are helping with the funeral arrangements.'

A day or two later, Dorothy told them it was fixed for two o'clock on the following Monday.

Edwin sent a wreath. 'You take the day off, Dorothy,' he said. 'Miss Pinfold will need support. Tell her I'll come to the church service and if we aren't busy I'll bring one of the girls.'

Dorothy was there by late morning helping Miss Pinfold fill rolls and cut cake for a small buffet for the mourners. She'd been with her for an hour when a rather tearful Miss Bundy arrived, with a sad tale of how she'd fared since she'd left Jardine's to take care of her father.

'You looked after your mother for years,' she said to Marjorie Pinfold. 'I was so sure I could look after Dad.' She was full of guilt that she'd found it impossible to cope with him. He was suffering from Alzheimer's and it had changed his personality. 'He used to be such a mild and polite man.' She shuddered. 'I couldn't manage. I had to put him in a home.'

'Now she's living in Wigan by herself,' Miss Pinfold told Dorothy, 'while most of her friends are in Liverpool. It must be lonely for you, Alice.'

'I visit Father every day.' She was defensive.

'Mr Jardine said you could have your job back if you ever wanted it,' Dorothy reminded her.

'Yes, I'd like to, but it's difficult. I've given up my little flat here and it's not so easy to find another these days. I'm living in Dad's house in Wigan.'

Dorothy was glad when the funeral was over. Edwin brought Miss Lewis with him to the service but apart from a few of Miss Pinfold's neighbours there was nobody else. 'Mother outlived her friends,' she said sadly.

Jane felt stressed. She spent most of the day in Miss Pinfold's office doing her work, and when that was finished she sat on over the typewriter. There was a letter she wanted to write although Dad had said she must not. Now Mrs Thorpe was wearing his engagement ring there could be no holds barred. She'd never gone against her father's wishes before, but she was afraid that, this time, it was essential that she did.

She guided a fresh sheet of paper into the platen and wrote to the manager of Woolton Park Golf Club, asking if Mrs Thorpe was known to him. She typed her father's name on it and signed it on his behalf before putting it in the post.

Jane had invited Dorothy to have her evening meal with them again this Thursday. She'd come every week and Dad had taken her to choir practice afterwards. She knew the rest of the staff were agog at this. The boss was inviting Miss Hadley to regular meals with his family and taking her out afterwards. Like Jane, they were dying to know how they were getting on together, but none felt they could ask Dorothy directly.

Instead they asked how she was enjoying being in the choir. 'I love it,' she told everybody, 'and singing the *Messiah* gives us all a lift. I'm getting to know the Choral Society people too. They said they'd be happy to have me join them if I wanted to.'

Miss Hadley seemed full of life these days, and a happier person. 'Doesn't Mrs Thorpe get you down?' Miss Jessop asked her.

'Well, she was doing just that, and turning me into a thoroughly unpleasant person, full of hate and envy and itching to do her down. I told myself I mustn't let her. Now I try not to think of her.'

'Quite right,' Jane said. 'We don't want you

changed.' How could Dad be so blind? How could he not see how caring Dorothy was? Jane knew she was doing the right thing by throwing them together, but she was afraid she'd left it too late, now Honor Thorpe was flaunting his engagement ring.

When she asked Dad how the *Messiah* rehearsals were going, he told her the choir was shaping up well and he thought they'd give a competent performance when the time came.

Kitty got up late and went to collect the ferry tickets from their travel agent. She spent the rest of the morning going round the big department stores in the city, buying more things to equip the camper, before she took the bus to Menlove Avenue.

Jason was always tired these days and had asked her not to wake him too early. 'I'm working nights,' he'd said. 'Last night I did two jobs. I need most of the day to catch up on my sleep.'

It was two o'clock and Kitty was hungry. As she walked along a parade of local shops she caught a waft of fish and chips, and the delicious scent made her stomach rumble. She bought two helpings and with watering mouth hurried on to Jason's house, where she lit the oven to keep the food warm. Upstairs she threw back his curtains and jumped on his bed to wake him up. His juddering intake of breath told her he was in pain.

'What's the matter?' She was alarmed.

He grunted as he turned over. 'I've hurt my ankle. It wasn't all plain sailing last night.'

'What d'you mean? You were nearly caught?'

He pulled himself up the bed, his face screwing in agony. Then, pushing his foot out from under the bedclothes, he studied his ankle.

'It's swollen,' Kitty said. 'Very swollen. What happened?'

'We were doing a garage in Bootle—'

'You said you did fencing jobs because it was safer.'

'Kitten, that changed when we decided to leave for Spain in a hurry. You knew I was ready to do anything.'

'But—'

'I'm in with a smart crowd. They aren't going to get caught.'

'Things can go wrong.'

'They did last night, but I got out, didn't I? Neither of us were caught.'

'But look at your ankle. How did you do that?'

'Getting out of a window in a hurry. It was high up at the back of the building.'

'What building, for heaven's sake?'

'The garage I was telling you about. It's a small place with only one door into a shop where they sell oil, car mats, batteries, that sort of thing. Jon and I walked in just before closing time. The shop closes at half past five but the garage stays open until eleven to sell petrol. I distracted the old codger serving there while Jon went into the storeroom behind and slipped the catch off the window so we could get in later on.'

'Don't they check the windows before they lock up?'

'He didn't open it, just unlocked it, so nobody was likely to notice. We came back around half past ten. It was near enough dark when we got into the storeroom. Next to it, also at the back, is a small office where they make hot drinks. The takings from the shop were in the desk. We found them and stashed the bag ready by the storeroom window, but we wanted to get the petrol money too.

'The cashier has a small room at one side of the shop with a window looking out on the forecourt where customers come to pay. He had his light on and the door to his room open so we could see what he was doing. The forecourt was all lit up too, of course, so it was only semi-dark in the shop. There's not much trade at that time of night so he should have been cashing up ready to go home. Jon knows because he has a mate who used to do part time there. Then suddenly the cashier got up and came towards us and we had to shoot back and hide in the storeroom.'

'This sounds dangerous.' Kitty had a sinking feeling in her stomach.

'It's hard on the nerves, but he hadn't seen us. He went in the office and made himself a cup of coffee. He was quite a young lad, weedy-looking and wearing glasses. With hindsight we think he must have been pretty new in the job. He drank his coffee leaning against the counter in the darkened shop, staring out across the forecourt. Then he thumped his mug down and went outside, locking the shop door behind him. It wasn't what we were expecting – we were waiting for him to cash up and put the money in a bag. That makes it easier to snatch, and we know we've got the lot.

'We were growing edgy hanging about on the premises. It gets to you, you know? The lights were still on in the cashier's cubby hole, so we shot in there. Jon had the till open when we heard the lav door slam round the back, so we knew the guy would be back in a couple of minutes. I wanted to grab what we could and get out, but Jon said no, it was two to one, and pulled me back to the shop. "Surprise him when he comes back, knock his glasses off," he said. "We can get the lot."

'But the next minute a car pulled up outside. Not in front of the pumps but outside the door. It was the owner – I could see him trying the door handle. Then the lavatory flushed. We had to get out of the shop before they came in. Jon was first through the storeroom window and the owner was shouting and coming for me. I got out just in time but it was quite a drop down and there was concrete underneath. I twisted my ankle. It hurts like hell – d'you think it's broken?'

'Could be. It's very bruised and swollen. You ought to get it seen to.'

'Jon wanted to take me last night, but we were both shaken up and I let out a screech, so they'll know somebody's hurt. What if the police are watching the hospitals?'

'Would they bother? It's not as though you've murdered somebody.'

'How would I know?'

'The worst you could be charged with is burglary or breaking and entering. How much cash did you get?'

'Two hundred and fifteen from the shop and four hundred from the petrol till. There was a lot more we didn't get.'

Kitty groaned. 'So your share is three hundred? That's not worth cricking your ankle for. Especially not when we're due to leave in five days.' It was his right foot. 'Can you drive?'

Jason grimaced. 'I expect I could if I tried. We used Jon's car last night.'

'Oh, lord! Me possibly pregnant and you with possibly a broken ankle. We can't set out for Spain until you find out whether it is or it isn't. Get dressed and come downstairs. I'll drive you to hospital when we've eaten the fish and chips I brought.'

'I'm not hungry,' Jason said.

'Neither am I, not after seeing your foot. But we'll have to eat them now or throw them away.'

After much discussion they decided to go to the Accident and Emergency department at the Liverpool Royal. Jason gave a false name and address, and when asked for the name of his GP gave the name of the new practice Honor had booked Kitty into.

They had to wait to see a doctor, and they spent the time whispering together about their plans. Kitty was worried. What if his ankle was broken and he had to have it plastered? He wouldn't be able to drive for weeks.

'We'll get across to France,' Jason said, 'and find a campsite near a beach. Nobody will think of looking for us there.'

He thought she'd be able to drive the camper that far, and the prospect didn't calm her nerves.

When their turn came, the doctor examined his ankle and asked, 'How did you do this?'

'I fell downstairs last night,' he said. 'Missed the last eight steps.'

Kitty asked, 'Is it broken?'

'Possibly a Pott's fracture, but there doesn't seem to be any displacement or dislocation, so possibly not. You'll need an X-ray before I can be sure one way or the other.'

They had to wait again for that, and then again to get the result. The doctor clipped the film on the screen. 'Well, you're in luck. There doesn't appear to be any sign of a fracture.'

Kitty breathed a sigh of relief.

'What you've done is twisted the tendons in your ankle. You need to rest it, keep off your feet. It'll settle down, but you should keep your leg up supported on a stool for two or three days.'

'What about the pain?'

'Paracetamol should do it.'

Jason hopped back to his MG and Kitty drove him home. 'Jon and I were going to do another job tonight, but it involves driving to Sheffield. I don't think I can.'

'You can't. Cancel it,' Kitty said.

'We've got to get more money . . . or I suppose we could postpone our Channel crossing for a month. Give my ankle time to mend and claw in more funds.'

'And what would I do?' Kitty spat. 'Live with you and your father or go home and live with Ma?'

'I'm worried we might not have enough cash.'

Kitty thought he was beginning to lose his nerve. 'What we need to do is the job at Jardine's. It's local and the seventeenth is still three days off. D'you think your foot will be better by then?'

'It could be.'

'We might never get another chance like this. And now we've got the camper, we don't even need to come back here. We could pick up everything we can of value and head straight down to Birmingham.'

Jason rubbed his eyes. 'OK then. I'll ring the jeweller I know there. We could stop off and see him on Sunday morning. I could sell off some of what we'd picked up and then we'd go straight down to Portsmouth.'

'Spain, here we come!'

Kitty was counting the hours until they'd leave. Jason had sat with his leg up on a chair since Wednesday and had not been all that much fun.

'I'm brassed off,' he said. 'It's boring sitting here all day.' But he was complaining less about his foot.

'Work out our route and mark out the campsites,' Kitty suggested.

'I've done all that, but I've thought of something else. I'll post a key of the house to Pa, with a note telling him I've paid the rent for two months and left my car in the garage for him. I'll tell him I've got a job in Africa and you're coming with me.'

'Why?'

'We don't want Pa to guess we're in Spain and come looking for us, do we?'

On Friday morning Kitty went shopping for food to equip the camper for their journey. She filled the van up with diesel, and pinpointed some hiding places for their money and the valuables they hoped to acquire.

She still had a few belongings left in the Queen's Drive house that she wanted to take with her, so she drove Jason's car round on Friday afternoon and parked it where Ma wouldn't see it. On the way she stopped to buy some steak and some cream cakes. This was to be her farewell meal with Ma, although her mother wouldn't know it.

Kitty was careful to get there before her mother came home from work so that she could take the ruby ring from behind the dressing table. It didn't look as though Ma would need the money she could get for it. Edwin was going to provide a life of luxury for her. She peeled back the Sellotape carefully and replaced the empty envelope in the same position. She didn't think Ma would notice even if she looked. Not unless she tried to take the ring out. Then Kitty packed what she wanted to take in a bag and took it out to the car before making herself some tea.

'Hello, stranger,' her mother said when she came in. 'Where've you been all this week?' She seemed none too pleased to see her.

Kitty asked about Edwin in order to find out if her mother was still expecting him to spend Saturday night with her. She was, and Kitty was more convinced than ever that her plans for Saturday night would go well.

Saturday, 17 August dawned, and Jane was up before her alarm went off. She was excited at the thought of going to Chester with Nick again tonight. She dressed quickly, got ready for work, and packed her overnight bag before going to the kitchen to make breakfast.

She could hear her father singing in his bath. He seemed happy. She hoped it wouldn't be short-lived, but was afraid it might. Enhanced by the echo from the tiles and the steam, his voice sounded strong and hearty. 'For unto us a child is born . . .' Jane recognised it as a chorus from the *Messiah*. She'd heard Dorothy humming it in the shop.

Dad was in a good mood as they ate breakfast. He talked about the arrangements for her wedding. Had she chosen a photographer yet?

'No, but Nick and I like the idea of hiring the church

hall for the reception, and that firm of caterers you suggested.'

'Yes, they've done a lot in the church hall recently, and they put on a good spread. I'll make firm bookings, then. Time's going on.'

They went down together to open the shop. Customers flooded in almost as soon as the doors were opened, and Jane was kept busy serving with Miss Hadley on the ground floor for most of the morning.

At lunch time, when she and Dad went up to the flat to eat the pork pie and salad Mrs McGrath had laid out for them, he told her he'd just had a phone call from their Aigburth branch manager to say that his stock of engagement rings was low and he was in need of more.

'They've sold more than they expected, then?' Jane asked.

'More likely bad stock control,' Edwin said. 'I'll just have a bite to eat and then I'll take some out to him. I might go round and see how Nick is after that.' He smiled at her. 'Always good to pop in when I'm not expected. I see what really goes on in my shops then. Don't you ring and warn him.'

'No, Dad. I won't.'

They ate quite quickly and were downstairs again half an hour later. The post came late on Saturday mornings, usually just before lunch. Jane went to Miss Pinfold's office and found a small heap of letters waiting on the corner of the desk. Miss Pinfold had taken a week's holiday following her mother's funeral but was expected back on Monday.

Jane slit open the envelopes and threw them in the waste-paper basket. Giving each letter a cursory glance, she sorted them into those she needed to show her father, and those she could deal with herself. She'd almost finished when she opened a letter from the Woolton Park Golf Club. Her heart began to race.

With regard to your enquiry about Mrs Honor Thorpe. We employed her as assistant catering manager in our clubhouse from 1 April 1972 to 24 April 1973.

We found her to be very competent and had no complaints about her work. However, we found it necessary to dispense with her services because of her behaviour.

That took Jane's breath away. She'd been an assistant catering manager! A competent one. Why hadn't she told them she'd worked so recently for a local golf club? But wait, she couldn't, she'd been dismissed for bad behaviour.

What sort of behaviour? Fraud and theft sprang to mind, but apparently she hadn't been charged with anything.

Jane's first thought was to lift the phone and ask to speak to the manager. She had his name, Mark Layton; he'd signed the letter. He might well tell her. Obviously he hadn't wanted to put it in writing, or Mrs Thorpe might claim it was defamation of character. But even if he told her, Dad would never believe ill of Honor.

She shot to the next office to show him the letter. She meant to suggest he ring the club manager himself. If she tried to tell him anything bad about Mrs Thorpe she wouldn't believe her. Better if he heard it direct.

Honor had been sacked from the golf club and Dad had taken her on without a reference! He was always so cautious about taking on new staff – or she'd thought he was.

But his desk was cleared and the safe locked as if her father didn't intend to return in working hours. She went down to find Miss Hadley. She had to tell somebody. The shop was quite busy but she insisted on taking her back to Miss Pinfold's room. 'It's important.'

'What have you found out?'

Jane sat her down and pushed the letter into her hands, then watched her expression change to one of amazement and shock. 'I knew it. I knew she must be hiding something.'

They speculated at length as to what behaviour had led to her dismissal. Jane could feel her curiosity growing.

'I think I'll ring the manager myself. It's Saturday afternoon, but it's a golf club. It's probably a busy day for them too.'

Dorothy groaned. 'Your dad will say you took too much on yourself,' she warned. 'Shouldn't you leave it to him?'

'Aren't you curious?'

'Desperately.'

'I'm going to do it. I just need a moment to psych myself up.'

'I'll leave you.'

'Why don't you make a cup of tea?'

'It's a bit early for afternoon break.'

'Go on, we might need it.'

Jane waited until Dorothy had shut the door firmly behind her, then nudged the letter closer to the phone and dialled the number on the heading.

'May I speak to Mr Mark Layton, please?' she asked and had to wait a few moments to be put through to his office.

'Mr Layton? I'm Jane Jardine,' she said when he picked up the phone. 'Of E. H. Jardine & Son. We employ a Mrs Honor Thorpe as a sales assistant here. We wrote and asked if you knew her and I received your reply today.'

'Oh, yes.'

'I was wondering if you'd enlarge on what you mean by having to dispense with her services because of her behaviour?' There was a moment's silence, and she added, 'You found her dishonest?'

'No, not that. It's a bit difficult, but . . . Well, she was using the club premises for the purpose of prostitution.'

'What?' Jane felt cold sweat break out across her forehead.

'I know, I couldn't believe it to start with. She was soliciting for sex in our bar and restaurant. Offering it in exchange for money and favours. We had several complaints from members.'

'Oh, no!' Jane hardly knew what to say. 'Thank you for telling me,' she said. 'It explains a lot. Oh, dear!'

Dorothy Hadley came in with two cups of tea on a tray. 'It was theft?' she asked.

'No.' Jane shook her head.

'Fraud?'

'No. You'll never guess. He said she was soliciting for sex on club premises in exchange for cash and favours. Prostitution.'

'Oh, my giddy aunt. Oh!'

'How do I tell Dad about this?' Jane wailed. 'He thinks she's an angel. He won't believe me.'

'Just show him that letter and tell him what you've done. It's the first proof we've had.'

'Oh, yes, I know I'll have to tell him, but I wish I'd waited and let him ring the golf club himself.' Jane still felt shocked. 'Prostitution, though. I'd never have thought it of Honor. She looks too wholesome. I bet Dad doesn't have an inkling.'

Dorothy gulped at her tea. 'Of course he doesn't. But it explains how she managed to get such quick results. She'd be offering – her wares. Diamonds and a promise of marriage were the price she extracted from your father.'

Jane could feel her mouth falling open. 'Dorothy! Dad's too old! He wouldn't be interested, would he?'

She could see that Dorothy was trying not to smile. 'He's not too old.'

Jane exploded. 'If she marries my dad, it'll be over my dead body.'

'And mine,' Dorothy added fervently.

CHAPTER TWENTY-FOUR

KITTY KNEW Jason was on edge before they were out of bed.

'I'm not sure about doing Jardine's,' he worried. 'I've got a bad feeling about it.'

Kitty frowned. Jason had had too much time to sit and think. It had given him cold feet.

'Why? I mean, what could go wrong?'

'What if the keys don't work, for a start?'

'The fellow who made them thought they'd probably be OK. It's worth a try, isn't it?'

Jason sighed. 'I hope you're right about nobody being at home tonight.'

'I am.' He was making Kitty nervous. She wondered if she'd been right to persuade him to do it. 'But if you're really not sure we could just forget Jardine's and go straight to Birmingham now with what you already have.'

'But doing it could make all the difference to us.' Jason pulled a face. 'It could put us on easy street.'

'Make up your mind, Jason.'

'OK, we'll do it then.'

'Look, on the way, we'll drive past Ma's house. If Edwin's there, his car will be on the drive. He wouldn't come to stay the night if Jane was at home. That should set your mind at rest, shouldn't it?'

'Yes. Sorry. Doing a job doesn't usually get to me.'

'It's because you had trouble on the last one. Was that the first time things have gone wrong for you?'

'Yes, and it brings home that I could get caught like Pa.'

'This will be the last job you ever need to do. We'll go straight when we get away from here. But this one could set us up for life.'

'If we can get in.'

Kitty was thinking. 'Instead of just passing Ma's place tonight, I could go in. When I got those soap imprints, Edwin's jacket was hanging in the hall and the keys were in his pocket. If he does the same tonight, I might be able to get the originals.' She groaned. 'But then I'd have to replace them.'

'Would it matter?' Jason asked. 'He's going to find out he's been robbed anyway.'

'Yes it matters, it would tell both him and Ma too much. His keys were all on one ring, he'll have used it to drive there. Who but me could get in the house to spirit them away? It might be safer to leave the keys where they are.'

They got up and had breakfast. Kitty took out the floor plans she'd drawn of Jardine's building to get everything straight in her mind. They had already provisioned the camper van and packed their clothes and belongings in the wardrobe inside. There was very little left for them to do today.

Jason said, 'My ankle feels better. I'll be able to drive now.'

'It still looks swollen.'

'We've got to do something,' he said. 'I'll try driving round to the local shopping parade, get some food for today. I don't want to go to the pub. The temptation to have a beer would be too strong, and today I must not. We need to be absolutely on our toes tonight.'

Kitty would have liked a last trawl round the big Liverpool department stores, but Jason didn't want to walk too much as it might make his ankle worse again. They watched television and ate a big meal, but time hung heavily.

After lunch, they went back to bed. 'To have a sleep,' Jason said, 'as we're going to be up for most of the night.' Kitty snuggled up and kissed him, but for once Jason was too stressed to make love.

At seven o'clock Kitty got up, had a hot bath and changed into black jeans and a black pullover. She'd even dug out her old black school gym shoes and borrowed some black socks from Gary's drawer. Jason had said there was less chance of being seen if they wore black. He already had the right outfit for this sort of work. Then she started to cook another meal.

There were a few bottles of beer left in the fridge.

She saw Jason eye them longingly, but he slammed the door shut and walked away. He was chain-smoking.

'We can still walk away from it.' Kitty shivered, feeling almost ready to back off.

'No,' he said.

After supper she turned on the television again. 'We don't want to get to Ma's place too early. I think she intended to cook for him, but what if he takes her out? We've got to give them time to get to bed. If they were still out jugging up, we could be misled into thinking he'd stayed at home in his flat.'

They waited until after eleven before they set out to pick up the camper van. Then Kitty drove the MG back while Jason followed in the van. They shut the car in the garage and walked round the house to make sure everything was locked up.

It was after eleven thirty when they drove past Honor's house. 'His car's here,' Kitty breathed. 'And all the lights are off, which means they're in bed.'

Jason pulled up a little further along the road and switched off the engine and the headlights.

'Shall I go in and see if I can get his keys, or not?' Kitty's heart lurched. She had the heebie-jeebies herself now.

'Don't forget you'll have to put them back.'

'I could just leave them on the gravel.' She gave a nervous laugh. 'He'd think he'd dropped them, wouldn't he?'

'Perhaps.'

'Well, he couldn't be sure he hadn't. Let's do the job properly.' Her heart was pounding. 'I'm not going to bottle out now.'

She picked up her torch and felt in her pocket for her front door key, then slid out of the camper, closed the door softly and walked back to the house. She was careful to walk on the grass instead of crunching on the gravel. She reached the front step without making a sound. Her key turned easily in the lock and the door swung silently open. She stepped inside, pulled the door to behind her and eased the lock on again without making it click.

It was dark now she was indoors, so dark and silent that it no longer seemed familiar. She shone her torch round. His jacket was there on the hallstand. She couldn't believe her good luck, but as she crept forward she reminded herself that his keys might not be in his pocket. But they were! Unbelievable!

She gripped them firmly before withdrawing them; she mustn't let them clash together. Then she retreated to the door and listened for a moment. What was that? Her heart lurched again before she realised it was her own breathing she could hear, shallow and fast. She held her breath. Thank the lord, now there was dead silence. Out again then as fast as she could without making a sound. Victory was sweet: she was brimming with joy. She jumped from the step to the little patch of lawn and fled back to the camper.

'I've got them.' Her voice sounded too loud and

breathy. 'No reason now why we shouldn't set ourselves up for life.'

Jason drove the van down Church Street. Kitty had never seen it so empty of traffic and pedestrians. In the harsh glare of the street lamps, it seemed ghostly. Jardine's building, like many of the others, was in total darkness. Kitty was scared stiff now the time had come. She'd never done anything like this before and it was a comfort that Jason must be used to it.

He turned right into Whitechapel. 'I had a recce last week for a suitable place to park. In this district, a white camper will stand out like a sore thumb, so we don't want it too close to Jardine's. I thought this would be a good place.'

He tucked the van neatly into the shadows. 'Right, let's get ready.' He put on his large black tea-cosy hat and pulled it well down; Kitty tucked all her blond hair inside her own black beret.

'Gloves on, and don't take them off until we get back here. We don't want to leave fingerprints.' He gave her a pair of thin rubber gloves. 'These were the darkest I could get.' They were deep pink. 'So there's black woolly mitts that leave the fingers free to go on top. Haversacks now.' Kitty slid out of the van and tossed hers up on her back. 'Torches and keys? I don't think we'll need anything else.' They closed the van doors quietly.

'Aren't you going to lock it?' Kitty asked.

'No, in case we need a quick getaway. There's nobody about and we won't be that long.'

Here in the city it was never completely quiet. An ambulance siren screeched in the distance, a car could be heard in the next street. They went quietly into the alley, their gym shoes making no sound. Suddenly, a cat shot across their path and disappeared into the gloom. Kitty jumped involuntarily.

'I think it was a black one,' Jason said. 'That should bring us good luck.'

The back of Jardine's building rose like a dark cliff in front of them. Jason used his torch for a mere second to find the dead lock and get the key to turn in it, and again to find the Yale lock. That key turned easily too and the door swung open. Kitty pushed inside after him and the Yale lock clicked behind them.

She could feel herself quaking. The darkness seemed thicker, as black as soot now they were inside. She put her hand out in front of her.

'Lead the way,' Jason whispered, taking her arm. They'd agreed to go straight up to Edwin Jardine's office and try to open the safe. The smallest and most valuable jewellery was what they sought.

The carpet felt thick underfoot and the place seemed to reek of scented luxury. Kitty found the heavy closed-up atmosphere and lack of light disorienting. 'It's like a fur-lined tomb in here,' she whispered.

Jason had told her, 'Only use your torch if you have

to. Somebody might be able to see it from outside.' She did have to. Even the stairs didn't seem to be where she remembered them. They went up hand in hand.

'Think of Edwin Jardine tucked up in bed with Ma.' She giggled. She was glad he wasn't in the flat above them, and kept telling herself they were perfectly safe. 'That was the first floor, now we're coming to the second.' In the flash of her torch she caught a glimpse of round clock faces and a flash of silver. 'Third floor now. His office is this way, I think.' She opened a door. 'This is it – no, it's the secretary's office. Must be the other door.'

This was definitely it. Jason let his torch play round the room. 'Hell, there's a window here.' He snapped it off.

Kitty had glimpsed the wire mesh covering it on the outside. 'No curtains, either.'

Jason was trying to open the safe and not finding it too easy. 'I wish I could see what I was doing.'

'Would it matter if we switched the light on? We're at the back of the building – there's nobody out there to see it.'

'No, we'll manage with the torches. Just shine yours this way.'

At last Jason got the safe open to reveal the display trays of rings and brooches all neatly fitted in together.

'Wow, just look at this!' he breathed. 'Enough to take your breath away.' The gems glittered and sparkled in the torchlight.

Kitty was overwhelmed to have such treasure within reach; it banished her fears. She tried to push a diamond ring on her finger, but it would only go as far as her nail because of her rubber glove. 'Isn't this beautiful?'

'For God's sake, Kit, you can play later. Let's get them into our haversacks.' Jason had his open and was pushing jewellery in as fast as he could go.

Kitty did likewise. 'We're going to get a marvellous haul here. What's in these boxes?'

She unclipped the fastener on a shagreen case and a stupendous necklace set with yellow diamonds glowed in the light of her torch.

'Gosh, I know what these are. They're the Sun Diamonds. There's a ring and some earrings too. They're given pride of place in the shop when it's open. Ma says they're worth a small fortune.'

'Put them back,' Jason said. 'It's easier to fence more ordinary stuff.'

'They're absolutely gorgeous,' Kitty breathed, holding the necklace to her neck. 'I'd love to keep these for myself. What d'you think?'

'No, Kitten, they're too recognisable. Keep one of these clear diamonds if you want. There're some real knuckle-dusters here.'

She returned the necklace to the case and clipped it shut. The deep yellow stones were the most beautiful things she'd ever seen. Ma had told her how everybody raved about them and how expensive they were. She was pushing the case in her haversack when a bell

435

shrilled through the building. Kitty froze, but not before she switched her torch off.

'What's that?' Her voice was a panic-stricken squeal. The bell rang again, and for longer. 'Is it the doorbell?' Her mouth had gone dry.

'Oh, my God!' Jason said. In the sudden pitch darkness, they clutched each other. 'It sounds as though someone's checking up. Could they have seen our light?' He pulled away from her to go to the window. 'There's somebody with a torch down there.'

The doorbell rang again. 'Sounds as though they're keeping their finger on it now.'

'What are we going to do?'

'There's more than one person now.'

'Oh, lummy! We've been caught, haven't we?'

Jason was relocking the safe. 'Not yet.' He swung his haversack up on his shoulder. 'Keep calm. Is there a window at the front, looking out on Church Street? We've got all the keys, so if there's no one there we could get out that way.'

Kitty tried to think. 'No – yes. Up in the flat above us.' She went to the stairs, stumbling in the dark. The windows in the living room meant it was not totally dark; it was possible to see the furniture. From the window they looked down on the glow from the street lamps. A police car was parked on the opposite side of the road.

'Hell,' Jason said. As they watched, two police officers walked towards it and got in.

Kitty felt the strength ebb from her knees. 'How do we get out of here?' Fear was washing over her, and she couldn't get her breath.

Jason's voice was calm. 'There's nobody else in the car, just the two of them. We go back to the office and look to see if there's still somebody at the back. If there isn't, we get out pronto and make a run for it.'

'Jason, I'm scared.'

'We might still be all right – with a bit of luck.'

This time Kitty followed him as he almost slithered down the stairs. He limped along the passage and into the office. She pushed her head up against the glass, and could no longer see any lights below at the back.

'Right,' Jason said. 'Time to get out. We'll run for it. You'll be quicker than me with this foot. Here's the key to the van. You'll have to drive. Get the engine started and be ready to take off as fast as you can. If I get nabbed, just save yourself, OK? I'll swear I was alone.'

'Jason! You've got to run.'

'Don't worry, I'll be as fast as I can.' He switched on his torch and left it on the desk. 'If they're watching, they'll think we're still up here.'

'What if they're waiting for us? We won't be able to see . . .'

'All is not lost yet. Do as I say and don't panic. You've got to keep calm. Come on.'

She knew he was limping as they went down to the back door. She pulled him to a halt and they listened.

A police siren wailed in the distance. Kitty went rigid. Was it coming nearer?

No. She could breathe again. Jason opened the door a few inches and peered out. 'It's OK. Go on.' She hung on to his arm, pulling him after her. 'No, you run for it. It's easier for both of us on our own.'

Kitty took to her heels and went then. Fear increased her speed. The van was round the corner where they'd left it and there was nobody in sight. She had her haversack off before she reached it. Snatching the door open she threw it in and scrambled up after it. The engine leaped to life and throbbed, but where was Jason?

She was breathless and frightened and thought for one awful moment he'd not followed her, but he was opening the passenger door and struggling inside. She tossed her haversack off the seat out of his way, then slid in the gear lever and moved off. She could hear Jason struggling to get his breath.

'Are you all right?'

'Yes, just this damned ankle.'

They came to the end of the road. 'Which way? I don't know where we are.'

'We're all right. Can you turn round?'

There was no traffic at all, so she swung the camper in a circle. It swayed but rocked back on four wheels. 'Slow down a bit. Better put your lights on.'

The road was suddenly filled with light. It took Kitty a moment to realise that it wasn't all from their own headlights. A car was coming towards them.

She felt blinded, and looked to the side.

'Oh, my God!' Jason was agitated. 'It's a police car.'

'No! Oh, heavens.' She went cold with terror. 'Are they looking for us?'

'Don't know but don't panic. Just keep going.' He sounded as though he was panicking himself. 'Hell, I think it's turning round.'

They were coming to a T-junction. She screamed, 'Which way? Which way?'

'Right . . . now first left here, and turn off your lights. Put your foot down a bit. We've got to lose them.'

'How, for heaven's sake? How?' Kitty could feel the blood rushing to her head. 'I wish you were driving. I don't like this!'

'You're doing fine.'

'But where are we?'

'This is Sir Thomas Street. You're coming up to Dale Street, turn right here and put your lights back on. There's other traffic.' There was very little. 'Left here into Hatton Gardens and then straight on up Vauxhall Road. We'll come out on the Southport Road.'

'Southport? But that's north. I thought we were going south to Birmingham.'

'We will be. Don't worry.'

The next minute Kitty saw a car coming out of a side street to her right. There was a blue light flashing on the roof and its headlights were full on.

'It's the police,' she screamed. 'They're after us!' It pulled out in front of her. 'They're trying to block my way.'

'Don't stop. Turn into the road they've just come out of,' Jason said. 'Go on, keep going.' They heeled over on screaming tyres. 'Good, they'll have to turn round again now. Keep calm. Put your foot down a bit harder.'

Kitty tried to follow his instructions, thankful there wasn't much traffic. They covered a couple of miles.

'OK, Kit, you're doing great, slow down a bit and turn right into this road.'

'Have we lost them?'

'I hope so. Keep going, straight on here.'

'Won't they call on other police cars to help?'

'Yes, probably. We can't go through the Mersey Tunnel – they'd be able to cut us off at the other end. We'll have to go up to Runcorn to cross the river.'

'D'you know where we are?'

'Sort of. I think we're going in the right direction now.'

They were coming to a major road, crossing the one they were on. 'Straight over,' Jason said.

Kitty could see traffic lights and they were turning red. 'Oh, goodness, I can't—'

'Go on, you'll have to jump them,' Jason said. 'There's nothing coming.'

But there was. Kitty didn't see the heavy goods vehicle travelling along the main road until she'd pulled out in front of it. For it the lights had gone green.

'Christ!' Jason swore.

Kitty was wrenching at the steering wheel to avoid it, but she didn't quite succeed. She clipped the back of the trailer and felt the weight of the camper veer over on two wheels. She was going much too fast for this. She was fighting with the steering wheel then but the camper wouldn't turn. She knew she was hurtling across the major road towards the building on the opposite corner. She felt a savage jerk as they mounted the pavement; heard the ear-splitting crash, the splintering of glass, the tearing of metal and the terrible crunch of stone, as they slammed headlong into it.

CHAPTER TWENTY-FIVE

HONOR WAS wearing her new engagement ring in the bath. She was well pleased with the way things had gone last night. Of course, it had been hard work. She had to do a lot of preparation when she wanted to put on, single-handedly, a stylish meal for Edwin, and at the same time focus all her attention on him.

If he'd planned to go home last night she'd have left most of the clearing away until this morning. Instead, she'd had to flit prettily round the kitchen putting the remaining food in the fridge and stacking the dishwasher but leaving the roasting pan and several other cooking pots shut in the oven out of sight. She'd have them to do when he went.

But it was well worth it. Not only had she convinced Edwin Jardine that she was an excellent cook and an efficient housewife, but he thought her the most beautiful and desirable woman in the world. He'd told her so several times last night.

She'd stocked her fridge in order to meet his wishes

this morning. Should he want breakfast, she had eggs and bacon; if they got up late and he preferred to have a brunch, she could offer scrambled eggs with smoked salmon. Honor felt both well rested and very content after the long lie-in they'd had this morning.

When she swished the bedroom curtains open and the sun poured in, Edwin had said, 'I think tea and toast is all I could manage. I'm not hungry after such a wonderful dinner last night.'

'I'm not either.'

'It's just the day for the seaside. Why don't I drive you out to Southport? I know an excellent restaurant where we can have lunch and then we could walk it off along the prom.'

'Lovely,' Honor had said. She'd rather walk along the beach, but she wouldn't push her luck on that.

She stepped out of the bath and towelled dry; Edwin would want a bath too and she mustn't keep him waiting too long. She rinsed the bath round, tossed her damp towel in the laundry basket and got out her best bath sheets for him to use.

Edwin came downstairs, bringing his overnight bag neatly repacked and leaving it in the hall. His bald head looked pink and polished, and he was rubbing his hands with satisfaction. Honor gave him the toast to carry and led him out to a small table she'd set on the patio. When he'd eaten, she watched him sit back to enjoy the sun on his face.

Turning to look at her, he said, 'It's time we thought

of ourselves, Honor. I'd like us to be married quite soon.'

It made Honor prickle with anticipation.

'Jane has made her plans and will be married on September the eighteenth. I'd like her to be back from her honeymoon so she can be with us on our day. In fact, she and Nick will have to be here to run the business before I can think of going on honeymoon.'

Honor felt her heart skip a beat. On one hand she was thrilled that he wanted to rush her into marriage, on the other a little nervous. Paul Thorpe was safely locked up awaiting trial, but it would still be bigamy. She'd not made up her mind whether she should go ahead and risk it, or whether she should wait until his case was heard. If only the death sentence hadn't been revoked.

She moistened her lips. 'What d'you mean by quite soon?'

'As soon as you can be ready. Can we set a date?'

Honor tried to think. This was what she'd been aiming for, wasn't it? Dare she risk it?

'Yes.' She smiled, making up her mind in that instant. 'At our age it's silly to wait, isn't it?'

'Yes. The run-up to Christmas is always busy in the shop and I couldn't go away then. So what I'd like us to do is to be married as soon as Jane and Nick get home. Otherwise we'd need to delay it until early January.'

Honor bit on the bullet. 'Why wait till January if we don't need to? What about early October?'

'Dearest Honor, I'm so very pleased. Early October it shall be. You've made me a very happy man.' Edwin took one of her hands between his own and leaned across to kiss her cheek.

'I'd like a quiet wedding,' Honor said. That was not really her taste, but she didn't want to draw attention to what could be a bigamous marriage.

'That's what I'd like too. In church, St Cuthbert's, but with just the family. Perhaps the vicar would agree to holding it in the lady chapel. I won't close the shop; we'll just slip off one morning, and instead of a reception I'll book a table at the Adelphi for lunch. Then Jane can arrange cream cakes at tea break and we'll tell the girls.'

'Yes.' She'd enjoy watching their faces when they learned she was Mrs Jardine. That would be a moment of real triumph. 'But aren't we to have a honeymoon?'

'We will. I wouldn't cheat you of that.'

'Where shall we go?'

'Wherever you like. You can choose.' Honor had visions of tropical islands and was about to suggest the Caribbean. 'I'd prefer the Lake District, or perhaps Wales, but we can't take longer than a week.'

He wasn't on her wavelength. Honor felt she'd been brought back to earth with a bump, but perhaps he could be persuaded.

'I'll have to think about it,' she said, and then, with a big smile, she added, 'It's all so exciting.'

*

445

The speed at which they were arranging this would shock Jane, Edwin thought, but could she blame him for wanting the same happiness she had for himself?

Honor's beautiful eyes looked into his. They were at one. She wanted the things he did.

She asked, 'And where shall we live? Will you come here and live with me or shall I move in with you?'

'That's a difficult question. I'll need to discuss it with Jane and Nick before we make any decisions. I'd feel happier if someone was living over the shop. There are so many things to consider. What would you like to do?'

She was shaking her head. 'I really haven't thought much about it.' He smiled, feeling overwhelmed with good fortune to have found happiness again at his age.

'My dear, it's almost midday. Why don't you get yourself ready and we'll go to Southport?' He watched her spring to her feet – she had such youthful energy.

'I'll just put the butter in the fridge so it doesn't melt. Then I'd like five minutes to change into a new dress I've bought. It's just the thing for a celebratory lunch.'

Edwin helped her carry everything indoors, and when she went upstairs to change he picked up his overnight bag and took it out to his car.

He had a little laugh at himself. He was so thrilled with the way everything was going that he'd forgotten he'd need his keys to unlock the car.

He went back, found his jacket on the hallstand and felt in the pocket. His keys weren't there. He tried the other pocket. No, not there either. He felt again in his right pocket more carefully and had another little laugh at himself. He'd been full of anticipation when he'd arrived last night, quite excited in fact. He must have put them down somewhere.

He looked round the sitting room, the dining room and the kitchen and drew a blank; neither were they on the floor under the hallstand or on the washbowl in the downstairs loo.

Honor was coming downstairs. 'You look absolutely radiant. That dress is lovely.' He kissed her cheek. 'I shall be very proud to have you on my arm.' He laughed again. 'I've put my keys down somewhere, and I can't find them. I think they must be upstairs.'

'I didn't see them.'

She followed him up. She'd made their bed and tidied the room. There was no sign of his keys on the bedside table he'd used, nor on the dressing table or the chest of drawers. She followed him to the bathroom. 'I don't think they're likely to be there,' she said. 'There's nowhere much to put them down.'

'How silly of me,' he said. 'They must be somewhere. I used them to drive here yesterday.'

'Not silly at all, it's the sort of thing I do. You must have dropped them somewhere.' They both went carefully over every inch of carpet and thermoplastic tile.

'Perhaps you dropped them outside before you ever came in.' She was out at the front again, kicking over the gravel with her high-heeled patent leather sandals.

447

'It's a big bunch of keys; they shouldn't be hard to see.'

Honor was going to think him an old fool who couldn't look after his own possessions. He tried the door of his car. It was locked, and the keys were not hanging in the ignition. He felt exasperated with himself. 'What a stupid thing to do.'

Honor's radiance was fading, and she was beginning to look exasperated too. 'They must be somewhere here. You didn't put them in your overnight bag?'

'Oh, that'll be it,' he said. 'I've packed my night things on top. What an ass you must think me.' He'd put his bag down on the gravel by his car. He took it indoors and emptied the contents out on her sofa and then wished he had not. He'd changed into the clean clothes he'd brought and the bag now contained his dirty washing and crumpled pyjamas. Not a romantic sight. But even worse, his keys were not here. He felt humiliated. To have this happen in front of his super-efficient fiancée made him look like a bone-headed idiot. On this day of all days, which he'd wanted to be special. Searing frustration had replaced his earlier happiness.

Honor was watching him minutely. 'You haven't looked in your washbag.'

'I know they're not there.' He couldn't keep the note of irritation out of his voice. He shook his washbag. There was no rattle of keys, but he looked anyway.

'They must be somewhere here.' Honor could no

longer hide her irritation either. Edwin knew she was going slowly round everywhere again, but he buried his head in his hands feeling defeated.

The next thing he knew, Honor was pushing a gin and tonic into his hand. 'Come on,' she said, and he sensed she was making an effort to appear brighter than she felt. 'I've put the chairs out on the patio again. You can take me to Southport another day. It's getting a bit late now to go there for lunch.'

He followed her out into the bright sunshine. 'What an ass I am. I'm so sorry, I meant to celebrate, give you a good time.' He was upset.

'Don't worry, we'll have lunch out here in the sun. I've got cold pork left from last night, and I'll make a salad to go with it. Never mind your keys.'

'But they must be here. I can't drive home until we find them. And I wouldn't be able to get in anyway.'

Honor was frustrated and disappointed. Where were his wretched keys? This was winding them both up.

'Let's forget about them for the time being and try to relax.'

'Honor, you're a saint to take it like this.'

Honor felt she had to take it like a saint to stay in character. She was pretending to be a compliant woman who would make a dutiful wife; a woman who was thrilled with everything Edwin did.

It wasn't easy when he was a bumbling old fool. God only knew what he'd done with his keys. He was now talking of ringing Jane when she came home to ask her to bring him his spare set.

But the gin worked its magic. She began to feel calmer and knew he was too. The lunch helped. It was great to be out in the fresh air and sunshine, and they were hungry. She offered ice cream to follow and he accepted. She was in the kitchen getting it out of the freezer when the doorbell shrilled through the house.

As she went up the hall to answer it, she glimpsed the uniform through the glass in the door. It took her breath away. She stopped dead and had to fight the need to flee. The bell rang again. What could they want? She had to force herself to carry on and open it. There were two police officers on the step, one of them a woman.

'Yes?' She did her best to look innocent. They introduced themselves, flashed their identity cards at her. Their names didn't register, but that the man was a police sergeant did.

'Good afternoon. Could you tell me if Katrina Thorpe is known to you?'

'Katrina? Yes, she's my daughter, she lives here.'

'We have some bad news, I'm afraid. May we come in?'

That was the last thing Honor wanted while Edwin was here. Kitty was with Jason. What had they been up to? She stood her ground.

'Could you just tell me here?' She could see they were surprised at that. 'What's happened to my daughter? Has she done something wrong?' Goodness, she must have done for a pair of them to come round. 'I have a visitor at the moment . . .'

What if Kitty had been caught shoplifting? It wouldn't help if Edwin heard of that. If he hadn't lost his keys they'd be in Southport now and she'd have avoided this.

The woman stepped forward. 'It's bad news, Mrs Thorpe, I'm sorry. I think we should come in.'

Reluctantly Honor led the way to her sitting room. 'You'd better have a seat.' She could see Edwin outside on the patio. She sat down with her back to the window.

'I'm glad you've got a friend here with you. Would you like him to come in?'

'No,' she said. 'No. What's this about?'

The policewoman stood up. 'But I think he should be here. Do you mind if I fetch him in?' Before Honor could think of a reason to stop her, she had left the room, and a few minutes later she came back with a worried-looking Edwin in tow. He stood awkwardly just inside the door as the police sergeant opened his notebook and began to read.

'At two-twenty this morning we were called to a road traffic accident that had occurred at the junction of Leeds Street and Prescot Road. The driver of a camper van had clipped the rear end of a heavy goods trailer and lost control of the vehicle. It went through the window of Barclays Bank, destroying the counter and taking down part of the wall. The driver was a young woman—'

'No,' Honor said. 'You've made a mistake. It can't be my daughter. She's only sixteen, she hasn't learned to drive.' She half rose, ready to usher them out.

'Bear with us, Mrs Thorpe, if you would. There was a youth in the camper van with her.'

'But she doesn't know anybody with a camper van.'

The officer looked up and his dark eyes seemed to bore into her. 'We found several documents in the van, including a driving licence in the name of Helen Swift of Wessex Road, Maghull. We visited that address this morning but were told the licence had been stolen some six months ago. There was a bus pass for a school child in the name of Katrina Thorpe of this address, and also a passport in the same name but with an address in Sandfield Pavement.'

Honor felt the blood rush into her face. Sandfield Pavement was where they'd lived with Gary before going to Spain.

'Perhaps it is Kitty,' she allowed. 'Is she in hospital? Is she badly hurt?'

'I'm afraid it was a fatal accident.'

Honor felt as though the wind had been knocked out of her. 'No, no, you can't mean Kitty's been killed? It can't . . . It can't have been her.' She felt ill, confused, unable to think.

'I'm very sorry, Mrs Thorpe. We think it is, but she must have died instantly.'

'Oh, God! No, no . . .'

'She wouldn't have felt any pain.'

Honor was aware that Edwin had come to sit on the sofa beside her and had taken her cold hand between his two warm ones. She heard him murmur, 'I'm so sorry, my dear. Poor Kitty. And such a shock for you.'

'The camper was registered in the name of—'

Honor sat up straighter and with her hand in front of her mouth choked out, 'Jason Bolton?'

'His body was in the passenger seat.'

'He's dead too?' She felt sick with horror.

'Yes. Do you know him?'

She could only nod.

'Do you know where he lived?'

Honor gave them the address in Menlove Avenue. She knew she should be thinking about what information it was wise to give and which it would be better to withhold, but her mind wouldn't work.

'Will we find his family at that address?'

'No.'

Kitty was dead! Hadn't she told her that Jason was dangerous? Why hadn't she listened to her?

'So nobody else lives there? We need to contact his next of kin. Can you help us with a name and address?'

She burst out, 'His father's in Walton prison. He's due out soon, his name's Gary Bolton.'

Tears came flooding down her face then. She couldn't stop them. Edwin put an arm round her shoulders and pulled her closer. He said gently, 'You've had a terrible shock, my dear.' He patted her hand. 'Can I get you something?'

Honor pulled away and ran blindly to the downstairs cloakroom. She could taste bile, hot and bitter, rising in her throat. Oh, God! This was awful, and what was it telling Edwin? She shouldn't have said that in front of him. Now he knew she moved in circles where people served prison sentences.

The next moment she was violently sick, her half-digested lunch rejected. She only realised then that the woman police officer had followed her in and was offering her a glass of water. She flushed the lavatory while Honor washed out her mouth and drank.

The woman said, 'I'll put the kettle on, if I may, to make you some tea.'

Honor rinsed her face in cold water and tried to pull herself together. The mirror reflected a woman she hardly recognised as herself. She looked half dead. She was being led back to sit beside Edwin, but veered away to sit on the other sofa where the policewoman had been.

The male officer flashed his identity card at Edwin. 'Sergeant Dransfield,' he said. 'So you're Edwin Jardine, owner of E. H. Jardine & Son, the jewellers? We've been knocking on the door of your shop in Church Street since the early hours of this morning.'

'Why?' Edwin asked.

'We found quite a lot of jewellery in the camper van, which we believe might have come from your shop.'

'From my shop? Surely not.'

'In other words, you and your shop seem to be connected to this accident.'

Honor stiffened, aghast at what she was hearing.

He was frowning, but his cheeks were flushed. 'Everything was fine when I left last night.'

'At what time would that be?'

'Around half past six, I think. Are you saying these two youngsters broke into my shop and sto—' Honor saw him glance at her, 'took some of my stock?'

'I'm sorry,' she cut in. 'I just can't take it in. My beautiful daughter! Kitty was only sixteen, you know. Only a child really.'

The woman police officer turned to her. 'Did you know your daughter and her companion were going abroad?'

'No, no. Why should they?'

'We found tickets. They were booked on a cross-Channel ferry this evening. They had foreign insurance for the vehicle and foreign currency. That's why they had their passports with them.'

Honor was devastated that Kitty had planned to go abroad without even telling her. Sergeant Dransfield was blowing his nose. 'I'm afraid I have to ask if you'd come and identify them officially. You do understand? Because they had their passports with them, we don't think there's much doubt.'

Honor nodded, 'Now?' She wouldn't believe Kitty was dead until she saw her.

'Is it wise to do that straight away?' Edwin protested. 'After such a shock?'

'If you don't feel up to it today, we could leave it until tomorrow.'

'I'd rather do it now,' Honor said firmly. 'It won't help me to lie awake half the night dreading it and wondering if it's really her.'

'Mr Jardine, let me get this straight in my head,' the sergeant said. 'Two weeks ago your shop window was broken but nothing was taken?'

'That's right.'

'And you asked for our Sergeant Mellor to call and advise on security?'

'Yes, he came. As a result of his advice I'm in the process of updating security measures in all my shops.'

'Did you warn us there would be nobody in your premises last night and ask us to keep an eye on the place?'

'Yes. I was afraid another brick might be thrown through my windows.'

Honor cringed back into the seat, a ball of ice in her stomach. She was one jump ahead of them now and was appalled at what she thought they were about to say.

'In the early hours of this morning, staff in one of our patrol cars reported seeing what they thought was moving torchlight in a room on the third floor at the back of your premises.'

'That would be my office.'

'They rang the doorbell but there was no answer. It seemed suspicious, although they could see no sign of breaking and entering.'

Edwin's voice was flat. 'I've lost my keys.'

'The patrolmen decided to keep the premises under surveillance to see if anyone came out. They returned to their car to radio in and ask other patrol cars to keep an eye out for a suspicious vehicle in the neighbourhood. If there were burglars operating inside they'd need a getaway vehicle and they couldn't see one immediately outside.

'Shortly afterwards, the camper van was noticed. We don't see many of those in the centre of the city, especially after midnight, so it was followed.'

Edwin jumped to his feet looking really agitated now. 'Did they get in by using my keys?'

'Well, we don't know that yet.'

'We've searched high and low for them here. I remember locking my place up when I left, and I drove here so I certainly brought them.'

'And you've been here with Mrs Thorpe since yesterday evening?'

'Yes. We intended to go out for lunch, but without my keys we couldn't.'

'Where did you put your keys after locking up your car last night?'

'I thought I'd put them in my jacket pocket. That's what I usually do.'

'Did Mrs Thorpe take your jacket from you when

you arrived? That's what a hostess would usually do, isn't it?'

Honor knew from that moment that she was going to lose Edwin Jardine and the share of his fortune that she'd had almost within her grasp. But she must keep her wits about her and not allow him or the police to unearth any more of her past.

She felt as though she was being kicked in the stomach. Kitty, her own daughter, the one person she'd tried so hard to help, had dropped her in this hole. Damn damn damn Jason Bolton. She blamed him. He'd have put Kitty up to creeping in last night to steal Edwin's keys. She didn't like the way this was going. It was ominous.

'Is it possible, Mrs Thorpe,' the police sergeant asked, 'that your daughter could have come here last night? Did you give her Mr Jardine's keys so that she could enter his premises?'

'Certainly not.' Honor was indignant. 'Of course I didn't.'

'Did you take them from his jacket pocket and leave them out on the front step, or under a doormat or in the hedge? A convenient place where she could pick them up?'

'No, no. Edwin, I wouldn't do such a thing. This is as much of a shock to me as it is to you.' She could see he was averting his eyes, and it made her feel worse.

'Mr Jardine, you had better come to the station with us to confirm that the jewellery is your property, though I understand the name of your business is stamped on some of the display trays. In fact, I think both of you had better come. We'll need you to make statements. This case is turning out to be more complicated than I'd first supposed.'

Honor started to cry. She often resorted to tears in a crisis; it was always the safest option. But with all her plans collapsing, she couldn't have held them back even if she'd wanted to.

CHAPTER TWENTY-SIX

EDWIN FELT upset and confused. He hardly knew what to make of the facts that were unfolding. He felt sorry for Honor, confronted so baldly, as she had been, with the death of her daughter. He'd put out his arms and tried to comfort her; offered his handkerchief when she collapsed in tears.

He was sure she was as innocent as he was; they'd both been caught up in some complicated scheme to burgle his shop that had ended in tragedy. By the time Sergeant Dransfield was ready to take him to the station, another police car had arrived at Honor's gate, and she was whisked off in that to confirm officially the identity of the couple killed in the camper.

As they arrived at the station, Sergeant Dransfield said, 'I'm going to show you the goods we recovered from the camper van. I want you to go through them methodically, and tell me if any of them belong to you.'

Edwin followed him into a bare room. The sight of so much of his jewellery spread across a plain table made him gasp with astonishment.

'It's mine.' He felt quite shaky. 'You say it was stolen from my safe?'

'Is that where you kept it?'

'Yes, overnight.'

'Is all of it yours? Go through it carefully, please. We need to establish the ownership of each piece.'

Edwin sat down on the chair he was offered with a little bump. 'It's part of my stock in trade. The most expensive items I have. Oh, my goodness! The Sun Diamonds too!'

The officer put out a hand to lift the shagreen case. 'Don't touch them.' Edwin stopped him. 'They're said to be cursed, to bring bad luck to those who touch them. It's a myth, of course, but . . . well, things do go wrong for some who do.'

Sergeant Dransfield was smiling indulgently. 'Are you suggesting that having cursed diamonds on board the camper caused the accident?'

'Terrible things do happen to people who touch them.' Edwin was remembering Elena. 'Yes, this all belongs to me. I put it out for sale every morning.' There was only one ruby ring. He picked it up, and felt shocked to the core. He recognised it immediately as the one Mrs Carruthers had chosen as a gift for her wedding anniversary.

'This wasn't in my safe last night. It disappeared weeks ago.' His mouth was dry and his hand was shaking as he remembered how it had been lost. He couldn't go on for a moment. Then he blew his nose, and haltingly said, 'My insurance policy paid up on it. I'll have to give them the money back.'

He told Sergeant Dransfield how Mrs Carruthers had fallen down the stairs in his shop and had fainted. 'She didn't discover her ruby was missing until the next morning. She reported it and a member of your force came round, but . . .'

How had Kitty Thorpe come to have it? The answer left him struggling for breath.

'Can you prove this is the actual ring?' Sharp eyes bored into his.

'I . . . I don't know.' He realised that if he said yes, he'd implicate Honor, and even now he found that hard to do.

'I take it, then, that other rings will have been made to this design?'

'Yes, it's a fairly common one.' He took a deep breath, knowing he must be truthful. 'But yes, it would be possible to determine whether this ring and the one bought by Mrs Carruthers are one and the same.'

'Could you be sure enough to swear in court that it was or was not her ring?'

Edwin swallowed hard. Every gemstone was different and his records would describe both the ruby and the diamonds round it. Also, Sam had enlarged it for her.

'Yes.'

He picked it up and took another look. Sam had made a good job of it. There was no visible sign that it had been made bigger, but he ordered rings in average sizes and this was extra large.

There was only one answer. Honor must have stolen it from Mrs Carruthers. Hadn't Jane pointed out that she was the first person to reach her after she'd fallen? He still found it hard to believe ill of her, but this was proof. Honor was not at all the sort of woman he'd thought. He felt sick. Jane had been right all along. He had to drop his head on his hands and take deep breaths.

The officer was talking to him again. 'Mr Jardine, you say all the rest of this jewellery is yours.' He waved his hand across the table and tapped the list that had been made. 'Can you prove that it is?'

Edwin sighed and tried to concentrate. 'I can. I buy mostly from suppliers in Birmingham. I'll have purchase orders, certificates of authenticity, delivery notes and bills, all that sort of thing, in my business records. Not for the Sun Diamonds, though; they're family gems that I've been trying to sell for the last few years. Many of my customers will confirm that they've been on show in my shop for that time.'

'Right.'

'Or . . . My wife's family bought the Sun Diamonds before the First World War, but I might be able to trace a record of that. I've got quite an archive in the cellar.'

'If you can get witnesses to say they've seen them on show in your shop . . . How much is all this stuff worth? Roughly speaking.'

Edwin did a few mental sums and told him. The sergeant whistled through his teeth. 'Blimey. As much as that?'

'I'd better tell my insurance company what has happened and where it is now. I suppose it's safe enough here?'

'Hopefully, yes.' Sergeant Dransfield smiled.

'They'll be pleased you've recovered it, anyway.'

'It's quite a haul.'

'When can I have it back? The cream of my stock is here. It won't be easy to run my business without it.'

'Normally we'd keep it as evidence until after the case had been heard, but since the main suspects have been killed . . . Well, before we return it, we'll have to check that it really does belong to you.'

'You could come to my shop and check my records now.'

'I will, Mr Jardine, but I also have to make sure nobody else will be charged in relation to this robbery. That may take a little time.'

'Who else could be?'

'Well, the mother, Honor Thorpe, for one.'

Edwin could feel the knot in his stomach growing bigger. 'She said the robbery came as a shock to her.'

'Well, she would, wouldn't she? But it was her daughter and her daughter's boyfriend who were in possession of your stock. They appear to have used your keys to let themselves into your premises and open your safe. We'll need to talk to her.'

'You've got my keys?'

'Well . . . I now presume they're your keys. When I first saw them I assumed they belonged to the owners of the motor home. What did I do with them? Ah, yes, here they are. There are two sets which appear to be identical.'

'Two?'

He put two heavy bunches on the table in front of Edwin, who picked up the one with a red tag. 'This is my key ring, the one I always use. My daughter gave me this tag some years ago.'

'And the other? Is that your spare set?'

'No. I do have spares, but the house, the shop, the car, they're all separate. I've never seen that set before.'

'These all look new. They must have had them made, which means they'd been planning this burglary for some time. But why, then, did they need another bunch? We'll try them both in your locks.'

The sight of his keys was bringing back images of Honor and her house, and the time they'd spent this morning searching for them, and the frustration and upset he'd felt.

Had Honor known all the time what had happened to his keys? Had she and her daughter deliberately planned the theft for last night, when she knew he and Jane would not be at home? It was beginning to look as though she had.

The officer said, 'There were other things found in

the vehicle, money for instance. Was any cash stolen from your premises?'

'I don't know. I haven't been home . . .'

'They had thousands in cash stashed round that van. The side was torn open in the crash and it flew all over the floor of the bank. We collected up several bundles.'

'I don't think it's mine. I don't keep large amounts of cash on my premises; we routinely drop it into the night safe. Generally my customers pay by cheque anyway. There'd be only a few pounds in change that we keep for the tills and a bit for household expenses up in my flat.'

Edwin was about to stand up, feeling the interview was at an end, when the officer suddenly barked, 'What is the nature of your relationship with Honor Thorpe?'

He shivered. 'I employ her as a sales assistant.'

'So she'd know the shop routine and where expensive items were kept?'

Even now he was slow to answer. 'Yes.' Hadn't he sat her in front of the open safe in his office and shown her exactly what he kept there?

Questions about her came thick and fast. He felt a fool admitting he'd employed her without references.

'I'll take you home now,' Sergeant Dransfield told him. 'In view of the value of the goods stolen, I want to bring some of my staff and a forensic specialist. I'll need to keep all these keys for the time being, and I want you to show me where you keep your purchase orders, delivery notes and such like. Also your staff records. You and I will take a look round to see if there's anything else missing and then I want you to stay out of the way until we've finished.'

Jane had been troubled all weekend. She couldn't get what she'd learned about Honor Thorpe out of her mind.

'She was dismissed from a golf club for offering sex for money and favours,' she'd told Nick, 'and now I have to make Dad believe it.'

When alone, they'd hardly talked of anything else. She'd asked, 'D'you think Dad was showing great interest in Honor because of what she was offering?'

'Yes – or giving.'

'Oh, Nick! You don't think Dad's too old for that?'

'Too old for sex? No, of course not.'

That confirmed what Dorothy had said, so it must be right. Poor Dad. She could understand now how Honor had swept him off his feet. As they travelled back to Liverpool, Jane tried to work out what she'd say to her father. It surprised her to find he wasn't home when they got there.

'It's five o'clock. Where can he be?'

Nick's eyebrows lifted. 'I'd guess with Mrs Thorpe,' he said.

'I think he'd try to be here before we got back,' she worried. 'You know what Dad's like.'

She was making a cup of tea to fill the waiting time when she heard him coming up from the shop. She shot out on to the landing to meet him and was shocked to see he had an escort of police officers. 'What's the matter, Dad?'

'We've been burgled, love.'

'What?' That was another shock. 'I didn't notice anything as we came in. Nothing out of the ordinary. Did you, Nick?'

'No, but really we didn't look. We came straight up here.'

'Has much been stolen?' she asked.

Her father looked pale and ill. 'Yes, but I think it's all been recovered.'

'Mr Jardine, will you and your daughter check your stock now? Do have a good look round and tell me if you find anything else missing.'

'I don't think anybody's been in our flat,' Jane said, going round the rooms and opening a few cupboards. 'Everything's exactly as it should be.'

'You and Nick look round the shop,' her father said, 'while I check the safes.'

Fifteen minutes later they both confirmed that nothing else seemed to be missing.

'Right,' Sergeant Dransfield said. 'Would you go up to your flat and leave us to finish off down here?'

Jane saw her father hesitate. 'I'd like to collect my car from Mrs Thorpe's drive. Would that be all right? I've got a spare set of keys.'

'All right.'

But when they went upstairs, instead of collecting the car keys Edwin groaned and sank on to his armchair. Jane made fresh tea and pressed a cup into his hands. 'What's been going on, Dad?'

'My mind's in complete turmoil,' he said. He looked shocked and upset but he managed to get the sorry tale of the last twenty-four hours out bit by bit.

'Kitty Thorpe has burgled our shop? Oh, my goodness!' Jane's mouth had fallen open with shock and disbelief.

'With the help of her boyfriend,' he added.

'And used your keys to get in? Dad!'

'I've been an utter fool,' he admitted. 'What you and the girls kept telling me about Honor is true. How could I have been so completely taken in?'

'You were conned,' Jane told him. 'Honor Thorpe was very good at that.' She told him about the conversation she'd had with the golf club manager.

'Soliciting for sex? Prostitution, you mean? Surely not!'

Jane saw her father's face collapse in anguish. She put an arm round his shoulders and gave him a comforting hug. She said, 'I was shocked too. I can't associate Honor with that sort of thing, but it could be worse. I was afraid you'd marry her and she'd be grinding you down for the rest of your life. I thought she meant to get control of your business and your money and push me out.'

'I'm sorry. I knew you were all concerned. I suppose you'll say I'm lucky Kitty tried to steal our stock – it blew everything wide open and let me off the hook?'

'I wouldn't dare, Dad.' Jane tried to smile. 'Let's say you were unlucky Honor picked on you in the first place.'

'You stay here and rest,' Nick said. 'If you give me your spare car keys, Jane and I will take the bus out to Mrs Thorpe's house and I'll drive it back to the garage.'

By Monday morning, Edwin felt very down, and couldn't bring himself to talk about Honor to the girls.

'It makes me feel such a fool,' he said to Jane. 'You tell them what happened, but keep it to a minimum.' He then shut himself in his office, but Sergeant Dransfield came to see him almost as soon as the shop opened, bringing the ring and the earrings in to show him. 'What d'you know about these?' he asked. 'Are they your property too?'

They glittered up at Edwin in their little leather cases with the name E. H. Jardine, Purveyors of High Class Jewellery in gold lettering in their lids. He felt mightily embarrassed having to say, 'I gave them to Honor Thorpe. They're legally hers.'

Sergeant Dransfield's face said it all. No fool like an old fool. How had he managed to get embroiled with a woman alleged to be a prostitute and a thief?

Through the nightmare of these happenings, normal life was going on. He stayed well away from the shop, leaving everything to Jane and Miss Hadley. He felt safer in his office out of everybody's way. The only

470

useful thing he did was to decide to send the Sun Diamonds down to Sotheby's when they were returned to him. He'd rung up to find out when their next specialist jewellery sale would be and was told early November. He made tentative arrangements, hoping he'd get them back in time.

Miss Pinfold had returned to work, and when he tried to sympathise about the loss of her mother, she'd said, 'We all have our hard times, don't we? We have to forget about them, put them behind us and remember the good times we enjoyed.'

'Very wise,' he said, wondering if there was a message there for him.

'I've seen Miss Bundy several times,' she told him. 'She's had a sad time recently too. She couldn't cope with her father, and she's had to put him in a home. She feels guilty about that and everything else. I've told her she'd feel better if she came back to work.'

'That's easily settled if she wants to. I'd be glad to have her back – I need a replacement for Mrs Thorpe.'

'She does want to come.'

'But I thought Miss Bundy had given up her flat in Liverpool?'

'She's asked if she could rent a couple of rooms from me. I've got plenty of space now, a three-bedroom house to myself.'

'That would be good for both of you,' he told her. 'When she's ready, ask Miss Bundy to come in and see me so we can fix it up.'

'I will. She'll be very pleased.'

It brought a little relief. At least he didn't have to worry about Miss Pinfold any more.

As her father had asked, Jane told Miss Hadley why Mrs Thorpe would not be coming to work this morning or any time in the future, and left it to her to tell the other girls. She heard little whoops of astonishment from various corners of the shop, followed by voices full of relief that Mrs Thorpe's marriage to Edwin would not now take place.

'I was dreading that,' she heard Miss Lewis say. 'She knew we'd taken against her; she'd have made our lives a misery.'

Jane thought her father must have heard them too. He came through the shop with his briefcase. 'I can't settle here,' he said. 'I'm going to visit the Southport branch. I'll take Eric Bannerman out for a spot of lunch.'

When she went to the rest room for her break, half the girls were talking with great animation about the local murder. It was nearly two weeks ago since the national dailies had been full of stories about a murder in Liverpool. The girls had been very interested, as had half England. Now reading about further developments was gripping the nation.

At the other end of the rest room table the girls were jubilant and full of questions about what exactly Mrs Thorpe had done. Jane knew they would not have questioned her father, but they felt no need to hide their curiosity from her. As she'd been instructed, she was as brief with her replies as good manners allowed, but soon discovered the shop was awash with facts about Mrs Thorpe that she hadn't known herself.

It seemed Miss Pinfold had glimpsed her father's copy of *The Times*. As a result of what she saw, she consulted Miss Hadley who asked Pam Kenny to slip across the road to W. H. Smith's and buy them each a newspaper. That sent Jane scurrying to her father's office to retrieve *The Times*.

Now Jane read that there had been further developments in the Baby Millie case.

On Saturday night there'd been an apparently unconnected burglary from E. H. Jardine's jewellery shop in Liverpool. Katrina Thorpe, aged sixteen, had been driving the getaway vehicle when she crashed after running through a red light, killing both herself and her passenger Jason Bolton, aged twenty. An amount of jewellery was recovered together with a large sum of money. A bus pass and a passport were found in the vehicle in the name of Katrina Thorpe, but giving different addresses, and she also had in her possession a driving licence carrying a different name and address.

When trying to establish Katrina Thorpe's true identity, it was discovered that she was Paul Thorpe's adopted daughter, and had lived with her mother

Honor Sarah Thorpe, Paul Thorpe's estranged wife, in Queen's Drive.

Jane shot back to the rest room with the newspaper. 'We've seen it.' Miss Hadley's voice was horrified. 'Leonard Thorpe is a murderer?'

'Alleged murderer,' Miss Pinfold cautioned. 'And an unemployed barman.'

Miss Hadley was aghast. 'No wonder we couldn't find any trace of him working as a solicitor.'

As far as Jane was concerned, the biggest shock of all was that Mrs Thorpe was still married to Paul Thorpe.

'Yet she'd accepted an engagement ring from Dad,' she kept on saying.

By the following day, articles and reports on the Thorpes were everywhere and everybody was talking about them. It was revealed that Honor Sarah Thorpe was employed at Jardine's jewellery shop.

Police searching the house found nothing more to incriminate Katrina, but when seeking evidence which might connect Honor Thorpe with the burglary found a passport, birth certificate and marriage certificate in her real name of Hilda Sarah Thorpe, now aged thirty-one.

That astounded the girls. 'Gosh, she's younger than she said. She gave her age as thirty-six when she got the job here.'

'Not many women make themselves older.'

'That was why Wayne couldn't find any criminal

record for her,' Pam Kenny said. 'They couldn't trace her under the new birth date.'

Miss Pinfold was reading the article to them all. 'In 1968 she was charged with stealing money from her employer, and failed to attend court when her case came up. She was found guilty in her absence. It appears that she moved to Spain and lived there for some years.'

'She's in real trouble now,' Dorothy Hadley said.

Jane was learning facts she hadn't even suspected. 'It must be awful to find you're married to a murderer,' she said. 'Awful too to lose a daughter like that. Poor Kitty.'

'They both deserve all they get,' Miss Jessop said, and most of the others agreed. 'You'd have got short shrift, Jane, and so would your father, once he was her husband.'

'She wouldn't have dared to marry Dad,' Jane said. 'That would have been bigamy. I wouldn't have worried so much about him if I'd known she was already married.'

A day or two later, further developments were reported in the papers. Sharon Burke had died of her injuries in hospital and that made Paul Thorpe a double murderer, and Katrina Thorpe was found to be two months pregnant at the time of her death.

'What a naughty girl Kitty was.' Miss Jessop pulled a disapproving face. 'Driving at sixteen! And using a stolen driving licence! She was an accident waiting to happen.'

'That was as good as guaranteed,' Pam Kenny said, 'once she'd stolen the Sun Diamonds. With that curse on them she was asking for trouble.'

CHAPTER TWENTY-SEVEN

THE FOLLOWING Monday, Dorothy was late going up for her afternoon break. When she reached the rest room she found Jane on the point of leaving. She smiled at Dorothy and said, 'I spent my lunch time looking at bridal gowns today, but I didn't have time to try them on.'

Dorothy was pouring herself a cup of tea. 'Did you see anything you liked?'

'Yes, but all the other girls trying on wedding dresses were with their mothers.'

'It's a mother's job, isn't it, to arrange her daughter's wedding?'

'Yes, but as I don't have one, I was wondering if you'd come to help me choose my dress?'

'Jane! Of course I will. I'm flattered to be asked.'

'Good. This week then, on your day off? Dad says I can take time off to do that.'

'Right. It'll be Wednesday this week.'

'Good, and do come for supper on Thursday. I don't want Dad to stop going to rehearsals. I suppose it was understandable that he cancelled last week, but he's still hiding himself away, burying his head in the sand over this Honor Thorpe business. It isn't good for him.'

Jane went flitting back to work leaving Dorothy still sipping her hot tea. She was enjoying the *Messiah* rehearsals. To open her mouth and let her voice ring out was an experience she hadn't enjoyed for years, and the music itself was wonderful. She was seeing new people and making new friends, but best of all it had brought her closer to Edwin and Jane. She was absolutely loving it.

Dorothy smiled to herself. It was Jane who'd invited her to have a meal with her and her father every week. Jane who had encouraged him to drive her to rehearsals. Jane who was doing her best to bring them together. Honor Thorpe, she ruminated, had not been good for any of them, but she was beaten now.

Edwin was having a terrible time. He cringed every time he heard the name Thorpe mentioned on the radio; it quite put him off listening to the news. Even worse was television, seeing Honor's photographs there as well as in the papers. He'd even seen pictures of his own shop, for he was being portrayed as a victim because Kitty had stolen the cream of his stock and might have got away with it had she not had a crash.

He hadn't been able to face the *Messiah* rehearsal last week, but on Wednesday evening Jane said, 'Dad, I take it you'll be going to rehearsal tomorrow as usual?'

'Oh, I don't think so. Everybody will have heard . . . They'll all know . . .'

Jane said briskly, with all the fervour of a teenager who thinks she knows it all, 'Dad, you can't keep avoiding people. Nobody there knew Honor and how things were between you. Dorothy's coming to supper as usual. The sooner you get back to your normal routine, the better you'll feel.'

Edwin wasn't convinced. Dorothy was one of the people he found hardest to face. She must surely understand that he'd turned his back on the companionship and loyal friendship she'd offered over twenty years in favour of Mrs Thorpe's more obvious glamour. She'd know he'd been foolish enough to believe Honor really loved him, and that he'd thought they were each going to have a passionate second marriage. Dorothy would be aware he'd gone overboard for sex as offered by a prostitute. Edwin was deeply ashamed he'd allowed himself to be so utterly taken in.

By Thursday evening, Edwin was still in a cold sweat about making such a fool of himself over Honor Thorpe. It was all very well for Jane to say he must face his friends in the choir, but it didn't stop him feeling uneasy about it. And in particular, he was afraid of being alone in the car with Dorothy. He was sure she must despise him.

He heard her and Jane closing the shop and going in and out of his office with stock to lock in his safe. He found a little job to do in the storeroom and hovered there out of sight until they finished and went up to the flat. When he went back to his office, he found a note of the day's takings on his desk.

He was still seeking the courage to join them ten minutes later. As he went slowly up the last flight of stairs, he could hear them in the sitting room, which was unusual, so he pushed the door open.

'Dad, there you are.' Jane was a vision in white. She'd changed into the wedding dress she'd bought the previous day. 'We've been waiting for you. I've got dressed up in my wedding finery to show you.' Miss Hadley was fixing the veil to her hair.

'I couldn't show you last night because I had to rush out to meet Nick. Do you like it?'

It took Edwin's breath away. He'd never seen her look more like her mother. 'My dear, you look absolutely beautiful.'

'Dorothy helped me pick this dress out.'

'Because it suits you, Jane. It looks very regal.' It was of ivory satin and had a tightly buttoned bodice with a mandarin collar and long sleeves.

'It's not all it seems,' Jane said. 'The bodice is covered with this little jacket. Underneath it's a strapless evening dress.' She took the jacket off to show him that too.

'I thought Jane might wear it again later as an evening dress,' Dorothy said. 'There were plenty of low cut gowns that could have been used as evening dresses as they were, but she wanted to be a traditional bride.'

'You couldn't have chosen better, But should you be showing it to me?'

'Why not?' Jane laughed and gave another twirl. 'It's Nick I shouldn't show it to. You're the father of the bride, Dad, not the groom.'

That brought the Honor Thorpe problem slamming back at him.

Jane smiled and said, 'I'd better get my ordinary togs on and get the supper on the table. You two don't have time to hang about.'

'D'you want any help getting out of it?' Dorothy was unpinning her veil.

'Could you get this zip down? Thanks, I can manage now. Would you mind starting to dish up, Dorothy?'

'Course not.'

Ever since that dreadful day Edwin had avoided being alone with Miss Hadley and now that he was, he didn't know what to say to her. She must think him disloyal to her, and an awful fool to be taken in by Honor.

He had to make an effort. 'Thank you,' he said, 'for helping Jane with her wedding arrangements. When it's frocks, I don't know where to begin. I'm very grateful and I'm sure she is.' He hesitated for a moment, and then added, 'You're the nearest to a mother she's had. She's very fond of you.' He almost added, but didn't quite manage it, *We both are.*

Dorothy went briskly to the kitchen. Edwin followed

in her wake. It seemed strange to see her taking the casserole out of the oven in his home.

She said, 'It's been rather a difficult time for us all, hasn't it?'

That seemed the understatement of the year. 'Very difficult,' he agreed.

She looked up and smiled. 'But at least the worst is over.'

'Is it?'

'Yes. We were all getting hot and bothered about Honor Thorpe, so suspicious of everything she did. We were spending too much time and energy trying to figure out who she was, and what she was up to. It's a relief to know the truth, though it's far worse than any of us imagined.'

'Yes.' It certainly was.

He watched Dorothy take the hot plates and then the bowls of vegetables to the table. She turned to get two tablespoons from a drawer, saying, 'I was a little frightened of her.'

'Were you? Why?'

'I knew she was determined to get what she wanted. She could bend things her way, make things happen, and at twice the speed we're used to. We couldn't keep up with her. And she so altered the friendly atmosphere in the shop. Spoiled it.'

And he'd gone along with it and allowed her to do it. He must have been blind.

Jane joined them wearing her jeans. 'Fancy her

being already married,' she said. 'D'you know, Dad, we got it all wrong.' She heaped cabbage on her plate. 'We really thought she had designs on you, and actually meant to marry you.'

That made Edwin catch his breath. He said, 'You kept telling me Honor wasn't genuine. I should have believed you. I'm sorry.'

It made him flinch to hear them talk openly about Honor Thorpe's plans, but if nothing else it would get it over and done with, and perhaps then he could put the whole sorry business behind him.

He tried to appear more at ease than he felt. 'She must have had a hard life, being married to a murderer.' What was he doing? He mustn't go on making excuses for her. He shut up.

Jane got up to take their dirty plates to the sink while Dorothy fetched some sort of sponge pudding from the stove. She seemed quite at home in his kitchen.

She said, 'I never thought I'd feel sorry for Honor, but losing her daughter in a terrible accident like that, she must feel her whole world is crashing in on her.'

Jane said, 'She got caught up in the mesh of theft and lies that Kitty made. That's what foiled her plans to batten on to you. You're far too generous, Dad. She'd have sucked you dry.'

Dorothy murmured, 'She was very beautiful and very good at manipulating people to get what she wanted.' He felt she was trying to support him.

Jane smiled. 'If I'd known she couldn't marry you I'd

have been less worried. I didn't fancy her as a stepmother, I can tell you.'

Jane's outspokenness embarrassed Edwin yet again. He was sure Honor Thorpe had meant to marry him, and he'd been ready to leap at the chance. More fool him.

Even now, Jane didn't realise Honor would have let nothing stop her. He was sure they'd have gone through the marriage ceremony even if for her it had been a bigamous one. She'd have tightened her grip on him to get at his money and his business. He could see now she had a ruthless streak, but had she really been a prostitute? He found that very hard to accept. He'd thought her quite ladylike.

'Would you have married her, Dad?'

'Would I have married her? As you've pointed out, she was already married to somebody else, so I wouldn't have been able to.' Was the white lie to protect himself, or to protect all of them? 'And now I know what she's really like, I don't want to.'

'Good,' Dorothy said. 'So now we can get on with our own plans.'

Jane sighed. 'I'm afraid Honor's landed herself in big trouble now.'

Her father said, 'She isn't going to be charged with burgling our shop. Sergeant Dransfield said there wasn't enough evidence.'

'So we'll be getting our stock back?'

'Yes, tomorrow, thank goodness.'

'She still has to answer for skipping off to Spain in 1968 with that fellow who's now in prison.'

'And with stealing Mrs Carruthers's ruby ring.'

Jane asked, 'Isn't it time you two were on your way?'

'Yes.' Edwin stood up. He felt better, more at ease with Dorothy now. He knew he could trust her. He ought to have married again years ago, found a new mother for Jane. Then this sort of thing couldn't have happened.

'A nightmare for Mrs Thorpe, I'm sure.' With a little smile, Dorothy took the dishes to the sink on her way out. 'But not the end of the world for the rest of us.'

Edwin knew she was right.

Preparations for Jane's wedding were going on apace, and Edwin knew it was high time he gave that his full attention.

Jane expected him to make decisions about where they would all live. He'd wasted time pondering whether Honor would want him to move in with her or whether he should buy another house. He'd known she wouldn't want to live over the shop and he'd come round to the opinion that with the new security system which was to be fitted next week, there was no need for any of them to live on the premises if they didn't want to. The outside electric shutters could be locked on to the pavement as they left each evening.

Changes would have to be made now, and it was

better if they were changes that would fit their lives well into the future.

'I still own the house your mother and I lived in,' he told Jane while they were eating their supper on Friday night. 'Being in Woolton, it's very handy. Would you and Nick like to live there?'

'Dad, I've never seen it except from the outside.'

'It's been rented since Elena died. I'd have to give notice to the tenants, and after all this time it would need a lot doing to it. A new kitchen for a start. Kitchens are very different these days.'

'It's a big house, isn't it?'

'Biggish. It's a family house. Six bedrooms.'

'Six?'

'There's a billiard room too.'

Jane put down her knife and fork. 'I think I'd rather have something smaller. Times have changed, Dad.'

'This steak and mushroom pie is very good.'

'It is, but I'll not be able to find another Mrs McGrath, not these days. The cooking and cleaning will be up to us.'

'I suppose so. You and Nick should start looking around. Find a place that would really suit you.'

'But can we afford it?'

'Yes, of course you can. One day, Jane, you'll inherit your mother's fortune and my business. You're a modern heiress. At one time I thought it might be necessary to keep fortune-hunters at bay, but with Nick Collins I didn't have to worry about that.'

'But can we afford it now?'

'Yes, now. This afternoon Sergeant Dransfield brought back the stock that was stolen and jolly glad I was to have it. I packed up the Sun Diamonds right away and sent them down to Sotheby's to be auctioned. I hope they'll be sold in their specialist jewellery sale in November. They should raise enough to buy you and Nick a home of your own.'

'Oh, Dad! That's marvellous!'

She and Nick lost no time in looking at what was on the market and making their choice. Within days they'd brought the brochure to show him.

Jane's eyes were sparkling. 'It has three bedrooms and it's being built on a small estate of detached houses with a bus stop close by.'

Nick too was thrilled. 'The location couldn't be better. It's on the way out to Speke airport with a train station just round the corner. It's easy to get anywhere from there, into town or out to Crosby.'

'Everything will be spanking new.' Jane was excited. 'And the house can be fitted out and decorated as we want it. It'll be easy to manage.'

Nick added, 'And cosy in winter.'

There had of course been the downside. It wouldn't be ready until January.

'It'll be worth waiting for,' Jane insisted. 'Do you mind if Nick pushes in here with us? Just for a few months while we wait for it?'

He'd said no, of course not. 'I'm not really looking

forward to being left here on my own. I'll welcome a little extra company for a time.'

As far as Edwin was concerned, Jane's wedding day was on him before he was able to banish Honor Thorpe completely from his mind. He was afraid it would take him a long time to get over her, but he meant to forget his own sadness and make it a very special day.

He got out of bed and padded across the passage to put his head round Jane's door. She was just waking up in the new double bed that had been delivered a few days ago.

'Morning, love. You stay where you are, I'll bring you some tea and toast in bed.'

'No, Dad, I'm getting up for breakfast.' She jumped out of bed and flung back her curtains, wide awake and radiant within moments. 'Great! It's going to be a fine day. Sunny but breezy.'

'I think there might be an autumnal bite to it. No need for you to come down to the shop this morning, by the way.'

'I want to. I don't want to spend any part of my big day by myself.'

He had to smile. It was wonderful to see her so happy and with such bounding energy. She had their breakfast on the table earlier than usual and had time to ring Nick before they opened the shop. The new security measures saved a lot of work. The electric blinds rolled up at the touch of a switch, revealing the plate glass windows with the stock already displayed. He did still keep a few of his most expensive items in the safe overnight, but those were never put in the windows.

All his girls were in a buoyant mood, and the shop seemed to fizz with excitement. Edwin found it infectious, his own mood lifting. The morning sped by, and when he closed the shop at twelve thirty he found they'd sold more than usual.

The ceremony was arranged for two o'clock. That allowed time for some of the girls to go home to change, but not all of them. Some had brought a sandwich as usual and worn their best clothes to work.

A couple of weeks ago, at breakfast, Jane had said that she wanted to invite Pam Kenny and Dorothy Hadley to have lunch in the flat with them today.

He'd said, rather wistfully, 'The rest of the day is going to be very full, very sociable. Wouldn't a quiet lunch with me before it starts be more to your taste? Or do you need help to get dressed?'

'No, I could probably manage on my own if you pulled my back zip up for me. But I can't let Pam rush home to eat and change into her bridesmaid's gown and then expect her to come back on the bus, can I?'

'No,' he said, firmly suppressing the impulse to suggest sending a taxi for her. 'Why Dorothy Hadley?'

'Well, I don't want her to feel left out on my wedding day. If I asked Pam and not her, she might. She's the nearest thing I've had to a mother, Dad. I've leaned on her.'

'Then of course you must ask her.' He felt proud of his daughter. She hadn't a selfish bone in her body; she was always thinking of others.

Mrs McGrath had made big bowls of chunky broth for them and followed that with Welsh rarebit. For those who needed more, she'd made a custard tart.

'You need something in your stomachs to build on before you start drinking champagne,' she told them. 'And I'm leaving as soon as I've washed up, so I can get to the church on time.'

Edwin sat down with a second cup of coffee. Jane had asked him to take his bath this morning so as to leave the bathroom free for the girls now. She'd also told him to hire a morning suit from Moss Bros.

'That won't be necessary,' he'd told her. 'I have one in my wardrobe.'

'Try it on,' she'd said, and nagged him until he did. The trousers wouldn't fasten round him, which had been a nasty surprise. 'I didn't realise I'd put on so much weight,' he told her.

'Just your bay window, Dad,' she'd laughed, patting it. Afterwards, she'd asked Miss Pinfold to hire what he needed. But of course it wasn't that simple, and he'd had to go along to be measured for it. She'd also insisted he bought himself a new shirt and shoes to complete the outfit. He dressed himself up now and felt quite the dandy.

It was Dorothy who came to tell him the car was at the back door and she and Pam were leaving for the church. She said, 'It'll come straight back for you and Jane.'

'Is she nearly ready?'

'I am ready, Dad.' She met him at the sitting-room door. 'Let's wait in here for five minutes.' She sat on the sofa with her long skirt and train spread around her.

'You look absolutely radiant,' he told her. Her dark shiny hair gleamed through the material of her short veil. 'Just like your mother on our wedding day.'

She smiled. 'I knew you'd say that.'

'I looked out our wedding photographs the other day.'

'Yes, I showed them to Dorothy. She thinks I'm like my mother too.'

'You're right about Dorothy,' he said. 'She's fussed around you like a mother hen.' He could see real affection on both sides.

'Fussed around you too, Dad.'

'Yes.' Why had he not seen that sooner? Perhaps it wasn't too late for him after all.

Jane couldn't sit still. 'Is it time to go downstairs? It's a long way down.'

'Everybody is willing to wait for you today, Jane.'

'I'm going to need help with this train.' She was gathering it up to help him.

'I've got it all, thanks.' He kissed his daughter's

cheek. 'I hope, love, you'll have a long and happy married life.'

The wedding car stopped in front of the undistinguished facade of St Cuthbert's church. Jane found it more difficult to get out than she'd expected, hampered as she was by unaccustomed long skirts. Pam Kenny, looking elegant but unfamiliar in the blue georgette dress they'd chosen together, came out to help her father stop the train from dragging along the pavement. From outside, Jane could hear the organ playing.

'For once it's not you,' she murmured to her father.

'Mrs Biddolph,' he said. 'I have more important things to do today.'

Jane knew the first one would be to give her away. When they reached the porch, Dad peeped inside and asked, 'Are we ready?'

'No, hang on,' Pam said, 'the train's all rumpled. Do you want me to let it fall to the floor now?'

'Yes.' Jane felt a shiver run down her spine.

'Right, we're ready then.' Pam gave her a wavery smile. 'Everything's shipshape now.'

The organ stopped momentarily, then struck up more vigorously. Jane gripped her father's arm as he led her slowly up the aisle. The congregation were turning to smile at her. All the girls were here, dressed in their best. Dorothy looked surprisingly pretty in a dark red suit, and a lovely big wedding hat. They were all her dear friends. Then she caught sight of Nick waiting at the front of the church, with the old school friend he'd asked to be his best man.

He turned to smile at her as she reached his side. She was very conscious of his love and support. They were about to be married and there was nothing they both wanted more.

'Dearly beloved, we are gathered together here . . .'

Jane had been thinking about this moment for so long that now the solemn ceremony was on her, it seemed as though it was happening to someone else.

Until, that was, Nick took her right hand in his and said clearly and confidently, 'I Nicholas take thee Jane to my wedded wife, to have and to hold from this day forward . . .'

The rest of the ceremony passed in an emotional haze for Jane. With the wide gold wedding band on her finger she signed the register. The sun was shining brilliantly when they went out into the grounds for the photographs.

Across then to the entrance to the church hall, where she and Dad stood with Nick and his mother to greet their friends as they went in. A waitress stood just inside offering each guest a glass of sherry.

When at last Nick led Jane in, the hall seemed sparklingly bright and fresh. She remembered then that it had been redecorated and refurbished last month as soon as the centenary celebrations had raised sufficient funds. A new music system had been installed and Dad had arranged the programme of soft background music.

A buffet lunch had been laid out and looked delicious. There was to be lobster and champagne but the magnificent wedding cake took pride of place. It dwarfed everything else. Five tiers, each made and decorated with love and care by her friends. Dorothy had put herself in charge of it, and she'd decided that the bottom, largest cake must be the first one cut today. That was the one she had baked.

The champagne was coming round. Everyone was raising their glasses to her and Nick, and murmuring their congratulations and best wishes for the future. Dad was organising the girls towards the food in much the way he did on occasion in the rest room.

'Mustn't let them drink too much on an empty stomach,' he said to Jane. 'Weddings are said to make the ladies weep emotional tears.' Quite a few were mopping at their eyes with lace handkerchiefs.

Nick put a glass of champagne into her hand. 'Here's to us,' he said. Jane took a sip and the bubbles went up her nose. She was able to relax then, and give herself up to the happy moment.

EPILOGUE

Christmas Eve 1980

J ANE KNEW married life was suiting her very well. She wasn't working at the moment, but she planned to return in a few months. Today, she'd brought her new baby daughter to show to the girls, knowing there wouldn't be a better occasion for this than the little party they always had on Christmas Eve.

'Meet Elena. We've called her Elena Jane after my mother.'

'Isn't she lovely?'

'Absolutely gorgeous.'

'What does she weigh now?'

The girls were all fascinated. Dorothy had walked round the rest room nursing the baby for the last half-hour, and the others kept folding back her shawl to have another look. They wanted to hold her tiny hands and stroke her pink cheeks. The infant's blue eyes stared silently up at them all.

The girls had given Elena her first Christmas

presents: a crocheted shawl, an embroidered gown, three bonnets, two matinee jackets and several pairs of bootees, all hand-made.

Jane had always loved Christmas Eve at the shop. Her father was slicing the two rich fruit cakes she'd made back in October. One she'd covered with marzipan and iced to the best of her ability. Dorothy had praised her work. The other she'd decorated with glazed almonds and cherries because Dad said he was not so fond of icing these days.

She'd never seen her father look so happy. He and Dorothy had been married in the spring. A very quiet wedding in the lady chapel at St Cuthbert's with just family members and a few friends round them. Instead of a reception, he'd booked a lunch-time table for ten at the Adelphi and they'd taken cream cakes back for the other girls to have in their tea break. Dorothy had moved in to live with Edwin in the flat, and said she was very happy there.

Jane knew that in the months after she and Nick were married, life had not been easy at the shop, though much had continued to go well. The Sun Diamonds had been sold at auction by Sotheby's for a spectacular price. Two wealthy Russians had competed to buy them.

'I hope they won't bring the new owner bad luck,' Jane had said.

'Of course they won't.' Dorothy had always been

one for common sense. 'It's the human lot to fall ill or have bad accidents. Who in their right mind would believe a few chips of rock could have any effect on the person who wears them?'

The Sun Diamonds had more than paid for the new house for Jane and Nick, and they'd loved it from the moment they'd moved in.

Dorothy had told Jane that she was enjoying the rehearsals for the *Messiah* so much that she didn't want the actual performances to come. Jane knew it was because she'd see less of her father then.

In early December they gave two very successful performances, one at St Cuthbert's and the other at the Philharmonic Hall. Jane and Nick went to both and had to congratulate everybody concerned. They'd achieved a very high standard.

'Since then, things have fallen a little flat,' Dorothy had admitted the following week.

'In a few months, when you've all had a rest, there'll be a new project on.'

'Yes,' Dorothy said, 'and it'll soon be Christmas.'

Jane had said, 'There are some orchestral concerts coming up at the Philharmonic Hall. You probably saw them advertised when you went there. Dad would love them. Why don't you buy a couple of tickets and ask him to go with you?'

She didn't often see Dorothy looking uncertain. 'Would that be a good thing to do?'

'I think so.'

'What if he says no?'

Jane smiled. 'I'll buy the tickets off you and take him myself. But he won't say no.'

He didn't, and it was as though Dorothy had shown him the way. After that he asked her out regularly.

Early in the spring, it had shocked her to see Honor come into the shop late one afternoon, after most of the girls had gone home. Her manner was more diffident than it used to be.

'I wonder if your father would spare me a few minutes of his time,' she said. 'Would you ask him?'

Jane was glad he'd gone to Southport that afternoon and she could truthfully say, 'He's not here at the moment. But I think it would only upset him to see you. It might be better if you didn't come back.' She sighed. 'I'd rather you didn't.'

Honor had burst into tears then and said her case was coming up in court next week and she'd been told she might get a custodial sentence.

'I'm dreading it,' she wept. 'But it's not just being sent to prison. I'll lose my house if I can't pay the mortgage. And if I can't work I definitely won't have enough money to pay it.'

Jane knew her father would immediately give her the lot. 'Well, I suppose we owe you some holiday money,' she said, making up her mind to give her a little on that pretext.

'It won't be enough.' Honor looked really woebegone. 'Please would you buy my earrings back from me? They're still a current design in your shop, so you could sell them as new. Nobody would know.'

'We would know,' Jane said gently. 'We don't sell second-hand jewellery as new. In fact, we don't sell it at all here in Church Street, but we do sell a bit of second-hand jewellery in our Southport shop. I could give you a price for your earrings that would reflect that.'

Honor mopped at her eyes. 'If you would, I'd be grateful.'

'On one condition,' Jane told her. 'I want you to sign a promise that you'll never try to make contact with my father again. I see you're still wearing his ring. I don't want you to come here asking us to buy that back. It would stir up a lot of unhappy memories for him. I want you to leave us alone.'

Honor nodded numbly. 'All right.'

'Come up to the office, then, while I make out the receipt and type out what I want you to promise.'

It was only when she was sitting at the typewriter that Jane added, 'If you ever do want to sell that ring take it to Morris Davenham's in Dale Street. They'll give you a fair price.'

She hadn't seen Honor after that, but her day in court was reported not only in the *Echo* but in several national newspapers. She was sentenced to six months' imprisonment for the theft of Mrs Carruthers's ruby ring. Miss Jessop thought it wasn't enough.

Jane cuddled her baby. The girls' happy chatter was

growing louder just as it always did after having the sweet sherry that went so well with rich fruit cake. Pam Kenny came round with the bottle to refill their glasses.

'Jane,' she said, 'you haven't had any yet.'

'I don't think I should,' she told her. 'I'm feeding Elena myself.'

'One mouthful won't hurt,' Pam said. She found a glass and poured her exactly that amount. 'It's Christmas after all.'

Pam had married her policeman two years ago, but was still working. 'I'm bowled over by your baby. We're planning to have one next year.'

'I recommend it. Elena has changed my life.' Jane laughed. 'But I've missed you all, the companionship, the gossip and the day to day bustle of the shop.'

'But you always planned to come back.'

'Yes, I'm going to start as soon as the Christmas holidays are over. Just for a few hours a day to begin with.'

'But what about Elena?'

'I'll bring her with me in her carrycot. Dorothy says she's looking forward to it and that she'll love helping me look after her.'

'So will I,' Pam said. 'We all will. It'll be lovely to have you back with us.'

Jane sighed with contentment. 'I think I've got everything in the world a girl could ask for.'

The Best of Fathers

Anne Baker

Mary and Jonty have battled against the odds to be together. Forced to run away when Mary's father disapproved of their relationship, they've managed to build a life for themselves. And their happiness would be complete if they were blessed with a child. Tragically, it seems that's not to be.

Then one night a yacht is shipwrecked near their home. Mary and Jonty rush to the rescue and, amid terrible carnage, they save a baby. Although they know it is wrong, they keep the child. Despite feeling guilty they cherish the little girl they name Charlotte.

Charlotte grows up to be an attractive young woman, devoted to her parents. But fate is to intervene when she decides to train as a nurse in Liverpool. For Liverpool is where her 'real' family lives, and it seems that secrets and lies are to be uncovered – with shocking consequences.

'[A]n immensely enjoyable read' *Coventry Telegraph*

978 0 7553 4077 4

headline

A Labour of Love

Anne Baker

Flora Wilcox has recently remarried but already has doubts about her husband and now has less time to support her daughters, Hilary and Isobel. They are each bringing up a family that seems to be heading for disaster.

Hilary is a budding novelist helping her husband run his market gardening business. She's very worried about their dyslexic twin sons Andy and Charlie, who find school and getting work afterwards a major struggle. While Andy works hard, Charlie falls in with a bad crowd – with shocking results.

Isobel is happily married to Sebastian and loves their two daughters, teenage Sophie and little Daisy. But Sophie is secretly dating a man who's not willing to face the consequences of their relationship, and finds herself in a nightmare situation. If only she knew that her mother had once stood in the same shoes . . .

Acclaim for Anne Baker's novels:

'A shining example of why the family saga genre is eagerly devoured by so many readers' *Newbury Weekly News*

'A heart-warming saga' *Woman's Weekly*

'An atmospheric and charming saga' *Coventry Evening Telegraph*

978 0 7553 3339 4

headline

The Wild Child

Anne Baker

1961, Liverpool. Flora Wilcox's daughters, Hilary and Isobel, couldn't be more different – Hilary is serious and hardworking, while Isobel seeks fun and excitement.

When Isobel's boyfriend drops her to take up with Hilary, a rift develops between the girls, and even their mother can't find a way to build bridges. While Hilary settles into wedded bliss and motherhood, Isobel escapes to London, where she begins a passionate affair with a much older married man. At first, she's happier than she could imagine, but trouble lies ahead . . .

As Isobel worries about whether her secrets will find her out, Hilary has a shock. Her lovely twin boys are struggling at school and, with no understanding of dyslexia, Hilary doesn't know which way to turn.

Can the sisters support each other when they need it most? The bonds of family are at their strongest in testing times . . .

Praise for Anne Baker's previous sagas:

'A heart-warming saga' *Woman's Weekly*

'Another nostalgic story oozing with atmosphere and charm' *Liverpool Echo*

'One of romantic fiction's most popular authors' *Lancashire Evening Post*

978 0 7553 3337 0

headline

Carousel of Secrets

Anne Baker

It's 1931, and as the Depression grips Merseyside, Greta Arrowsmith's family battles to make ends meet. The girls at the laundry where Greta works are unanimous about one thing: the *only* way out of poverty is to marry money.

One cold winter's night, Greta takes pity on a lost dog, little realising her decision to take it home will change her life for ever. For the dog belongs to Mungo Masters, the handsome, wealthy owner of a chain of funfairs. He is instantly attracted to Greta and, despite her mother's warnings, she soon finds herself caught up in a heady romance. Lavished with luxuries, Greta dares to hope her dreams have come true – especially when Mungo gives her brother a job at one of his fairs. But Mungo's past returns to haunt him, sweeping Greta into a dangerous world of secrets, violence – and murder . . .

Praise for Anne Baker's previous sagas:

'A heart-warming saga' *Woman's Weekly*

'A stirring tale of romance and passion, poverty and ambition' *Liverpool Echo*

'With characters who are strong, warm and sincere, this novel is a joy to read' *Coventry Evening Telegraph*

978 0 7553 2468 2

headline

Let The Bells Ring

Anne Baker

1941, Merseyside. Eighteen-year-old Hannah Ashe and her mother Esme are lucky to escape when their home is destroyed in a bombing raid. Forced to move in with Esme's difficult sister-in-law, they make the best of things. Hannah thrives in her new job repairing damaged fighter planes and becomes firm friends with vivacious workmate Gina Goodwin. While Hannah enjoys spending time with Gina and her handsome brother Eric, she's a little afraid of their stern father, who acts strangely when he hears mention of Esme's name. What does he know that Hannah doesn't?

When Hannah starts to ask questions, Esme clams up and forbids her daughter to visit the Goodwins again. Strong-willed Hannah refuses to obey, but, as she is pulled closer into their circle, she realises the Goodwins are hiding many secrets . . .

Praise for Anne Baker's previous sagas:

'A heart-warming saga' *Woman's Weekly*

'Another nostalgic story oozing with atmosphere and charm' *Liverpool Echo*

'With characters who are strong, warm and sincere, this novel is a joy to read' *Coventry Evening Telegraph*

978 0 7553 2466 8

headline

Now you can buy any of these other bestselling books by **Anne Baker** from your bookshop or *direct from the publisher*.

Moonlight on the Mersey	£6.99
A Mersey Duet	£6.99
Mersey Maids	£6.99
A Liverpool Lullaby	£6.99
With a Little Luck	£6.99
The Price of Love	£6.99
Liverpool Lies	£6.99
Echoes Across the Mersey	£6.99
A Glimpse of the Mersey	£6.99
Goodbye Liverpool	£6.99
So Many Children	£6.99
A Mansion by the Mersey	£6.99
A Pocketful of Silver	£6.99
Keep The Home Fires Burning	£6.99
Let The Bells Ring	£7.99
Carousel of Secrets	£6.99
The Wild Child	£5.99
A Labour of Love	£5.99
The Best of Fathers	£5.99

TO ORDER SIMPLY CALL THIS NUMBER

01235 400 414

or visit our website: www.headline.co.uk

Prices and availability subject to change without notice.